THE

BEDLAM DETECTIVE

THE

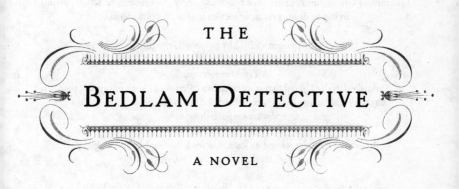

BEDLAM DETECTIVE

A NOVEL

STEPHEN GALLAGHER

BROADWAY PAPERBACKS
NEW YORK

Copyright © 2012 by Stephen Gallagher

All rights reserved.
Published in the United States by Broadway Paperbacks, an imprint of the
Crown Publishing Group, a division of Random House, Inc., New York.
www.crownpublishing.com

Broadway Paperbacks and its logo, a letter B bisected on the diagonal,
are trademarks of Random House, Inc.

Originally published in hardcover in the United States by Crown Publishers,
an imprint of the Crown Publishing Group, a division of Random House, Inc.,
New York, in 2012.

Library of Congress Cataloging-in-Publication Data
Gallagher, Stephen.
The bedlam detective : a novel / Stephen Gallagher. — 1st ed.
        p.   cm.
1. Private investigators—England—Ficiton.   2. Rich people—England—
Fiction.   3. Eccentrics and eccentricities—Fiction.   4. Murder—
Investigation—Fiction.   I. Title.
PR6057.A3B93B43 2012
823'.91—dc22   2011018605

ISBN 978-0-307-40665-1
eISBN 978-0-307-95278-3

Printed in the United States of America

Book design by Lauren Dong
Cover design by Whitney Cookman
Cover photography © Stephen Mulcahey/Arcangel Images

10 9 8 7 6 5 4 3 2 1

First Paperback Edition

It is no good casting out devils. They belong to us, we must accept them and be at peace with them.

D. H. LAWRENCE
The Reality of Peace
1917

THE

SOUTH WEST OF ENGLAND
SEPTEMBER 5TH, 1912

ONE

SEBASTIAN BECKER'S TRAIN HAD BEEN STANDING IN THIS LITTLE English rural stop for fifteen minutes or more. When he looked out through his compartment's window the view fogged and cleared, fogged and cleared, adding an illusion of movement as the locomotive's idling boiler vented its unused energies and a breeze drove the cloud vapor on down its flanks. Sebastian saw a landscape of field and hedgerow, hedgerow and West Country field, all the way out to the blue distant hills.

There was a railway guard working his way down the platform toward them, stopping at each compartment to ask the same question.

A glance around Sebastian's companions in first class showed strangers, all. A fat man in tweeds. Two clerical men, and a woman with a child. The child was about eight years old and wore a sailor suit, much as Sebastian's own son once had. A pint-sized sailor, on his way to the seaside. The plush fabric of the seat made the child's bare legs itch. Whenever he squirmed his mother would reach for his arm and shake him, once, in silent remonstration.

She was a widow, still in the attire. The boy was pale and blue, like the cloth of his suit. It was as if he were his father's only memorial, and she exercised her grief by keeping him scrubbed down to the marble.

She met Sebastian's eye.

"Forgive me," he said, and once more looked out the window.

How far were they now, from the sea? Fifteen, twenty miles?

The sprung latch on the carriage door opened with a sound like the bolt of a rifle. The door swung out and the train guard hauled himself up to stand on the footboard. He'd bypassed the third class compartment next door.

He was a man of some girth, and he was shining with perspiration. His thinning hair was the dark brown of a much younger man, but his thick mustache was mostly gray and ginger. He wore a watch chain and waistcoat and the uniform of the Great Western Railway.

"Pardon me," he said breathlessly. "But is anyone here a medical man or an officer of the law?"

He spoke to the company in general but when his gaze lit upon Sebastian, his manner changed.

No one moved.

"I thought perhaps you, sir?" the guard persisted when Sebastian made no response.

Sebastian Becker could sense the eyes of everyone in the compartment upon him.

"I'm sorry, but no," he said.

The guard seemed to hesitate, as if about to say something else. Then he accepted the rebuff and moved to withdraw.

One of the clerical men called after him.

"Excuse me," he said, "but why have we stopped?"

"Just a slight problem in the baggage car, sir," the train guard said. "The stationmaster and I are having a difference of opinion over what's to be done about it."

The door closed with a bang. And that was that.

There was some shifting and throat-clearing in the compartment, but apart from something murmured by the fat man no one spoke. Back in America, Sebastian thought, the guard's departure would have been the cue for some lively speculation and debate between strangers. But here, there followed a strained and British silence.

The guard was repeating his question next door to the third class people, this time with no *Pardon me.*

Sebastian opened his book and pretended to read, but it was of no use.

Eventually he closed the book and got to his feet.

"Excuse me," he said, and opened the compartment door to climb down after the guard.

SEBASTIAN HAD once seen half of a man's head blown clean off, gone from the eye sockets up. It had been done from behind, with a shot from a hunting rifle at a range of inches. Two men held the victim's arms and forced him to kneel. The man with the rifle called a warning as he fired, so that his friends might turn their faces away—not to be spared the sight, but to avoid the spray. Sebastian could do nothing. He was part of a mob that had, only minutes before, been a peaceful labor meeting. To drop his disguise would have been certain suicide.

Although his evidence had later helped to hang two of the men, the hour stood in his memory as one of shame. He might have intervened; he had not. The fact that he was a Pinkerton man and undercover, and that the mob would have turned on him in an instant, somehow counted for little after the event.

Others agreed. Complete strangers were generous with their views on how he could and should have acted. *You could of said something abt. the sky and then taken the gun off the shooter when he was looking up and turned it onto him,* wrote one correspondent. *That is surely what I would of done in yr place.* And after his court appearance, another with differing loyalties wrote, *On your word two good men will hang. The scab only got what he deserved and some day so will you.*

A return to England, the land of Sebastian's birth, had been Elisabeth's idea. She sold her jewelry to buy them steamer tickets. It meant a fresh start, but a step down in fortune. Sebastian Becker now lived in London, and drew his modest pay from the coffers of England's Lord Chancellor.

They were not rich. But he had his one decent suit of clothes, and a certain authority. An agent of justice once again, he now served as the special investigator to the Masters of Lunacy.

"I WAS a detective once," he said. "But a mere civil servant now."

"Nevertheless, sir," the guard said, "I'll ask you for your guidance and I'll value your opinion."

"On what?"

"Please. This way."

As they began to move, he signaled to the stationmaster. The stationmaster saw the wave and broke off an argument with a third class passenger hanging out one of the end carriage windows.

The train was a cross-country set, pulled by a tank engine. A full quarter of its length was taken up by the luggage van. British holiday passengers rarely traveled light. They'd arrive at their lodgings in a caravan of trunks, suitcases, and hatboxes, more appropriate to a house move than a weeklong stay. Many would even pack food, as if a Minehead or a Weymouth were some far-off and foreign place with unreliable supplies.

But this was the season's end. And a wet and disappointing season that 1912 summer had been. The train was less than half full.

As they walked up the platform the guard said, "I expect you're wondering how I had you singled out, back there."

"My travel warrant," Sebastian said, to the guard's disappointment. "I assume you noted the crest on it."

The stationmaster caught up, and by the time they reached the luggage van they were four: Sebastian, the guard, the stationmaster, and the stationmaster's gormless-looking lad who'd appeared from nowhere. The lad wore a porter's uniform and a haircut that looked as if it had been inflicted on him in a dark alleyway. He couldn't have been more than sixteen, but he was wiry.

"In here," said the stationmaster, and once they were inside the station's baggage room he closed the doors behind them and drew down the blinds.

There was a wall of numbered cubbies for bags and suitcases, but most of the room was open floor space for setting out baskets and dry goods. A second set of doors opened into a lane behind the station.

And there was a stink; a pungency somewhere between vinegar and turpentine, without quite being either. Sebastian knew it, and knew it far too well. It took him back to his first job in uniform, and memories of mortuary visits on hot summer evenings.

"Here, sir."

The station's platform cart had been dragged into the room. A leaking crate stood upon it. The side of the crate had been opened, with some of its boards prized off and then replaced loose to shield the contents from view.

The three railway employees stood watching him, and none offered to explain. So he moved the loose boards and looked inside.

Inside the crate was a cylindrical, glass-lidded tank, roped into place. Folded blankets had been wedged in around the sides to cushion it. Staring out at him, crammed in like so much colorless fruit in a preserving jar, was a small dead freak.

Or two dead freaks that shared a head. Opinions might vary. It was as if in creation their faces had been mashed together to make one three-eyed, two-mouthed horror. Their bodies, as far as he could see, were normal.

To get them into the jar they'd been arranged in a tight embrace, arms wrapped around each other as if clinging in terror to the only reassurance that either of them knew. Their limbs must have softened, to fit the space in the jar so closely. The lid had been sealed on with strips of tarred linen.

The stationmaster said, "There are five more boxes like this on the train. We're supposed to hold them for collection."

Sebastian looked up at him.

"And?"

"That *is* some kind of a human child, is it not?"

Sebastian considered. He'd been expecting something suspicious concerning a trunk. Trunk murders, most of them involving dismemberment and left-luggage offices, were an enduring British obsession. He could recall one that had proved to be a consignment of theatrical costumes, unlaundered and reeking of glue and the sweat of performance.

This was something else.

He took a moment longer. Then he said, "I believe this should properly be called a specimen. Do you not recognize that rank smell?"

The three looked blank.

"It's formaldehyde."

Two of the three did their best to look enlightened.

He indicated the stain around the crate. "It's either leaked or spilled. What happened here?"

With a pointed look at the lad, the guard said, "There was a mishap as the box was taken from the wagon. The box was dropped, something broke, and the smell came right after."

The boy might have been looking embarrassed, but it was hard to tell. His expression barely changed.

The stationmaster said, "I stopped the unloading and took a decision to open the box. Specimen or no, sir, is there no special law to cover the transport of the dead?"

"You'd know that better than I would," Sebastian said. "Who's the owner of the crate?"

The guard handed him the consignment papers, and he gave them a quick look-over. The boxes had been packed and shipped by a carrier in New York. The contents of the six crates were described as "curiosities" and were to be collected by one Abraham Sedgewick or his representative.

Sebastian looked at the stationmaster. He said, "Do you know this Abraham Sedgewick? Is he a local man?"

The stationmaster made a small and helpless gesture, but the lad chipped in and spoke for the first time.

"Sedgewick's Fair is passing through on Thursday," he said.

Sebastian considered for a moment. "Well," he said. "A fair. That makes a kind of sense. Does it not?"

They were all looking at him and expecting more.

Sebastian went on, "Created as specimens, bought to be exhibits. Destined for display in some fairground sideshow."

"Specimens, exhibits," the stationmaster said. "I don't care what you call them. They're dead bodies, and I don't want them in my station."

"Well," the guard said, "they can't stay on my train."

They looked to Sebastian for some kind of adjudication. He realized that what they'd been seeking was neither a doctor nor a policeman, but a Solomon.

Meanwhile, his train stood waiting. And there was an urgency to his mission that, though he could not advertise it, argued against delay.

The fact of it was that he had no answer. Freak or not, these were human remains and there was probably some law to govern their storage and use. His employer might know. But Sir James was up in Dundee for the week, giving an address to the British Association.

He gave the bottled specimen a more intense inspection. Here, only inches from the glass, the smell of formaldehyde was almost overpowering.

He had an idea.

He said, "Have you opened any of the other boxes?"

"No," the stationmaster said.

"Have you taken a close look at this?"

"As close as any man would care to."

"Look," he said, and beckoned the man in. "Get close enough and you can see a faint crazing pattern in the surface of the skin. What does that tell you?"

The stationmaster opened and closed his mouth and then was about to shrug, so Sebastian told him.

"I think you'll find that what you're looking at may not be flesh, but . . ."

"Wax!" the guard said suddenly.

The stationmaster seemed doubtful. He regarded the freak through its glass and said, "They're waxworks?"

"Have you never heard of such a thing? Anatomical models. Bottled up in spirits of alcohol for a showman's trick. Of course," he added for safety, "that's only my guess."

Then he looked into the milky eyes of the three-eyed freak, and the dead freak stared ahead and through him as if refusing to meet his gaze.

He felt a touch of guilt.

But hadn't he witnessed worse things in this world? And the freak was long dead.

And as for the guard, he had all the answer that he needed.

He clapped his hands together. "Right," he said. "I'll have the rest of your goods off my train and we'll be on our way."

As the lad went to unload the other crates, the stationmaster crouched down and peered more closely into the jar. All of his reticence was forgotten now.

"A waxwork," the stationmaster said, and he looked up at Sebastian with a face of wonder where, before, there had been only disgust.

"Indeed," said Sebastian.

"Who'd have imagined that?" the stationmaster said. "You don't see it till you really look."

THE UNLOADING of the boxes took another fifteen minutes. Once the train was moving again, Sebastian opened his book and tried to read.

The reading was not for pleasure; behind the content of the book lay one of the reasons for his journey. If he arrived too late to seek out the author this afternoon, he could finish it in his hotel.

He was keeping alive a glimmer of hope for a decent supper. His warrant might give him first class travel out of London, but the restaurant car was beyond his means.

To those hopes of a quiet evening and a decent supper he added another, which was not to dream of carnival freaks in a strange bed.

In the event, he did not. But only because worse was to come, before the day was out.

TWO

AFTER THE GOODS DISPUTE AND AN UNSCHEDULED CROSSROADS stop to pick up some soldiers, Sebastian reached his destination almost an hour late. There was an address on the slip of paper that he'd been using as a bookmark. He took it out to check it now. He had a room reserved by telegram at the Sun Inn, Arnmouth.

Arnmouth was a resort that had been established close to an estuary, where the lack of a suitable bridging point had sent the railway line inland. Which meant that the station was more than a mile from the town, with a horse wagon service to carry passengers and their luggage over the final leg of the journey.

Sebastian had no luggage to speak of, just his usual leather Gladstone. While the other passengers were seeing their bags onto the station wagon, he watched the soldiers climbing into the back of a waiting motor truck. They were a squad of teenaged boys and a gray-headed sergeant. All had ridden the last few miles together in the baggage car. Their transport now was a petrol-driven three-tonner with cart wheels and a canvas cover, and an engine noise like spanners tumbling in a drum.

A young railwayman closed up the tailgate after the soldiers. He'd been blasted with soot at some point in his working day, so that when he turned around to the horse wagon his eyes were a startling blue in contrast to his blackened skin and shirt collar.

"Sorry for any delay, ladies and gentlemen," he called up to the passengers as their horse shied and stamped.

"No apology required," one of Sebastian's fellow passengers called back. "We don't argue with the King's Own. Is it for the maneuvers?"

"A little local emergency they're helping us out with," the railway-man said. Sebastian felt his senses sharpen. But the young man was already walking away.

The final leg of Sebastian's journey took about twenty minutes through country lanes. Arnmouth was a onetime fishing village that had grown for the summer crowds as far as its situation would allow. His first sight was of a clock tower and municipal welcome garden at the top of the main street. A dense bed of roadside flowers spelled out the town's name on a sloping bank.

Their wagon made its way down the street, which wasn't long. An observer could feasibly stand at one end of it and hail to a friend at the other. The street was lined with fancy shops, fine hotels, and tall houses made of the local stone.

Something was definitely amiss. Shopkeepers were outside their doors, exchanging words while their shops stood empty. A group of women had gathered on a corner. None of them paid the station wagon any attention as it went by.

The Sun Inn was at the end of the main street, where the street made a sharp turn down to the harbor. It was an old coaching inn, with an archway to its stables and a view out over dunes and the estuary strand.

Sebastian tipped the driver sixpence and climbed down with his bag. Then he glanced back up the street. The local women were too far off for him to do more than read their attitudes. Some stood with their arms folded. They glanced around as they talked.

The driver inspected the sixpence, sniffed wetly, and then pocketed the coin as he flicked the reins to move on.

THE TWO STEPS up from the pavement into the inn were edged with heavy iron. Once off the street, Sebastian found himself in a low-ceilinged and gloomy interior. Except for a few stuffed sea birds on a shelf above the mantel, he was alone. There was a mahogany bar counter with a backdrop of bottles, mirrors, and crystal. On one paneled wall was an engraved print of the barquentine *Waterwitch*, and on another a picture frame with samples of sailors' knots behind glass.

He'd found solitude, but not silence. At the far end of the saloon bar was a partition. Beyond the partition was the snug, where the floor would be bare wood and the beer a halfpenny cheaper, and from which came the noise of a crowd of men. Sebastian paused for a moment to listen in case he could make out what was being discussed with so much enthusiasm, but he could not.

He reached over the bar to where a brass ship's bell hung, and tweaked the clapper so it rang once.

All went quiet. Then a head popped around the bar side of the partition. It belonged to a large, unshaven man wearing—from what Sebastian could see—a parish constable's uniform with a touch of the rummage-box in its fit and condition.

His expression was of one poised for abuse, but that changed at the sight of a gent.

"Just hold on," he said, and disappeared again. A few moments later Sebastian heard the muffled shout of a name somewhere in the back of the inn. Moments after that, the noise in the snug returned to its previous level.

A woman in cook's whites appeared, bringing with her a waft of warm kitchen air. She was short and broad and homely.

"Good afternoon, sir," she said.

"Sebastian Becker," he said. "I've a reservation."

"A reservation?"

"Sorry. A booking. I sent a telegram."

She went behind the bar counter and reached down for a visitors' book. "A reservation," she said, as if it was a word that she didn't hear too often. "You speak a little like an American gentleman, Mister Becker."

"My wife's American. I spent some years there. I often slip."

He scratched his name in the book with the pen that she gave him.

As he was writing she said, with due apology, "I'm afraid there's no one to take your bag upstairs."

"I can manage that for myself," Sebastian said. "What's going on?"

"Two children are missing," the cook said.

Sebastian abruptly laid down his pen.

"Tell me more," he said.

"Oh, it's probably something and nothing," she said. "They didn't come home for supper last night. It's a family that takes Rose Villa every year. The girls run wild all summer and Mister Bell comes up at weekends. Everyone in town knows them. They're always out and about." And she blew on the ink of his signature to help dry it before closing up the book and returning it to its place under the counter. "You watch. They'll appear. In tears and all sorry for the trouble they've caused."

Sebastian said, "How long have they been gone?"

"Only since yesterday. My opinion is that they're on an adventure. Stayed out all night and now they're scared to come home." She tried to give a little smile, but anxiety betrayed her.

"And in there?" He indicated the activity on the other side of the snug partition.

"They've sent us a county detective," she said. "He's organizing a search. Or trying to."

With the guest book safely away, she took a room key from a hook board behind the bar. All the keys had wooden tags and all the tags bore the names of sea birds in handwritten script.

Sebastian said, "Tell me something. How do I get to Arnside Hall?"

"Sir Owain's house?" the cook said.

"Sir Owain Lancaster, yes."

"You won't get there today. There's no one to drive you."

"Because everyone's on the search."

"They've even called in some soldiers."

"Now I understand," Sebastian said.

THE WOMAN had expressed hope. But knowing what he knew, Sebastian already feared the worst. Up in the Sandpiper Room, which was of a generous size and had an oak-framed bed and plain whitewashed walls, he laid out his soap and his razor on the washstand and placed Sir Owain Lancaster's notorious book on the bedside table. Next to it he laid a handwritten list, and a typewritten letter.

He could hear voices from below. This room was directly above the snug. Every now and again, a phrase or a few words would come through. Someone was trying to organize the volunteers, and all the volunteers seemed to be arguing with their directions.

Sebastian moved to his window and looked out. His window overlooked the shore. From here he could see the river snaking out through a deep cut in the sand toward the distant sea. Beyond the river, fanning out toward the far horizon, stretched an enormous and probably treacherous tidal beach. Way out across the flats, so far off that they were but sketchy figures in a vast landscape, a dozen men with staffs had formed a line and were moving across the bay, checking pools and quicksands. The local police would be few in number, bolstered by volunteers, and none would have been trained for such an operation.

Sebastian looked back over his shoulder at the bedside table. Sir Owain's book purported to be an account of an ill-fated expedition somewhere in the region of the Amazon basin, led by its author. Its publication had caused a scandal and the destruction of Sir Owain's reputation, forcing him to abandon his town house in London and retreat out here to his country home. The implications for its author's mental state were a significant part of the reason for Sebastian's visit. His regular duties involved investigating the background and circumstances of persons of interest to the Lord Chancellor's Visitor in Lunacy.

In this instance, the list and the letter added a sinister dimension to his mission. The disappearance of children now added another.

The lock on the bedroom door was hardly substantial, and the board of keys behind the bar was far from secure. He went over to the table and gathered up the list and letter, slipping them inside the pages of Sir Owain's book. Then he hid the book under the pillow bolster and remade the bed over it, tucking in the sheets, blankets, and coverlet to make them as ruthlessly taut as before.

Then he went downstairs and across the empty saloon and opened the door to pass through into the snug.

And to the sudden silence that greeted him, he said, "Who's in charge?"

THREE

I AM. WHO ARE YOU?"

The man who'd spoken up was sitting behind a map table in the snug, a Bartholomew sheet for the area opened out before him. Another man, the parish constable in the hand-me-down uniform, stood looking over his shoulder. The rest of the company, and the source of most of the noise, were local men who appeared to feel that wetting their whistles in the bar was an essential prerequisite for a successful search. A door stood open to the inn yard outside, and more of them stood out there.

Sebastian said, "My name is Sebastian Becker. I just arrived. I'm staying in this hotel."

"What of it? You can see we're busy here, Mister Becker."

"I heard about the children. I want to join the search."

The seated man was around thirty, perhaps even younger. The detective from the county force. The parents of the girls must be people of some influence.

He said, "Do you know the area?"

"I can read a map," Sebastian said.

"This is the only map we have."

"Then put me with someone who knows the land," Sebastian said, his irritation rising. "Preferably one not doing his looking in the bottom of a pint glass."

As a couple of the whistle-wetters made indignant noises, the parish constable moved toward the yard and beckoned for him to follow.

"I'll send him out with Endell's men," the constable said. "This way, Mister Becker."

Sebastian followed the man out. He would later learn that the parish constable was also the Sun Inn's landlord, and that when required the snug became a makeshift police headquarters. The cellar had served as a lockup until a seafront cardsharper had spilled an entire barrel of ale in a bungled attempt to get a drink out of it.

They joined a waiting company of searchers around the back of the inn, just as a horse-drawn farm wagon with a twelve-year-old boy at the reins came clattering into the yard.

"One more for you, Ralph," the constable said.

Ralph Endell was a middle-aged man who moved like an old one, dressed for outdoor work. His fair hair was mostly sheared close and he had a mustache that Lord Kitchener might have envied.

"Aye?" he said.

"Aye. Don't lose him."

All climbed on, and Endell offered Sebastian a hand to scramble up.

"Where are we going?" Sebastian said.

"We're taking the woods and quarries," Endell said. "There's a few wrong places up there where two kiddies might come to grief."

As their wagon climbed a cobbled street that turned into a dirt lane behind some houses, Sebastian said, "Who's the detective giving the orders back there?"

"Stephen Reed?" one of the others said. "He's a county copper, but he grew up local. He was the harbor master's son."

Another man said, "It was a mistake to send him. People who knew him as a lad can't take him serious now."

Ralph Endell said, "You're never a prophet in your own land," and the others all made a knowing chorus of agreement.

They were an assorted bunch. Most were obviously outdoor workers, dressed in layers of their oldest clothing. One man was an oystercatcher, and a couple worked on boats. Endell had been the local blacksmith; he still shod horses, but now he also sold petrol in gallon cans along with parts and tires for motor vehicles.

They'd have about four useful hours of daylight. The first volunteers had ignored police orders and set out to concentrate their efforts along the shoreline. These were the people that Sebastian had seen from his window.

"Why waste time looking on the beach?" one of the men said. "It's live bodies we're needing to find."

HIS COMPANION was right. It made far less sense to search in the obvious place for drowned girls than in the less likely places for live ones. Sad to say it, but a drowned girl would come to no further harm. The boy soldiers, he learned, had been called in from a local barracks. Some of them had received less than three weeks' training. They'd been sent farther up, to comb through the open heath above the woodland.

After a bumpy quarter of a mile, their cart came to a stop by an overgrown gateway. The wall here had been pushed over long ago, and greenery had forced its way up through the stones.

When the oldest member of the party began to climb down, Ralph Endell said to Sebastian, "You go with Arthur. His eyes aren't what they used to be."

"Nothing wrong with these eyes," Arthur said without looking back.

"Nor with your ears, when it suits you," Ralph Endell called after him.

Arthur was like a rangy old whippet. Not fast, but once he'd set the pace, he didn't flag. They climbed to the ruins of a farm that had been abandoned for so long that a tree had grown right through one of its broken walls. This gave the building an air that was both commonplace and magical. It was exactly the kind of fairy-tale setting that might attract children of some imagination.

A low wall enclosed a jungle of riotous weeds that had once been a kitchen garden. Here Arthur lowered himself stiffly and sat, lips compressed and breathing loudly through his nose, while Sebastian went ahead and did the exploring.

The farmhouse itself was only a partial shell. The most complete of the outbuildings was a low stone structure built around a wellspring. He pushed in the rotten door to look inside. The small building was windowless, its walls thick with moss and mold. Water spouted from a lion's-head carving in the back wall to fill an overflowing stone trough beneath. The ground for yards around the doorway was spongy and soft.

Otherwise, the site was a ruin. The main building's roof had collapsed and taken the floors with it, right down into the cellars. In the shelter of its walls, Sebastian found evidence of several campfires; but these were old, and the carbonized bones in them were rabbit bones. He looked around for clothing, for marks of any kind.

When he found an opening to a part of the cellar, a wide mouth into complete darkness, he crouched before it and called the girls' names.

"Molly? Florence?"

He'd learned them on the cart. Molly Button and Florence Bell; best friends, spending their summer in a villa rented by Florence's parents.

His voice echoed in the space under the old house. But he expected no reply. The dirt that he could see around the opening had been smoothed by heavy rain and hadn't been disturbed by anything other than birds' feet in some time. Their fine toes had patterned the mud, imprinting a thousand tiny trident shapes without ever sinking in.

"No one's been here," he told Arthur when he rejoined him in front of the site.

"No one?"

"Not for some time," Sebastian said. "Tell me something. Do people often go missing in these parts?"

"Things happen that you don't always hear about," Arthur said.

"What does that mean?"

"Folk come here to spend their money," Arthur said. "Bad news hurts trade."

And so they moved on to the next place.

A proper search over a wide area was a hard thing to organize. Taking a map and squaring off the landscape for methodical investigation guaranteed a kind of military thoroughness but could take days or longer when speed was essential. Much better to start with the places that children frequented, where mishaps might occur. Check every barn, well, quarry, and gully. Stop and question every suspicious character. And if you could get them, use dogs. Nothing could beat a well-trained dog.

Meanwhile, in a place like this, there would always be the sea to consider; close to hand, not to be overlooked, but offering little in the way of a hopeful outcome.

They crossed a field and entered a copse. The two men separated and spent the best part of an hour going through it. Some of the trees here had been marked for felling, but there was no sign of the woodsmen. Sebastian scared off a fox.

After making certain of the copse, they moved on. A track from the wood led to a disused set of rails, which in turn led to a mine shaft about a quarter of a mile farther on.

"How far is it to Sir Owain Lancaster's estate?" Sebastian said.

"You're on it," said his garrulous partner, and that was that for a while.

This place was more menacing than magical. The shaft was a vertical hole in the ground capped with wooden railway sleepers. The middle beams of the cover had collapsed in, and when Sebastian looked through the rotted hole he could see black water fifteen feet down. He cast all around looking for signs, but saw none.

He stepped back. Arthur was plucking at his lips, thoughtfully. He saw that Sebastian was watching him, and stopped doing it.

"Anywhere else we can look?" Sebastian said.

"There's not a lot more we can do before nightfall," Arthur said, and then, sadly and unexpectedly, added, "God bless them."

Suddenly he was no longer a surly old local, but some child's grandfather. And the places they were visiting might well have been his own remembered playgrounds, from a life spent on this land.

As they crossed a field to join a lane that looked very like the one that they'd left, they saw someone running down the hill. A lad, by the looks of him. He saw them at the same time, and diverted to meet them.

As he drew close, Sebastian could see that it was the youngest-looking of the boy soldiers. He was white-faced and flustered.

He said to Sebastian, "Are you the detective?"

"No," Sebastian said. "He's down at the inn. What's the matter?"

"We found them," the boy said.

Then was violently sick.

FOUR

THE TWO BODIES HAD BEEN PULLED FEET-FIRST FROM A SCRUB-filled gully, and now lay side by side. They were like white china dolls in a woodland clearing. Their cotton dresses had been dragged upward to cover their faces as they were pulled out of the gorse. One still wore underthings, the other none. Their feet were bare. Half a dozen of the boy soldiers were picking around the site to no convincing purpose, and a couple were staring at the exposed parts of the unclad child.

"Hey," Sebastian called out across the clearing. "Who's in charge, here? Has someone moved those bodies?"

Most of their faces turned his way, but none of them responded. There they stood, all pale and slack in their ill-fitting khaki. As Sebastian drew closer he could see that a soldier near the bodies had emptied a wicker picnic basket onto the ground at his feet and was stirring through the contents with the toe of his army boot, nosing them around like the muzzle of a clumsy dog.

"Stop that!" Sebastian said. "Put everything down!"

He was breathless from his dash to the scene, but not too breathless to shout. The soldier looked up and the others continued to stare, as if Sebastian were some madman who'd come crashing into a private function to blurt out obscenities.

Good God, was there *nothing* they hadn't disturbed? One was down among the gorse bushes in the gully and had lifted a bloodied cotton bag of some kind on the end of a stick. He appeared to have been poking around in the undergrowth and passing up anything he could find.

This included a wooden box that one of the others had paused in the act of trying to open.

"For God's sake!" Sebastian said, turning here and there to address them all, his voice so sharp and loud that it scared a bird or two out of the trees above their heads. "Am I talking to myself? Stop trampling the ground and handling all the evidence! This could well be the scene of a crime! You have two dead children here! How do you expect anyone to account for them?"

Not one of the young men showed any sign of having understood, and he was beginning to wonder if he'd come upon some regiment of mutes or simpletons. He took three long strides and grabbed the wooden box from the soldier's hands, and he called down to the boy with the bloodied sack on a stick.

"Put that back wherever it was," he said. "As close as you can manage it. Step out of there and don't touch anything else."

At that moment he heard the engine of a motor truck, laboring hard, and turned to see the vehicle coming into sight at the other end of the clearing. It was the same truck that he'd seen collecting the boys from the station. At the wheel was its operator and beside him was the youngest soldier, the one who'd been sent down the hill, now returning to act as guide.

The truck pulled into the clearing and stopped, and from around the back there was a crash as the tailgate dropped. A second later a figure swung into view, followed by another. One was the gray-headed sergeant, and the other, in a rather sharp tan overcoat, was the detective from the Sun Inn's snug.

Stephen Reed looked first at the bodies, and stopped. Some of the will seemed to go out of him, just for a moment, as if he'd absorbed a blow, and Sebastian saw the youth behind his authority. Serving officers quickly grew hardened and could view wasted adult life with little emotion. But a dead child was a grief to all the world.

From the bodies, he looked up to Sebastian. He saw the box in Sebastian's hands, and his face grew dark.

Before Sebastian could speak, Stephen Reed was walking toward him. His expression was one of fury.

"That man!" he said, and he pointed a finger. "Tampering with evidence! What do you think you're doing?"

Sebastian stood his ground. "In your absence, I was doing your job," he said.

Stephen Reed looked back at the army sergeant and said, "Arrest this man."

"You heard him, boy!" the sergeant said to the nearest of his squad. "What are you waiting for?"

So they weren't deaf after all. Having borne his abuse, here was their license to respond. The box was knocked from Sebastian's hands and he was seized by the arms and collar and rushed toward the back of the waiting truck. He could hear Stephen Reed saying, "Sergeant, I need you to remove everyone from this place, now," and he tried to call something back over his shoulder, but a sly punch in his side made it impossible to speak.

He was shouted at and forcefully propelled into the back of the motor truck, where he just about managed not to land on the dirty floor but made it onto one of the side benches.

Two of the boys climbed in after and sat, one with a rifle, to guard him. Sebastian's last sight of the scene, as the truck made a bumping circle and returned to the lane, was of Stephen Reed crouching and gingerly starting to uncover the face of one of the dead girls.

He took a deep breath and relaxed back against the side of the wagon, as much as he was able. The seat was hard and the track was rough, and every now and again he had to grab the slats to keep from being thrown around. The only light came from the open back and through vents cut into the canvas, making the wagon a moving box of musty shadows.

The boy soldiers were watching him with dead eyes. Their manner had changed. They were no longer passive but had been given the upper hand.

One said, "What do we do with him?"

And the other, the one that he'd berated, shrugged and then blew air out through closed lips in a gesture that said, *Don't ask me.*

Sebastian said, "If there's a police station, you take me there."

"You shut yer mouth," the second one said.

So Sebastian settled back for the rest of the grim ride, and closed his eyes and looked inward, where he saw again the uncompleted moment as the county detective reached to uncover a dead child's face.

Molly or Florence. He didn't know which.

Perhaps he should have stayed in his room. For he'd surely achieved nothing for anyone by leaving it.

FIVE

T HE MOTOR TRUCK STOPPED RIGHT BY THE SUN INN'S COACH-
yard gate. In the absence of the parish constable, who was now
out on a bicycle making house-to-house visits to all of Arnmouth's
holiday villas, Sebastian was placed in the charge of the cook.

"What am *I* supposed to do with you?" she said.

"Strictly speaking," Sebastian said, "you ought to lock me up. Tempers were frayed up there and I'm supposed to be under arrest. Don't
fear, ma'am. It was a misunderstanding in the moment. And I'm not the
most pressing thing for the authorities to deal with right now."

"Have they found the girls?"

"I don't think that's for me to say."

"It's something bad, isn't it?"

"I'm afraid so."

"Did they drown?"

"It's worse than that."

She knew. Her hand flew to her mouth, and for a moment she
looked drained and ill.

Sebastian said, "I'm sorry. I gather it's not the first time that children have come to grief?"

But she left him then, too upset to say.

AFTER ANOTHER fifteen minutes or so, a rocket was sent up from the
harbor. It burst high above the town and came down in a shower of
light, like an angel winged by grapeshot. It was the signal for all of the
search parties to abandon their efforts, for whatever reason. It was to

be a good two hours until Stephen Reed returned. In that time, Sebastian obeyed the letter of his arrest and did not leave the inn. He did, however, go up to his room.

He could not settle, nor even think of returning to his reading. Sir Owain's book would have to wait. He went through to the upstairs dining room and watched through various windows as the Specials gathered on the street and climbed into cars and wagons to be transported up to the site.

Only the Sun Inn's landlord wore the police uniform. The others wore volunteer armbands and apprehensive looks. Missing children were one thing, murdered children another. Those who'd willingly joined a search party now found themselves being shepherded up the hill to less welcome duties.

There was a telephone close by. It was across the way in the house of the preventative officer, the town's own customs official, and was in constant use with people running back and forth with messages.

After about an hour, activity began to center on a large building three doors down, separated from the customs house by a row of alms cottages. This building was tall and churchlike, with high windows and a bricked-up Gothic doorway. The entrance in use was to the side of it, and much less striking.

Gaslights were lit inside, and all the doors were thrown open. After a while a cart arrived, bearing a number of well-used trestle tables. By now a crowd had gathered, and some lent a hand to carry them. Blackout curtains were raised at the windows to create a private space within.

Throughout all this time, the light was fading; and at the point where the day was all but extinguished in the sky, a number of the Specials returned and moved everybody back. They set up a ring around the building, where they stood facing outward and looking uncomfortable at this implied confrontation with their neighbors. But the small crowd complied, as if they, too, had a role to play here, and wished only to be told what was proper.

Where were the parents, Sebastian wondered? Not here and waiting on the pavement for news, that was for sure. But no one would ever envy them this day. In fact, Florence Bell's mother was in their rented villa, and her father on his way up from London. The parents of Molly Button—childhood friend, now fixed in her childhood forever—would know nothing about anything until the next morning, when a telegram would reach them at their hotel in Aix-les-Bains.

And now the light was gone. It was not so much like the fading of the day as the looming of a terrible shadow, rising from the woodland on the far side of the hill and inking out the sky.

The wagons came then, down from the hill in a silent convoy. The one bearing the stretchers led, and the ring of volunteers opened to let it pass through. The bodies were taken into the hall and one of the Specials gave a hand to help the vicar, who'd made the journey with them, to climb down and follow after. He was elderly, and the climb was difficult for him. The girls were fully sheeted, but their small forms were unmistakable. Some of the women turned away. The men stared, bleakly.

Boxes and bags were taken in, all the evidence collected from the scene. The local doctor arrived from the hill a few minutes later and followed the bodies into the hall.

There was little to see after that. The doors were closed, the volunteers dispersed, the wagons all sent away. There was a general move toward the church. One man remained to guard the door of the hall.

After a while, the church bell began to ring.

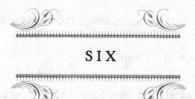

SIX

STEPHEN REED ENTERED THE SUN INN'S ILL-LIT AND DESERTED snug about half an hour later.

He'd left papers and his briefcase on the map table. No one had been in to light the gas, and the only illumination came from the passageway behind the bar.

He started to gather his few effects together, and then he seemed to lose heart. He kicked out the chair and sat, heavily.

Sebastian said, startling the officer a little, "Is this your first murder?"

Reed recovered himself. "No," he said.

"But your first with children."

He peered at Sebastian in the gloom. Sebastian moved forward, the better to be seen.

"Sebastian Becker. I'm the special investigator for the Lord Chancellor's Visitor in Lunacy."

"Oh?"

"You had me arrested for trying to protect your evidence. What happened to the camera I was holding? Please tell me you didn't let those boys interfere with it."

"That was a camera?" the detective said.

"I believe so."

"It was like none I've ever seen."

"Where is it now?"

"Over in the assembly rooms, along with the bodies. Everything's there."

"It's a slim chance," Sebastian suggested, "but the plate may carry an image from those girls' last hour. Has anyone been stupid enough to open it?"

Stephen Reed's distraction fell away, and his sense of purpose seemed to return.

"Oh, Lord," he said. "I hope not."

He went out onto the street. A reasonably bright-looking child in a cadet's uniform was passing, and Stephen Reed collared him. He sent him at a run with a message for the man on the door at the hall. Then he came back inside.

"You're not a policeman?" Stephen Reed said.

"I used to be."

"But you work for the Lord Chancellor now."

"For his Visitor in Lunacy. Sir James Crichton-Browne."

"What does that mean?"

Sebastian took out the letters of authority that he always carried with him.

"When the sanity of a man of property is questioned," he said, handing the letters over, "it's the Visitor's duty to determine whether such a man is competent to manage his own affairs. Sometimes the mad can be devious in concealing their madness. I investigate those cases."

Stephen Reed looked at the papers.

He said, "Insanity in our town? I'd say your investigation has implications for mine."

"If there is evidence to support such a notion, trust me to share it. There's a telephone across the way. Call the Bethlem Hospital. They keep an office for me there. If you're in any doubt as to my character, they will confirm what I'm telling you."

Stephen Reed handed the papers back to Sebastian.

"I jumped to a hasty conclusion," he said, while managing not to seem too unhappy about it.

"No apology required," Sebastian said, aware that none had been offered. He returned the papers to the inside of his coat. "Are they definitely the girls you were looking for?"

"I believe so. But I can't say for certain until we reach Mister Bell to arrange a formal identification. It's not a thing I can ask of a mother."

"I heard say that Bell's a judge in town."

"A barrister. Florence was his daughter and Molly her best friend. Molly's parents are abroad. Bell won't be here until morning and I can tell you, that will not be an easy hour of any man's life. Their faces have been disfigured."

"Do you have children of your own?"

"Not even married. Which does not make it any less hard to look upon."

Sebastian said, "It'll go well with your superintendent if you can offer a theory."

"I know," Stephen Reed said. "Some clothing is missing. I'm thinking this may be a crime of child-stripping gone too far. These were well-dressed girls. Except . . ."

"What?"

Stephen Reed shook his head, fully aware that his theory was not a good one. He seemed about to say as much when his young messenger reappeared in the doorway. The boy seemed reluctant to cross the threshold into licensed premises.

"Well?" Stephen Reed said.

"Your man on the door says to tell you that someone's in there looking at the girls."

Stephen Reed was shocked. "He was to open the room to no one," he said, and the boy could do no more than look helpless.

"He says it's Sir Owain, sir."

Stephen Reed set off for the hall, with Sebastian following close behind.

SEVEN

THERE WAS NOW A MOTOR VEHICLE ON THE STREET OUTSIDE the hall, a landaulet tourer with a silent chauffeur seated in the open behind its wheel. The chauffeur was gloved and muffled against the elements. There was no one in the passenger cab behind him. Stephen Reed went past the vehicle and bore down on his man at the door.

"I said to let nobody in," Stephen Reed said.

"I know," the man said, "but it's Sir Owain, sir. How was I supposed to stop him?"

"Nobody means nobody!"

Sebastian followed Stephen Reed inside.

The construction of the public assembly rooms was honest and unfussy. The floors were of scrubbed bare planks, the walls of painted boards. A large public chamber with seats and a stage and open rafters stood dark and empty. They passed along a corridor beside it to a suite of rooms behind the stage.

A second volunteer watchman sat on a chair in the corridor. He rose as Stephen Reed was approaching and began to give a halting explanation of his conduct.

But before the man could say much of anything, the detective said, "I'll be speaking to you later," and swept on by. Following a few paces behind, Sebastian was able to see the special constable's unhappy expression as he sank back to his seat.

One of the rooms was a scullery. It had tiled walls and a sloping floor with a drain at its center. Its windows were small and high with frosted glass and metal bars. It was into this room that the two girls had been brought to spend their first night as objects of mourning and evidence of murder.

They lay much as they'd lain in the woods, side by side, only now on folding tables, and covered by shrouds. Someone had placed a single flower on each.

Two men were in the room with them.

One man stood back and played no part. In the soft, unsteady glow of gaslight the older of the two had raised a corner of one of the shrouds and was looking on the face beneath. In the time since the bodies had been brought in, a small amount of blood had risen through the fine linen and now marked the positions of the features and the girls' extremities.

"Sir," Stephen Reed said, "this is a criminal investigation. I have to ask you to leave."

Without dropping the material, the man looked up. He was somewhere past his sixtieth year. His eyes were almost without color, his hair sparse and white. Sebastian could see that, at least until recent years, he'd been a man of some vigor. He still had the frame of one, but now an older man's flesh hung on it. The same slight air of misfit could be seen in his starched collar and heavy tweed suit. The suit was—had been—of the most expensive weight and cut. A suit fit for a gentleman of the shires.

"And you are . . . ?" he said.

"Detective Sergeant Stephen Reed. I'm the officer in charge of this case."

The man holding up the shroud gave a sweet smile. Which Sebastian found unsettling, given the circumstances.

"Albert Reed's boy?"

"Sir," the young man said, testily.

"No harm done, Sergeant Reed," Sir Owain said. "We're men of science. And these girls were found on my land."

During this exchange Sebastian was eyeing the second man, standing over against the wall. This man was some ten years younger. An educated professional, by the look of him. He stood with arms folded, his expression betraying no emotion. But his gaze flicked from his companion to the detective, and back again. As if ready to step in with a word or more, should anything more than a word be needed.

Stephen Reed said, "I know who you are, sir. But for the moment this is not a public place and you should not have entered it."

"Your policemen let me in."

"They were at fault in doing so. Please replace the sheet as you found it."

The corner of the shroud was lowered with the greatest delicacy.

"You don't want to hear my theory, then," Sir Owain said.

"I need to hear anything that will help me to find those responsible. But please."

Stephen Reed gestured toward the door. The second man had unfolded his arms and now stepped forward from the wall to murmur something into his companion's ear. Sebastian was unable to pick up what was said, but it had the air of a gentle suggestion.

At that, the older man nodded. He didn't so much lead the way out as move ahead and allow himself to be steered. Sebastian followed, and Stephen Reed stayed behind for a moment to check the room and then lower the gas.

In Stephen Reed's position, Sebastian would have been happy to hear any theory, too. This was no incident of child-stripping. That had been a common crime once, taking advantage of a child's size and weakness to steal and sell its clothing. But even then it had rarely ended in death, except incidentally as a result of exposure.

The volunteer Special was on his feet again. Stephen Reed came out of the room and closed the door behind him. He closed it gently, as if not to disturb the sleep of those inside.

He straightened and said to the first of the two intruders, "Now, sir. What can you tell me?"

And the older man leaned forward and put his hand on the detective's arm. He looked intently into Stephen Reed's eyes and said, in a tone as if imparting a deep confidence, "Those children were torn by beasts."

Stephen Reed's expression did not change.

"Beasts," he said.

"Of a form that the human mind can barely encompass. Your search parties won't find them. They arise, do what they will, and then vanish away."

He waited for a reaction. The second man stepped in close and touched his companion's shoulder; the older man was aware of it, and the shift in his posture acknowledged it, but he did not take his eyes from Stephen Reed's. He would stay there until he had a response.

The detective said, "Thank you, Sir Owain. I'll make a note of that."

The other man had a proper hold on Sir Owain, and Sir Owain, satisfied that he'd been heard, allowed himself to be drawn away. Not so much by a friend or a companion as by a keeper.

Speaking out for the first time, Sebastian called after him, saying, "Sir Owain Lancaster. Yes?"

Sir Owain turned back on hearing his name.

Sebastian went on, "My name is Sebastian Becker. You should be expecting a visit from me."

The second man, whom Sebastian assumed to be Dr. Hubert Sibley, Lancaster's personal physician, said, "Surely not tonight?"

"We'll make it tomorrow morning," Sebastian said. "I'm staying at the Sun Inn. Can you send your car to pick me up at ten?"

Sibley didn't try to argue. "I'm sure that will be acceptable," he said. "We'll be ready for you then."

As for Sir Owain, it was as if he'd said his piece. Now he was happy to do whatever he was told.

Dr. Sibley finally succeeded in drawing his patient away and ushered him out to their waiting car. Stephen Reed let out a breath and then closed his eyes, taking a moment to settle his mind. Outside, Sebastian could hear the Daimler being started on its crank.

Here in the corridor, there was a moment's silence. The Special waited for the reprimand that he probably didn't think he deserved.

Then, choosing his words with care, Stephen Reed said, "You know more of this than you've been saying, Mister Becker, and you've known it all along."

"The camera?" Sebastian prompted.

Stephen Reed hesitated, wary of saying anything more that the Special might overhear and repeat.

"This way," he said to Sebastian, and led the way to a storage room adjoining the scullery.

The room was small and had been cleared of its usual contents in order to fit in two more of the folding tables. All the pieces of evidence from the woodland scene had been laid out separately, like parts of a puzzle or a toy requiring assembly. Shoes, the contents of the wicker basket, the bloodstained cloth bags fished from the gorse.

Stephen Reed surveyed the arrangement.

"Any sign of interference?" Sebastian said.

"I don't believe so."

In the middle of one table stood the varnished wooden box that Sebastian had taken from the boy soldier, and which had been taken from him in turn.

"Is that the camera you meant?" Stephen Reed said. "I took it for some kind of an instrument case. It's not like any camera that I've seen."

"Nor me," Sebastian said. "But there's a maker's plate and a patent number, and that surely is some kind of a lens on the side. We shouldn't try to do anything with it. This calls for professional advice. Did I see a photographer's studio on the main street?"

"The local photographer went out with the search," Stephen Reed said, turning the box around and squinting to read the maker's plate in the poor light. "I'll have him look at this first thing in the morning."

Carefully, he set the box back in its place. Sebastian was looking at the two bloodstained bags. The blood had dried and the print was difficult to read, but they appeared to be flour bags.

"Those were lying close to the bodies," Stephen Reed said.

"Not covering the faces?"

"I think they probably were. They may have been pulled from the heads of the children as they were dragged out into the open. But I can't get the soldiers to say."

"Why did the soldiers move them at all?"

"Because they thought it was required of them. Like corpses from the field of battle. They'd have put the bodies on a cart and brought them back into town if they'd had one."

"This is not a consequence of child-stripping," Sebastian said. "You surely can't think so."

"I'm sorry we got off on the wrong foot, you and I. But I suggest that now it's time to share your knowledge."

"That is awkward," Sebastian said, "given that it involves both Sir Owain and your own superiors to some degree."

"In what way, exactly?"

"Come to the inn when your business here is done," Sebastian said, "and I can show you what I mean."

EIGHT

A s Sebastian Becker was leaving the assembly rooms in Arnmouth, back in South London his wife was locking away the ledgers that she'd been studying for the past two hours. The heavy books with their pages of close writing went into a cupboard in the receiving office of the Evelina Hospital on Southwark Bridge Road.

Elisabeth Becker had been working late, getting the August report for the Committee of Management into order. Elisabeth was the clerk to the hospital's receiving officer, whose role it was to assess each patient's family for their ability to pay. Treatment was free to children whose parents were without means. The Evelina was a charity hospital, and most of its patients were the children of the poor.

The office was on the ground floor, close to the house surgeon's rooms. This was an odd-shaped building, designed to fit a donated site in a crowded and busy part of Southwark. It was tall, with long curving sides and a flattened front end. Seen from the appropriate angle, its lines could remind a visitor of the rear view of an old-fashioned galleon towering overhead.

On her way out Elisabeth bade a good evening to Mr. Briggs, who supervised the porters and kept order in the public areas. A onetime military man with no family, he lived in sparse quarters behind the postmortem room but was rarely to be found there. By day he stood in the hallway and directed visitors to their various destinations. By night he patrolled the stairwells and corridors. He had a straight back and a stern eye, but a bout of pneumonia last winter had left him perceptibly frail. Now he patrolled with the aid of a stick, and had been discouraged from passing through the wards after his shadowy figure and the steady thump of his staff had raised nightmares in some of the children.

"Good night, Mister Briggs," she said.

"A good night to you, Mrs. Becker," he said, with a slight bow of his head.

It was a pity about the nightmares. They were understandable, but undeserved. Mr. Briggs always had a kind word for the children. It was their guardians who sometimes needed a reminder of authority. Most were respectful of being in a hospital, but some showed behavior that was affected by guilt, grief, drink, or any other of those factors that can render the human personality unpredictable under pressure.

At the door, she passed two of the nurses coming in. They wore blue uniforms with white caps and aprons. They'd probably been over to Guy's; Guy's Hospital was only a few streets away, and staff often had cause to pass between the two.

She stepped onto the street. Her head buzzed with figures, and her eyes ached from the strain of close work. It was already dark outside. But at least she was in the open now, if this busy and noisy road could be called such. Despite the racket of a passing tram, she felt a little of the tension lift.

Her eyes hadn't always ached so. Elisabeth's last birthday had been her fortieth. She'd approached her forty-first year without any special apprehension, but now she didn't know what to make of it. Every Englishwoman of forty or over seemed to regard herself as old, and to behave accordingly; but Elisabeth was a Philadelphian American, and didn't care to consider herself among them.

Was this reasonable? Or did she fool herself? The mirror showed lines, but not so many. Her mind was sharp, and she was still trim. But on the inside, there was a kind of dismay.

She regretted none of the choices she'd made in her life. She might, however, have appreciated some advance warning about the speed with which life's options would narrow.

Heading up Southwark Bridge Road, she breathed in the air. South London air, a chilled brew of river and coal smoke and horses and fog. Ahead of her, several lines of railway track passed above the road on a mighty iron viaduct that roofed over the world as she entered the space beneath. For the next hundred yards ran a low riveted sky. Here in its shelter stood the all-night pie stand where cabbies stopped to refresh themselves and where Sebastian, when he was around, had an arrangement to pick up his messages.

Once she'd had a goal, which was to find some excuse to bring their troubled son to London. A bad turn in her husband's career had provided it. Now they were here, and she was finding it hard to settle on any further purpose to her life beyond the day-to-day.

She often wished she could discuss these matters with Sebastian. But whenever she felt able to speak of them, Sebastian was always away on Lunacy business; and when he spent a few days at home, it was as if all the wrong feelings came rising to the fore.

And she knew how he would respond. He would make suggestions. Tell your troubles to a man, and to the best of his ability he'd advise you how to fix them. Complain at that, and you'd bewilder him. Why seek advice, only in order to reject it? What, otherwise, could have been the point of the conversation?

The evening fog put a hazy ring of light around every streetlamp. Five minutes' walk ahead was the river. Beyond the river, the great shining capital, while behind her spread Southwark's unhealthy warren of tenements, warehouses, and overcrowded dwellings, along with its churches, workshops, and gilded public houses.

She rarely crossed the river. When she reached Southwark Street, she turned right. These days her journeys were always the same; from home to the Evelina, from the Evelina to her home.

Such as it was. Four rooms and an attic above a wardrobe maker's, reached by a stairway between two shops. It was her second home in London, and their sixth or seventh in the past nine years. Back when Sebastian had been the rising British Pinkerton man in the Philadelphia office, they'd rented a neat row house in a nice part of town.

Life was different now. And in at least one respect, it surely was better. It was for Robert's sake that she'd sold her mother's emeralds to get them here, and there could be no question that he'd gained by the move.

She was passing the chocolate factory, a Victorian building that was straining to be something more French and fancy. Its windows were busy with flutes and fruit and columns and added detail. She was close to home now. Her last turn would be into a side street after the next railway bridge, across from the Borough Market.

Their son, Robert, had recently turned eighteen. He'd been a child of fearsome intelligence and overpowering obsessions; loving, articulate, and blessed with a phenomenal memory. But he was also a child who could be rendered mute and uncooperative by any attempt to impose discipline upon him. Rare was the teacher or physician who'd spare the time or the patience to understand the boy's needs. Everyone to whom they turned would class him as subnormal, or as feebleminded at best.

Elisabeth had read journals and learned papers, but it was a chance remark by her own clinician that had led her to the work in London of Dr. John Langdon Down. In a series of lectures to the Medical Society the doctor had described many of Robert's attributes, concluding that the condition was the product of something other than the congenital or the merely accidental. Here, at last, she'd thought, was someone who might understand.

Down had founded an institute for his patients, a family-run community on the outskirts of London, based on principles of education and compassion. Elisabeth had written to him there, only to learn that the doctor had passed on. His sons were continuing his work. Reginald Langdon Down had advised caution over her hopes for Robert. He might be helped, but it was wrong to hope for anything so conclusive as a cure.

After an hour spent with Robert, mainly discussing the dime magazines of which the boy had an encyclopedic knowledge, Dr. Reginald had recommended a private day college run by a colleague in South Hampstead. They'd managed to secure him a place. Robert had begun to flourish there and, for the first time in his life, to be happy outside the home.

It had been a struggle for the family. They had no income and were four in number, including Elisabeth's unmarried sister, Frances. But then, with letters of introduction secured from the Down brothers, her husband had found employment with Sir James Crichton-Browne, the Lord Chancellor's Visitor in Lunacy.

Crichton-Browne's investigator was on the point of retiring, and the Visitor had need of a man with Sebastian's talents. The work suited his skills, but the pay was not good. Elisabeth had taken her job at the hospital, and Frances, when not accompanying Robert across town, took in piecework for a local haberdasher.

Here was their street. Some would call it an alley. She looked up at the windows above the wardrobe maker's and saw that the sitting-room lamps were lit. Their previous lodgings had been wired for electricity, but they hadn't been able to afford to use it.

This was not the life that she'd dreamed of, but this was the life that she had. Her son seemed happy, and only in her worst moments did she find herself resenting him for it. Sebastian would be home in a day or two.

It was far from perfection. But what would she change? Here was one aspect of her existence that she never could have predicted: that so many of the things that she valued would have been born out of her disappointments. Which made it impossible for her to wish her disappointments away.

And now she was home.

She let herself into the tiny hallway between the piano shop and the wardrobe maker's, and ascended the stairway to her waiting family.

NINE

It was Sebastian's habit, when away from London, to send a postcard home at the first opportunity. His wife would be assured of his safe arrival, and if it was a picture card then Robert could add it to his collection.

His Arnmouth card that evening was a plain one from a sixpenny packet in his luggage, and when writing it he made no mention of the afternoon's events. He addressed it in his room and then took it downstairs to give to the landlord for the morning collection.

He walked into a fug of beer and smoke. In the hour since his return from the assembly hall, the bar had been opened. The saloon and public rooms were now filled with local men, some the whistle-wetters from that afternoon, others still in their volunteer armbands. Despite the shadow that had been cast by the day, there was nothing subdued about their conversation. Tragedy always sharpened a community.

"Will you take a drink, Mister Becker?" the landlord asked him over the roar. The landlord's name was Bill Turnbull, and he'd shed his constable's jacket to work the pumps.

"I was hoping to get some supper," Sebastian said. "Is there any possibility?"

"I'll send Dolly out when she's got a minute," Bill Turnbull said, "if you don't mind a wait."

Supposing it would make no difference if he did mind, Sebastian agreed that he didn't. He ordered a brandy and then, turning from the bar, spied Ralph Endell. The blacksmith was behind a table with three or four others, in a nook between the fireplace and the dining room. Endell made a gesture of invitation, and Sebastian went over.

They made space for him. Sebastian supposed that he'd be expected to stand the group a round at some point, and that point came rather quickly. He called Dolly over. She fetched the drinks on a tray and took his order for a sandwich and a bowl of the local fish stew.

They knew that he'd been to the spot where the bodies were found, and wanted to know more. He gave them an account of his arrival at the scene and his treatment at the hands of the army, with as little of the indelicate detail as he could include. In return he picked up the tap-room gossip and speculation, which had no real substance to it at all. No local man could ever do such a thing, so it must have been gypsies, tinkers, or German spies.

"We'll see what happens tomorrow," one of the party said. "When the proper police get here." He had small hands, wire spectacles, and a hank of hair that he'd arranged across his balding head in the hope of persuading the world that it grew there.

Ralph Endell had spoken the truth when he'd said that no man was ever a prophet in his own land. Penny Dreadfuls and story papers had recreated police detectives as exotic figures of adventure. A local boy like Stephen Reed could never expect to be taken seriously as one of their number.

After twenty minutes or so, and with no sign yet of his supper, Sebastian saw Stephen Reed enter. Reed called the landlord down to the end of the bar, and the two of them were in conversation for a while. Then Bill Turnbull reached under the bar and brought out the residents' register.

Sebastian excused himself to the company and went over.

He found that Stephen Reed was arranging rooms for the senior detectives and other officers who'd be arriving in the morning to take over the case. The young detective sergeant didn't seem despondent about it. If anything, he seemed relieved. A weight would be off his shoulders. He explained as much to Sebastian and declined to join him in a brandy.

He said, "I'm not here to drink. I'm here for what you know."

"Upstairs," Sebastian said, and led the way.

THE RESIDENTS' corridor was as silent as it could be with a public bar directly beneath. As Sebastian stepped first into his room, he took a moment to look around before touching anything.

"What?" Stephen Reed said.

"I was downstairs for less than an hour," he said.

He went over to his Gladstone and looked inside. The bag was exactly as he'd left it, but there was no mistaking that the contents had been disturbed. Sebastian knew his own packing. Or rather, he knew Elisabeth's. She folded everything with precision and stowed it to a certain plan. No intruder could ever hope to recreate the effect.

He looked at Stephen Reed.

"I do believe I've been searched," he said.

"Not by me," Stephen Reed said.

The bedcovers didn't appear to have been touched, and when Sebastian tipped over the bolster, his book and the papers were still there. "Do you know what this is?" he said, holding the volume up.

Stephen Reed shook his head.

"It's Sir Owain's account of his Amazonian adventure. Though it purports to be a factual account, it's actually a fantasy of the most extreme order. He leads an expedition party into an unknown land. They find that they've ventured into a territory where monsters roam. The party is cut off from civilization and attacked from all sides. His men are carried off, one by one. At first the creatures move by night but then openly, by day. In the end, Sir Owain barely escapes with his life."

"And he presents all that as truth?"

"He offers photographs and documents as proof of his story, all manufactured. The truth of it seems to be that these are the facts as he believes them."

"Hence your interest."

"He's been of interest to my employers since the book was first published. You heard nothing of this? It caused quite a stir at the time."

"All I know is that he lost his wife and child under tragic circumstances in South America. I can imagine that being enough to damage any man's reason."

"Not just his wife and son. His entire party, from the mapmakers and surveyors right down to the cook. There's no true account. The inquest took place in a town where the British consul appeared to spend his nights in local whorehouses and his days sleeping off the drink, and his reports were useless.

"Questions from the bereaved families were met with offers of generous settlements. But the families have never been satisfied. There's a thirdhand rumor of a Portuguese bearer. He's supposed to have walked out of the jungle with a tale of the mad white captain who turned on his own crew when the river took his mind."

"More storybook stuff."

"That's how it's been dismissed," Sebastian said, taking the papers from out of the book. "Your police commissioner's response was a robust exoneration based on his personal knowledge of Sir Owain's character. I have a copy of his letter here."

"Let me understand this," Stephen Reed said, with no more than a glance at the letterhead. "You're telling me that Sir Owain is no mere eccentric. He's known to be mad."

"There are degrees of lunacy."

"But you've known this for some time and he's allowed to go free."

"One needs a good reason in law to deprive a man of his liberty."

"Especially a prominent man."

"Prominence should have nothing to do with it," Sebastian said. "But unfortunately, that's not always the case. This list was compiled by my predecessor. A more meticulous man than I." He gave the handwritten sheet to Stephen Reed.

As the young policeman scanned it, Sebastian went on, "My predecessor toured every parish with a border adjoining Sir Owain's estate and noted every death or disappearance in recent years. Suspicious or accidental, report or rumor, they all went in. A woman drowned in a pool. A girl who set off for school and neither arrived nor returned. The disappearances were always at a time when Sir Owain was at home."

Stephen Reed looked up from the list. "I know two of these names," he said.

"You do?"

"Grace Eccles and Evangeline May Bancroft. Local girls. They're my age. I knew them growing up. We went to the same school."

"Do you know what happened to them?"

"I remember some concern when they were lost on the moors one night. But it turned out they'd each misled their parents and gone camping together. They were found the next morning, miles from anywhere."

"Where are they now?"

"Evangeline's gone. She went away to London. And Grace is not an easy woman for anyone to speak to."

"Easy or not, this is no time for reticence. What if today's crime has a precedent?"

"It's not a matter of reticence," Stephen Reed said. "Believe me. If you were to meet Grace, you'd understand. May I hold on to this?"

At that moment, there was a knock at the door. It was Dolly, to say that Sebastian's supper was waiting for him in the dining room.

"Keep it," Sebastian said. "And do with it what you can."

TEN

IT WAS the morning after the night attack on our camp. The dead and the injured lay where they had fallen. Everyone came down out of the trees and out of their hiding places and began to share their stories of what they had seen. One of the *camaradas* told, in his halting English sprinkled with phrases from his native Portuguese, of seeing four of our fellows carried off alive.

I had witnessed no such thing myself. I am ashamed to say that the attack had been too sudden, and too overwhelming, for any response other than hasty self-preservation. One moment we had been sitting by our separate campfires, doing our best to raise each other's spirits for the further trials ahead; the next, it was as if a combined landslide, whirlwind, and stampede descended upon us, all at once.

You might say that, after our earlier experience upon the river, we should have been more prepared for something like it on dry land. In our defense, I should say that even the most fertile and apprehensive imagination could never have anticipated what came to befall us. First had come the sound, like the thunder of an approaching wave, to which had quickly been added the crashing of falling trees. We had barely time to rise to our feet and then the herd was upon us, charging through the camp, scattering bodies and trampling our fires.

What little I saw, I saw by firelight. I could make no estimate of their number. Each of those beasts was a giant, of a species hitherto unknown to science. They seemed to move as easily on two legs as on all fours, their long tails providing balance and their forelimbs as well adapted for gripping as running. At the time their attack appeared to have no purpose other than to terrify and destroy.

But now, as we counted our number that morning and found no less than three of our fellows and one of the *camaradas* missing, it seemed that the simple *peon*'s story was true. There was a purpose to the attack after all; we had been harvested. There was much grieving and wailing, and a great sense of gloom and despair settled upon the camp, and I resolved that if I did not act to dispel it, our adventure might end there, and all the struggles we had endured and the losses we had borne would be for nothing. I gathered everyone together and addressed them thus:

"We have already lost many of our number and most of our supplies in that terrible incident upon the river. Last night, we suffered losses again. But for those of us who have survived, let us remember that a certain providence has brought us this far. We live because it is clearly God's purpose that we should, and to give up now would be to go against his plan."

I saw hope in their faces as I spoke. Truth to tell, we had all been through a dreadful ordeal. To see one's comrades torn by beasts is a terrible thing. The river serpents that had upset our boats and taken our companions had left many in a state of shock, and I knew that from now on a few among us would need to have courage for the many. And with that in mind I set out the following plan.

Those injured in the night's attack would be moved to a new camp on higher ground. Dr S——— would supervise their care and set about the gathering of certain plants and herbs that would alleviate their injuries. I, meanwhile, would take my buffalo gun and follow the clear trail left by the night's attackers, in the hope that I might find and rescue some, or even all, of our fellows.

I credited those rampaging creatures with some dim intelligence, in that they had surely taken their victims alive for some purpose. What that purpose might be was too horrible to contemplate, but it gave me all the more reason to proceed without delay. I loaded the buffalo gun and gathered my remaining ammunition, after which I devised a way to hang it around my shoulders in a makeshift bandolier.

My enemies would be formidable, but thus armed I was confident that we might be evenly matched. My greatest danger was that they might come at me all at once, for the buffalo gun carried but a single round and required a reloading after every discharge. I was, however, banking on the prospect that the devastating effect of a large-bore hit upon one of the creatures would be enough to cause its fellows to turn and flee.

The others pleaded with me and expressed fear for my life, but I grew stern with them as if they were so many children, and reminded them of my authority as their leader.

"Enough," I said. "Bury our dead and fortify our camp against further attack, and I will return by nightfall, either with our missing comrades or with news of their ends."

With that they were resigned. Each man insisted on shaking my hand and wishing me well, and I saw tears in the eyes of more than one. As the effort of cutting wood to build a stronger stockade began, I took a half-day's ration of food from our meager supplies and set off to follow the trail left by the attacking herd.

Tracking them was no difficult job. No Roman army ever blazed a road so straight, nor so clearly defined, as those great primitive monsters in their advance through the jungle.

As I made progress, and as the sounds of the camp fell behind me, I began to realize that from tragedy there might yet arise some benefit to those who had survived. For this early part of the trail at least, it seemed that the herd had followed the line of the river and done much to break the way for us. Normally we had to move at a slow pace behind the Indians and *camaradas*, as they cut a path through the jungle with axes and machetes. But where the creatures had rampaged, they had left us a broad avenue along which we might pass with ease.

Within the hour, I had covered the kind of distance that otherwise would have taken us a day, and though I lost sight of the river for long stretches at a time, I was never beyond the sound of it. This was most important. Though we had lost our boats, the river was our God-given guide out of the wilderness. Without it we might circle forever, with the trees blocking out the sun and a steady madness descending for want of us having any purpose or direction.

Shortly after that, I saw my first signs that the creatures were near. I shall not go into detail. Suffice it to say that waste, flies, and steam played a part in my deductions. I moved onward with great caution, hoping not to betray my presence.

I had reasoned that, since the creatures had attacked us at night, then surely they must sleep by day. The night-adapted eye fares less well in the noonday sun, and the energies expended in night hunting must be recouped at some point.

My hope was that if our fellows had been taken as prey for future consumption, then there had been some purpose in taking them alive, and that keeping them alive was a part of the creatures' plan. If the creatures slept and I approached with sufficient stealth, I might yet be able to free my party and lead them back to our new camp, where a second attack would find us more prepared.

It was with these thoughts in mind that I crept forward and met a sight for which nothing could have prepared me. Had I realized how close I was, and how the creatures had moved to conceal themselves from sight, I would have been even more conscious of the need for silence in my progress. Fortunately the spot they had chosen for their day-nest was close to the river, where an unusually raucous set of fast-moving rapids made a noise that easily masked my movements.

The creatures had smashed down vegetation covering an area about the size of a tennis court, in order to make a type of bower. Within this jungle hollow all lay curled and sleeping, a dozen or more of them, their limbs and tails intertwining. A hasty count was impossible. I wish that I could have taken the time to make detailed observations and sketches. The ones that I reproduce in this volume are made from memory and not from life. Alas, all thoughts of science had deserted me in that moment, for it was now that I saw the fates of our comrades.

The creatures had, indeed, taken four men with the intent of preserving them alive. However, their method for this had evolved for use with prey more robust than man. Each member of my expedition lay pinned to the ground by an outstretched limb or tail, in a move calculated to prevent any from escaping while the creatures slept. But the crushing weight of those monstrous limbs had caused them to bear down with devastating effect. Our men had survived their kidnap only to be suffocated under the enormous weight of the creatures' extremities. In the case of one man (I shall not name him for fear of further distressing his widow), he had been pressed down onto broken vegetation so forcefully that the sharpened ends had passed through him like so many spears.

Fearsome though the scene was, I could not leave it without satisfying myself that no spark of life remained in any of my former companions. I crept as close as I dared, and then gathered my courage and crept closer still, until I was so close to those great beasts that I might have reached out and laid a hand upon their thick hides, had I been so inclined. Alas, it seemed that my daring was in vain. C————, our instrument-maker, was cold to the touch. The injuries sustained by R———— the cartographer and Dr B———— were only too obviously mortal. As I moved from one to the other, one of the creatures stirred in its sleep and gave a huge sigh. The beast's hot breath washed over me, as when a wind changes direction over a bonfire and one is bathed in the heat that it carries. But what a fire! One that stank of putrid swamp, and rotting meat. Being now on the riverward side of the nest, and in danger of being cut off from the jungle, I was almost persuaded to withdraw without further investigation, when I noticed a wasp landing on the nose of the sole non-European among the abducted, our mule-driving *camarada*. It lit there for only a moment, but was met with a definite twitch of the nostrils.

I never knew his name—for the purpose of this narrative I shall call him Pablo—but he opened his eyes and, upon seeing me, stretched out a hand in entreaty and began to call to me. I quickly motioned him to silence, and such was the discipline that I had imposed upon our party that he immediately obeyed.

I took a moment to assess our situation. I could not leave him to his fate, there was no question of that. No loyalty had been fiercer than that of these bare-footed, uneducated bearers, many of whom had already laid down their lives in the service of white men whom they did not know, for an expedition whose purpose their simple minds could never hope to understand. To abandon him now would be a poor reward for such devoted support.

Pablo lay with the tail of one of the creatures pinning him to the ground, as a fallen tree might trap an incautious logger. By signs I managed to get him to move his legs, thus proving that his back was not broken and that, once freed, he would have a reasonable chance of continuing his escape.

I considered, and quickly dismissed, any idea of provoking the creature in the hope that it might raise its appendage without being fully roused from its slumbers. To risk waking one was to risk waking all, so closely were they intertwined. Instead I noted that the part of the riverbank on which Pablo lay was of soft red sand, and might be dug away with some care. To this end I retreated into the jungle, and searched around for anything that could be used as a makeshift spade. As I was unable to explain my purpose to him, the despair on Pablo's face as he saw me withdraw was a pity to behold, and I spent no longer than was necessary in securing a broken gourd that would suffice for the task. I returned with it and, once more signalling him to silence, began to scoop out the river dirt from around and under his body.

Once he'd realized my purpose, he attempted to help by digging away with his bare hands. Too late, the inadvisability of his action became obvious. Thick though the creature's hide was, it had enough sensitivity to register Pablo's movements and transmit them to its distant brain. After a while its great sides began to stir, and I stopped all movement for a second or two; but when I saw that this would not be enough to make the great beast subside again, I threw caution to the winds and resumed digging as quickly and as carelessly as would be required to get the job done.

Waking, the creature gave us unexpected aid; the flick of its tail as it began to raise itself had the effect of releasing Pablo completely, and I flung the gourd aside and dragged him out. As I picked up my buffalo gun, Pablo struggled to his feet; his movements were mirrored by those of the waking creature before us, struggling to disentangle itself from its fellows and causing them all to stir in their turn.

Now we were in a pickle. The creatures were rolling over, and the

Celtic knot of their daytime nest was rapidly unravelling. The jungle was only yards from us, but our chance of reaching it was quickly vanishing. "Run, Pablo!" I cried, bringing my buffalo gun to bear on the heart of the tangle, and whether or not he understood my words, my dusky friend was in no doubt as to their meaning. As he leapt for the foliage, I fired at the head of the biggest and most dangerous-looking creature at the center of the herd, reasoning that this roughest of beasts must surely be its leader.

As I had predicted, the roar of the gun threw the half-awake beasts into an immediate state of panic and confusion. They fought each other to get free, and I saw Pablo reach safety and disappear into the green without seeming to be noticed.

My own situation was far less certain. Forcing myself to remain calm, I dropped to one knee and reloaded. I was aware of a tail sweeping over me like the boom of a yacht, missing by inches. Within moments, the gun was back to my shoulder and I fired again.

That second shot did it. There was a sudden scream, like no animal sound that I had ever heard before, and the creatures scattered like a mob, crashing off into the jungle on every side. All except for one, this being the beast that I had hit.

The beast did not panic like the others; instead, pain had concentrated his attention on me, his tormentor. I had the river at my back, while the beast stood between me and any chance of escape. I saw it clearly for the first time. Its shape lay somewhere between that of an ape and a dinosaur, only one of the many fantastical forms that I was to encounter in the dark days ahead. Blood was leaking down its hide from a chest wound. Its yellow eyes were fixed upon me, and they blazed with fury as the creature lunged.

I had no chance to load and fire again. I could only run in one direction, and that was to the river. The river held terrors of its own; they were beneath the surface and out of sight, but those terrors were there nonetheless. I had, however, noted the presence of a line of rocks in the shallows and the rapids, that when taken together might serve as a series of islands in the manner of large stepping-stones. Of course, a pursuing creature might cross these as easily as I; but this creature was wounded, and though it could run on two legs, on less certain footing

I was gambling that it would be happier on four, and so would be unable to reach for its prey.

As I leapt from rock to rock, I was aware of the beast following me; and when I reached the largest of the rock islands with the rapids all around, I looked back to see that it had left the shore. Along with all the pain and rage, there was a growing uncertainty in its movements. With more confidence, it might have strode across this natural causeway through the boiling stream and reached me in seconds; but by attempting to gain its balance with all four of its limbs on one stepping-stone at a time, it was severely compromising its ability to progress.

Here was my chance. And just as well, for I had reached the last island and could run no farther. With my back against the rock, I reloaded and took aim. Spray from the river was lashing me, but while running I had kept the gun held high, and my ammunition was dry. My target was no more than fifteen yards away, and the size of a house.

My gun spoke, and my bullet did not miss. And yet my pursuer did not drop; he roared in pain, again that terrible sound that I'd encountered nowhere else in nature, and rose to his full height so that those great, broad claws could clutch at a second chest wound. Though my large-bore rounds were doing certain damage and had the power to drop an elephant, even these were not enough to stop him on their own.

Fortunately, I had two good allies to come to my rescue; the force of gravity, and the forces of the river. In rising so hastily, the creature caused himself to overbalance and now he lost his footing. He hit the surface with an almighty splash and immediately began to tumble away from me in the raging current. That on its own would have been enough, but there was more to follow. Within seconds, shadow-shapes were rising from the depths and flocking to him.

What I felt then was something close to pity, as teeth fastened on his body and one tentacle after another wrapped over the beast and finally drew him under, silencing his dying cries. He went down like a pig among crocodiles, the whole angry, battling mess being borne away around a bend in the river as I watched.

I took the precaution of reloading before I returned to the bank. There were more of the creatures about, after all, and one or more of them might return. However, all was silent as I crossed the site of the nest, and after listening for a while I was confident that all had flown. I called out to Pablo, and after a few moments was rewarded with the sight of his cautious face peeping out from the bushes.

I do not think that any man has ever expressed his gratitude to another more eloquently, or with greater enthusiasm, than that simple *peon* in his moment of deliverance. While he did not quite grovel at my feet nor place my foot upon his head, his actions left me in no doubt as to his feelings. I raised him, and by one means and another gave him to understand that while I appreciated his thanks, there were still dangers all around us. In this more somber mood, I supervised as he used the broken gourd to scrape out shallow graves for the remains of those fallen Englishmen. After a few simple prayers, to which a lack of comprehension didn't prevent Pablo from adding a broken and charming *Amen*, I led our way back to the main camp.

There was a cheer when we were spotted emerging from the jungle and it was seen that I had not returned alone, but the general jubilation turned to sadness as my party learned the fate of their own people. That night, while Pablo celebrated with his fellow *camaradas* and no doubt embroidered the tale of his rescue until my actions gained some heroic stature, ours was a more subdued campfire gathering. During my absence, this new camp had been set up within a palisade of sharpened pickets with their points angled outward; though we heard many a worrying sound from the jungle that night, we suffered no further attack.

When all of our injured had either died or recovered sufficiently to travel, we broke camp and moved on. We followed the trampled "road" until we reached the clearing by the river. I was surprised to see how the broad avenue was already beginning to vanish, and how all signs of the creatures' nesting were gone. Fresh bamboo was growing up through the broken vegetation, and I was unable even to locate the shallow graves of our lost companions in order to point out their final resting places. Everything in the jungle consumed something else, I concluded; and failing that, the jungle consumed itself.

My name among the *camaradas* was now *Assassino da Alimárias*, which I'm given to understand means "slayer of beasts." I received the news with grim amusement.

We had far to go, and many more such perils to face. I decided then that where the slaughter of such monstrous game was required, I would forever stand ready.

ELEVEN

Breakfast the next morning was taken in the bar, because the dining room was in use. The true prophets, those senior detective officers with the city's glamour on them, had arrived to take over.

Sebastian sat behind his kippers at a corner table and watched all the comings and goings with mixed feelings. The tall, straight detectives in their immaculate overcoats and bowler hats were attended by a squad of clerks and sergeants that ran ahead of and around them. Messages were flying, and there were scenes to be visited. Despite the tragedy at the heart of it all, he felt a certain nostalgia. Such had been his life, once.

After that he went up to his room and prepared himself to go out. This time, he found his belongings undisturbed. There was little he could do to protect himself against further searches, whether by curious staff or by someone with a more sinister motive, other than to ensure that he kept his notebook and valuables about his person. An intruder would find nothing of advantage in his shaving kit or linen.

He'd cleaned up his own boots, knowing that he could expect little in the way of extra service under the circumstances. He stowed his letters of authority in one pocket, his copy of Sir Owain's book in another.

An Amazonian expedition had taken place. That was beyond doubt. And that it had met with disaster could not be doubted either. But as he'd told Stephen Reed, no true or satisfactory account of that disaster had ever been given.

Lancaster had funded the trip himself, with the intended purpose of taking celestial measurements from one of several key points around the globe. The measurements were needed to support his patented system for aiming large guns by the stars. He had set off into the jungle with vehicles, mules, experts, porters, and an enormous caravan of instruments and supplies. He'd returned with none of them. Just himself, and one other survivor. The survivor had suffered injuries and a level of delirium that had left him permanently hospitalized.

As a consequence, Sir Owain's Royal Society lecture, in which all was to be revealed in detail, had attracted wide attention. The promise of sensational revelations, with no hint as to what those revelations might be, had stoked the public's interest. The original meeting-hall venue had been ditched in favor of the Queen's Hall in Langham Place, a concert theater of much greater capacity. Several newspapers requested advance interviews, but were turned down. Sir Owain's book was scheduled for publication within a matter of weeks, but no page proofs or early copies could be located.

Even the society's president had known nothing of what was to come. Following his introduction, Owain Lancaster had begun with a warning: that what followed might be hard to believe, but was true nonetheless. For much of it, he could offer no evidence beyond his own observations. His public testimony was underwritten by his private grief. He owed it to the dead to tell the whole truth.

The whole truth, as he told it, was that the expedition had been wrecked by an early accident on the river that was carrying them downstream, after which the party's survivors had been stalked by monsters. The monsters rarely showed themselves and were mainly known from the evidence of their attacks. Of all the party, Sir Owain was the only one who saw them fully with his own eyes. They included a serpent that tried to wreck the rescue boat that was carrying him home.

The first ten minutes of Sir Owain's talk were received in silence. The next five played to a growing rumble of conversation among the rows. His lantern slides were met with loud heckling and open derision, and the rest of his words went unheard; most of the audience was on its feet by then, and the ushers struggled to keep any kind of order. Some object was thrown, and something close to a riot followed. The speaker persisted and had to be stopped. Sir Owain was hurried from the building by a service door. His lantern slides, which featured some photographs but were mostly artists' realizations of the monsters made under Sir Owain's direction, were stolen during the upset.

But they were no loss. Those same images appeared as plates in the published account, which went on sale shortly after. Its publishers, who'd been hovering over a decision to withdraw the book, found themselves with a runaway success.

They were half embarrassed, half elated; they did their best to follow a line that allowed them to keep both their dignity and their profits. And so, as Sir Owain suffered public opprobrium and the censure of the society and withdrew to his West Country estate, they continued to sell copies of "this remarkable document, the subject of so much lively and continuing debate."

Stalked by monsters, torn by beasts. And an estate on which, it now seemed, people vanished and young girls of a certain age and development could not play in safety.

As Sebastian's predecessor had first noted, there seemed to be something more than coincidental misfortune at work here.

WHEN SEBASTIAN stepped out into the main street, he could see that new activity had begun around the assembly rooms. Locals were again gathering outside. A hearse wagon and two undertakers' men waited by the doors. Becoming aware of two women passing behind him, Sebastian tipped his hat to them; they didn't even notice. He heard one telling the other that the parents had arrived and had gone in with the police. The women went on to join the assembly room crowd, and Sebastian turned away.

The grief of the parents would be a hard sight to bear. He understood that there was a low point in any journey such as theirs. Some called it the hour of despair; others, the suicide hour. The notion was that if one could pass through it, then hope would begin. The hour could be deferred, or it could be ignored for a while. But if life were to continue, it could not be avoided. How did one pass through a loss so profound? He couldn't begin to imagine it.

The town's one-roomed museum and library was on a steep little street that led down to the harbor. It was a humble whitewashed building with a surprisingly grand door. There was an imposing house above it, and less imposing houses below.

Sebastian tried the door. It was unlocked, so he went inside.

It was historical exhibition and reading room combined. Arnmouth's modest history was covered by six glass cases of coins and other objects, some Roman stones, and a dozen or more framed oil paintings of local estates. The farther part of the room featured two long tables with eight chairs to each. Beyond them was a counter, behind which was a woman. She seemed surprised by his presence.

Raising her voice to reach him, she said, "I don't open until nine thirty."

Sebastian glanced back. "Your door isn't locked," he said.

"I don't need to keep it locked," she said. "Everybody knows I don't open until nine thirty. What do you want?"

He'd reached the counter now. The woman had iron-gray hair, pinned up. She wore a high-collared blouse and she held herself straight. Despite his transgression, she didn't seem ready to order him out, and so he decided to press his luck.

Sebastian said, "Do you keep a local newspaper?"

"In the racks," she said, "over there." And she pointed to a frame where three or four broadsheets hung from rods, café-style. "Leave it out on the table when you're finished."

Sebastian glanced briefly and said, "I meant old newspapers. Whichever volume might have the story of Grace Eccles and Evangeline Bancroft."

The woman's manner seemed to chill, and her face became set.

"What story would that be?" she said.

"About the time where they were lost on the moors," he said. "I understand that it was a good few years ago."

"I'm afraid all those issues are at the bindery."

"Can you check that for me?"

Her face betrayed nothing.

"I don't need to," she said.

"Perhaps I'll talk to Miss Eccles, then. Can you tell me where to find her?"

"I don't advise it."

"All the same, I'd like to."

"Grace took over her father's cottage on the Lancaster estate. You can try talking to her, but I doubt she'll have much to say to you."

"Can *you* tell me what happened?"

"No," she said, "I can't." And she walked off into an inner room behind the counter, leaving him alone.

HE GOT back to the Sun Inn at five minutes before ten. Sir Owain's car was already waiting, its engine idling and Sir Owain's chauffeur behind the wheel. When the driver saw Sebastian, he hopped out and had the passenger cab door open by the time he reached it. There was no one else in the car.

"Thank you," Sebastian said, and climbed aboard. He settled back into the buttoned leather seat as the driver returned to his place.

Sebastian tried to look as if he were used to this. But of course, he wasn't. The landaulet was a rich man's transport, and Sebastian was not a rich man. It was, in essence, the coachwork of the finest horse carriage built onto a heavy motor chassis. The passenger rode in comfort while the driver faced the elements behind the engine, bundled up in leather and goggles with just a short windshield for protection.

But to drive one was a mark of prestige for any servant. And this man knew it. Small boys stopped to watch as the car swung around in the street and they headed out of town, along the road that Sebastian had come in by. Instead of crossing the river to the station, they turned inland.

Sebastian leaned forward and knocked on the glass that separated him from the driver. He had to knock again, and harder, before he was heard.

The driver unhooked a catch, and the window cracked open an inch or two. The wind roared through the gap. The driver cocked his head toward it, without taking his eyes off the road.

Sebastian raised his voice and half-shouted, "Where's the cottage that Grace Eccles lives in? Is it on this road?"

The driver shook his head. Then said, "It's over toward the river."

"Can we reach it by car?"

"Not without making you late. Sir Owain's waiting."

"Sir Owain can wait a while longer. I want to visit her first."

The road hit a patch of bad repair, and Sebastian did nothing to gain the driver's favor by having distracted him so that he failed to avoid the worst of it.

When they were done bumping, the driver said, "I can't do that, sir. I take my instructions from my employer."

Watching the man's gloved hands on the wheel, Sebastian said, "And do those instructions include rummaging through the hotel rooms of his visitors?"

He saw the driver's grip tighten for just a moment, which gave him his answer before the man said, "I have no idea what you can mean by that, sir."

"Never mind," Sebastian said. "Today your employer answers to me. So you'll take me first to Grace's cottage, please."

TWELVE

As they followed the course of the river inland, the estuary plain was wide and sandy. But the sand gradually turned to a mixture of sand and mud, that in turn grew a surface of moss and vegetable scum, that in turn became wide open fields where animals grazed. On a raised bank overlooking these flats, they passed a row of upturned boats and dinghies like the shells of sleeping turtles.

After another mile or so, a bare track led to an open place by the water. At the end of the track was a collection of mismatched wooden buildings, at the heart of which stood a ramshackle stone cottage. The roofs of the buildings had all been repaired with tarpaper. There was a straw-covered yard before the cottage and beyond the yard, a gate in a rail fence led out into open paddock and grazing land. This was poor land, low-lying and liable to flood.

As they were approaching, Sebastian thought that he saw a figure flit between two of the buildings. The track was growing rougher, and the driver stopped the car with at least a dozen or more yards still to go.

He clearly didn't expect to be staying here for long. He kept the engine running as he got out to open Sebastian's door.

As Sebastian stepped down, the driver said, "You should know this is a waste of your time."

"How so?" Sebastian said, noting the presence of horses far off in the paddock, right down by the water.

"Grace Eccles can be a bit wild. I'm telling you, she's known for it."

The driver closed the car door behind him. Sebastian started toward the buildings alone.

Before he'd taken more than a few strides, a young woman came out. She wore a full skirt and a man's jacket buttoned up tight, and her hair was so long and unkempt that it seemed so by intent rather than neglect.

Grace Eccles, he assumed. She had a rock in her hand.

She said, "This is my house. You come no closer."

Sebastian stopped.

"How close would be acceptable?" he said.

"I prefer you fuck off and far away, sir, and here's the proof of it."

He might have been shocked by her language, had she given him the chance to react. But she did not.

It was a good throw, overarm and with force in it. And accurate, too. It would have laid him out flat if he hadn't turned side-on and dodged it. It missed his head by a whisker. It missed the driver by more, but went on to smash through the Daimler's side window like a marble fist.

Whereupon the driver emitted a loud oath that was almost as foul as her own and scrambled to get back to the wheel of his vehicle. He crashed the gears in his haste to reverse up the track to a place of greater safety; and as the wheels spun and the Daimler slid around in its retreat, Sebastian remembered to look toward Grace Eccles in case there might be another rock coming.

But she was watching the car's departure with visible satisfaction.

Sebastian said, "That was uncalled for."

"Whatever you say," Grace Eccles replied. "How many motorcars can you muster? I've no end of stones."

With the aim of catching her unawares, Sebastian said, "I'm here on serious business. Two young girls were found dead on the estate yesterday."

She showed no particular reaction. She kept on looking at the car for a while, and then she looked at him.

"What's that to me?" she said.

"I thought you might be concerned to hear it."

She did no more than shrug.

"Can I ask you something?"

"You can ask."

Sebastian said, "What happened to you and Evangeline Bancroft? And why will no one speak of it?"

"I know why you're here," she said, ignoring his question. "Tell him I don't care who he sends. This was my father's house, and now it's mine. I've a piece of paper that a judge has looked at, and here I stay."

"I don't know what you're talking about."

"Then where's the point in you standing there and listening to me?"

She turned her back on him, walked across the yard and into her house, and slammed the door.

In that moment it was as if she'd walked out of the world completely; the house sat like a dead thing, abandoned and unlived in.

Sebastian waited.

Then he turned away and walked up the track to the car. The driver was beside it, pulling glass out of the door frame and examining his coachwork for further damage.

As Sebastian drew close, the driver looked up angrily and said, "How stupid was that? As if I didn't warn you."

"I know," Sebastian said. "Forgive me. I never listen."

He swept broken glass from the leather seat, and they continued their journey. The remainder of it was undertaken in silence—or as close to silence as could be achieved, save for the noise of the car's engine and the wind that whistled in through the broken window.

The car might be damaged. But not so damaged, Sebastian thought, as the young woman who'd thrown the rock at it.

OWAIN LANCASTER had been born the son of a Welsh corn merchant. As a young man he'd been sent away to study the law in Manchester, but an interest in science and engineering had prevailed, particularly in its application to long-range artillery. He'd sold the rights to his first arms patent, an improved breech-sliding mechanism for field guns, for thirty pounds. After seeing how much money it made for its new title holders, he never signed away another.

He'd risen to own foundries and factories and a shipyard, and had bought Arnside Hall and its estate from a bankrupt family some twenty-five years before. He'd meant it for a summer retreat and had spent a considerable amount on rebuilding the house and installing the most modern conveniences: ducted heating, electricity from its own plant, the first telephone in the county. Now he'd sold his London house and lived here all the time.

Sir Owain's entire life had been material proof of the value of science, a triumph of the rational. It had brought him a fortune, a fellowship in the Royal Society, and a reputation that, with a single publication, he'd managed to destroy almost overnight.

Where insanity threatened a fortune, the Lord Chancellor's Visitor in Lunacy was obliged to intercede. Distant relatives, alarmed at the endangerment of riches they might someday hope to share in, had written to the Lord Chancellor's office raising questions over Sir Owain's ability to manage his affairs. Their letter had been passed to Sir James, whose first move had been to send his man—Sebastian's predecessor, now retired—to investigate and report.

The drive ascended through farmland to grouse moor, and then from grouse moor to managed forest. Its last mile was up a narrowing valley, winding and switching until Arnside Hall came into view at the top of it.

It was a strange building. Half doll's house, half castle, perched atop an enormous rockery where a waterfall spilled down to a trout lake below. Sebastian looked up at it through the Daimler's good window and felt something between a chill and a thrill. After selling off his business interests at loss-making prices, Sir Owain had retreated here to live off his patents. As the income from these began to decline, his inventions superseded by newer technologies, he'd let estate staff go and allowed the building and its grounds to deteriorate.

Rich man's retreat or madman's hideaway?

Soon, Sebastian hoped to know.

THIRTEEN

ORIGINALLY, THE HOUSE HAD BEEN A LODGE. IT HAD BEEN EX-panded by more than one architect into something of a visual mishmash, its roofline a forest of chimneys and gables of different designs. It had bowed windows and Gothic windows and a bit of Tudor half-timbering thrown in here and there, with the final entry into the main courtyard being achieved through an archway that could have been lifted intact from a cathedral apse.

The courtyard itself was like the setting for an opera, with windows, outlooks, and balconies at every level and of every imaginable character. Here, with a carriage turn before it, was the main door of the house.

On the steps to the main doors, Sir Owain Lancaster waited to meet the car. As before, he was not alone. Behind him, lurking in the background like a diffident Iago, came Dr. Hubert Sibley.

The car stopped before the entranceway. The driver exchanged a few words with his employer, presumably to account for the damage to his vehicle, before returning to it and opening the door for Sebastian to step out.

Sir Owain did not offer his hand.

He said, "Permit me a grim smile at the irony of my position. I hold honors from three universities. My patents have amassed fortunes and my factories supply the armies of the world. But my fate and future happiness now lie in the hands of the watchdog to the Lord Chancellor's Visitor in Lunacy."

"There's nothing about my presence that should make you feel threatened," Sebastian said. "My function here is only to observe and advise."

"And yet my liberty will depend on the advice that you give."

"Think less of it as a matter of liberty, and more a matter of your well-being."

"It's very hard not to think about liberty when you face the prospect of losing it."

With the pleasantries dispensed with, Sir Owain led the way inside.

The entrance hallway had a stone-flagged floor with a rug on it and light oak paneling on its walls. A wide stairway led to a gallery above.

On the short walk to Sir Owain's study they passed a long glass case containing a scale model of a warship, the original of which had been built in one of Sir Owain's yards. The air inside the house was colder than the air outside and had a musty odor. Sebastian saw no sign of any staff.

Sir Owain's study was dominated by a large kneehole desk with a captain's chair behind it. On the desk were a typewriting machine and a binocular microscope in brass. There was a wall of books, with a set of green baize steps for reaching the upper shelves.

Sebastian said, "Do you understand why it's necessary for me to be here?"

Inviting Sebastian to sit while seating himself in the captain's chair, Sir Owain said, "I understand that any man with the taint of madness and a fortune is fair game for the Masters of Lunacy. As little as fifty pounds a year or a thousand in the bank will get their attention."

"You merely need to convince Sir James that you are competent to remain in charge of your own affairs."

"Convince him? Or convince you?"

Sebastian waited.

Sir Owain went on, "Given that I must, I believe that I can. Doctor Sibley, here, is my constant companion and the guarantor of my sanity."

By now, Dr. Hubert Sibley had joined Sir Owain behind the desk. He remained standing, more like a valet than a medical man.

Sebastian looked at Sir Owain again and said, "So do you consider yourself insane?"

"No," Sir Owain said. "But I can understand why others might. Is that in itself not some kind of proof?"

Dr. Sibley then spoke up and said, "I have prepared you a full report of my observations and a fair copy of Sir Owain's treatment diary."

Sir Owain looked at him, and Sibley nodded. Then Sir Owain opened a desk drawer and took out a folder of typewritten papers, tied with a ribbon. He placed the folder on the desk and slid it toward Sebastian.

"My life is in these pages," he said. "There is no part of it that is not subject to Doctor Sibley's supervision. Whether it's my health or my business or the management of the estate."

"No part of it at all?"

"None."

Sebastian was finding that Sibley's presence made him vaguely uncomfortable. Not so much a man, more a slimy shadow. Hanging around in the corner like an undertaker's mute.

He looked at the man and said, "Where are you living, Doctor?"

"I live here at the Hall," Sibley replied, "with Sir Owain. Constant companion means exactly that."

"I can't help observing that to ensure Sir Owain's liberty you seem to have given up your own."

"I am well rewarded. The work is light and the life is pleasant. I believe you'll find that our arrangement is the equal of any more oppressive or restrictive regime, and offers a humane and enlightened alternative."

"In other words . . . as long as you're steering Sir Owain and whispering in his ear, I should recommend against any form of asylum."

"Sir Owain is not mad," Dr. Sibley said.

"What is he, then?"

Sir Owain spoke up for himself. "I speak my mind, I say what I see, and for reasons of their own some choose to call me mad because of it. The mere whiff of the word around a rich man brings the Masters of Lunacy running. Lawyers and parasites with no other interest than to get control of a man's fortune and squander it. They are a plague, and it's the Lord Chancellor's Visitor who moves ahead of them and marks the foreheads of the doomed."

At that point he realized that Sibley was giving him a warning look.

"Is one possible opinion," Sir Owain amended.

"You can hold whatever opinion you wish," Sebastian said, and he reached for the folder on the desk. "Believe me. I have a duty to be impartial, and my employer is a fair man. I will read this report. I shall pass along the treatment diary for someone more medically qualified to assess. And I shall establish whether this live-in arrangement is a genuine form of care or a deliberate ploy to stave off the appropriate legal process."

Dr. Sibley said, "How can we convince you?"

"Don't try to convince me. Just conduct yourselves as you normally would. Sir Owain."

"Yes?"

"I've been reading your book."

A new and subtle tension seemed to enter the room.

"As have many," Sir Owain said with care.

"A well-wrought piece of fiction," Sebastian suggested, and waited to see Sir Owain's response.

Sir Owain could not help it. He looked at his doctor. His doctor said nothing, but the implication hung there. *I can't prompt you. Be careful.*

"If you say so," Sir Owain said.

"What do *you* say, Sir Owain?" Sebastian pressed. "Do you still insist on it as an honest account of your Amazon adventure? Is it a faithful memorial to those who failed to return?"

Sir Owain looked again at the doctor, who now was looking at the floor as if to show that any response was Sir Owain's, and Sir Owain's alone.

Sebastian went on, "Just between us. In this room. Do you still hold it to be the truth? Or is it, as so many say, a miscalculated hoax that has caused the loss of your position and earned you the scorn of your peers?"

Dr. Sibley could keep his silence no longer.

"This is unfair," he said.

"I know it, Doctor Sibley," Sebastian said. "It's not a choice that I'd care to be faced with. Stick to my story and be deemed insane, or abandon it and stand revealed as a fraud."

"And whatever I answer," Sir Owain said, "you'll have the option of calling it a response that I learned for the occasion, to achieve an end."

"And so we go round and round."

"If a man can feign sanity to perfection, is he not therefore sane?"

"Why did you view the bodies of those dead girls?"

The abrupt change of tack threw Sir Owain for a moment, as Sebastian had meant it to.

He floundered for a moment and then said, "They were found on my land. And I wished to offer my help."

"Ah, yes. Your theory. Torn by beasts." From the deep pocket inside his coat, Sebastian took his copy of Sir Owain's book and searched for the page that he'd located and marked. "You must be aware that the exact same phrase occurs here in your mendacious memoir."

"It's but a phrase, Mister Becker," Sir Owain said. "You saw the condition of those children. Tell me that the wording is anything other than accurate."

Sebastian regarded him for a few moments.

Then he closed the book.

"Please call your car for me," he said, and rose to his feet.

Sir Owain seemed bewildered.

"Is that it?" he said. "What happens now?"

"I'll be in the area for a day or two. Making my inquiries. You'll hear from me again."

"When will we know the decision?"

"That, I cannot say. The decision won't be mine to make."

HE DECLINED a tour of the house. He'd seen a sufficient number of great houses to know that the gentry were equally indifferent to magnificence and squalor, and that their homes were no guide to anything. He'd once reported on a marquis who kept a pig in his dining room, and Sir James had been happy to sign him off.

As the car was once more drawing up in front of the building, Sir Owain said, "Who will pay for my broken window glass?"

Sebastian said, "I think you will."

"You speak sharply to me," Sir Owain complained. "In a way I do not believe I deserve. But how can I respond in kind to a man who has power over my liberty?"

"If I seem sharp, sir, then I apologize. I do not mean to be. You can be assured that my only interest is in the facts behind the matter."

"Then," Sir Owain said, phrasing his courtesy in such a way as to leave no doubt that he was sorely aggrieved by the obligation, "I should support your discovery of the facts in full. My car and driver are at your disposal during your stay. Wherever you may wish to go. Just telephone the house and I'll send them out."

FOURTEEN

T HE OFFER OF THE CAR HAD BEEN MADE WITHIN THE DRIVER'S earshot, and he remained sullen and silent at his wheel throughout the return journey. The vehicle had been swept clear of broken glass during the interview, but the window was still open to the elements.

Sebastian looked through the pages in the folder. They were the work of a careful typist, but not a trained one.

After the car had dropped him off on Arnmouth's main street, Sebastian went into the first tearoom that he saw. Over lunch he studied the restaurant's copy of the *Daily Mail*, scanning it for any details of Sir James's address to the British Association.

There was no mention of the murders in the early edition. The rest of the news was much as usual—a new terrorist outrage in the Middle East, a ban on infected cattle movements in Wales. Army maneuvers continued in Cambridgeshire, mirroring those of the Kaiser's forces in Switzerland. If the shadowplay were ever to turn into real conflict, those boy soldiers from yesterday would probably be sent to join it. Meanwhile, the *Mail* saw German spies behind everything. The newspaper's estimate of their numbers regularly exceeded the total of German nationals in Britain.

Sebastian folded the paper and laid it down. Someone on another table asked for it, and he passed it over.

He looked out the window. Take away the shadow that hung over it, and this was a nice little town. Not exactly the kind of place that he and Elisabeth had dreamed of, but somewhere they might settle for. If they had the money. And didn't have Robert's needs to consider.

After checking the time by his pocket watch, he paid his bill and went outside. He walked up the street to the preventative officer's house, where he showed his credentials and begged the use of the telephone.

DESPITE THE fact that they'd agreed a time for the call, it took almost half an hour for the staff to locate Sir James in his Dundee hotel. Without any preamble, Sir James said, "So what do you make of our mad Sir Owain?"

"It's a rum setup," Sebastian said. "He's dismissed most of the staff and the estate's going to ruin."

"I could commit him for that alone."

"Except that his doctor now claims to be managing his affairs as well as his treatment. They've given me the books to look over. But, Sir James, I have to tell you that there have been other developments."

"Of what kind?"

"Two more bodies were found on Sir Owain's land yesterday."

"Bodies?"

"Definitely murdered this time, no question about it."

Sebastian explained further, including mention of Sir Owain's appearance at the temporary mortuary and his assertion that the victims had been "torn by beasts."

"One is the child of a prominent barrister," he concluded, "so I imagine we'll get to hear more about it. Sir Owain showed no sign of any guilt, only concern. I made little headway with Grace Eccles, but I'm hoping to track down Evangeline Bancroft. In the meantime I'd like to confirm the credentials of Doctor Ernest Hubert Sibley."

"Stay with it," Sir James said. "It's no easy matter to take a knight of the realm out of circulation. So let's hold off calling his doctor a quack until we can back it up with proof."

AS HE left the customs house and crossed the street, Sebastian was startled to hear his name being shouted from nowhere.

"Mister Becker!"

He looked all around. Then he looked up. Stephen Reed, the young detective, had opened a second-floor window above the photographer's studio in order to call to him.

"Yes?"

"Have you a moment? Can you come up?"

The studio was at the top of the house, combining attic space and a large skylight. It was reached by a gloomy staircase through the photographer's living quarters. His private rooms were screened off by a red velvet curtain with braid and tassels, like the dressing on a Punch and Judy booth. Sebastian ascended through the chemical odors of the photographer's trade, musty and unnatural, and the boiled-cabbage fragrance of his midday meal, even less appetizing.

Stephen Reed was waiting at the top of the stairs.

Sebastian said, "Did you pass on my suspicions to your superiors?"

"I did," Stephen Reed said, "and the rebuke was even sharper than I expected. My handling of the search has been roundly criticized and I've been demoted to evidence duties."

"I'm sorry. I'd hoped you might get a better hearing."

"I know. I blame no one. For what it's worth, I still think that your theory should be investigated before it's dismissed."

"Strictly speaking, Mister Reed, it's more hypothesis than theory. It'll be a theory when I can offer some hard facts in support of it."

The studio itself was a bright room with a square of heavy carpet on the floor. Potted plants and chairs stood before a canvas drop with a painted seascape on it. Just showing behind the backdrop was a rack of dressing-up clothes that included cloaks and Pierrot costumes.

"Mister William Phillips," Stephen Reed said, by way of introduction to the resort's resident photographer. Billy Phillips was a small man, in a baggy linen jacket with a wing-collared shirt and a bow tie.

"I'm sorry, but I can't do anything with this," Billy Phillips said, indicating the object of his frustration with a wave of his hand. Under the skylight stood the photographer's retouching table. On the table stood the camera from the murder scene. "It's a Birtac," he added, as if that explained it.

"What's one of those?" Sebastian said.

"A moving-picture camera," Stephen Reed said. "Of a kind that's designed for amateur use, apparently."

"It doesn't expose to plates," Phillips said. "And plates are all I do. I'm not sure what it uses. For moving pictures there's almost as many film types as there are devices. All I know is, it'll be on a long roll and I've no way of handling anything of that length. I could try to rig something up in the bathtub, but I can't guarantee I won't ruin it. I don't even want to risk opening the case."

Sebastian said, "Where does the camera's owner send his films?"

"That's almost certainly the father. I'm not allowed to speak to him."

The photographer said, "There's a footage counter. See? It's been run about fifteen feet into the roll."

"What does that mean?"

"That something has been captured onto the film."

"But we can't know what it is yet," Stephen Reed said, and he looked at Sebastian. "Unless you've any other ideas, I'll have to return it to the evidence store."

They walked out together with the camera parceled up in brown paper, to disguise it from view. The coroner, a local solicitor, had set a date for an inquest, and members of the national press had been arriving on the morning trains. A journalist and a photographer from the *Daily Mirror* had made the journey in a two-seater roadster. Hungry for story, they'd need little encouragement to speculation.

As soon as they were alone, Stephen Reed said, "I didn't only stop you about the camera. I checked, and there's a police file on Evangeline and Grace."

"Can you get hold of it?"

"I already have. I called Records last night and it came over this morning. I tell you, I had no idea."

"What do you mean?"

"They were not simply lost on the moors for a few hours, as we children were told. They suffered an ordeal, and had no memory of it."

"Memory or no memory, Grace Eccles is a damaged and defensive young woman."

"I knew Evangeline better."

"Well enough to approach her on such a subject?"

"We're not children now. I'd hope to engage her in a professional manner."

Sebastian said, "Then I'd better set my office to tracking her down."

"There's no need for that," Stephen Reed said. "We can ask at the library."

"They have London directories there?"

"I wouldn't know," Stephen Reed said. "But Evangeline's mother is the librarian."

FIFTEEN

SEBASTIAN WAITED OUTSIDE. IT SEEMED WISER. ALTHOUGH Lydia Bancroft hadn't shown him any actual hostility, he'd given her good reason to be cool toward him. How was he to have known that the subject of his insensitive inquiry—as she must have seen it—was actually the librarian's own grown-up daughter?

He stood at the bottom of the street, looking out across the harbor. There wasn't much to the harbor itself; a sea wall, some fishermen's huts, a low tidal jetty with its pilings hung with weed. The sea was a way out, the sound of its rollers like a distant train. Where the river estuary spilled across the sand, the masts of beached sailboats pointed this way and that.

After only a few minutes, he heard the faint sound of a latch and the opening of a door. He turned and looked back up the street, expecting to see Stephen Reed emerging from the library. Instead he saw a young woman in a short-waisted coat and a full traveling skirt. Her hair was up, with a hat pinned in place. She looked back as she emerged; Stephen Reed was right behind her, a small traveling bag in his hand, drawing the library door closed after them. As he stepped out to join the young woman, Stephen Reed gestured down the street, in Sebastian's direction. She looked his way and seemed suddenly confused. As they moved toward Sebastian, Stephen Reed was explaining something.

Sebastian did not need an introduction to tell him the young woman's name. With her hair pinned up, the resemblance to her mother was unmistakable.

Sebastian straightened up and made an effort to look pleasant.

"Mister Becker," Stephen Reed said. "This is Evangeline Bancroft."

Sebastian briefly took her hand and felt almost as much at a loss as the young woman looked.

"Evangeline heard the news and came up on the morning train," Stephen Reed explained.

"Heard it how?" Sebastian said. "I thought it hadn't reached the papers yet."

"The murder of a barrister's child," the young woman said. "It's all over the Inns of Court."

"You work in the Inns of Court? Are you in the legal profession, Miss Bancroft?"

"I carry out clerical work for lawyers," she said, and looked from one man to the other. "Forgive me. There seems to be something I don't understand here. Are you also a policeman, Mister Becker?"

"A servant of the Crown," Sebastian said, "with an interest in this case. I'd intended to seek you out in London, but instead I find you here. You came because you see a parallel with your own history. Am I right?"

"It's a shocking crime, Mister Becker," she protested.

"I know," he said. "And I know your own experience had a happier outcome. But there may be something we can learn from whatever you may remember."

Evangeline looked unsettled and uncertain. Then she looked back toward the library, as if half inclined to retreat to it.

"A happier outcome," she said, and there was no color at all in her tone.

Stephen Reed spoke then.

"Please, Evangeline," he said. "Trust us."

"Walk me to my mother's house," she said.

THEY FOLLOWED the shore road away from the harbor, overlooking the dunes and the empty beach beyond them. In the dunes stood posts where cork life preservers hung on weathered boards. The cork in the rings was old and splitting, but appeared to have been freshly painted for the season.

Stephen Reed continued to carry Evangeline's weekend bag. Sebastian held back and let him do the talking.

"Evangeline," Stephen Reed began, "forgive me. But for a moment I have to be a professional man and not your childhood friend. This may cause you some personal distress. But strictly in that professional capacity, I've had sight of the case notes from the time that you and Grace Eccles went missing. They tell a different story from the one in the newspapers. I wish I could spare your blushes, but there it is."

"I'm not blushing," she said, though she was. And so, for that matter, was he.

"This is very awkward," he said. "If you want me to stop, I will."

"No," Evangeline said, betraying that she was aware of Sebastian without quite looking at him. He felt that his presence was that of part intruder, part chaperone. "Forget my embarrassment," she said. "This is important."

"We need to know what you remember of that night."

The road made a steep and sandy turn and they began to climb away from the beach, toward a part of town where modest houses competed for hillside space.

Evangeline said, "That's very easy to answer. I remember nothing."

Stephen Reed said, "The doctor's notes are in the file. Please be assured, I didn't look at the medical details. But when he asked the two of you to explain what happened, he wrote that he saw a look pass between you. Evangeline, if there's something you know that you have never spoken of, I urge you to tell it to us now."

"With all honesty," she said, "I have no memory of anything that took place. Or even of the exchange of looks that he describes. I can't imagine what it may have meant. If it happened at all. Stephen, I'm concealing nothing from you. I've written to Grace several times over the years. She wrote back to me only once, to tell me that she'd taken over her father's business and to ask if I'd send her notices for London horse traders' sales. I imagine that in the usual run of things, we'd be strangers by now. I've done my best to keep our association alive, even though we've only the past in common."

"Then why persist?"

"Because I think Grace remembers more than I do. I'm sure of it.

I've been hoping that one day I can persuade her to share what she knows."

"Mister Becker's been out to speak to her," Stephen Reed said.

"I had to dodge a rock for my trouble," Sebastian said.

Though she'd been serious to the point of a frown until this point, this news transformed the young woman's expression. Her face lit up, and she let out a laugh that she quickly tried to cover with an apology.

"Grace is a tricky one," Evangeline said. "She always has been."

"Perhaps you can talk to her," Stephen Reed said.

"I will." She stopped and took the weekend bag from his hand.

"I'll walk on from here," she said. "I'd like some time to think."

As the two men walked away, Sebastian said, "The medical details?"

"Both girls were violated."

Sebastian looked back, but Evangeline was already gone from sight. "Does she know that?"

"I imagine it won't have escaped her, Mister Becker, memory or no memory. How does such an act fit in with your picture of Sir Owain's madness?"

On the walk up from the beach, they'd passed a board fence that had been set up to hold back the gorse and sand from the road. Its timbers had all but disappeared behind a pasted mass of notices and handbills for pier-end shows, political meetings, temperance rallies, Fry's chocolate, traveling circuses, and the Judgment of the Lord. They were passing it again now. The freshest, cleanest addition among the posted bills was the notice of the forthcoming inquest, placed within the last hour or two. The paste was still wet.

Sebastian said, "I don't have an answer for you. But let me take the machine."

"What machine?"

"The camera, if it won't be missed for a few hours. I think I may know where to track down someone with the expertise we need."

SIXTEEN

T HE NAMES OF THE HOUSES ALWAYS CHARMED HER. THEY hadn't when she'd lived here, but they charmed her whenever she returned. Prospect Place. St Cuthbert's. Puffin. St Elmo's. Evangeline was a city dweller now, a grown woman, and these names were her childhood. She wished that she could revisit them with simple pleasure. But between her childhood and the present stood a short passageway of lost time, where there was only uncertainty and pain. Something within her, some natural custodian whose name she did not know, had elected to close the door on that darkness.

As a result, she remembered nothing of her lowest hour. It was an act of consideration that she had not consciously authorized and did not appreciate. In speaking of the doctor, Stephen Reed had avoided mention of any results of the doctor's examination. Perhaps the doctor had been discreet in his notes. For that, at least, she could be grateful.

As she climbed the last few yards, the sun broke out for a moment. She remembered the summers here. They were endless. And summer society was always strictly divided according to class, position, and propriety. A widow and a widow's child had never quite fitted in. Which had brought freedom, of a kind. Her friendship with Grace Eccles would have been impossible otherwise.

Here was her mother's house. Right up at the back of town with steps up to the front door, a view mostly of rooftops, and a side garden that was just about big enough to put a shed on. The brickwork was neat and the paintwork was green. Lydia paid a man to keep it spruced, every other year. The front door was a heavy showpiece with two panels of etched glass like a funeral parlor or a public house, and was rarely used. Evangeline let herself through the side gate and entered through the kitchen door, which, as ever, was unlocked.

Lydia Bancroft's supper place was laid on the table, ready for her return. Supper for one. The house was silent, and Evangeline felt like an intruder.

But when she took her weekend bag up to her old room, she was surprised to find the bed already made up, and with fresh-smelling linen. She'd given her mother no warning of this visit, so Evangeline could only conclude that this was how she always kept it.

She laid out her nightdress on the bed, but otherwise she didn't unpack. She went downstairs and out to the garden shed, which was no more secure than the house; its door didn't even have a lock, but a small toggle of wood that turned on the frame to hold it.

From out of the shed, she wheeled her bicycle.

She hadn't ridden it in two years, but her mother made occasional use of it, so its condition was good. The tires were soft but the chain ran freely, and a drop of oil and a minute's work with the air pump had it ready for the road. She never rode in London, but back when she'd lived here she'd cycled everywhere. Evangeline was even adept at cycling in a skirt. Being neither rich nor eccentric, she owned none of the "rational cycling wear" that tended to draw ridicule onto women in public places.

When she set off down the hill, she wobbled a little at first; but within a minute she had the hang of it again and was soon sailing along.

If her mother had been surprised to have her turn up unannounced, imagine how Grace would feel.

ON HEARING where Sebastian wanted to go, Sir Owain's driver said, "But that's thirty miles from here!"

"Twenty-five," Sebastian said. "I just measured it on the map."

"I have other duties than this," the driver protested, but Sebastian was firm.

"As I recall it, the offer of the car was for anywhere I may wish to go."

The driver conceded, but did nothing to disguise his displeasure.

He went to get behind the wheel, and this time Sebastian had to open the passenger door for himself.

Once inside, Sebastian set the camera down on the seat beside him. The car had been fully cleaned up now, and the broken window given a running repair with a sheet of thick parchment. It was opaque, but it let in some light while keeping the wind out.

These were country lanes, but a good part of the route would be along the Bristol road. When they'd left Arnmouth behind, he slid open the window that divided the passenger cab from the driver's position.

Leaning forward and raising his voice almost to a shout to be heard, he said, "I fear we got off on the wrong foot, you and I."

"Did we, now," the driver replied without emotion. In his cap and goggles, facing forward in a scarf wound tight against the oncoming weather, he had the advantage over Sebastian, whose face was up against the little window with his eyes already beginning to stream in the rush of air.

Sebastian said, "I believe the fault is mine. It's easy to mistake loyalty for obstinacy. How long have you worked for Sir Owain?"

The driver took a while to respond. And then all that he said was, "Long enough."

"He said those girls were torn by beasts. What do you think?"

"I wouldn't know," the driver said. "I didn't see them. I stayed outside with the car." He glanced at Sebastian. "I take it they were bad."

"Torn by beasts or not. Someone meant to spoil them."

They passed over the bridge across the railway line. The estuary was behind them now. Beyond the station stood a hill dense with trees.

Sebastian said, "What's your name, driver?"

"Thomas Arnot, sir."

"Forgive me for the way I spoke to you before."

This belated touch of civility, along with mention of the suffering of the victims, seemed to temper the driver's attitude.

The man said, "If you want to talk about beasts, go to the post office and ask them to show you the book."

"The what?"

"The book where all the holiday people write down their stories of what they see on the moor."

"Are you joshing me?"

"No, sir, I am not. And I'm not claiming there's any truth in any of it, neither. I've never seen any such thing myself. But there's been many a sighting over the years. For all I know, there could be something in it. Some animal escaped from somewhere, going back to the wild. Strange things brought home from faraway places. It's not always peacocks and monkeys."

Sebastian was inclined to dismiss it. He'd seen the results of animal attacks. But before he could say so, the driver suddenly said, "Is that why we're going to the fairground? To see if anything's escaped from their menagerie?"

And his manner was so changed, now that he saw himself included in the thinking behind the plan, that Sebastian chose not to contradict him.

"Something like that," he said.

Then he closed the dividing window and sank back into the leather seat, steadying his mind for the drive ahead.

EVANGELINE WAS passing the upturned boats by the estuary. Out in the sand and the mud, a solitary rotted wooden post stood firm, worn down to a stump of two or three feet. A tangle of old ropes and knots festooned it like a merman's necklace. Even farther out, rising from the water, was a dune topped with a memorial cross. A chapel had stood there once, she'd been told, until floods and the shifting river had cut it off from the town.

There was another mile to go. She'd have to keep an eye on the time, or risk returning across the moor as night fell.

In the days following their misadventure, the newspapers had reported that she and Grace had been found safe and well the next morning, none the worse for their outdoor ordeal. But many details had been suppressed in the retelling. All that Evangeline knew was that she and Grace had actually been found terrified and shivering, with most of the clothes ripped from them. And this was knowledge that she'd gleaned from the questions she'd been asked; she had no direct memory of it herself. Her closest memory was of lying in her bed while adults talked downstairs.

It was a rough ride down the last of the track, and for the final hundred yards Evangeline had to dismount and walk the bicycle. There ahead of her was the old familiar cottage, with the paddocks and the great wide bay beyond. It had been dilapidated then, and it was dilapidated now. Any more dilapidated, and it would be derelict.

"Grace?" she called from the gateway, but there was no reply.

She left her bicycle leaning against one of the outbuildings. The front wall of the wooden stable was a rusty maze of bolts and hinges and iron catches. She walked around it and found Grace in the paddock behind the house, tending to one of her horses.

She hadn't heard Evangeline coming. Evangeline called out, "Are you well, Grace Eccles?" and Grace quickly looked toward her.

There was a moment in which Evangeline was uncertain of the reception she'd get. But it was quickly over.

"Better than some," Grace replied, turning to face Evangeline as she crossed the paddock. Grace looked as dark and as wild as ever. "What are you doing here?"

"Just a brief visit to see some old faces."

"And rattle some old bones?"

Instead of replying, Evangeline looked at the animal in the halter that Grace was holding. She'd been stroking its head and speaking soothing things into its ear. There was something odd in the way he held his head to listen, but Evangeline couldn't have said why.

"What's wrong with him?" she said.

"He kicked up and threw his owner. So his owner pulled his head around and had an eye out with his thumb. Who could do that to an animal?"

"That's appalling. Though I could imagine wanting to do it to some people."

Grace removed the halter. The horse didn't move until she gave him a push, and then he trotted off.

Evangeline said, "I don't know how you can keep a farm going on your own."

Grace shrugged, as if there were no choice involved. She said, "I can't sew and I can't sing. And they don't welcome riffraff like me in the kind of places you go."

It was said without resentment. They started to walk back toward the house.

Grace's father had bred horses. Grace herself did not. It was 1912, and the market for working animals was beginning to disappear. Tractors and buses and trucks were replacing more of them every year. With no capital to speak of, Grace scraped her living by taking in distressed city horses, nursing them back to health, and selling them on.

Evangeline looked out toward the estuary. The half-blinded horse had joined four others grazing down there, right up against the fence. With the sun going down, this felt like the sweetest, most isolated spot on Earth.

She said, "Does anyone ever come out here?"

"An earful usually sends them away. They don't expect it from a woman."

Grace had never been at a loss for a riposte. Evangeline could remember their school and the teacher who'd once said, when Grace had been scowling about something, "Now, Grace, what's that face for?" And Grace had replied, "It keeps all the meat from falling off my head, Miss." The entire class had laughed, and Grace had been sent to stand alone out in the yard for all of a cold March morning. Evangeline was the only one who could see her through the window, and the teacher would ask her every few minutes for a report.

"Just standing there, Miss," she would say.

And indeed, Grace had just stood there; unbeaten, unbowed, until finally she was recalled. Whereupon she returned to her desk without any sign of self-pity or contrition.

They walked back up to the buildings. After she'd hung the animal's halter up on a peg outside the stables, Grace said, "Come inside. We can have a glass of water."

So then they moved from the stables toward the house.

Grace went on, "I know the real reason why you came back."

"Do you?"

"Yes, I do. Can't you let it go? You'd do better to."

"You're sounding like my mother."

"Your mother's ashamed for you. Doesn't want people to think you've been tainted. She thinks you should feel the same way."

"Do *you*?"

"I used to."

"Don't you think about it?"

"I've been through worse since," Grace Eccles said, and they went inside.

Evangeline understood what Grace surely meant. Grace had nursed her father through his final months, right here in this house. They couldn't afford doctors, and there was little that a doctor could have done; it was the drink that had killed him, and his final weeks had been a harrowing time of jaundice and delirium.

The house was mean, but Grace kept it neat. Fresh rushes on the floor, meadow flowers in a small cracked vase on the sideboard. Evangeline was surprised to notice some books, but she didn't comment. She couldn't recall seeing a book in the Eccles house while Grace's father had lived.

Grace had water in a jug, kept cold on a stone. Alongside it were two fine glasses, polished.

Grace poured out two careful measures and handed a glass to Evangeline.

"Taste that," she said. "It's so clean."

Politely, Evangeline drank; Grace sipped at hers, and closed her eyes to appreciate it. She kept them closed for a while, long enough for Evangeline to drink again and wonder if she was missing something.

Then Grace said, "Did anyone tell you they're trying to get me off the land?"

"I thought Sir Owain made you a promise."

"It's not him. It's that doctor who lives in his house. Tells him when to eat, tells him when to sleep, tells him when to fart and make water."

"Grace!" Evangeline pretended to be shocked, and Grace to shrug it off. She'd always liked to play the outrageous child. Because her father was said to have been a settled gypsy they'd called Grace a *diddikai*, and she'd turned the insult into a badge of pride.

From her father she'd inherited his touch with horses and this cottage, and the dispute that came along with it. He hadn't owned the land, but he'd laid out hard cash for a lease that still had thirty years to run. He'd counted the money out before witnesses and made his illiterate's mark on a deed. When he'd died, there had been some immediate question as to whether it should revert to the estate or pass on to his heir.

Grace said, "Sir Owain was always as mad as a coot, but now he's getting worse. A man came out from London. Went over to the Hall asking questions, trying to get him locked up. It's supposed to be a big secret but everyone knows about it. Old Arthur told me." She smiled with some satisfaction. "The London man came to the house. I sent him off, too."

"What did he want with you?"

"Didn't give him a chance to say." They pulled out chairs to sit at the cottage's plain board table. It was heaped with brasses and bridles and a mass of other tack that Grace was attempting to clean up or repair. She had to clear a space for them to put the glassware down.

She went on, "That doctor friend of his keeps saying that my piece of paper means nothing now Father's gone. Says the estate has to be run properly or Sir Owain will lose it. He wants me paying rent or he wants me out. Well, he can want. There's worse than him to watch out for."

"Like who?"

"If anything ever happens to me, I daresay you'll know where to look to find out."

Evangeline looked at her. Lost, unhappy Grace. With her wind-scrubbed skin and her dirty fingernails. Evangeline felt a lurching reminder of the sisterly love she'd once had for her. Motherless Grace and fatherless Evangeline. At one time it had been as if they could read each other's thoughts. But now Evangeline looked and found the book closed, its pages blank, its text encrypted and hidden from her view.

Grace said, "Go back, Evangeline. Go back to London. The last thing you want is to find what you're looking for."

"I wish I could remember, Grace," Evangeline said simply.

"No, you don't."

"Won't you help me?"

"Nothing I can do."

Grace walked her as far as the gate, where Evangeline said, "Those two dead children. They could have been you and me."

"Sir Owain says they were torn by beasts," Grace said. "I don't think he's far wrong."

Evangeline gave it one last try. "What do you know, Grace?" she said.

"No more than you," Grace said.

Again, Evangeline had to wheel the bicycle over rough ground to the main track. Grace did not stay to wave her off. She felt a hollow space inside her for the friend she once thought she'd keep forever, but must now acknowledge that she'd lost.

So Sebastian Becker was actually the Lunacy Visitor's man and had his sights set on Sir Owain? That was a detail that he and Stephen Reed had chosen not to share.

Instead of pointing the bicycle toward Arnmouth village and home, she turned it toward Sir Owain and the Hall.

SEVENTEEN

THE FAIRGROUNDS CAME INTO SIGHT, OCCUPYING THREE FIELDS on the outskirts of a small market town. It was almost evening now, and the lanes all around were dense with people making their way to the entertainment. The car had to slow to nose through them; the crowd treated the Daimler as part of the day's spectacle, a piece of road jewelry as exotic as any sight they'd come to see.

First came the noise. Not one Marenghi organ, but a dozen, each one cranked up to drown out its neighbor. Heard at this distance, their tunes varied as the wind changed.

There was a gateway of painted scenery and electric bulbs that turned the entrance of a common field into a portal of wonders. Beyond it, a bazaar of light and noise. The fair was a portable city of tents and boards, of wooden towers and brilliantly decorated show fronts. Among the temporary buildings stood mighty engines like Babylonian elephants, all crashing pistons and blowing steam, powering the rides with their belts and dynamos.

The car didn't enter the grounds, but was waved on to a field above them where provision had been made for motor vehicles and wagons. It was grazing land, unplowed, and the ground was poor. Sebastian had to clutch at a hanging strap as the Daimler bumped over ruts to find a level spot in the grass.

When they came to a stop, Thomas Arnot turned off the engine and the two men climbed out.

The entire site could be observed from here. Looking down on the contained land of people, planks, and canvas, the driver said, "I don't see any menagerie."

"There's horses," Sebastian said.

"You get horses anywhere."

He took the camera and left the driver standing guard on the Daimler, observing the show field from its running board. Some boys were trying to get Arnot's attention, probably to ask if they could climb up and have a sit behind the wheel, but he was ignoring them.

Down in the field, Sebastian quickly found what he was looking for. Bordering one side of the fairground was an entire row of attractions, each with a walk-up platform and a show front. Each had a barker and some had demure dancing girls, in full white skirts and ankle socks. The barkers were playing hard to the crowds, but it was still early and the crowds were sparse.

The show fronts were decorated to an astonishing standard, every one a rococo basilica of gilt and paint and gingerbread. The grandest of them all was the Electric Coliseum, a veritable cathedral face built around an eighty-seven-key Gavioli organ. Little matter that it was pure illusion, all scaffolding and panels that would pack down into a line of wagons when it was time to move on. It promised awe and glory, and all for pennies.

The Electric Coliseum was a Bioscope show, exhibiting a program of moving pictures. A show would run around twenty minutes, each one containing four or five subjects, always ending with a comedy.

Still carrying his parcel, Sebastian went to the Electric Coliseum's pay booth.

To the woman in the booth, he said, "Who's in charge?"

"Why?"

"I want to talk to the boss."

"Mister Sedgewick's inside. Oi."

Sebastian was halfway up the steps to the walk-up platform.

"That's sixpence, thank you, sir," she said in a voice that managed to combine a superficial courtesy with a deeper sense of menace.

He went back to the booth and paid up.

So Sedgewick himself ran the show. That was no surprise. The man with his name on the fair was likely to own most of it, and from its size and its position in the grounds the Electric Coliseum was one of the fair's grandest attractions.

That said, the tent was only one-third full. Sebastian took a seat. The subject playing was a comedy chase titled *The Plumber and the Lunatics*. It was a simple story, and built around a single joke—that of a plumber dropping his knife in an asylum, and running in terror from two inmates who were merely attempting to return it to him. But the audience liked it well enough.

Then came a short film of some local parade, which seemed to last forever but which actually ran for three minutes. The grand finale was a novelty Vivaphone subject, in which film projection and a Gramophone record were roughly combined to present an actor in blackface and boxing garb performing *The Night I Fought Jack Johnson*.

When all was done, an imposing bearded man in a tailcoat appeared before the screen and called out, "Side exits, please, ladies and gentlemen, and tell all your friends that our program changes daily." Whereupon the Gavioli struck up and the floor shook with its bass notes as the audience flocked out into the fading daylight.

Waiting to be among the last of them, Sebastian stayed back and got the bearded man's attention.

"Are you Abraham Sedgewick?"

The man turned. He was half a head taller than Sebastian. His beard was streaked with gray and his morning suit was faintly shabby, as formal clothing would be if one's workplace was a field.

He said, "Who would be asking?"

"Sebastian Becker. I'm the one who stepped in to release your consignment of curiosities on the railway. Did you take delivery?"

"The specimens? Yes, I did. And I heard the story. Waxworks, eh?"

"I'm in the area on the Lord Chancellor's business." Sebastian took out his letters of authority and showed Sedgewick the crest. He said, "I'm trying to do something for those two girls killed in Arnmouth."

"An appalling affair. Is it a charity benefit you're looking for?"

"No!" Sebastian said quickly. "No. I'm looking for your professional help." He gestured toward the picture screen and said, "Over at the Wild West show they told me that you make these entertainments as well as screening them."

"We do."

Sebastian tore away the brown paper wrapping to reveal the Birtac camera.

He said, "Then I think you're the person I need. This was found at the scene. I'm told that it's a moving-picture camera. I believe there may be exposed images in it. I would very much like to know what they are."

Sedgewick took the camera from him and turned it around in his hands. Over on the other side of the tent, people were beginning to enter for the next show.

Sedgewick said, "Exposed film can be easily spoiled. Has anyone opened this?"

"I can't be sure, but I sincerely hope not."

Mindful of the paying customers, Sedgewick indicated for Sebastian to follow him. They made their way around to the projection booth, separated from the exhibition space by a fireproofed wall.

In this cramped room, dominated by the projection apparatus and smelling of ozone and naphtha and nitrates, a young man was cranking a handle to rewind a film spool for the next show.

Sedgewick introduced him as Will. Just Will. The young man was in white shirtsleeves and a buttoned-up waistcoat. Barely out of his teens, he had a wisp of a mustache and beard.

It took Sebastian a moment to recognize him as the Second Lunatic from the short that he'd just seen. Sedgewick showed Will the Birtac camera and said, "Ever seen one of these? Don't open it, there's film inside."

Will took it and looked it over, much as the older man had. He shook his head.

"It's amateur's kit. A new one on me, boss."

Sedgewick went on, "We're doing a good deed for those poor little girls. Sort this gentleman out with whatever he needs."

SEBASTIAN FOLLOWED Will out of the Bioscope tent and into the part of the showground away from the public area. The growing noise of the crowd and the steady roar of the fairground organs seemed muted here; the noise of the steam traction engines did not. Sebastian had to duck through washing and avoid tripping on heavy cables as he followed Will through.

Will looked back over his shoulder and said, "We don't develop much film these days. My father made a deal with Gaumont. They give us raw stock, we make the scenes, and they develop it for free. For that Dad lets them sell our subjects outside the area. Watch yourself. The third step's loose."

He was ascending to a door into a square-sided wagon that stood some yards apart from all the others. Despite the warning, Sebastian almost stumbled on the third step. Will switched on an electric light.

There was a bench down one side of the wagon. Strips of moving picture film hung from clotheslines above it, all of differing lengths, stirring in the draft from the door like the tails of so many kites. Metal film cans were stacked high on every surface, and on the wall a large hand-painted notice warned of the dangers of sparks and naked flames.

Will said, "This calls for the nuns' drawers."

"The what?" Sebastian said.

Will flushed slightly as he realized that he'd spoken without thinking. "Sorry," he said.

He reached under the bench and produced a black velvet bag with two sleeves. The camera went inside, and the bag was sealed. Will then put his hands in through the sleeves, which were elasticated for a light-tight fit around his forearms.

He fiddled around inside the bag for a while. Sebastian heard the catch go, and the sound of the camera body coming open. Will made faces and stared off into nowhere as he explored the innards of the machine, like a blind man feeling his way around the works of a pocket watch.

"Yep," he said. "It's amateur gauge."

"What does that mean?"

"Half the width of the film we use. Smaller film, smaller image, costs less money. Looks awful on a big screen but good enough in your living room."

"Is that a problem for you?"

"Give me an hour."

EIGHTEEN

"Miss Bancroft," Sir Owain said. "Never was there a fairer sight on a bicycle."

"I didn't think you'd recognize me."

"I barely did, you've so much changed. Quite the young city woman, now. Are you visiting your mother?"

"I am. But I want to talk to you about Grace Eccles."

"Ah."

They were in one of the house's galleries, long and vaulted and painted in a deep red. Sir Owain had been cataloguing when she arrived. The gallery contained his collections of seashells and geological specimens, stuffed birds under glass, and sculpture of a morbid character.

Sir Owain was much changed from the man she remembered. He'd always been a figure of consequence in the area. A vigorous presence, he now seemed diminished. She was moved by his air of vulnerability.

She said, "Grace is my oldest friend."

"Then perhaps," Dr. Sibley said, "you might have some influence with her?"

Even without Grace's forewarning, it would have taken Evangeline less than two minutes to form a dislike of Dr. Ernest Hubert Sibley.

She said, "To help you persuade her out of her home, you mean? Quite the opposite. I'm here to ask you to leave her alone."

"Now, Evangeline," Sir Owain broke in. "Nobody wants to force her to anything."

"However," Dr. Sibley said firmly. Sir Owain fell silent.

Dr. Sibley went on, "You may know that I'm responsible for ensuring that Sir Owain manages his affairs with visible competence. I can tell you there really is no question over Sir Owain's health. There are doubters, but they have their own motives. It's essential not to provide them with the means to do him damage. You do understand?"

She didn't understand. She said, "How does that concern Grace?"

"Grace Eccles is living on land that was granted to her father. The lease expired when her father died."

"She inherited."

"She imagines that."

"Is it a matter of money? You must know she has none. I've seen how she lives. She can barely keep herself."

"It's not a matter of money. It's a matter of good administration."

"Pardon me," Evangeline said. "But that sounds heartless."

"It's not heartless," the doctor said, unhappy with the turn that this had taken; he seemed to be a man more used to giving instruction than to being met with argument. "It's business. And an estate must be seen to be run in a businesslike manner."

"God forbid that we should value human decency over book-keeping."

Sir Owain, who'd grown visibly uncomfortable, said to Evangeline, "But what would you have us do?"

"Just let her be," Evangeline said, and she gestured to include the gallery and all its works and the great labyrinth of the house beyond it. "You have all this, and she has so little. Why would you deprive her of it?"

Dr. Sibley said, "I take it we needn't look for help from you, then."

"To see my best friend rendered destitute? No. And if your main concern is to keep your employer from looking bad, victimizing a tenant seems hardly the way to do it."

That shut him up, for a moment.

Sir Owain said, "Evangeline—you said it yourself. She *is* destitute. I had fears for her life last winter."

"With no home and no land for her horses, how would you expect her to live at all? Will *you* give her a job? Can you imagine Grace in service?"

"The parish would support her," Dr. Sibley said. "And Sir Owain has long been a great supporter of the parish."

"Then why not live and let live, and cut out the parish altogether?"

The doctor opened his mouth, found himself lost for a reply, and closed it again.

Then he tried a different tack. "I'm sorry," he said. "I assumed that a friend would help a friend. Especially two people who have been through so much." And he put a meaningful emphasis on that final phrase, as if he expected her to understand what he meant by it.

"Grace and I have not met in years," she said.

He persisted. "But some experiences can leave a permanent mark. Do you not find? Sometimes help is required to move forward. If you wish, I can offer you a consultation."

She felt herself flush. She said, "You may be Sir Owain's doctor, but you are not mine. So this is inappropriate."

His face didn't move. But his eyes went cold, as if she'd slapped it.

He made an *as you wish* gesture and withdrew from the discussion. He seated himself on a padded gallery bench and looked pointedly away, as Sir Owain inquired after her mother's health and attempted to rescue the occasion to some degree.

And when that was done, and Sir Owain escorted her toward the entrance hall, the doctor took his time before rising to follow.

When he believed they were out of the doctor's earshot, Sir Owain lowered his voice and said, "Forgive me for all this. My life is no longer my own."

She glanced back, to be certain they were not overheard.

She said, "What's brought you to this position?"

"Sheer necessity," Sir Owain said. "The Lord Chancellor will have my land and all my patents, and I a room with a lock on the door, if I am judged unfit. The Visitor's man came. He suspects me of many things, none of which I'm guilty of. But those children who died. They haunt me now."

"Why?"

"What if I could have prevented their suffering by speaking out when I had the chance? Instead of falling silent in my own best interests."

"I don't understand."

"I saw such things on my travels. Secret creatures that I fear may have followed me home. Capable of incalculable harm. But when I published my account . . ."

He said no more, because Dr. Sibley had caught up with them. They'd reached the steps outside the building.

"It's getting late, Evangeline," Sir Owain said. "Perhaps you should wait, under the circumstances. I can have Thomas drive you back, when he returns."

"Don't worry about me," she said. "I won't stop for anyone."

"Or anything," Sir Owain suggested pointedly.

Dr. Sibley offered to steady her bicycle as she climbed astride it.

As Sir Owain returned to the top of the steps, the doctor said to her in a low voice, "I do what I can. But perhaps now you can begin to understand."

SHE'D BARELY covered the first hundred yards before she was forced to concede, with some disquiet, that Sir Owain had been right about the hour. This had been an unplanned addition to her day, and she'd stayed out too long. The light had already faded to the point where the track was blending into the moor and the moor was blending into the sky.

There was an electric lamp on the front of the bicycle's basket. She stood up on the pedals so that she could reach over the handlebars to switch it on. It made no difference so she switched it off again, to save what remained of the battery until it might be more effective.

She wondered about the possibility of stopping on the way back and asking to spend the night with Grace in her cottage. Grace surely wouldn't say no. But given these recent events, what would her mother think if she didn't return? The worst, for sure.

Better to press on, and beat the fall of night. Evangeline tried to think more of her mother's worry, in order to dwell less on her own. She'd no fear of breezy open daytime spaces. The moors after dark would be another matter.

How far was it? Two miles? Three? Half an hour's ride, perhaps, if she kept up a steady speed and didn't coast. She'd surely have some level of visibility for half an hour. She might end the ride in deepening gloom, but by then there would be the town to aim for. She'd be like the fishing boats, making toward the harbor lights at the end of the day.

When she passed Grace's cottage, she didn't slow. Then realized that she hadn't even seen the turnoff until it had gone by. Looking down from the track she was able to make out the cottage roof by the gray smoke rising into the deeper gray of the sky, but no light escaped its shuttered windows.

By day the house's isolation had seemed romantic, almost poetic. But at night, simply unwise. A late visitor might cause a panic; she imagined being Grace, inside her home and hearing a sudden banging at the door. How brave Grace must be, to live so far out here alone, where no cry would be heard, and with no help at hand. If she was not brave, then she was foolish. Or perhaps simply desperate—as Grace herself had pointed out, her choices were limited.

Evangeline rose in the saddle as her wheels jolted over a rock. She dropped back hard, but did not slow. It was easy to imagine that something was behind her, breathing on her back, its presence growing as she pedaled. She might have a rational mind, but no one has a rational soul. Whatever dogged her, it did not go away, but kept a distance as if biding its time.

NINETEEN

T HE DAIMLER WAS NOWHERE TO BE SEEN. SEBASTIAN WANdered the field among grazing horses and factory trucks that had been pressed into service for workers' outings, thinking that perhaps Sir Owain's man had moved the car to a safer spot. But he had a growing suspicion that he'd moved it rather more.

He stopped a couple of people and asked them. No one had seen the man or the car.

He went back to the lower field and wandered the fairground for a while, keeping an eye open for the driver. Alone at the fair, he felt awkward.

It was a long time since he'd attended such a thing for his own pleasure. The freaks, the puppet shows, the hurdy-gurdy men. A father's role was to take along his family, and to stand back and draw his satisfaction from their amusement. He was too old to be a target for the flirtatious groups of factory girls, too respectable-looking to be hailed and challenged as he passed the boxing booth. The pitchmen on the stalls called over his head, to less sober and more likely-looking marks. He felt, to all intents and purposes, like an invisible man.

He passed the freak show a couple of times, and on the third pass he paid the money and went inside. Everyone was crowded in shoulder-to-shoulder: the nervous, the curious, the callow, and the near-hysterical. They shuffled around slowly under the harsh electric bulbs, following a course from entrance to exit. At the front of the show was a "six-legged calf," actually an animal with bifurcated forelegs that could not support its weight. It crawled about its stall on callused knees, trying to reach a few scraps of hay that had fallen from its feeding trough. Around the corner was the fat lady, seated on a stool and knitting to pass the time. She was large, but not so large as to be worth paying to see. Then there was the usual Fiji Mermaid in a glass case, half dead monkey, half dried fish, the two halves stitched together by a taxidermist's needle.

Last of all, in a partitioned area at the back, forbidden to children and costing an extra penny, there were the Seven Freaks of Nature. Their signage was freshly painted, so the smell of glue size mingled with the lingering odor of formaldehyde. Some balked at the extra charge, but most paid up and went through the bead curtain to see what was there.

The specimens of human tissue included a pair of lungs, one from a city dweller and the other belonging to a country person. The city dweller's lung was gray and mottled, rather like a bad green cheese. The countryman's lung was drained and lifeless but comparatively pink. There was a preserved half of a brain. A human uterus. A child's healthy heart, white as folded silk as it hung there in the preserving fluid.

Among the severed heads and flayed torsos and part-dissected limbs, Sebastian found his friends from the train. They now bore the name *Lusus Naturae, The Human Monster,* but were otherwise as before; their heads merged in some fantastical lovers' kiss, their arms around each other in a fearful embrace. Unable to function in life, earning their keep in death.

He stood before their jar for a while, until pressure from the crowd behind him moved him on. As he emerged back into the fairground, he saw Will pushing through on some urgent-seeming errand with a case of lightbulbs, and managed to catch his eye.

"Your film's done, it's drying now," the young man said. "If you can stick it out until the last show, we can put your pictures on the big screen afterward."

"I may as well," Sebastian said. "My driver appears to have abandoned me."

WHEN THE last comedy ended and the audience left, Sebastian stayed behind. All through the program of subjects, his heart had been hammering. Now he realized why. It had nothing to do with the show that he'd seen. It was for the show yet to come. Not an involuntary excitement, but an involuntary dread.

No one appeared for a while, and he wondered if they'd forgotten him. The lights on the show front were extinguished, one set after another.

But then Will arrived, carrying a heavy metal spool with not very much film on it. Sebastian followed him into the projection booth, where he watched as the young man loaded the spool onto the projector arm and threaded up the film. Sedgewick joined them before the operation was done, along with a couple of others, sideshow workers drawn by curiosity at the mention of the dead girls' moving pictures.

"Close the doors," Sedgewick said to them, "and put a chair across."

The tent was secured and made private. According to Will, the Birtac was an amateur's camera designed with a double function. With the addition of a suitable lamp housing, it could be converted into a projector to show the images it had taken.

But with no such accessory available to them, Will had made do with a carnival hand's ingenuity. He had exposed the half-width camera negative onto normal-sized film stock to produce an oddly proportioned, but viewable, positive image. At least, this was how he told it to Sebastian. Who still failed to understand until he saw the first, running-up-to-speed, flickering image on the big screen.

One entire side of the screen was blank while on the other, two near-identical images appeared. One above, one below—until Will put his hand before the projecting lens in a crude mask, leaving just one bright image in a quarter of the screen.

It was a garden scene.

"Are those the girls?" Sedgewick said.

"I believe they are," Sebastian said.

He could not easily relate the figures on the screen to the bodies that he'd seen the night before. Though made of nothing but light, these girls were life itself. Whereas those bodies, though flesh and blood, had borne the full weight of death.

Now here they were, in summer dresses and grown-ups' hats, with a backdrop of lawn and rhododendron. One bright girl, one dark one. Their antics would never change. Nor would they age.

Nothing really happened. The girls were doing the kinds of things that people do when someone points a camera at them for no special reason. Just standing there in the garden, hesitant, smiling, uncertain.

Sebastian was disappointed. These scenes had been made earlier in the summer, probably by Florence's father. They told nothing of the night the girls had died.

Then the scene changed. Though the film continued, the screen went dim.

Sedgewick turned to the open door of the projection booth and called out to Will, "What's the neg like?"

"Very thin," Will replied.

Satisfied, Sedgewick returned his attention to the screen.

Something was happening there. It was hard to make out what. Something seemed to move in the shadows, and then to rush toward the camera.

"My God!" one of the sideshow workers said.

The rest of the film was blank after that.

AROUND THE same time, back in her old bedroom, Evangeline May Bancroft sat on her bed with the curtains thrown back, looking at the moon across the rooftops. The moonlight caused roof slates to shine like polished iron.

She had made it home with nothing to spare. When she'd climbed off the bicycle to walk it back into the shed, her legs had been unsteady. Through the anxiety or the exertion, it was impossible to say.

After her conversation with Grace, the hunger to know was fiercer than ever. Something had once happened to her. Something had shaped her, but she couldn't say what. However awful, she needed to understand it. If she knew herself better, her life might be different.

This had been Evangeline's first return to Arnmouth in some time. A year, at least, since her cousin's wedding, where the local women had gathered at the church gate for a sight of the bride. She wrote to her mother every week, and received a letter in return, so she was reasonably *au courant* with local affairs—who'd left, who'd died, which of her contemporaries was now married and to whom. For her part, she wrote of exhibitions and concerts that she'd attended, of anything interesting that happened in her work, and the seesawing health of her landlady's cat, which was a fighter.

One time, when Lydia had written at unusual length about cousins and weddings and children, she'd responded, *Few men in London seem to care for a provincial girl with strong opinions about life. I rather fear, Mother, that you may have to resign yourself to having raised an old maid.*

She hadn't been entirely honest in writing it. She'd had no lack of suitors in London, despite her making no efforts to invite them. They appeared, they persisted for a while, and then eventually they gave up and looked elsewhere. She did nothing to drive them away. She actually preferred the company of men to women. But she did nothing to encourage them beyond a certain point.

In Evangeline, the prospect of intimacy raised complex emotions. Intimacy was like a ship to her. A picturesque thing on the horizon, but intimidating when it loomed overhead.

She'd indicated to her mother that a life alone—much like Lydia's own, in fact—was more appealing to her than any alternative.

And in that, she supposed that she'd lied.

TWENTY

"WHERE CAN I FIND DETECTIVE REED?" SEBASTIAN ASKED when he finally reached the Sun Inn, late the next morning. "I have something for him."

"He's over at the assembly rooms," Dolly the cook said. "He's been looking for you, too. I had to tell him your bed wasn't slept in."

"I spent the night elsewhere. Though not by design."

She looked him over.

"So I can see," she said, and she reached across the bar counter and plucked a piece of straw from his lapel. She said, "You missed all the excitement."

"What excitement?"

"Over the murderer, of course. They've caught him."

That snapped him to full attention. Sebastian had been fighting the urge toward a hot bath and a shave, after sleeping in his clothes in one of the traveling fair's spare wagons. Midmorning he'd transferred to a boneshaker of a bus that served the valleys. It had dropped him within half a mile of the town, and he'd walked the rest of the way. Sir Owain would be getting a strongly worded note about his driver's behavior.

"Who is it?" he said.

"Some gypsy," she said. "Just like everyone thought."

THE INQUEST had taken place earlier that morning, in the main hall of the assembly rooms. At one point the jury had trooped through to the back room to view the bodies. Even as the coroner had been reviewing the events leading to the girls' discovery, the detectives had been making their arrest. Now there was a police van outside the assembly rooms, and all of the doors had been thrown open to air the place. A caretaker was scrubbing down the corridors. Sebastian had to step around him to get to the back rooms, where Stephen Reed was labeling his evidence boxes for transfer to the waiting vehicle.

Sebastian said, "I'm told you've got your man."

"An itinerant," Stephen Reed said. "A rag-and-bone man with a puppet peep show. We're pressing him for a confession, but he's a simpleton."

"You're not happy."

"Of course I'm happy," Stephen Reed said with ill-concealed bitterness. "In my experience, a simpleton's good for a confession to anything. In fact the same can be said of any man, if you go at him for long enough."

Sebastian said, "Is there a witness? Or any evidence?"

"Evidence enough for an arrest," Stephen Reed said. "He had some of the girls' clothing on his cart. The parents have looked at the pieces and identified them." He tilted one of the unsealed boxes to show the tagged and labeled clothing inside it.

"I came to return this to you," Sebastian said, and set the moving-picture camera down on the table.

Stephen Reed looked at it. "Did you find anything?"

"A few domestic scenes. And, at the end, a few seconds of an indistinguishable shape, flying toward the picture-taker. The people I consulted did their best, but they're show folk. A scientific analysis might tell us more."

The young policeman nodded slowly.

"I see," he said, turning away. "Well, it's all academic now. As you say, we have our man."

Sebastian placed his hand on the younger man's arm and surprised him with the strength he used to keep him in place. He checked the room behind them and then lowered his voice. "What do *you* think?"

Stephen Reed hesitated for a while, as if at a door that he knew he might regret opening.

Then he said, "There's no way that the man we've arrested could also have carried out the attack on Evangeline and Grace. At that time he was in the king's navy, far overseas. Receiving the wounds that have addled his brain."

"Then perhaps they're unrelated after all?"

"Evangeline and Grace may not have died, but they were cruelly handled in a similar way. Their hands were tied behind them and bags were placed over their heads. And whether they remember it or not, someone interfered with them. A doctor inspected them and there can be no doubt of it. After the assault they were thrown alive into a gully where gorse bushes broke their fall. They struggled free and made their way back home. They reappeared all scratched and torn and claiming no memory of where they had been."

"Then what—"

"Both incidents even began with the same childish dare. The one back then, and the one this week. Both pairs of girls made a camp on the moors. Their plan was to sit up to watch . . ."

"For a beast?" Sebastian said, with a suddenness that surprised even him.

"Our local legend," Stephen Reed said. "Beasts, and rumors of beasts. But never any proof of beasts. Personally, I've never seen a thing on the moor. But then I've never been a drinking man."

"So who do you favor for it?"

"Oh, Mister Becker," Stephen Reed said. "Given a free choice in a perfect world, we both know who I'm starting to favor for it. Him and his beasts and his trail of the Amazon dead. The problem is, I don't have a scrap of evidence to offer in support."

"Where was Sir Owain on that first occasion?"

"All I can establish is that he was in residence at Arnside Hall," Stephen Reed said. "Fresh back from his South American jaunt but with his memoirs unwritten and his reputation still intact. But why should I worry? The rag-and-bone man did it."

"It's time I spoke to your superintendent."

"Good luck with that," Stephen Reed said.

THE MAN waxed his mustache. In Sebastian's book, that was never a good sign. His name was George Hartley and he accepted Sebastian's credentials at a glance, without seeming to be impressed by them.

"I know the Visitor's role," he said. "It's to protect the business affairs of lunatics. What have you to offer me? I can spare you five minutes."

"I fear that a wider issue is being overlooked."

"You think so? Convince me."

"I have a list of earlier incidents from this area. All of them with some aspect in common with your case."

"I've seen your list. There are no actual murders on it. Whereas for this one I have a culprit, and I have his confession."

"A confession from an ill-educated man who's probably yet to grasp, in any meaningful way, that his eagerness to comply with his captors will send him to a hanging."

"His education has nothing to do with it."

"There are many similarities between this and the one fully documented case on that paper."

"And many differences, too."

"They don't undo the comparison, or make it any less valid. I think they give a tantalizing picture of a madman's mental process. The differences make sense if you take them as evidence of an evolving state of mind."

Sebastian went on to explain. With Evangeline and Grace, their assailant had tied their hands and thrown them alive into a gorse-filled gully on a forlorn part of the moor. He had not killed them, but had surely meant for them to die. It was the action of a man who wanted a certain result, but not to feel responsibility for it. He did not consider himself a murderer. By some peculiar logic, he probably felt that he could avoid guilt by being elsewhere when death finally came.

It was their survival and return that had forced a change in his method the next time. Only luck had saved him from discovery. This time, he'd battered them to be sure. Bagging their heads had saved him from seeing their faces when he did it. He still did not consider himself a murderer. A man who killed when forced to it, perhaps. But in his mind the fault lay with the forces, not with him.

On both occasions, Sir Owain Lancaster had entered the story uninvited and shown his concern for the victims. He was a prominent local figure, and both discoveries had been made on land that was part of his estate. But the fact that he blamed imaginary creatures, and was now under investigation by the Lord Chancellor's Visitor in Lunacy, must surely call his innocence into question.

George Hartley said, "There's nothing here I haven't heard before. What's your game, Mister Becker? What exactly were you sent here to achieve?"

"I'll be open with you, sir. My task was to establish whether Sir Owain Lancaster is merely a harmless fantasist or a man capable of expressing his madness by causing suffering in others."

"And you have not done so. Good day to you, sir."

THEN SEBASTIAN and Stephen Reed took a shortcut up a winding flight of steps behind the Ship Hotel and the Methodist church to the houses above the town, with the intention of calling on Evangeline Bancroft.

She wasn't at the house. No one was. Stephen Reed looked in the shed, and her bicycle was there.

"Perhaps she's meeting her mother for lunch," Sebastian suggested.

"Perhaps," Stephen Reed said.

They went down to the library. There were four or five browsers, and one reader at the tables. Lydia Bancroft was busy in the restricted section, where the rare editions and the mildly racy subjects kept company on the shelves. She was visibly pleased to see Stephen Reed. Less pleased to see Sebastian. And she had surprising news for them.

"Evangeline's already gone," she said.

"Gone where?" Stephen Reed said.

"She took an early train back to London. She asked me to give you this."

She held out an envelope with Stephen Reed's name on it. The young policeman hesitated, and then took it. He hooked his little finger under the flap and tore it open to read there and then.

As Stephen Reed moved aside, Sebastian said to Lydia Bancroft, "I'm sorry that I missed her. We had something of great importance to discuss. Can you give me your daughter's address in London?"

"I'm sorry," Lydia said. "She specifically asked me not to."

"The address of her employer, then?"

"That, too. She doesn't want you contacting her at all, Mister Becker. No one appreciates being misled. Everyone knows who you are now. You're the special investigator to the Lord Chancellor's Visitor in Lunacy. You didn't come here to save children. You came here to harass a decent man with a view to depriving him of his liberty."

"I'm sorry you feel that way," Sebastian said.

"And I'm sure you imagine that's an apology," Lydia Bancroft said. She turned to Stephen Reed, who was now replacing Evangeline's letter in its envelope.

"Stephen," she said, "if you want to write to Evangeline, I can forward any letters."

"Thank you, Mrs. Bancroft," Stephen Reed said, and gave a glance to Sebastian that suggested they should leave.

OUTSIDE ON the street, he gave Evangeline's note to Sebastian.

In black ink with a neat hand, she had written,

> *I learned this morning that the police have their man and that is that. This alone would not have caused me to leave without further discussion, but I have to tell you that I do not appreciate the efforts of Mr Becker to make me his spy against a troubled man who has shown nothing but kindness to many. For you, Stephen, I will simply tell you this: you asked me to say if I remembered anything, and I think I have. I remember that Sir Owain came to the house after Grace and I had been found. I was lying in bed with that peculiar feeling one has when trying to remember a dream. I heard him speaking to my mother downstairs. I think he may have offered her some money in an act of simple charity. I expect he was more prosperous then. But my mother would not accept his offer. If he made the same financial gesture to Grace's father, I expect he drank it. Please watch out for Grace, and do not allow Dr Sibley to drive her from her father's land. She is a sad soul, and she has suffered enough.*

Sebastian said, "We can't lose her. There's too much at stake. An innocent man will hang and more children will probably suffer. I have an idea."

BUT THE local postmistress was unable to give them Evangeline's London address, even though she must have hand-franked a hundred or more of Lydia Bancroft's letters. Sebastian had a suspicion that she'd been warned and wasn't being entirely honest with them. She could remember that it was somewhere in Holborn, she said, but was blank on the name of the street.

"Thank you, anyway," Stephen Reed said. "And please don't tell Mrs. Bancroft that we were asking."

He'd already assured Sebastian that Lydia Bancroft would learn of their ruse before the day was out.

Sebastian said to the postmistress, "I understand you keep a monster book. A book of beasts?"

"I put it out in the holiday weeks," the postmistress told him. "For visitors to read."

"Did Florence Bell and Molly Button ever come in and look at it?"

"I expect they did," she said. "All the children do."

At his request, she brought it out. It was a scrapbook of handwritten stories and newspaper clippings, going back over some thirty years. He skipped the stories, which were mostly inconclusive observations, secondhand reports, or obvious fabrication. Some way back in the book he found something that caught his attention, a yellowed cutting from the area's local newspaper. The glue that fixed it to the album was old and discolored, and was showing through. But the print was still readable.

It was a diary piece, written to amuse, and it went:

If you lack for entertainment, go out to Arnmouth and spend a few pennies in the bar of the Harbor Inn. For the price of a pint of the local ale, horse breeder Edward Eccles will tell you his tale of a beastly encounter on the moors; and a fine tale it is, that grows in embellishment with every retelling. In fact, we are confident that

by the summer's end, the Beast of Arnmouth will have sprouted a
brood of fine children and be Mayor of the Borough. Tootle pip!

Edward Eccles, breeder of horses; almost certainly the father of the foul-mouthed Grace. At the foot of the column was a humorous note from the editor, offering a cash prize to any visitor or local able to provide a picture or other conclusive proof of the Arnmouth Beast's existence.

Four young girls, separated by time. Two survived, two now gone. All torn by some beast.

The police were leaving, the bodies were gone . . . the grieving relatives had ended their summer early and returned to the capital. Stephen Reed nursed his doubts, and a tinker sat in a police cell. The law was satisfied, even if others were not.

On the pavement outside the post office, Sebastian said, "Don't give up. I'll find Evangeline in London, and I'll press her for whatever was said. And I'll take the printed copy of the moving-picture film and see what it can yield."

Stephen Reed said, "Good luck with that. I have duties now. I'll be lucky if I even get to say good-bye to my dad."

SEBASTIAN COLLECTED his bag from the inn and made his way to the pickup point for the railway's station wagon, marked by a folding board on the pavement outside the apothecary's store. The wagon arrived a few minutes later. Its driver was not the sullen ostler who'd brought him here, but the blue-eyed young railwayman. He was in a clean collar and scrubbed of his layer of soot.

Sebastian shared the ride out with three newspapermen returning to London, and on the ten-minute journey he almost dozed. At the end of the ride, the newspapermen went into the waiting room and raised a fog of tobacco smoke while Sebastian stayed out in the fresh air.

He walked to the end of the platform and stood looking at the coal yard beyond it. There was a coalman's shed, with an iron roof and a stone chimney. It was a building that might easily have been a poacher's cottage in the country were it not for the fact that its kitchen garden was in walled sections, each section containing a heaped-up mountain of glittering black spoil.

When Sebastian came back down the platform, the young railwayman was lining up dry goods and mailbags for loading onto the branch line service.

He was a hard worker. Sebastian found himself thinking back to the half hour when the fairgrounds began to empty and the stalls to shut down, when he'd made his way to the Electric Coliseum and waited out the final show. Once again, the plumber ran from the lunatics. His antics never changed. But nor did he age, or get drunk on the job. And, Sebastian supposed, he performed nightly and forever for his single day's wage.

Sebastian said, "Do you know much about Sir Owain Lancaster?"

The young man didn't pause in his work. He said, "Anyone who grew up around here knows Sir Owain."

"And what do they think of him?"

"A kind man, and a generous one," the railwayman said. "We don't care what they say in London. There are things in this world that no one can dispute with any certainty. If he says he saw monsters in the jungle, then I for one am happy to believe him."

TWENTY-ONE

Attn: S Greenhough Smith Esq
George Newnes, Ltd
3–13 Southampton Street
London WC2

Dear sir,

I write to you at the suggestion of my employer, Sir James
Crichton-Browne, whom I serve in the capacity of Special
Investigator. This concerns my son, Robert, who is eighteen years
old. I will be grateful if you will consider him for a position in your
archive or editorial departments, should one become available.
Although his temperament is not well suited to responsibility, his
grasp and retention of detail will, I believe, make him an asset to
your editorial staff in matters of proofreading or record keeping.

I will welcome any opportunity to discuss the matter with you.

Sincerely
Sebastian Becker

TWENTY-TWO

S OUTHWARK, THAT "VAST AND MELANCHOLY PROPERTY" SOUTH
of the Thames, would never have been Sebastian's first choice for
an area in which to lodge his family. In any ranking of desirable London
boroughs, it could not be placed much above the lowest. But at least it
wasn't the East End. And for a weekly rent that might just have covered the meanest garret in Bloomsbury, they had a suite of rooms with
clean water and relatively honest neighbors. Compared to the squalid
courts and alleys and the tenement blocks that surrounded them, they
had hygiene and comfort. But that was only in comparison. One day he
hoped to move the household to some better address across the river.

One day.

Sebastian tried not to look too far ahead. Ambition was a young
man's game. These days he was more concerned with the continuing
survival and security of those he loved. It was no longer so much a
matter of dreaming of how high he might climb, as of always keeping
in mind how far they might fall.

Every morning, beginning at around five A.M., the population of
Southwark began to move. To the breweries and the printing shops,
to the wharves and the warehouses. To the vinegar works, to the iron
manufacturers in Union Street, to the leather factories in neighboring
Bermondsey, and across the bridges into central London and the City.

They were all kinds of people. Butchers, laborers, compositors, office cleaners, and artisans. Their hours were long and their pay was
small. At the end of the day, when all were coming home, the Thames
bridges grew so dense with bodies that it was hard for one person to
cross against the flow.

Most were honest. Many were not. Almost all shared the same thought: to better themselves, and to leave.

On his way home that evening, Sebastian stopped by the pie stand under the railway bridge on Southwark Bridge Road. Though he had an office of sorts in the nearby Bethlem asylum, the accommodation was in a basement room that he shared with the unclaimed belongings of deceased inmates. He visited it as infrequently as possible. The pie stand opened all hours to cater to the cab trade, and he had an arrangement to pick up his messages there. He was given three, including a note from Sir James Crichton-Browne.

Crichton-Browne was one of three Lord Chancellor's Visitors— two eminent doctors, and one lawyer—who carried out a yearly examination of every detained psychiatric patient of significant means. Their remit covered those in institutions as well as those, like Owain Lancaster, in private care. Any deemed incompetent to manage their own affairs were placed under the control of a Master of Lunacy appointed by the Lord Chancellor. Sir James was the busiest of the Visitors; even at the age of seventy-two, he kept a punishing schedule.

Sebastian was the first of the family to arrive home that evening. Their rooms over the shop were empty. The fire was laid, so he lit it.

Frances and Robert arrived shortly after. Frances acknowledged his greeting and then busied herself preparing the evening meal, leaving Sebastian alone with his son.

Observing the boy's mood, he said, "A good day today, Robert?"

"The best, father," Robert said. "Absolutely the best. Even though Frances was late and I had to wait."

Sebastian glanced toward the kitchen. "Is she upset about something?"

"I don't know," Robert said. "Is she?"

"Hang up your coat."

Robert had turned eighteen now. Almost a grown man, and not so much a boy anymore. He attended a private institution in South Hampstead where he received an education designed around his needs. Here, for once, his talents were recognized, and his abilities explored and developed in ways that no one else had ever considered. The only advice they'd received, when Robert had been small and manifestly strange, had been to treat him as feebleminded and hide him away.

After he'd hung up his coat, Robert said, "I'd like to read for a while if I may, Father."

"Wait until after supper."

"But that will leave me with nothing to do now."

"Ask Frances if she needs any coal brought up."

Last year, under the supervision of the college principal, they'd tried Robert in a brief period of employment. Very brief. Placed in a job as a waiter in a middle-sized commercial hotel, he hadn't lasted a morning. He'd taken everyone's orders and then sat down to his own breakfast.

Returning from the kitchen, Robert said, "Frances says she brought in coal this afternoon. What else can I do?"

"Tell me what you're reading."

"There's a serial in the *Strand*. I'm collecting all the parts. The Smith's lady is ill and no one had saved my copy, so we had to go to Waterloo."

Ah. No wonder Frances seemed irritated. Elisabeth's sister was a saint, but Robert's obsessions could wear out the patience of one. In America, he'd collected dime magazines. Here he'd transferred his obsession to the likes of Rider Haggard, Verne, and Wells.

He said, "May I read my serial now, father?"

Sebastian gave in.

"Be sure to stop when your mother gets home," he said.

Robert settled in a chair by the window with his magazine, and Sebastian took a letter opener and started on the day's post. When Elisabeth arrived a few minutes later, Robert didn't even notice.

When he saw her coat, Sebastian said, "Is it raining?"

"When is it not?" Elisabeth said, and went into the kitchen.

Within a minute he heard voices being raised. Then he heard Elisabeth's affronted cry of "Mince?" Moments after that, Frances emerged from the kitchen and stamped up the back stairs to their attic rooms.

Sebastian went into the kitchen.

"What's this about?" he said.

For no reason he could see, Elisabeth was moving all the evening's raw food from the place where Frances had laid it out to another. She said, "The butcher gave our order to someone else. So forget your chops, it's mince."

"I don't mind mince."

"What's the matter with her? I can't trust her with the simplest task. I have to do everything myself."

Sebastian knew better than to defend one sister to the other right now, but he was still at a loss to see the younger woman's crime.

Elisabeth added, "And if there's a shirt you want to wear again, you'd better go and rescue it from the wash."

He went upstairs. Frances heard him and, when he entered the larger of the attic bedrooms, stepped back from the laundry basket with her hands lifted in the air in an end-of-the-tether, *All right, what now?* gesture.

He said, "May I speak?"

Frances waited without moving, looking down.

Sebastian said, "Forgive your sister, Frances. She spends all her days being harsh with people. It takes her a while to return to herself."

For a moment, he thought she wasn't going to reply.

Then she said, "Then perhaps we should move away from the borough."

"Why?"

"So she'll have a longer walk home and more time to adjust her foul mood."

Then she gave him a glance, to see how that had gone down. He realized that she was making a joke, of a kind. It was hard to tell with Frances. She was the quiet sister, the younger one. But she was in her thirties now, with a gray hair or two that she didn't bother to conceal. Somehow along the way, without anybody planning it, the younger woman's practical room-and-board arrangement had turned into a spinster's life.

He said, "It could be worse. Wait until she next sees the butcher. I wouldn't want to be in his apron."

That drew another look, and a rueful smile. Or a half smile, anyway, which he suspected came more out of politeness than anything else.

As he descended the attic stairs to the smell of frying mince, it seemed to Sebastian that such fallings-out were becoming more frequent these days. He was required to play the peacemaker whenever he was at home.

Since the household seemed to run perfectly well during his absences, he wondered if these arguments flared up only because, with him around, they could. Elisabeth and her sister were like two fighters who would never engage without a ring and a referee. Without those, to strike out would be to injure. But with Sebastian in the middle, they could vent their feelings in relative safety.

AFTER THEY'D DINED, Frances took up her sewing and Robert went to his bedroom, an extension to the apartments that was little more than a cubby built out over the shop's front. He took his newest magazine with him, to read for the second time.

When Robert was out of their earshot, Sebastian said, "I've had a reply from the publishing house."

"Saying they won't take him."

He showed her the letter. "They'll write to us if a position becomes available," he said.

She looked at the letter, but she didn't take it from him or read it.

"They always say that," she said, and gathered up the last of the plates to take back to the kitchen.

He rose, and followed her. All through the meal he'd been sensing that there was more to this than weariness or frayed nerves.

He said, "What happened today?"

"Nothing."

"Elisabeth."

"I said, nothing."

He waited, and then she said, "We had to have the police in."

"For?"

She stopped what she was doing, and took a moment.

Then she said, "A man came in wanting to take his child away. He was stinking of beer and he wouldn't be told. He said that the doctors were killing her and her place was at home. Said he had a knife, although he didn't show it. Two of the nurses kept him talking while I ran for the police."

"What's wrong with his child?"

"She's dying."

"Nothing the doctors can do?"

"No."

"Then why not let him take her, if there's nothing to be done?"

"His home is a sty. And his children only matter when he's drunk. And the more drink he takes, the more sentimental he becomes. He's the kind of man whose love is all noise and self-pity; at least she'll die where the sheets are clean."

He touched her shoulder. "You're worn out," he said. "You should go to bed."

"I think I will."

She went about half an hour later. In many people's minds, working in a charitable children's hospital was an extended fantasy of rescued orphans and grateful Tiny Tims. But the truth of it was not for the soft of heart.

Sebastian was left with the publishing-house letter in his hand. There was no point in pushing Elisabeth to read it; unlike him, she wouldn't take courtesy for encouragement. Not today, at any rate.

He became aware that Frances had paused in her work and was looking at him. Then she quickly pretended that she wasn't and returned her attention to her decorative embroidery, held only inches from her face.

He said, "Have you enough light?"

"Enough for what I need," she said.

He had a rolltop bureau in the corner of the room. When he was home, it served him for an office. He put the letter in one of its drawers and then picked up his copy of Owain Lancaster's book.

It was a nice piece of binding, in blue cloth with printed boards and a number of tipped-in illustrations on slick paper. He'd bought it at

Wilson's on Gracechurch Street, billing it to his employer. He opened it at the copyright page. Due in part to the scandal that had driven its author from town and from London society, the book had sold in its thousands and was now in its fifth impression.

He closed up the desk and then moved to the doorway.

"Good night, Frances," he said.

She laid the fancy work in her lap. "Good night, Sebastian."

Before going upstairs, he moved toward Robert's room with the book in his hand. It was "fancy work" of a different kind. As fiction, it would be a commendable account of a fantastical expedition to a far-off land. One that had involved perils and wonders, tragic loss and heroic survival. The maps and doctored photographs would have enhanced its grip on the imagination.

But Sir Owain had insisted it was no fiction. He'd even been prepared to take the Royal Society to court for casting doubt on his word. His vigorous defense had led to a public accusation of fraud and the equally public destruction of his reputation. He'd sued the Society and several newspapers, and lost every action.

And now here he was, withdrawn from public life, struggling to preserve his liberty and to retain control of his fate and his finances.

Sebastian tapped on Robert's door before going in. Robert was writing. His bed was covered in slips of paper, all crammed with lines in his neat hand.

"I thought you were reading," Sebastian said.

"I've read my serial. I'm not ready for anything else just yet."

"I know what you mean," Sebastian said. "It doesn't do to rush onward. It's nice to stay in the tale."

"At least for a while. My favorite time of the day is when I'm waiting to go to sleep. I like to just lie there and think."

"What about?"

"Things," Robert said.

Sebastian knew that he made stories of his own, but he wouldn't share them. Sebastian had sneaked a look at some of his writings, once. It was all gangs and pirates and Martian war machines, jumbled together in a single tale.

Sebastian said, "I have a job for you. It's worth a shilling or two." He handed over Sir Owain's book and said, "Tell me what you think of this. Have you read it before?"

Robert turned it around and looked at the title.

"No," he said.

"The author would have us believe that it's a true account of his adventures. He travels to the Amazon, and his party is attacked by monsters unknown to science. He speaks of members of his expedition being discovered, torn by beasts. See if you can tell me the point where the truth ends and his fantasy begins."

"All right," Robert said.

Sebastian had half-expected him to argue. It wasn't often that Robert read a book. It was periodicals that fascinated him. To his mind a book was a dead thing, fixed, detached from real time.

The boy laid the volume aside and returned to his writing.

"Good night, Robert," Sebastian said, and Robert murmured something that Sebastian couldn't hear. He didn't take his eyes from the page.

ELISABETH WAS sleeping when Sebastian went upstairs. Or at least, her eyes were closed and she didn't open them. He undressed in the dark and lay down beside her. She was turned away.

He wondered how the world must seem through Robert's eyes. He could not imagine it. Elisabeth's hope had always been to see Robert take his place in ordinary human society. But now Sebastian sensed a reluctance in her whenever there was any real suggestion of letting the boy go. As if she wanted to see him stand, but would not risk seeing him fall.

His request had been a serious one, not meant simply to indulge or occupy the boy. Robert's knowledge of such fantastical literature was detailed and comprehensive.

Sebastian stared up at the ceiling until shapes started to form. Then he closed his eyes.

The shapes did not go away.

In the forests were various beasts still unfamiliar to zoologists, such as the *milta,* which I have seen twice, a black doglike cat about the size of a foxhound. There were snakes and insects yet unknown to scientists; and in the forests of the Madidi some mysterious and enormous beast has frequently been disturbed in the swamps—possibly a primeval monster like those reported in other parts of the continent. Certainly tracks have been found belonging to no known animal—huge tracks, far greater than could have been made by any species we know.

From the manuscripts and letters of
Lt. Col. P. H. Fawcett, DSO, FRGS
Written 1909–1925
Collected in *Lost Trails, Lost Cities,* 1953

TWENTY-THREE

SEBASTIAN HAD RETURNED THE MOVING-PICTURE CAMERA AND its developed roll of negative to Stephen Reed, but he'd retained the positive copy. He now had the film roll in his pocket, wound tight in its wrapping of stiff paper, and a number of questions about its content that the fairground people hadn't been able to answer.

Kelly's London directory listed several film companies. Most of them were out in the suburbs, but there was a cluster of office addresses in Warwick Court. This was a stone's throw from the records department of King's College Hospital, where he intended to begin his inquiries about the medical training of the disagreeable Dr. Sibley, and from the Inns of Court where Evangeline Bancroft had let slip that she had employment.

As it turned out, the King's College records had all been boxed up and sent across the river, ahead of the hospital's relocation to Denmark Hill. That would have to be a job for another day. The shortest way to Warwick Court from here would be through Lincoln's Inn Fields.

The morning was cold and dry. Lincoln's Inn was a walled enclave of legal offices and chambers made up of town houses, alleyways, and green spaces. The grander chambers had large ground-floor rooms with chandeliers. The others packed in their lawyers from ground to gables, like warehouses of litigation. The adjoining fields were actually a fashionable square with a public garden, like a parade ground to the barracks of a lawyers' army.

A high wall and a gatehouse separated Lincoln's Inn from the actual fields. He stopped by the gatehouse and spoke to the porters and other servants of the inn, but none recognized Evangeline by name.

As he cut through, looking this way and that on the off chance that he might spot her, black-robed "benchers" flitted through the gardens in their twos and threes like carrion birds, crossing on their way to the Courts of Justice; strollers moved more slowly, and sometimes got in their way.

Like the hospital, Warwick Court was a disappointment, but also a lead onto more promising things. The court itself was little more than a glorified alleyway on the north side of High Holborn, ending in a tall cast-iron gateway with yet more lawyers beyond it. The alley's buildings were wedding-cake heavy with carved stone features and fancy Victorian brickwork.

In a second-floor film sales agency office that he picked at random, he explained his needs and was given an address and a note of introduction. The address was for the Walton Film Studios, the note of introduction to a Mr. Cecil Hepworth.

He was urged to "tell Cecil that Joe sent you, and sends his regards."

"I'M LOOKING for Mister Hepworth?" Sebastian said.

Cecil Hepworth's Walton Film Studio was so close to the Walton High Street that a two-minute walk out of the center had taken Sebastian some way past it. Walton on Thames, just a twenty-five-minute train ride out of Waterloo, was part riverside boating village, part office workers' suburb. Along the river were inns, moorings, and great rafts of empty rowboats herded up against the banks awaiting weekend rental. Beyond the main street of shops and public houses spread a semirural outskirts of villas and smallholdings.

The film studio had grown up around one modest dwelling in an outer cul-de-sac, absorbing the other houses in the row and then expanding into the gaps between them and onto the land behind. Now the original buildings contained offices, cutting rooms, and workshops. Blocking out the sky behind these, risen from the suburban clay like airship hangars, were Hepworth's number one and two covered studio buildings.

A young man in flannels and a cricket jersey led Sebastian from one place to another until they finally located the boss. They found him in an automated film-processing laboratory on the ground floor of one of the studio buildings. The long room was an elaborate and noxious-smelling laundrylike plant of racks and tanks and spindles, with exposed and processed film zigzagging through it in an endless flow. Hepworth was discussing some critical adjustment with one of the women operating it. He proved to be a tall and bookish-looking man, quietly spoken and with a pale gaze.

Sebastian introduced himself, took the small roll of film from his pocket, and explained its significance.

"There's barely a minute's worth of activity there," he said, raising his voice over the clatter of the machinery. "But I need an expert's opinion on the last picture. There's a chance that the girls may have photographed their attacker before they were murdered."

The young man let out a whistle.

Hepworth opened up the roll and drew it out to arm's length. The young man in the cricket jersey scooted around behind him to look as he held it up to the light.

"What do you reckon, Geoff?" Hepworth said.

"It looks like someone printed a seventeen-point-five neg onto thirty-five mil stock," the young man said.

Sebastian said, "A lad copied it for me in a show van on a fairground. He said it was unusual. The camera was called a Birtac."

"That's Birt Acres' old camera," Hepworth said, still studying the images against the light. "He made it for the amateur market about ten years back. Cost about ten guineas and it never took off." He looked at Sebastian. "You don't have the negative?"

"It was evidence. I had to give it back. This is all I could keep."

Hepworth studied the strip again, pulling out several more feet of it until he reached the scene in question. "Is it all like this? It's very dense."

The young man said, "We could try making a copy and printing it up a bit."

Hepworth nodded and Sebastian said, "What does that mean?"

"It means putting more light through it to bring out any detail that's hiding," Hepworth said. "But it's not guaranteed. If it's not there in the image, then there's nothing to find. But we can try it for you, if you like."

Hepworth sent the young man off with the roll, and gave Sebastian leave to wander for the hour or so needed to make and process the copy.

Sebastian went upstairs to look into the studio, hoping to see a scene or two being made, but the doors were wide open and carpenters were at work inside. The interior light on the stage was soft and gray, diffused by the clouded glass of the skylight roof. But there was nothing of great interest to see.

He saw a handcart load of costumes being taken off toward the river, but didn't follow it. He had more luck in the other studio, where a boy had been posted at the doors to keep out visitors and signal for quiet; from inside the studio came the sound of Gramophone music. The music lasted no more than a couple of minutes and then the doors were thrown open. No one paid any attention to Sebastian as he wandered in and took in the scene.

The studio was airless and hot, due to the electric arcs that burned to supplement the autumn light. There was a crowd of shirtsleeved men around the camera, and a large Gramophone with an enormous brass horn beside it. Two young women, in costumes and heavy white makeup, were studying a song sheet. A man in a checked cap positioned the Gramophone's needle arm over the record and played them a burst of song, to which they listened intently before exchanging a glance and nodding. One was dressed as some kind of dancer or chorus girl, the other as a suffragette.

Sebastian had spotted something of significant interest to him, and he tried to make his way through to speak to one of the young women; but a cry of "Close all doors!" and the sudden galvanization of all around him made him freeze to the spot. Everyone who'd been lounging, chatting, or arguing out a problem suddenly turned to some professional purpose. Sebastian alone was left without a role.

He eased his way to the back of the crowd as the two young women took up their positions before a music-hall backdrop. No one challenged him.

There was a further call for silence; the camera operator began to crank, the women struck a starting pose, and then, as the Gramophone music began, they went into a dance and mime to the song they'd been studying. The silence was far from perfect, but it allowed the performers to hear and follow their words.

Sebastian recognized the song; it was called "I Do Like to Be Where the Girls Are" and it was strange to hear the far-off, voices-from-the-ether sound of the Gramophone apparently issuing from the lips of the all-too-solid young women before him.

So the people on the screen in those novelty Vivaphone subjects weren't speaking or singing at all. It was an illusion of living sound, not a record of life itself.

The song ended without applause. A man by the camera called out, "That's a good one, let's check it," and then all stood around doing nothing until, at some secret signal, everyone sprang into movement again. The studio doors were thrown open and the two young women headed for the outside air.

Sebastian stepped forward to catch the attention of the one wearing the high-waisted jacket, hobble skirt, and *Votes for Women* sash of the music-hall suffragette. She had brown wavy hair and arresting gray-blue eyes, and a face that was a perfect oval. Seen this close, she was a girl of no more than sixteen or seventeen years.

"Excuse me, miss," he said. "That pin you're wearing. What exactly does it signify?"

She looked down. It was as if he'd drawn her attention to something that she hadn't even been aware of.

"Sorry," she said. "I couldn't tell you. It came with the wardrobe."

THE SCREENING took place in the inspection room, above a wooden garage on the front of the property. It was a new building, replacing one taken by fire a couple of years before. Heavy drapes blocked out the light from a square bay window, and the young man in the cricket jersey operated the projector. Only he, Sebastian, and the studio's owner were present.

Sebastian said, "Do we see anything more?"

"I don't know," the young man said. "I haven't looked at it myself yet."

He'd somehow dealt with the new copy so that a single picture appeared on the screen before them. No twinned image, no large area of dazzling blank screen. With the room's short throw, the picture was no more than three feet across and its edges were unusually crisp and bright.

Here were the girls, happy in their garden again. The screen was so washed with new light that in this section they were now without substance, like ghosts.

Sebastian leaned closer as the critical scene approached. At first he didn't realize it had come; where it had been black-on-black the first time that he'd seen it, now the screen was filled with a swirling gray fog like filings in a jar. But in the fog, something moved. There, and there. It was all over too soon.

Cecil Hepworth said, "That doesn't look like a man to me. Perhaps they were trying to make a trick film. Wouldn't you say?"

"A what?" Sebastian said.

"Run it back and let's see it again."

Sebastian turned to the young man at the projector. "It went by too quickly," he said. "Can you make it go more slowly?"

"If I run it too slow, the lamp will burn the film and blow a frame."

He shut off the lamp and backed the roll up a few feet, then ran it again as slowly as he dared.

It was slow enough for the illusion of motion to be replaced by a sequence of frozen flicker-images, as if time had been sliced and laid open before them. A smoke-figure that was almost certainly one of the children seemed to turn in the fog and dash toward the camera. As she passed from the picture, something else burst out of the fog behind her and rushed at the lens. It took much less than a second.

They ran it back and looked again. Even more slowly, this time. Five, six frames at the most, and then it was gone.

Hepworth said, "Are you in focus?"

"I'm as sharp as it'll go," the young man said. "That's motion blur."

"Can't be a puppet, then."

"A puppet?" Sebastian said.

Hepworth said, "For a trick film you photograph a puppet one frame at a time. Nothing's actually moving so everything's sharp. But when you run all the frames together, the puppet seems to move."

"That doesn't look like a puppet to me," Sebastian said.

"It doesn't look like *anything* to me," the young man said from behind the projector. "Shall I run it again?"

He ran it again. Even more slowly, this time. The shadow-child ran from sight again. The shadow-thing burst from the bushes behind her and enveloped the world. Fire burst from its heart and the screen blistered like skin.

The heat of the projector was burning the film. It bubbled and foamed and the young man quickly shut down the lamp, before the highly flammable nitrate stock took flame.

"Sorry," he said.

"Don't be sorry," Sebastian said.

TWENTY-FOUR

T HE TYPEWRITERS' WORKPLACE WAS IN THE BASEMENT OF THE South Chambers, and Evangeline's machine was under a barred window in a lightwell that ran along the front of the buildings. If inclined, she could look up through its railings and glimpse the feet of passing benchers, as the senior lawyers were called, and the occasional clerk pushing a trolley of beribboned documents from one part of New Square to another. But in the interests of her employment, she resisted the inclination. Noticed at the wrong moment, it might be taken for idling.

She'd hoped to complete her work early so that she could square everything away and leave on time, but extra papers had come in and kept her late. Now she drew out the last typewritten page and its two carbons and pulled the cover over her everyday dancing partner, the Remington Standard.

She was by no means the last to leave. As she hastened her way up the basement stairs, young Barnes, one of the articled clerks, called after her, "Don't keep that young man waiting, Miss Bancroft!"

She did not reply, or even acknowledge him. Barnes was, in essence, a solicitor's apprentice, and many of his remarks to the women employees were in poor taste. But reprimand had no effect on him. His uncle had a partnership and so, one day, would he.

Evangeline's lodgings were in Holborn, no more than ten minutes' walk away, but she had plans for the evening. The pavement outside was wet and slick and the New Square gaslights had been lit, each one bearing a halo like a hovering angel in the damp September air. As she walked along, she doubled her scarf and pinned it in place.

She boarded a Central Line tube train at Chancery Lane, and changed at Oxford Circus for Baker Street. The second train was crowded, but a man gave up his seat.

The Great Room and hall of the Portman Rooms had once housed Tussaud's exhibition of waxworks and Napoleonic relics. Now the waxworks had moved across the road, and these rooms were a spacious venue for dancing, concerts, and public gatherings. As she hurried up the ballroom-wide stairway, she could hear that the Women's Freedom League meeting was already in progress. She cracked open the door to the hall as gently as she could; it made a sound like a gunshot to her own ears, but no more than one or two people sitting close by seemed to notice.

The seating was around two-thirds full. Attendance always varied. The WFL was a breakaway movement from the Women's Social and Political Union, its members dissatisfied with the growing autocracy of the Pankhurst leadership and dismayed by Emmeline and Christabel Pankhurst's advocacy of violent protest. Though she supported the principle of democratic equality, Evangeline had found herself ill at ease with a leadership that resisted democracy within its own ranks and saw consultation as "interference"; while to her mind, the use of violence in a cause dishonored it.

Tonight's speaker was making a case for a program of social disobedience that defied the law, but stopped short of vandalism and arson. The building's steam heat was fired up and the big room was warm and stuffy, in contrast to the nipping air of the street.

"I ask you," the speaker on the stage was saying, "what is the good of the constitutional policy to those who have no constitutional weapon?"

She was a tall, strong-boned woman, and no stranger to public debate. Her references were impeccable: twice arrested, and once sent to prison where she'd been pinioned and photographed, with her picture being distributed to police forces and institutions across the land.

Evangeline slid along into one of the empty seats in the back row as the speaker went on, "When someone does not listen, you can request their attention. But when they *will* not listen, then their attention has to be compelled. They say they will not deal with us unless they have to. So we must make it that they have to. When the subject of the forced feeding of women in prison is met with laughter in Parliament, we know that we can expect neither grace nor courtesy from those we address. It is the government alone that we regard as our enemy, and the whole of our agitation should be directed to bring just as much pressure as necessary upon those people who can deal with our grievance."

A woman farther along the row caught Evangeline's eye.

"Thought you weren't coming," she mouthed.

"Sorry," Evangeline whispered back. "I'll stay after and help clear up."

The address went on for about another twenty minutes. Evangeline listened intently for the first ten, struggled to keep her attention in focus for the next five, and fought against drowsiness for the remainder. It was too hot in here, and her day had been a long one. But the talk ended with some spirited questions, most of them from the first three rows of the audience, and the change in tone helped to rouse her.

"We *have* to agitate," the speaker concluded in response to an earnest young telegraphist in the second row. "We can organize a peaceful demonstration as well as anyone. But when we fill Hyde Park with ten thousand voices and our own prime minister affects not to hear, what then are we to do?"

After the talk, tea was served. Some women left early. Many of those who stayed behind were young and single and fired up by what they'd heard. Usually Evangeline would have been an eager contributor to their conversations. But tonight, it was as if she hadn't the heart or the energy to join in. Instead, she offered to help with the refreshments.

At one point she set an empty cup on a table, forgot that it was there, and knocked it to the floor with her sleeve only a moment later.

"What's the matter?" said her earlier companion from the back row. She was a Yorkshirewoman, and her name was Lillian. She worked in the drapery department of Derry and Toms department store, over on Kensington High Street.

"Just tired," Evangeline said.

Lillian cocked her head in the direction of the doors. "Go on, then," she said. "I can manage here."

"No," Evangeline said with a half-serious smile. "This is all the fun I ever have."

At nine o'clock they set about collecting and stacking chairs; most of those remaining began a halfhearted effort to help and then discovered the time with surprise.

Emptied, the big room took on a more melancholy character. It was said that when Tussaud's had vacated these rooms for its new premises, the entire move had been carried off in a single weekend. Sheeted figures on the floor, when prodded, had proved not to be the mannequins they appeared, but exhausted members of the staff.

"*Now* go," Lillian urged her when the stacking was done. "I'll stay and find the caretaker to lock up."

So Evangeline went, thinking wistfully of her rooms and her bed and a novel from the Boots circulating library. Out into Baker Street, past the studios of Elliot and Fry, the Court photographers next door, imagining as she always did the great and the good who daily crossed the pavement she was passing over now. Usually she'd have a companion for her journey back to Holborn, Lillian or a lady whose husband worked in the advertising office at the *Daily Mirror* building and supported their cause. But in the lady's absence, tonight Evangeline walked out alone.

There was some traffic on Baker Street, much diminished at this hour. So much had changed in the few short years since she'd come to London. Most of the hansoms were disappearing, supplanted by motor taxis. Horse wagons were still used for deliveries, but fewer of those as the months went by. Where would all the animals go? Wherever they went when their usefulness was done, she supposed, only not to be replaced. Theirs would not be a happy fate. Grace Eccles couldn't take them all. It would be the tanner's knife and the bone merchant's cauldron, rather than grazing out their days in a field.

And in a moment that struck her as both absurd and sincere, *God grant them Grace*, she thought.

It was then that she heard a man's voice call out, "There's one of them."

TWENTY-FIVE

A<small>FTER A LONG WAIT FOR HIS TRAIN IN</small> W<small>ALTON STATION</small>, S<small>EBAS</small>-tian walked home from Waterloo. There were no messages at the pie stand, but he stopped and exchanged a few words with a couple of cabmen. By now Sebastian was a familiar enough figure to have earned himself a nickname; to the cabbies he was the Bedlam Detective.

Walking on in the late-evening darkness, he thought about trick films and puppets. Something had been said about the tinker having puppets. About how children would bring him rags, and he'd make the puppets dance for them.

But a trick film? That seemed like the least likely explanation of all.

Frances was sitting before the fire, her clenched hand raised to touch her lips, gazing into the flames. The room smelled of coal smoke, along with the ever-present smell of moldering wallpaper that hung around the suite of apartments. She didn't seem aware of him at first. He stopped to look at her; and in the second or more before she registered his presence, he had the sense that her innermost thoughts would be within his reach, if he were only to ask.

But then she looked at him; and when their eyes met he smiled briefly and found some reason to look away as he spoke to her, much as he always did.

"Where's Robert?" he said.

"In his room," she said, "reading the book you gave him." And then she returned her gaze to the flames.

ROBERT SAID, "I can't do what you asked for."

"That's all right," Sebastian said. "I know it was difficult."

"It's not a matter of being difficult," his son said. "You asked the wrong question."

"Did I," Sebastian said.

Usually as tidy as a bug collector's cupboard, Robert's room was in some disarray. But it was disarray with a purpose, as Sebastian could see. Spread out across the bed were a dozen or more of his magazines, arranged in some kind of significant order. Some lay open, others had pages marked with slips of paper. There were books close to hand as well, and he had a notebook in which he'd been writing. Sir Owain's memoir carried even more annotation slips. By the looks of it, Robert was still only halfway through.

Sebastian said, "And what question should I have asked?"

"It's not a matter of where truth ends and fantasy begins," Robert said. "You should have said where *fact* ends and fantasy begins. If that's what you wanted to know."

"Isn't it the same thing?"

"No, it's not. Mother's like a spring flower. That's not strictly a fact. But it *is* true."

The phrase sounded familiar. "Where'd you hear that?" Sebastian said.

"I heard you say it once."

And it was true, he had. He remembered now. In another life entirely.

Robert went on, "In the book, the narrator's party is dogged by all these various trials and they see terrible destruction along their way. He listens to the stories of the natives and draws conclusions about the causes. He imagines these great creatures and then he looks for the evidence. What you're calling his fantasies are actually how he pictures his fears. So they may not be factual, but to his mind they represent the truth."

"Read on," Sebastian suggested, picking up one of Robert's older dime novels and looking at the cover. "He becomes more explicit."

"I hope he *does* produce some monsters," Robert said. "A dinosaur or two can gee up a tale no end. There's not a single one in *Along the*

Orinoco, and it's all the poorer for it." He looked up. "Will there be dinosaurs?"

"Not exactly," Sebastian said, and held up the story magazine. It was issue number 130 of the Frank Reade Library, dated April 3, 1896. Authorship of *Along the Orinoco* was credited to "Noname," as well it might be; a glance inside showed the lines to be brief, the language vigorous but rudimentary.

"Where did this one come from?" he said.

"I brought it with me. From home."

He meant Philadelphia. Laying the magazine down again, Sebastian said, "I can see you've been researching the subject."

"You said you'd pay me a shilling or two for an opinion," Robert said, reaching out and returning the issue to its proper place in the order. "If I don't put in the effort, how else am I going to form one?"

"All I'm trying to resolve, Robert, is whether the man who wrote that story believes it to be his actual experience."

"You want to know if he's intending fiction or deception."

"Exactly."

"Is this for your Lunacy work?"

"It is."

"Why don't you ask him?"

"Because I can no more trust in his answer than I can believe in his book."

Robert turned around and reached for a bound volume that lay on top of a stack of others on his bedside table.

He said, "This one's called *Among the Indians of Guiana*. It's exploration, not fiction. Mister Everard Im Thurn says of the Guiana Indians that they make no distinction between their dream lives and waking lives. If a man dreams of being hurt by his neighbor, he'll go round and punch him the next morning."

"Trust a savage not to understand the difference."

"They don't believe there *is* a difference. But their thinking is quite sophisticated. In their world it's the spirit that's responsible for the deed, not the body. And the spirit can live in all kinds of forms and cross from dreams to life and back again."

Reaching into his pocket, Sebastian said, "So a man gone native may lose his sense of what's real. That's worth a shilling."

"I don't want it," Robert said. "I haven't earned it yet."

"But you've given me something that I can tell Sir James. Does this Mister Im Thurn have anything to say about the state of mind of a man who sees monsters?"

"Oh, yes. That's half the fun of a lost world. The Indians say that every inaccessible place in their jungle is inhabited by monstrous animals. They say there are huge white jaguars and eagles on the plain of Roraima, high above the Amazon. And down by the rivers there are monkey men and water beasts. It's like Challenger's world in the serial I'm collecting. That has dinosaurs."

"Have you not yet reached the episode with the nest of monsters? Or the sea serpent that pursues the rescue boat?"

"No," Robert said. "But don't spoil it for me."

TWENTY-SIX

"THERE'S ONE OF THEM."

She was just making the turn into Paddington Street. Lights burned in some of the upper windows, but the pavements were empty. It was now almost half an hour after nine o'clock. She looked back and saw a group of three men. They were crossing Baker Street toward her.

"Oi," one said. "Miss. You. Come here. I want to talk to you."

As they passed under a streetlamp, their foreheads and faces lighted up like bone and their eyes were plunged into deep shadow. They wore cheap suits, and cheap boots. The one who'd spoken had a lock of hair in his buttonhole, worn like a trophy.

"Not tonight," she said.

She turned away and put on speed.

"Don't you walk away from me," she heard. "I'll bloody teach yer."

She could hear their boots on the pavement. She glanced back and saw the three of them striding after her. The foremost of them, the one with the lock of hair on his lapel, was balding and had a wide, dense mustache over a weak chin. His two friends were giggling behind, and one was checking behind them to see if anyone was watching.

She looked ahead and saw that the short length of Paddington Street was empty of people.

She broke into a run, to reach the next corner before they could reach her. If she could get around the corner they'd be seen, and she'd be safe.

But the next street was empty as well. There was a dray pulling along at its far end, but it was heading the wrong way. Right behind her and even closer now, she could hear the delighted snorting of her pursuers at their own outrageousness as they flouted all that was holy. For she was only one of those suffrage hoydens, come from the place where they were known to gather, alone and fair game for any sport.

She saw the etched glass and dim yellow lights of a public house, and in that she saw sanctuary. Without any hesitation she slammed open the doors and fell inside.

She looked around. She was in a small snug with aged woodwork and gleaming brass, and room for about a dozen men. She saw old men, bearded men, men squat as toby jugs, some with caps, some with pipes, all with stolid, phlegmatic expressions as if their lives had run out early and they wished nothing more than to sit out the rest of their days in silence, right here, with little to say.

"Hey, Captain," one of them called out. "Woman on the bridge."

And another one added, "She's out on her own."

Any hope of sanctuary was dashed by the appearance of the land-lord, all brawn and shirtsleeves and red-faced perspiration. His eyes were hard and his face was set.

"Come on, you," he called from behind the bar. "Out."

"I'm being followed," she said.

"I don't care what you are," he said, speaking over her and shout-ing her down. "No women in the snug."

"Nor gentlemen either," she retorted, whereupon with a "Why you—" he threw back the counter flap with such violence that she felt a sudden and genuine fear for her safety, even more immediate than the threat she'd felt on the street. She dashed through into the adjoin-ing public bar rather than face him down.

It was as if the world had tipped and turned over in the space of a minute, and she'd fallen into London's shocking through-the-mirror counterpart. From the public bar she came out into the street and al-most collided with a night-patrolling constable.

She stopped. Relief flooded through her like a laudanum rush.

The policeman looked at her and then at the public house behind her and said, "What's this?"

"Ask the roughs who decided to chase me," she said.

He didn't look around. "Where?"

She was gathering her breath now. "Back on the street," she said. "They were waiting around outside the Portman Rooms. I was at a meeting there. I made the mistake of coming out alone."

Now he looked around. But pointedly. Suddenly she didn't like the way that this was going. He was a big man, as all of London's policemen tended to be. And he had a country accent, as so many of them seemed to have. There were very few sharp-witted cockneys walking the streets for the Metropolitan Police, but there were a great number of these slow-moving, blue-caped and helmeted oxen.

He said, "Where are they, then?"

A glance, and then she said, "Gone."

"Gone, are they?"

"They chased me from Baker Street."

"If they ever existed."

"What do you mean?"

"There's no man safe from your kind," he said. "Is there?"

She was shocked.

She said, "Is this how you respond to every woman who asks for your help?"

"There's women and there's women," he said, glancing down at her coat. "I know where you've come from. And I know what you are. So move on. Go home to your husband. If a woman like you can get one." He leaned forward slightly. *"Whore."*

He said this last word low, and between his teeth, so that even if anyone had been standing close, they'd be likely to miss it.

As fast as the relief had run through her, she was now flushed through with ice.

"What did you call me?"

"I called you nothing," the policeman said, straightening up again. "You must be hearing things."

She glanced down and realized what he'd been looking at. Her suffragette pin with its green, white, and violet colors. Some wore amethyst and pearls. Hers were paste.

She walked, unsteadily, the rest of the way to the Underground station, knowing that the constable was following and watching her from a distance, but taking little comfort from the fact. His presence might deter anyone from approaching her with ill intent; but were they to do so, he'd probably turn away.

Her train carriage on the return journey smelled of sweat and leather, like cooking bones. She caught herself shaking, and made herself stop. The short walk home was a new trial.

Safe in her rooms, she did not burst into tears as she was thinking she might, but was violently sick into the basin from under the washstand. Her landlady was partially deaf and unlikely to hear. Evangeline sank to the floor by her bed, hugging the basin, teary and miserable with the vomit searing her sinuses, and sat there without any sense of the passage of time. It might have been for minutes, it might have been an hour.

Eventually she rose, and cleaned everything up, and washed her face in cold water.

With her self-control regained, Evangeline looked to her future. Fear would turn to anger. Perhaps not tonight, but in time. She would take care not to be caught so again. She would continue to wear the badge of her belief, though not, out of prudence, at her place of work; if its significance were to be understood, her dismissal would probably follow.

She undressed and put on her nightgown, and then quickly climbed into her cold bed and shivered under the layers of heavy blankets until her own body heat warmed the space she lay in and made it into a nest. She told herself she was safe. She'd felt threatened, but she had not been hurt. She tried to compel herself to appreciate the difference.

Eventually, Evangeline slept. Inevitably, it was troubled sleep.

She had a nightmare of her childhood, the first in a very long time.

Grace was screaming, and Evangeline could not bring herself to turn around and see why.

That was all.

TWENTY-SEVEN

LYING IN THEIR BED AND WATCHING THE LACE PATTERNS CAST across the ceiling from the streetlamp outside, Sebastian sensed that Elisabeth had an inclination to talk. So he stirred a little, to signal that he was wasn't asleep.

"Are you awake?" she said.

"I suppose," he said.

"Frances tells me that Robert's teacher has been talking about finding him employment again."

The last time he'd raised the subject, she'd had no enthusiasm for it. But now her tone was optimistic.

"That's encouraging."

"Yes. It is."

Sebastian said, "I wish someone could say where he'd fit in. I know he's good for something. If I didn't know the boy was troubled, sometimes I would think him a genius."

"He's no longer a boy."

"If he were merely slow, employment would be no problem. There's many make a living with a shovel or a broom that can barely speak their own names."

"He isn't slow."

"Anything but," Sebastian agreed.

After a moment, Elisabeth said, "I do have a strange feeling that all's going to be well."

Given her recent moods, Sebastian was surprised to hear this. "What's caused that?" he said.

"Nothing I can begin to explain."

Then she began to explain.

"I went up to see the little girl. The one I told you about? The one whose drunken father came in and threatened the nurses. She's a beautiful child, the way so many consumptives are. Large eyes and a lovely transparent complexion. She said that she hoped her sisters won't cry too much when she's gone."

"Who told her she's dying?"

"No one's had to. She just knows. We understand nothing, Sebastian. We don't know where we're going or why. We think that what we know is all there is. But sometimes you just get a sense of what's beyond it. And that can take your breath away."

They lay there in silence for a while. And then he felt her leg against his own. He laid his hand on her stomach, and she rose to press against it; and from there the journey of intimacy took its familiar, though of late less frequent, course.

Afterward, they said nothing. Within minutes, she was breathing deeply and he knew she was asleep.

Sebastian could not sleep. Normally his work did not prey on his thoughts. But this case was different.

He found himself constructing a rough sequence in his mind. How old was Grace Eccles now? Twenty-six, twenty-seven? Evangeline would be the same. Their ordeal had taken place two years after Sir Owain's return from his South American expedition. Then a gap of years in which deaths and disappearances had certainly occurred, but none that drew so much notice as these present murders.

Something troubled him. He could construct a narrative in which Sir Owain roamed his estate in search of the beasts that lived on in his mind. But try as he might, Sebastian could not reconcile this narrative with the indecencies that had been practiced upon the victims.

Perhaps he simply lacked the necessary education in man's psychological complexity. He certainly knew of man's capacity for harm, and he'd heard rumors of soldiers abroad whose actions beyond the sight of God and country were a disgrace to their flag and their uniform. But try as he might, he could not quite believe it of the man he had met.

Evangeline had returned to London, and was somewhere close. One way or another, he would find her.

After that afternoon's visit, he even had an idea for how he might go about it.

Perhaps the nature of these beings is best made clear by saying that they correspond very closely to the dragons, unicorns, and griffins, and to the horned, hoofed, and tailed devils of our own folk-lore. . . . The one common quality which these animals have for us is that they are all fabulous and non-existent. But our knowledge of this fact is derived entirely from science. The Indian, being without even the rudiments of scientific thought, believes as fully in the real existence of an animal as impossible as was ever fabled, as he does in that of animals most usual to him. In short, to the Indian the only difference between these monstrous animals and those most familiar to him is that, while he has seen the latter, he has not himself seen the former, though he has heard of them from others. These monstrous animals, in short, are regarded as on exactly the same level as regards the possession of body and spirits as are all other animals.

EVERARD F. IM THURN,
Among the Indians of Guiana:
Being Sketches Chiefly Anthropologic from the Interior of
British Guiana
KEGAN PAUL, TRENCH & CO., 1883

Sᴇʙᴀꜱᴛɪᴀɴ ʜᴀᴅ ɪɴᴛᴇɴᴅᴇᴅ ᴛᴏ ʙᴇɢɪɴ ʜɪꜱ ꜱᴇᴀʀᴄʜ ꜰᴏʀ Eᴠᴀɴɢᴇ-line Bancroft as soon as his other duties allowed. But when he read the midmorning message waiting for him at the cabmen's stand, he forgot all else and ran. There was a crowd on the street outside the Evelina, and half of it seemed to comprise policemen. One of them tried to direct him away, but he pushed by and ignored the angry shout that followed him into the building.

In the hospital's chaotic entrance hall he stopped the first sergeant that he saw and said, "Where is she?"

"Who are you?"

"Sebastian Becker. I'm the husband."

"Who of?"

"Elisabeth Becker! The receiving officer's clerk! I had a message to say she was attacked."

"Ah," the sergeant said. "One of the doctors is stitching her up."

The entire place seemed to be in turmoil. By contrast the dispensary wing was almost empty, and the outpatients' waiting area had been completely cleared. It was in one of the adjoining treatment rooms that Sebastian found his wife receiving care from one of the senior medical men. Sebastian recognized him; he was one of the doctors from Guy's.

For a moment, Sebastian stood in shock. Elisabeth sat with her dress cut away to her bodice and her arm raised; her arm was bared, but covered in so much dried blood and iodine that it might have belonged to a terra-cotta statue, freshly dug from the wet earth. By contrast, her face was deathly white. Her expression was calm and serious. A few flecks of blood had peppered her neck and chin. A blood-spattered nurse held her steady while the surgeon, in waistcoat and rolled-up shirtsleeves, made at her arm with a needle that looked as if it might belong to a sailmaker.

"Oh my Lord," Sebastian said.

The nursing sister, whom he didn't know, was about to speak, but Elisabeth saw him and said, "Sebastian. Don't be too distressed. It looks much worse than it is."

But a brief glance up from her surgeon seemed to suggest otherwise. He met Sebastian's eyes for a moment and then returned his attention to the work.

The fresh wound spiraled all the way around the length of Elisabeth's forearm, like apple peel. Her fingers were bent, her wrist cocked. The surgeon had sutured about three-quarters of the slash. The wound above the stitches gaped, like a shallow rip in a cushion.

Sebastian said, "Can I stay?"

"If you're prepared to help," the surgeon said without taking his eyes from his work.

"How can I do that?"

"Hold her other hand. She's got my knee squeezed down to the bone."

She hadn't realized. "Sorry," she said, and released her grip on him. She might have blushed, if she'd had the color to spare. The surgeon smiled briefly, to tell her he wasn't serious. Then the smile was gone.

Sebastian pulled over a chair and sat beside them. She gripped his hand tightly, and squeezed it even tighter whenever the needle passed through her skin.

"Not much longer now," the surgeon said.

Sebastian said, "What happened?"

Elisabeth said, "It was the father of the consumptive girl. He showed up drunk again and demanded his daughter. He evaded Mister Briggs and found me in the receiving office. I asked him to leave and he set off for the wards. I didn't know his knife was out when I tried to stop him."

"You should have called someone."

"There wasn't time. Who'd imagine a man would turn on a woman like that?"

The surgeon paused in his work and asked her to move her fingers. She managed to flex them just a little, at the cost of some considerable discomfort that she tried not to show. But Sebastian felt it in her grip. He could feel every transferred nuance of her pain as the procedure went on.

He said, "I don't mean to question your treatment. But would this not be better carried out in the operating room?"

"It would," said the surgeon without taking his eyes off his work, "if we had the use of it. But the man's still in the building. They've got him trapped upstairs."

Sebastian needed a moment or two to take that in.

"Trapped?"

"On one of the wards, I was told."

Then Sebastian was on his feet, with Elisabeth still clutching his hand; and the Guy's surgeon, who'd been about to pass his needle into the skin of her forearm where the line of the wound passed over the tendons of her wrist, drew back with an unintended oath.

"Forgive me," Sebastian said, prizing himself free, "but I deal in madmen. I may be able to give advice to bring about a safe outcome."

"Sebastian, no!" Elisabeth said. "Stay with me!"

"Let me make the offer," Sebastian said. "For the truth of it is, I know it's a necessary pain, but I can't watch you suffer like this."

"Let him go," the surgeon said to her, adding, without rancor, "because frankly, Mister Becker, you're being neither use nor ornament here. If you can help the situation, please do. But be warned. Two minutes after he attacked your wife, the man killed a nurse."

FIRSTLY SEBASTIAN had to find a way up to the wards, avoiding the pandemonium of the entrance hall. Because of his wife's employment he had a better knowledge of the building than a casual visitor might, but he didn't know it well. Making a turn out of the dispensary, within a few strides he found himself witness to a scene of exodus via the hospital's back ways; all of the hospital's sick children were being ushered down service stairs and through kitchen corridors by policemen, nurses, and some of the hospital's civilian staff. They shuffled in near-silence, like a night-marching army. The children were mostly in nightshirts with blankets thrown around their shoulders. Some were carrying toys, while many of the smaller ones were being carried themselves.

There was Mister Briggs, big, stern Mister Briggs, craggy as a statue with a cracked heart full of well-hidden love, standing before a doorway with a hospital screen across it.

To those looking frightened by this strange experience he added to the strangeness by booming, "Go on, now, boys and girls. Go with the nurses. They will look after you. There's nothing here to see."

Then he glanced back at the folding screen, saw that its coverage of the opening behind it was not complete, and moved to make a careful adjustment.

"Mister Briggs, I need to pass," Sebastian said to him.

"I wouldn't," the old soldier advised.

"I'm afraid I have to."

"How is Mrs. Becker?"

"Bearing up better than I would in her place."

Briggs nodded, and turned away.

"Do as your nurses tell you," he called out in a ringing tone, overlooking the fact that the nurses were urging the children to conduct themselves quietly. "Obey them as you would your own mother."

Beyond the opening was a wide corridor with offices along one side of it. Chairs stood against the opposite wall for those awaiting their turn with physicians and dressers. The chairs had been pushed askew and some personal items abandoned when the area had been cleared.

Toward the corridor's far end lay the body of a nurse. Beyond it stood policemen and white-faced members of the Evelina senior staff and at least one member of the governing board. Someone was sobbing, and Sebastian couldn't immediately see who. The body was uncovered and a police artist was making a sketch of its position with measurements, stepping over and around the blood to get them. It was life's blood, an enormous static pool of it under and about the body like the satin lining of an outspread opera cloak.

Sebastian tilted his head to see the dead woman's face. He could not say that he knew her. She looked around nineteen years of age, but was perhaps older.

His heart, already chilled, grew even more cold.

A magnesium flash lit up the corridor's far end. They were photographing the knife that had been used on her, and presumably upon Elisabeth. A scaled measuring rod lay on the floor alongside it. No one gave Sebastian a glance. He went no closer, but returned through the screen.

The service stairway was empty of children now, and he ascended without obstruction. On the next floor was a passageway running beside a long, high-ceilinged ward. The ward had four fireplaces so that it could be divided up as needed, and there were further side rooms for the smallest infants and the isolation of whooping cough cases.

As he walked the empty length of the building, Sebastian became aware of some slight, small noises. Then as he approached the end of the passageway he saw that the children who could not rise or walk had been rolled to safety on their beds, all of which were now marshaled in the infants' room like ships in a crowded harbor. Two nurses were among them, and a policeman with a pistol guarded the door. All their eyes were on Sebastian, like those of frightened creatures in a burrow.

The armed man on the door first gave a warning signal for Sebastian to make no sound, and then waved for him to go back. But instead of turning around, Sebastian held up his Lord Chancellor's papers with their visible crest. He made a silent face of inquiry.

The officer decided against a challenge to this stranger's authority—though in truth, Sebastian had none to exercise—and pointed the way.

Treading softly, he entered the main stairwell. The noise from the entrance hall below drifted up, like echoes from a different world. He saw no one until he reached the next landing.

The floor above was a close counterpart of the one below. At this end of the passageway, the police had set up their siege base. The corridor's windows looked into the ward. About half a dozen detectives and two sergeants were dug in at this spot, crouched low or pressed up against the walls, watching anxiously and craning to hear, trying to observe without drawing any attention to themselves.

Sebastian stood at the back and craned along with them. Right down at the far end of the ward he could see two men and a child, just about. Of the three, he could see the nurse-killer most clearly. The man was sitting on a bed with the child beside him, a controlling arm across her shoulders. The other man, whose back was toward Sebastian, was speaking earnestly to him.

The man holding the child was sallow and unshaven. The other, a well-dressed man, was silver-haired and broad-shouldered. They were too far away for Sebastian to make out anything of what was being said.

In a low voice he whispered to the nearest detective, "Is that his own child?"

"His child died last night," the detective whispered back.

At that moment, the unshaven man on the bed was making some point. He was emphasizing it by stabbing at the air with a surgical scalpel. The silver-haired man quickly held up his hands and rose to his feet. The hostage-taker was growing increasingly agitated, and only began to calm when the other backed off to a distance. Sebastian heard a snick of metal on metal, and looked to his side.

He saw that one of the sergeants held a Lee-Enfield army rifle and was sliding the bolt as slowly as he could, though slowing the action did nothing to make it more discreet.

The superintendent of M Division Southwark came striding out of the ward with his face set and grave. In contrast to his hair, his brows and mustache were mostly black.

Even as their commander rejoined them, the sniper sergeant with the Lee-Enfield was murmuring under his breath, "Just say the word, sir." But the superintendent waved him down, and hardly needed to give his reasons why; not at this distance, and not with the child so close.

Keeping his voice low, he said, "I can't bargain with him. With the nurse dead, he's for the drop and he knows it. What can I offer a man in that position?"

"God's mercy," one of his detectives suggested, "if he spares the child."

"I fear he's given up on that. We'll have to rush him."

At which point, Sebastian spoke up.

"Sir," he said, and the superintendent's gaze swung to him.

"Who are you?"

"Sebastian Becker, sir. From the Lord Chancellor's Visitor. May I speak to your man?"

"To what end?"

"I'm used to reasoning with lunatics. I don't think your man's so different. I can suggest a case for his survival if he'll give up his hostage."

"And if he won't?"

"Then I have more experience with firearms than most. If he so much as lowers his guard to think it over, I can put a bullet between his eyes with no risk to the child. But for that I'll need to be close."

The superintendent was looking at him without warmth or, indeed, giving any sign of his feelings at all.

"A Visitor's man?" he said.

"Sebastian Becker. Once of the Detectives Division where I served under Clive Turner-Smith. And later of the Pinkerton Detective Agency in the United States of America, where I learned how to use a pistol." He glanced over the superintendent's shoulder, to see that the sallow man was looking down and explaining something to the child. The child was rigid with fear, a fact that the man seemed not to notice.

Sebastian said, "I wouldn't wait, sir. I can see he's growing maudlin."

The superintendent considered his options.

"America," he said. "They're all gunslingers there."

Sebastian said nothing.

Then the superintendent turned to one of his detectives and said, "Give him your pistol."

They moved out of the sallow man's sightline, and a fair detective with a wispy mustache handed Sebastian a Webley pocket revolver. Sebastian checked the load and then flipped back his coat to secure it in the back of his waistband.

He said, "Do we know the man's name?"

"Hewlett," the Superintendent said. "Joseph Hewlett. He carts waste from a tannery, when he works at all. He came drunk into the building, but this last hour has sobered him. You'd think sobriety would bring reason. But it's merely allowed him to see how desperate his position is."

Sebastian let his coat fall, swinging his arm a few times to see how easily he might reach for the gun at his back.

"One way or another," he said, "the life he knows is over. He needs to understand that."

TWENTY-NINE

No big room had ever sounded quite so empty as the Evelina children's ward when Sebastian was making his way down it. The floors were of scrubbed board with a central linoleum walk. The ceiling was a full fourteen feet high. In that great space, the hard leather of his boot heels made a sound like pegs being driven into wood.

Joseph Hewlett watched him approaching, sharp-eyed as a squirrel and tense as a watch spring.

"And who've they sent me now?" he said as Sebastian drew near.

Sebastian stopped, not so close as to offer a threat. He could see the scalpel better from here. Not so long an instrument as the tannery blade the man had used on Elisabeth, but at least as sharp. And the girl under his control was a much smaller subject. Around five or six years old, she was big-eyed and as thin as a sparrow.

Keeping his voice even, Sebastian said, "Are you prepared to hurt that child?"

"The child is on my knee and this butcher's knife is in my hand," Hewlett said, "so I suppose the proposition is on the table."

"I don't believe that," Sebastian said. "From a father of children."

"Am I? The father of a child like this one? Then have those doctors bring her to me."

Sebastian risked moving to another of the beds and lowered himself to sit. There was one complete bed's width between the two of them, and by seating himself he immediately reduced the tension just a little. At this distance, Sebastian would be unlikely to spring for the knife.

He could smell the gin on the carter, hours old and leaking from his pores, sweet and pungent like a cheap perfume. In response to the man's attempt at irony, Sebastian said, "You know they can't bring her to you. You know she died."

"Ay," Hewlett said. "And I know who to blame."

"Who would that be?"

"Doctors." He spat the word with contempt.

"No doctor killed your daughter. They fought for her life and lost the battle."

"I would have fought harder than any of them. But for my want of a rich man's learning."

"We can all say what we'd do in another's shoes. When we've no fear of ever being tested."

You could of said something abt. the sky and then taken the gun off the shooter when he was looking up and turned it onto him. That is surely what I would of done in yr place.

Sebastian looked at the floor for a moment.

Then he said, "I can help you."

"No one can help me."

"You don't even know who I am."

"I know a bobby when I see one. Come to charm me out so they can hang me."

"I'm not a policeman. I'm an investigator attached to the Lord Chancellor's Visitors in Lunacy. And listen to this, Hewlett. We do not hang those we find to be of unsound mind."

"You'd have me play the madman? I will not. I'll keep what dignity I have."

"I can tell you there's no dignity at the end of a rope. The bowels empty. And in death the male parts become aroused for all to see."

This was something that Hewlett did not like to hear. It seemed to dismay him more than the prospect of death itself. Death was an experience for which his imagination had no precedent; whereas humiliation had a reality for him, being something that he probably experienced daily.

"You've seen this?"

"I have."

He said, "Then what am I to do?"

"The child is afraid," Sebastian said. "Will you let her go?"

"She's not afraid," Hewlett said, and he looked down at the girl. "We're friends, you and I," he said. "Are we not?" And he clumsily chucked her under the chin with the same hand that held the surgeon's knife. His nails were black with grime and chewed ragged.

Sebastian said, "If you speak of hanging, then you must know the nurse is dead."

"They tried to tell me she was not. So I said, produce her, then. Because I know what's what. And the other? The receiving officer I cut?"

"You cut the receiving officer's clerk."

Hewlett gave a shrug.

"'Tis all the same to me," he said, and Sebastian fought with the urge to reach for his pistol and end their conversation there and then.

In a tight voice he said, "You have scarred her badly. But she lives."

"No matter. They can only hang me once."

Sebastian rose to his feet and let his hand fall by his side. His coat was pushed back and would not foul his move. He kept his face composed. Let the child move away, and let Hewlett give him the slightest cause to act, and he would drop the man where he sat. His success would be a small gift of apology from an inattentive God.

"No matter, you say. Do you really care for no one's pain but your own?"

Hewlett said, "It is the only thing I have, that gentlefolk do not seem eager to take for themselves."

Sebastian said, "You have killed a woman today. But I am willing to argue that you killed her in a frenzy. Harm that child for any reason and you will have no such defense. Let her go."

"No."

Sebastian looked at the girl.

"What is your name, child?" he said. "Tell this man."

"Dora," the girl said, trying to speak normally but managing little more than a whisper.

"Do you miss your brothers and sisters?"

Hewlett said, "Stop it." He spoke sharply and the girl flinched. But then he grew more calm. He looked up at Sebastian.

"I only wanted to hold her for a while," he said. "As they would not allow me to hold my own."

Then with a gentle shove, he pushed little Dora from his knee. She slid to the floor and landed on her feet. There she stood, uncertain; with a movement of his head, Sebastian indicated for her to go.

She did not run. She walked, straight-legged, with her hands balled into fists by her sides.

As soon as the child had passed by him, Sebastian moved out around the end of the empty bed that separated Hewlett from him and said, "What's it to be, Joe? Will you lay down the surgeon's knife and walk out with me?"

He heard doors bursting open at both ends of the ward as the child hostage was judged to have reached a safe distance, but he kept his eyes on his man.

"No need," Hewlett said.

Sebastian could not move quickly enough. If Hewlett had intended to pass the blade across his own throat, he misjudged the stroke; he planted it in and hacked it deep, causing a sudden sideways fountain.

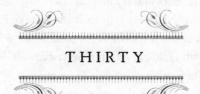

THIRTY

THREE OR FOUR HURTLING BODIES SEEMED TO HIT THE CARTER all at once, bearing him backward onto the bed. Striding in after, the superintendent ordered, "Get the snaps on him."

"Fetch him a doctor," Sebastian said. The blood was coming out of Hewlett like wine from a bladder.

"Snaps first," the superintendent said, and they turned Hewlett over on the mattress to cuff his hands behind his back.

The sniper sergeant said, "This doctor. How fast do you want me to walk?"

Sebastian grabbed a folded cloth from one of the bedside tables and moved in. He half-knelt on the mattress and jammed the cloth against Hewlett's neck to stem the spray. The superintendent considered his options for a moment and then, with some reluctance, chose a path of decency.

"Better run," he said.

Hewlett slid from the bed to the floor and Sebastian went with him, holding the cloth in place. He feared that he was doing little good.

Hewlett looked sideways at Sebastian and said, "Is this madness enough for you?"

When he spoke the wound moved like a second mouth, mimicking his speech with the imperfection of a ventriloquist's doll. Sebastian struggled to reposition the cloth and close the wound, but the cloth was already sodden and his efforts seemed pointless.

Hewlett then said, "I apologize for the trouble I've been causing to all," and slipped out of consciousness.

The doctors came then, and Sebastian stepped back. One or two of the policemen gave him comradely slaps on the shoulder, and he remembered his manners and nodded in acknowledgment. On the inside, he felt only confusion. He'd been ready to take Hewlett's life, but when the moment came he had fought hard to save it. Here was the self-pitying beast who had carved into Sebastian's wife. Yet at the core he was a man like any other.

He walked away through the empty ward and found the children's bathroom. There he tried to clean himself up. But he realized with a sinking heart that his one good suit was ruined. No amount of sponging would ever take out the blood. It had clotted into the fabric and he was spoiling the hospital's towels just by trying.

He heard noise outside the bathroom. When he emerged it was to find that Hewlett had been taken out of the ward. Most of the police had gone with him. The mess that Hewlett had left behind had not yet been cleaned up, but the ward sister was in charge again and normality could soon return.

Sebastian descended the main stairs. When he reached the entrance hall, the superintendent spotted him and came over. His look was far from congratulatory.

"You're the husband of the wounded woman," he said, making an accusation out of it.

"I am," Sebastian said.

"And you didn't think to tell me?"

"I thought I identified myself well enough."

"Not well enough for me. I'd never have let you near him if I'd known."

"The child is safe. What other outcome would you have?"

"I like to know what risks I'm taking when I take them," the superintendent said. "I'll be having words with your employer."

"Do that," Sebastian said.

THEY'D MOVED ELISABETH. Once the needlework on her was completed, her surgeon had sent for a cab and moved her to Guy's. The hospital was less than a quarter mile away and Sebastian walked the short distance, entering through the St. Thomas Street gates. He felt weary and light, at the same time. In the tiled and colonnaded passageway that ran under the main building, he met the surgeon coming toward him. No longer in shirtsleeves, no longer alone, the man was dressed for authority and trailed by assistants. But as soon as he spotted Sebastian, he stopped.

Sebastian said, "Sir Edward. Thank you for your attentions."

"And we can all thank you for yours," the now visibly eminent Sir Edward said. "I heard of what happened."

"I fear the police are not so impressed with me."

"Ignore the police. Your wife will be very proud."

"How is she?" Sebastian said. The younger assistants were eyeing him, and he was again made aware of his shabby state. "Can I take her home now?"

"I want to keep her in," the surgeon said. "Until we know she's over the shock and there's no risk of infection."

"Ours is a tight ship, sir," Sebastian said, though it pained him to admit it before strangers. "We've nothing spare for a hospital stay."

"I know about your situation. You needn't worry. Your wife is one of our own. I'll see she's taken care of."

He found Elisabeth in a room off the women's ward, where he had to seek the permission of the ward sister for an outside-of-hours visit. Unlike the Evelina, Guy's had an air of security . . . though its original purpose as a "lock" hospital for incurables meant that the measures designed into its construction had been intended to keep its patients in, rather than intruders out.

The side room was light, with a large window and a shiny linoleum floor. Elisabeth lay with a mountain of pillows elevating her tightly bound arm. She was drowsy but aware. Her heavy-lidded gaze followed Sebastian as he set a chair by the bed and sat upon it. He took her uninjured hand and looked into her eyes.

"Well," he said.

Elisabeth managed a smile.

Sebastian tried the same, and hoped it would show him as he wanted to seem, rather than betray the truth of his fragile feelings.

She said, slurring her words a little, "Are you thinking the same thing as me?"

He nodded. He didn't need to say it aloud. Both were thinking of the Hotel Dieu, in New Orleans. The Louisiana hospital where she'd finally managed to locate him, days after a near-fatal wounding almost a decade before.

She said, "This time I get the bed and the morphine."

"And I get to do the worrying. Please agree that you won't go back there."

"New Orleans?"

"The Evelina."

"Let's not talk about it now, Sebastian," she said, in a tone that suggested that if they should talk of it at all, it would only be to have his point of view discouraged.

He said, "How can I ever feel at ease after what happened today? We'll find you something else."

"And how will you support the four of us if nothing comes along? It's not just about the money. They actually need me there, Sebastian. I know I wasn't bred to be useful. But in that position, I am. What's happened here isn't a consequence of the job. This is misfortune. And misfortune strikes where it will."

"Why did that argument never work for me?"

"Because in your case it wasn't true. You went seeking misfortune out. Now go home. And change that shirt before Robert sees it. He'll have nightmares."

FRANCES TOOK the news badly. Though she set out an evening meal for Sebastian and Robert, she ate nothing herself. After a visit to the hospital, from where she came away with a list of Elisabeth's housekeeping instructions, she did what she could to sponge the blood out of Sebastian's suit and rescue his bloodstained shirt with soap and a bag of Dolly Blue bleach. In fact, for the rest of that evening she showed an unusual level of personal concern for Sebastian, as if near-tragedy had driven her usual shyness away.

Robert did not go to the hospital, by mutual unspoken agreement.

He had the situation explained to him, but seemed unaffected. This, they knew, could be misleading. Emotion tended to hit Robert like winter squalls; suddenly, at unexpected moments, and hard.

For now, his main concern was for who would be taking him to his piano lesson while Mother was away.

THIRTY-ONE

THE BETHLEM HOSPITAL, THE THIRD OF ITS KIND TO CARRY the name and function, stood in St. George's Fields with its main gates and gardens facing the Lambeth Road. Columns and a long Georgian frontage gave it the look of some enormous Quaker meeting hall. As "Bedlam" the old place had become synonymous with chaos and disorder; in art and in the public mind, it was nothing less than a living hell upon Earth.

The present-day truth was not quite so dramatic. Wards for the dangerously insane had been closed after the building of a state criminal lunatic asylum at Broadmoor, and most patients in the Bethlem were now private admissions from among the educated middle classes. Standards were high. Some even believed that they were living in a hotel. The hospital's governors were fighting a slow battle to separate Bethlem and Bedlam in the public mind.

Sebastian's avoidance of his basement office had little connection with the lunatics in residence. The "furious and mischievous, and those who have no regard to cleanliness" were now accommodated elsewhere. But the room made available to the Visitor's man, as a favor to his employer, shook when trains passed under and stank when the heat came on. The blame lay with the Bakerloo Tube and the boxes containing unclaimed effects of long-dead patients, stacked floor-to-ceiling against the rear wall and filling almost half of the room. While the owners might be long gone, their odor survived them in their goods.

For this reason, Sebastian called by only when required to, or when his employer was on the premises. Several of the Bethlem patients were on Sir James's list, their estates taken under the control of the

Lord Chancellor's department. It was entirely possible that Sir Owain might end up here, or somewhere like it, if investigation showed his reason to be compromised and his affairs incompetently handled.

They met between interviews in the doctors' room, situated between the galleries for male and female patients. Sir James had co-opted the office as his own for the morning.

"Sebastian!" he said. "Don't dawdle in the doorway. Time's a-wasting. What can you tell me?"

Sir James Crichton-Browne had held the post of Lord Chancellor's Visitor in Lunacy for some thirty-six years, securing the job over fierce competition. Prior to that, he'd been the youngest-ever medical director of Wakefield's West Riding Asylum. A broad-domed, silver-haired, bewhiskered Scot, he was something of a professional whirlwind. His intervention in any situation always guaranteed some form of action or change. But, like a whirlwind, he could leave considerable upset and disarray in his wake.

Sebastian said, "On the face of it, Sir Owain seems coherent and well cared for. His affairs are properly managed. No one that I spoke to gave anything but a good account of him."

"What about this companion of his? Doctor Ernest Hubert Sibley. Is he sound?"

"He *is* a doctor," Sebastian conceded. "After he qualified he spent a number of years in general practice in the provinces. His name disappears off the medical register for four years from 1888, but there's no record of any disciplinary action."

"Nor need there be. A man can drop off the register for any number of reasons. Changing address and not informing the General Medical Council, for one."

"With that in mind, I checked to see if he might have spent those years in prison."

"And?"

"You know I found nothing."

"Doctor Sibley has written to me," Sir James said, "forwarding these." He moved the typed pages of Sebastian's report aside, uncovering an assortment of handwritten notes. He slid these forward to place them within Sebastian's reach.

"A letter from the parents of each dead child," he said. "And one from the county's chief constable. All thanking Sir Owain for his kindness and support in a difficult time."

Testimonials. Of a kind. Out of politeness Sebastian picked up one or two and scanned them, but the words passed before his eyes and he took nothing in.

He said, "Are we to set these against our appeals from the families of his expedition's members?"

"I promised them a full investigation, Sebastian. I didn't promise the result that they wanted."

"I should have made faster progress," Sebastian said. "I fear I've been distracted."

"How is Elisabeth?"

"Home, now," Sebastian said, "and able to move around. She doesn't complain but I can tell she's still in discomfort."

"When she starts to carp about it," Sir James said, "you'll know she's on the mend."

"Yes, sir."

"We know that Sir Owain's own wife and child accompanied him on his Amazonian jaunt and that neither returned. I'm in no doubt that what happened out there saw the beginning of his mental undoing."

"I agree, sir."

"Do you, now? Stick to the detective work and leave the diagnosis to me, Sebastian. I'm an old-school psychiatrist. I believe that life's too short for psychoanalysis. But I can't deny the value in a certain kind of therapy. If writing his book served some such purpose, then so be it. There may be comfort in blaming monsters for a grief one cannot bear. Though publication was clearly unwise."

"I've one avenue still to pursue, sir."

"Then pursue it until the end of the week. After that, we'll have to move on."

THIRTY-TWO

That night he sat with Elisabeth before the fire in their rooms above the wardrobe maker's, staring into the falling coals. Elisabeth wore a heavy dressing gown with a rug over her knees. Though allowed home, she was still fragile and her appetite was slow in returning. On the day of her return, Sebastian had carried her up the stairs from the street. Once he'd been able to sweep her up and spin with her, perfused with a joy of life and youth that defied gravity. But this time his knees ached, and they'd been aching ever since.

Elisabeth said, "Lucy came to call this afternoon."

Lucy? Sebastian hunted through his memory for a few moments before he was able to place her among the Evelina's staff.

"Good," was all he could think of to say.

"I may have to appear as a witness. We all will."

The maudlin Joseph Hewlett, despite his best efforts to take his own life, had fared better than the young nurse that he'd killed. The timely work of those present had managed to preserve him for justice.

Sebastian said, "You won't have to face him if he pleads guilty. Don't be swayed by gossip."

"Gossip's all I'm living for right now!" Elisabeth exclaimed, though not with ill temper. "I haven't been out that door in three weeks."

"Less than two."

"See? I'm even losing track of the days. I'll have to scratch a calendar on the wall. Like the Count of Monte Cristo."

They both smiled. He saw that she was looking at the shabby jacket of this, his second-best set of clothes.

She said, "Frances couldn't save your good suit?"

"She tried. The blood wouldn't sponge out. I told her to burn it."

"She could have taken it to the rag shop."

"She did. No one here listens to me."

There was a silence for a while. Some of the coals shifted and fell in a cokey shower, right at the heart of the fire where the heat was the whitest.

Elisabeth said, "Something's troubling you."

"What do you expect?" Sebastian said. "I want to see you well again."

But she wouldn't be deflected. "Besides that."

Sebastian contemplated further evasion, and concluded that it would be a lesser drain on his energies to simply give her the story. He told her of the suspicions surrounding Sir Owain, of his own arrival and the events in Arnmouth, and of the arrest that had brought a premature end to official police interest in the case.

"What proof is there?" Elisabeth said when he'd concluded the tale. "Aside from your predecessor's suspicions?"

"None," he admitted. "It's stupid to persist, I know."

"It's not stupid. Not if a man's life now depends on it."

"A tinker," he said.

He stared into the fire for a while and then Elisabeth said, "Is a tinker's life worth less than any other man's? I've never known you to speak like that before."

He said, "I'm weary. That's all. Grace Eccles wouldn't talk to me and I've no power to compel her."

"What about the other young woman?"

"She claims no memory."

"Memories can be jogged."

"I know. I should have been more open with her, but I wasn't and I drove her off. She's somewhere in London, but that's all I know."

"So you've looked."

"I even asked the census office to check for me. Under the guise of official business."

"What's her name?"

"Evangeline May Bancroft. Not exceptional. But not so common either. For all I know she may have married and changed it."

"Or she may simply have avoided the census."

"The census takers are terriers. Few people escape their attention."

"You can find her, Sebastian. You used to be able to find anyone. How will you feel if the tinker hangs and then it happens all over again?"

They sat in silence for a while.

Then he said, "She had one of those purple pins the suffragettes wear. I saw one on the costume of an actress at the film studio. She couldn't tell me what it meant, but the wardrobe mistress did. Didn't suffragettes boycott the census?"

"There may be some record at the Old Bailey," Elisabeth said. "Those women get arrested all the time."

THIRTY-THREE

THE MEETING ENDED EARLY. SEBASTIAN STOOD ON THE PAVEment outside the Portman Rooms, and from there he watched the women coming out. He'd hesitated to enter, thinking that he'd be conspicuous, but now he saw that a small number of men had been in attendance. Evangeline Bancroft was one of the last to emerge, arm-in-arm with another young woman of around her own age. This second woman suddenly hesitated on the steps, as if remembering something; with an apology she disengaged herself and hurried back inside.

This left Evangeline alone in the lighted half circle at the foot of the entranceway steps. Seeing an opportunity as she waited for her companion's return, Sebastian started toward her.

"Excuse me," he called out, and as she spun around to face in his direction he was surprised to see her draw a short length of heavy chain from her bag.

"I suggest you pass on by," she called back. "And don't imagine I'm afraid of you."

He stopped, with his hands raised.

"I can see as much," he said. "You misunderstand. My name is Sebastian Becker. Surely you remember me?"

She peered at him suspiciously, and he moved more fully into the light.

"Mister Becker?" she said.

There followed a few moments of silence. Then the dull clink of the polished chain as Evangeline Bancroft gathered it up and returned it to her bag.

He said, "We parted on bad terms. You were right to criticize my honesty. I beg forgiveness. Will you give me a chance to explain myself and make amends?"

Her companion emerged at the same time as two others. After a brief exchange of words, Evangeline sent her off with them.

"We've learned the wisdom of watching out for each other's safety," Evangeline explained.

She consented to let him walk her to her train. The evening was clear and the pavements not too crowded, the stars overhead blotted out by the smoke of a million September stoves and fires.

She said, "How did you find me?"

"You were part of a suffragist demonstration in Downing Street six years ago."

"I was never arrested."

"No, but the police have a record of your name. I went to the address they had, but it was out of date."

"That was a hostel for young women. I have my own rooms now."

"I know. So I found you this way instead."

She said, "I was new to life and London and full of anger then. It's an incident that could damage me in my present position."

"Not through me," Sebastian promised. "I know you think I meant to draw you into a plan to gain control of Sir Owain's fortune. But I can assure you, it's not his wealth I'm interested in. You know they're set to hang a tinker for this latest attack."

"But he's confessed."

"He'll say anything that he thinks will gain him favor with his interrogator."

"Mother said he had the girls' clothing on his cart."

"That's true. But not the clothes they were wearing."

"How so?"

"I saw the clothes. They don't match the description that Florence Bell's mother gave before the search. I think that when the detectives showed her the evidence, she changed her story."

"Why would she do that?"

"I'm not saying she lied. And I'm not saying the dresses don't belong to the girls. But the rag-and-bone man had a peep show for the children. They'd bring him old clothes, and he'd let them look through the spy holes while he pulled a string to make the puppets dance. What if Florence and Molly had traded him their castoffs without telling Mrs. Bell? And Mrs. Bell, at the sight of them, was moved to correct her own memory?"

"If the tinker didn't kill them, who did?"

"I believe it could be the same man responsible for your own misfortune," Sebastian said.

THE BELOW-GROUND buffet in the station concourse was open for tea, toast, or a three-shilling supper. Evangeline declined them all. She sat forward on the edge of her seat and did not unbutton her coat. The buffet was paneled in rich, polished wood, with stained glass in the concourse windows and electric light from bronze fittings. Their table was not in the best spot, but it was separated from the others and they would not be overheard.

Evangeline began, "Grace Eccles was my best friend. We didn't choose each other, we just made a pair. Chalk and cheese. Mother didn't approve. She was never a snob, but she's always been proper."

"What about your father?"

"My father died when I was very small. I don't remember much about him at all. He was in the foreign service and they sent him out to India. He was supposed to send for us when he got settled, but a fever took him six weeks after the boat landed. Mother got a telegram to say he was dead. A week after that she got a letter from him, the last one he wrote. I'll always remember that."

"Stepfather?"

"You're looking for a man to blame for my situation."

"Just trying to understand it better."

The waitress brought coffee, and Evangeline waited until she'd gone before continuing. As she started to speak again, she undid the top button of her coat and unwound the scarf from around her neck, reaching up and over her head to do it.

"People misjudge Grace," she said. "They always have."

Evangeline told of how her mother had reason to disapprove of her daughter's friendship with Grace Eccles. Grace's father was a man of poor reputation, though Grace loved him as much as any daughter ever could. Grace's mother had run off with another man. Her father had been a hard worker and a Saturday-night drinker before that, and became an all-week drinker thereafter. This didn't sit well with Lydia Bancroft, who was a member of the Temperance League.

Evangeline said, "The story is that Grace's father was making his way home from the Harbor Inn one night and swore he saw something cross his path in the moonlight. Big and black and it looked at him with yellow eyes. He said they shone out like lamps. You can imagine what everyone thought. But the more people ridiculed him, the more he insisted. Until the story found its way into the paper, and then he shut up. The reporter let him think they were going to take his side. But they only mocked him like everyone else."

"I read the article."

"Where?"

"In the post office book."

"That would be the one. To this day, every visitor gets to read it. They destroyed him with that. But Grace never doubted him. Stood up for him at school. She fought with boys as equals and beat them, too. She was always determined to prove him right and clear his name.

"So the two of us hatched this plan. The idea came from Grace, but she needed me for the camera."

The fine hairs rose on the back of Sebastian's neck. "You had a camera?"

"The *Advertiser* made an offer to encourage visitors. One hundred pounds for a genuine picture of the Arnmouth beast. Grace didn't care so much about the money. She just wanted to prove something for her father. It was my father's Box Brownie. He'd bought it for Mother to make photographs of me, so she could send them to him as I grew. I don't think she ever got to use it."

Evangeline explained how she and Grace had each lied to their lone parent, each saying that she'd be spending the night at the other's house.

"We had blankets and some food tied up in a tablecloth, and a little lantern with a candle in it. Grace knew where there was a dead lamb, up near some old mine workings, and we had some bread and cake to throw around as extra bait. For some reason we thought that might bring out the beast of the moor.

"We found a sheltered place to set up camp. It had been a building, but the roof had fallen into the cellar and there were only three walls standing. You could look up and where there should have been a ceiling, you could see the stars. I think I remember looking up and seeing something move across them. Something dark, like it was making them go out. Like a figure standing over the world. But I could be inventing that."

Evangeline went quiet for a few moments, recalling the memory.

"And then?" Sebastian prompted.

"Then I was at home," she said. "In my bed, in my bedroom, with the curtains closed even though it was daytime. And that felt all wrong. I could hear voices through the floor. When they came upstairs I pretended to be asleep. But I think my mother knew. She touched my shoulder and I pretended to wake up. It seems I'd been awake before, from the way they talked to me. But I don't remember."

"Were you in physical pain?"

"I prefer not to discuss that."

"Forgive me. Was this when Sir Owain appeared at your house?"

"His was the voice that I woke up to hear. Is that why you're pursuing him? I've read detective stories. Is he your suspect?"

"Do you find the idea completely beyond belief?"

"Before I went out to the Hall, I'd have said it was. Until then all my memories were of a man who acted like a father to the whole town. But now there's that doctor of his . . . watching over him and guiding what he says. It's like they've made a private world up there. Just the two of them. They're on their guard when you enter it and they can't wait for you to leave. And there's something . . . I don't know, there's an atmosphere in that house. It made my flesh creep."

She sat back in her chair and picked up her scarf. As she'd been speaking, she'd absently folded and refolded it into the neatest of squares. Now she shook it out again. "Will you tell me what you discover?"

"If there's a way I can reach you."

"I'll reach *you*. Tell me where."

Sebastian took out his pocket pad and scribbled a few lines on a blank page. Then he tore out the sheet and held it out to her.

"Here's where I pick up my messages," he said. She read it, and then looked at him.

"A pie stand?" she said.

"A man has to eat."

"Not quite the Criterion Grill."

"I'm not quite your Criterion type. Thank you."

"For what?" Evangeline said, rising to her feet, and he quickly scraped back his chair to rise with her.

"Your patience and your openness," he said. "I'd expected less. But I can see that you're an unusual young woman."

"I would like—someday—to be not so unusual. Outwardly I live a life of independence. Inwardly I live in fear. In my life there is no intimacy. I don't know how I can even say this to a stranger."

"With a stranger it's often the way," Sebastian said.

THIRTY-FOUR

FRANCES WAS STANDING BY THE WINDOW WHEN HE GOT HOME. She had the lamps turned low and was looking out across the rooftops of the borough. She'd once told Sebastian that it eased her eyes to look at distant things, when too much concentration on close work had tired them.

She looked toward the door as he came into the room. For a moment, in this light, he was reminded of some familiar painting. But he couldn't have said which one. Sebastian wasn't a gallery man, and got most of his art from magazines.

She said, "Elisabeth's reading. I've been trying to get Robert to his bed. He insisted on waiting for you."

"You should have left him to it," Sebastian said, hanging his overcoat on the stand. "He's old enough, and capable."

Frances gave a brief, tight smile.

"Tell that to Elisabeth," she said, and moved to gather up her sewing.

As she was leaving the room, Sebastian's son was trying to enter with an armload of books and documents. He was so eager that he forgot to be polite, and did not step back to let her through.

"Father," he said, "I think I have earned my money."

"That's very good to hear, Robert," Sebastian said. "Can we talk about it in the morning?"

"But I've been waiting for you. Didn't Frances say?"

Sebastian began to frame a reply. But Robert was bursting with energy, and Sebastian had none with which to resist. So he said, "All right."

Robert started to clear a space on the table for the papers he'd

brought. Sebastian saw that they included Sir Owain's book. It was
bristling all around with slips of paper, like a hedgehog.

"The author's observations of the seasons are very precise," Robert
said. "And I think the few actual dates he gives may be accurate. Unless he's fabricated Christmas."

"How is Christmas significant?"

"From one date I can work out another. He refers to five days on
the river, two days in camp, a week spent wherever. With enough detail like that I can make out a rough chronology."

"Can you indeed," Sebastian said.

"I made you this to explain everything."

In the cleared space, Robert unrolled a makeshift chart made from
several sheets of paper gummed together. He placed a book on either
end of it, to pin it down. The chart was somewhere between a vertical
time line, and a family tree. Robert's writing was minuscule and filled
many boxes, between which he'd drawn connecting lines.

He said, "Over on the left-hand side are all the dated events that
I can pin down exactly. On the right are those story events that clash
with the calendar and can only be false. I've positioned all the other
events somewhere in between them on a scale of credibility. Farthest
to the left is your certain truth; over to the right is your certain fiction.
Most things lie somewhere in between. It's the closest you'll ever get to
a simple answer. Isn't that what you wanted?"

Sebastian's head swam.

"This is . . . very well done, Robert."

But Robert, who was odd but no fool, could see that his father
hadn't yet grasped the point.

"It's not just an exercise, Father," he said.

"Of course not."

"It's practical," Robert persisted, "For example. Match your firm
dates to shipping records and you can track down the crew of the rescue ship that took Sir Owain to safety."

Suddenly, Sebastian understood.

It was brilliant. With patient analysis, Robert had deconstructed
the author's method and performed a fractional separation of fact and
fiction, with a precise grading of all the shades in between. It was

detailed and obsessive, and—professionally speaking—a significant piece of detective work.

"That's very impressive, Robert," was all he could say. "Thank you."

"And I don't want the money," Robert said. "It's my contribution. To help us get by."

Happy now, Robert went back to his room.

Alone, Sebastian paced for a while. Then he added a piece of coal to the fire, which was beginning to die. He wasn't ready for sleep yet, and with the fire gone the room would quickly lose its heat to the night. This was one of those occasions when he could be dazed by Robert's flights of intellect.

He thought he might tell Elisabeth. But when he went to check, she'd turned out her light. He backed off quietly, not wanting to risk disturbing her.

Back in the sitting room, he picked her rug off the chair and shook it out. Elisabeth's recovery seemed worryingly slow. Sebastian wasn't sure whether to blame her actual injury or the degree to which it had shaken her, but he'd seen no real improvement since the day he'd brought her home. She hardly slept. Any movement or disturbance during the night would cause her pain.

He took the poker from the grate and gave the fire one last rake-over. Then he wrapped the rug around himself and settled into a chair for the night.

The river now widened so that in places it looked like a long lake; it wound in every direction through the endless marshy plain, whose surface was broken here and there by low mountains. The splendor of the sunset I never saw surpassed. We were steaming east toward clouds of storm. The river ran, a broad highway of molten gold, into the flaming sky; the far-off mountains loomed purple across the marshes; belts of rich green, the river banks stood out on either side against the rose-hues of the rippling water; in front, as we forged steadily onward, hung the tropic night, dim and vast.

THEODORE ROOSEVELT, *Through the Brazilian Wilderness*
JOHN MURRAY, 1914

ॐ

No less than six weeks were spent in slowly and with peril and exhausting labor forcing our way down through what seemed a literally endless succession of rapids and cataracts. For forty-eight days we saw no human being. In passing these rapids we lost five of the seven canoes with which we started and had to build others. One of our best men lost his life in the rapids. Under the strain one of the men went completely bad, shirked all his work, stole his comrades' food and when punished by the sergeant he with cold-blooded deliberation murdered the sergeant and fled into the wilderness.

THEODORE ROOSEVELT, LETTER OF 1 MAY 1914
TO GENERAL LAURO MULLER
MINISTER OF FOREIGN AFFAIRS, RIO DE JANIERO

THIRTY-FIVE

THE TRAFALGAR TAVERN, ON THE GREAT BEND IN THE THAMES at Greenwich, was a large Georgian inn with dining rooms downstairs and a ballroom above. It had balconies and a terrace that overlooked the river, and to save her from waiting alone on the public embankment, the management allowed Evangeline to take a seat and watch for the ferry from there. The balconies were said to be copies of the stern galley of the HMS *Victory*. The river was low, and pauper children were picking for coal on the mud banks directly beneath her terrace view.

There was a train off the rails at Deptford, so she was hoping to see Sebastian Becker among the Greenwich steamer's next batch of passengers. They had agreed a time to meet, and he was late.

A waiter came out onto the terrace. He wore a long white apron, like a Parisian *serveur*. He said, "Will there be anyfink, madam?"

"Nothing, thank you," she said. "I see a mist beginning to rise. Is it likely to get much worse?"

"I daresay it will," he said. "On the other hand, it may not."

"Does it interfere with the steamer service?"

"Sometimes it do, sometimes it doesn't."

"That's very helpful," she said. "Thank you."

"My pleasure," he said, and went back inside.

Evangeline's law chambers handled some maritime business, and through records and by telegraph she'd been able to make some progress in fleshing out the real-life details of Sir Owain Lancaster's movements at sea, as deciphered by Becker's son from the man's fictionalized narrative.

Though there was nothing improper about it, there was a clandestine element to her support for Becker's inquiries. She preferred not to have it known that she was helping him, or how he'd managed to trace her. Evangeline's arrest at the Downing Street protest had been the result of an early militancy; she'd been swept up in the Women's Social and Political Union when a stenography student, and, at that young age, she'd been eager to compel change by the most immediate means. But now the nature of her employment put her in an awkward position, forcing her to balance conscience and necessity. Three years ago she'd given up the WSPU for the more pacifist Women's Freedom League. She remained committed, and continued to wear the discreet badge of her allegiance. But she'd break no more windows, and would take care to avoid the risk of another arrest. It was wrong that her employers might dismiss her for political reasons, but dismiss her they would.

Looking toward the Pool of London from the Trafalgar's terrace, she thought she could see a plume of white. She suspected that it might be from the smokestack of the London Bridge passenger steamer, but it was hard to be sure. The smoke was barely distinguishable from the general heavy mist that lay across the busy waterway today. The vessels that had passed close to the inn on their way upriver had weight and substance, their timbers groaning faintly as they glided by almost close enough to hail; ships farther off were more like pencil sketches of masts and rigging, lightly made on coarse paper.

Through the naval register, Evangeline had traced the British merchant vessel stationed off the South American coast and assigned to transport and collect the Lancaster expedition party. Its captain now had another command, and was at sea. But the master's mate had been injured, and retired from the service; a former navy man, he taught navigation and seamanship to officer cadets at the Royal Naval College, Greenwich.

It was, indeed, the steamer. As it came about to the pier, Evangeline made her way through the inn to the river walk, and was almost at the pier gates when Sebastian Becker emerged through them.

"I know I'm late," he said when he saw her. "Forgive me."

Evangeline said, "I was curious to see who'd come rolling in first. You or the fog."

SEBASTIAN SAVED his explanation. He saw no reason to burden Miss Bancroft with his troubles. His wife had suffered a bad night, and he'd felt unable to leave her without first arranging for one of the Evelina nurses to call by.

From the pier it was no more than two hundred yards' walk to the West Gate of the Royal Naval College. Built as a hospital on the site of a palace, the complex had been run down as such and its great Corinthian halls and domed buildings converted to other uses. All of the pensioners were long gone, and a part of the college was now dedicated to the instruction of naval officers. One hall was a museum, and many of the suites of rooms stood empty.

To enter the railed boundaries of the college was like walking into a small renaissance town, but with broader streets and English weather. A glance from the main avenue toward the building known as the Queen's House brought an arresting, disconcerting sight: in the square before it stood a full-sized three-masted corvette, landlocked but fully rigged, under full sail with boys manning her yards. In the Queen's House was the Royal Naval School, the so-called cradle of the navy, where boarded a thousand sons of British seamen and marines. The training vessel *Fame* had been assembled by shipwrights on solid ground and had nets strung, circus-style, to catch any white-suited unfortunate who might fall from the rigging in the course of his training.

They made their way to the Painted Hall, a public space within the college where anyone might linger between ten o'clock and four. The hall's polished wooden doors led them into an immense ornately painted chamber, its walls a riot of trompe l'oeil on plaster. Fifty feet above them was a ceiling of even greater dark detail and intensity, paintings in which gods and angels and eighteenth-century heroes fought, flew, and frolicked in one seething mass. A century before, Lord Nelson had lain in state here for the three days before his funeral. Some ten thousand souls were said to have been pressing at the gates on the morning they were opened.

The floor was gray marble. If any part of the interior was not painted, it was gilded. A few visitors browsed at the far end of the enormous room. Sebastian had a cadet sent out with a message for the man they were to meet. With barely a glance at the glories around her, Evangeline said, "I had a letter from Mother."

"Is she well?"

"She says that the day-trippers have started returning. Not in spite of the murders. Because of them."

"It happens," Sebastian said.

"I think it's awful," Evangeline said. "The tearooms have stayed open, and old Arthur and some of the others make a few shillings by guiding parties up to the spot where the bodies were found. The people openly admit the reason for their visit. Paying their respects, they call it. They didn't even know the girls! Yet they've read all the newspaper stories and want to gawk at where they lay. What kind of respect is that?"

"I've seen it before at the scene of a tragedy," Sebastian said. "People making a day out of it. They get all the exercise of grief, without personally having to suffer anything."

"I don't know who's worse," Evangeline said. "Them for making the journey, or those who welcome their money."

HIS NAME was Albert Wilder, and he'd been the master's mate on the expedition's support vessel. Another cadet fetched them to him, in an empty classroom overlooking a cobbled yard. A man of some thirty-odd years, Wilder had been aged by suffering and yet seemed in no way infirm. He wore the instructor's uniform of double-breasted jacket and peaked cap. He removed the cap in acknowledgment of Evangeline's presence.

The classroom had a plain wood floor and no desks, only a single square table and a couple of benches. Crowded into the room were four huge and fully detailed ship models, the largest of them with a masthead almost touching the ceiling. These were no toys, but were for the purpose of instruction. On a raised platform stood a complete and functioning ship's wheel.

Sebastian said, "Thank you for this interview. Did my note give a sufficient explanation?"

"It did," Wilder said, "though I wondered if you might be better served by reading the surgeon's log for the return voyage."

"We're pursuing everything, Mister Wilder," Sebastian said. "And I'd like to hear whatever you may have to say."

He saw Wilder glance at Evangeline. "There are some disturbing details," Wilder said. "How plainly should I speak?"

The question was addressed to Sebastian, but Evangeline answered it.

"As plainly as the story requires," she said. "Make no special consideration for me."

They sat on the cadet students' benches, and Albert Wilder told them his tale.

He said, "From the moment I saw the nature of Sir Owain's preparations, I believed that I was looking at a disaster in the making. I've lived a modest life, but I've observed something about prominent men. They become convinced that their success in business proves the superiority of their opinion in all other things. It doesn't matter what your skills are, or what it is that you do. They'll not hesitate to tell you how you ought to be doing it."

Evangeline said, "I take it you weren't impressed by Sir Owain?"

"I found him charming, in what little contact I had with him. But when I saw the way that he'd equipped his expedition, I knew that it was doomed in one way or another."

Sebastian said, "Others must have seen what you saw and reached the same conclusion. Did no one warn him of it?"

"There's no advising a man who's rich enough to take a coastal feeder out of service and have it at his disposal for most of a year. Sir Owain was determined to conquer the interior in high style."

At this point, Wilder paused for a moment. He seemed to feel that he was getting ahead of himself. After regathering his thoughts, he began at the beginning.

He said, "Our company was based in Liverpool. Our sea routes were all along the eastern side of South America, from Venezuela down to Brazil. Our officers were mostly British and our crews a mix of all nations. Are you familiar with the landscape of South America?"

Evangeline said, "Only to recognize the shape of it on the globe."

Wilder faltered a little. Consciously or not, he'd been addressing himself almost exclusively to the other male present.

With an attempt to include Evangeline, he said, "Our orders were to meet Sir Owain's party in Caracas and transport them and their equipment to a set-down point on the coast. From there, they'd journey overland to the source of one of the Amazon's tributary rivers. From the headwater they'd travel all the way down the river in boats, taking measurements as they went."

"Measurements of what?" Sebastian said. "I've never fully understood the purpose of the expedition."

"Sir Owain was developing a system for aiming big guns by the stars. He was compiling a set of tables that required observations from specific points on the globe. I didn't understand his system then, and I don't understand it now. And I teach navigation for a living."

"Do go on," Evangeline said.

Wilder said, "When we arrived at Caracas, all of his cargo was lined up on the docks and waiting for us. It took us most of a day to load. One net alone was filled with crates of fine wines and pâtés, and English cheeses soldered into tins. One crewman swore that he looked between the bars of a crate and saw a child's playhouse and a rocking horse packed in straw. Someone came up the gangplank with a crystal chandelier, holding it up high like a birdcage. They had carpets for their tents and a fully equipped field kitchen with a French chef to go with it. A box the size of a small pantechnicon was said to contain a selection of outfits for Sir Owain's wife. Sir Owain's personal luggage included a mahogany gun case, which no doubt explained the two springer spaniels that we hoisted on board in a cage."

"He took the family pets?" Sebastian said.

"His gun dogs. His plan was to shoot birds, and he had hopes of bagging a jaguar. The dogs were let out on their first night on land, and one of them didn't return. The other one wouldn't leave the camp after that, but within a week something had come in and taken it."

Evangeline said, "With all that cargo, how large was the party?"

"Thirty Europeans in the main party, with a hundred and fifty Portuguese-speaking laborers set to join them for the land and river journey. As well as the guides and quartermasters he had an astronomer, a chief engineer, and a surveying team with an instrument maker to maintain and repair the survey equipment. He had a mapmaker and a botanist who doubled as the expedition's doctor. It seemed as if Sir Owain's plan was to overcome all challenges by simply assembling the full weight of modern civilization and driving it through them."

"All the same," Sebastian said. "Who'd take a woman and child into such a situation?"

"I think he took a landowner's attitude to the world. Wherever he might care to go, he would have it tamed to his purpose like one vast country garden. He and his family would picnic in the jungle, if he so chose."

"For most men," Evangeline observed, "planting a flag will usually suffice."

"We sailed along the coast to the point he'd selected for the start of the land journey. His Portuguese-speaking *camaradas* had a camp set up and had been waiting there for a month at half pay. They set about the unloading with eagerness, happy to break the tedium and impatient to start earning their full rate. But as the riverboats were disembarked, and the gangs of men struggled to manage the weight and the bulk of them, I could see looks being exchanged.

"Over the boats, for one. They were of a badly chosen design. The Amazon is a broad, slow river that's easy to navigate. Its tributaries are anything but. They twist and drop through falls and rapids, and the only way to make progress is to leave the water and carry your boats and cargo down to the next calm stretch. These boats were made of steel, and very heavy. It took six men or more just to lift one.

"But there were other, more immediate problems. They faced two months of overland travel before they'd even reach the river; they had a hundred mules and fifty oxen and, most spectacular to our eyes, five huge steam cars each carrying two tons of freight."

He shook his head, as if the memory of those great mobile machines impressed him still.

He said, "They ran on wheel-driven tracks that made short work of mud or dense foliage. But of the seven steam cars that had set out, two of them had already failed on the way.

"Without the full complement of vehicles, there was insufficient hauling power for all of the gear. We crew watched from the rail as a hasty conference was held to determine what should be taken and what left behind. Sir Owain ordered the erection of a canvas gazebo so that his wife and child might have shade. And there they sat, on drawing-room chairs in their linen and buttons and lace, waving away mosquitoes like abandoned French royalty.

"A number of boxes were finally separated out for leaving behind. These were stacked up on the shore with a net thrown over them. For all I know, they're standing there still.

"Sir Owain and his family were to ride in a sprung observation car that was towed by one of the engines. It had a sumptuous interior and a daybed, and various private facilities. He'd designed it himself and had it constructed at the Great Western works in Swindon, and shipped it out in advance of the expedition.

"They went without a smile, a wave, or even a look back at us. The great steam cars led the way, huffing and roaring like monsters, breaking down jungle as they went, while the *camaradas* walked behind with the mules. The pace was such that the mules had no problem keeping up. Even when the caravan had passed from our view we were able to track their progress by the plumes from the steam cars' smokestacks, rising above the trees. When it came time for us to leave on the next tide, their smoke was still within sight."

Wilder took a moment. Sebastian wondered how often he thought on these images. The master's mate seemed to have been drawn into his own tale and it was almost as if, in his mind, he was back there now. Then:

"Our orders were to sail on down the coast to the mouth of the Amazon. We were to travel up the river as far as our ship could safely navigate, and then send a boat party onward to meet the expedition at the end of its journey. I was assigned to lead the greeting party. Through circumstances outside our control, we reached the point of confluence some fifteen days late.

"It was of no matter. Sir Owain and his people had not yet appeared. The captain sent me inland to look for them. I took my men some way farther up the tributary river and we made camp at a convenient spot, where we settled down to wait.

"Days passed, and then weeks. I stopped expecting them to appear around the river's bend at any hour and was gripped by an increasing certainty that something terrible must have happened. As our presence became known in the area, Indians came to our camp and showed us items that had washed downstream. A straw hat. Some rope. A champagne bottle with its label washed off—it had miraculously survived being smashed in the rapids.

"I sent a message back to my ship, asking what I should do. The captain's reply came back. He said that we were being paid to wait, so I should wait. So we did.

"Finally, the survivors came floating out of the jungle on a crude raft. There were only two of them. Sir Owain, and one other. They'd been deserted by the *camaradas* and their boats and equipment were lost. Everyone else in the party had perished. Sir Owain's wife and child were dead. The other man was limping on a gangrenous foot."

Evangeline said, "Who was the other man?"

"The botanist, I think. Sir Owain was delirious and raving, and both had to be carried. We got them back to the ship as quickly as we were able, where our ship's doctor dealt with them as best he could. Sir Owain was terribly thin but seemed physically intact, though he raved and rambled and made little sense, and eventually had to be doped and tied to his bunk.

"That was after he'd got hold of a gun from somewhere and run to the stern, blasting away at the sea and swearing that there were great serpents following us. It was a tragic sight."

Sebastian said, "Was anything actually there?"

Wilder shook his head. "Nothing at all," he said. "Over the next few days, Sir Owain seemed to recover. He was more or less rational by the time we reached port. As his mind cleared he asked for ink and paper and began to write furiously. Our ship's doctor spent a lot of time with him, reading the pages as they came."

"What of the other man?"

"That same doctor saved most of his foot. Our ship's carpenter made him a crutch. Neither man would say much about their ordeal. They acted like men walking away from a battle with most of their scars on the inside."

Evangeline said, "Do you remember your doctor's name? Can we locate him?"

"The botanist? It was Doctor Summerfield, I think. Or Smithfield. Something like that."

"I meant your own ship's doctor."

"Oh, *him*," Wilder said. "Of course. That was Sibley. Doctor Hubert Sibley."

THIRTY-SIX

So that was Wilder's tale. He walked them out, through long corridors in need of repair, emerging into a part of the college that felt to Sebastian like a massive Roman cloister. Greenwich was a place of tides and fog, and the fog had filled the cloister up while they'd been inside. The air hung still, and in this stillness was a creaking sound. It came from large iron lamps that hung from plaster roses in the ceiling of the colonnade, moving slightly under some imperceptible influence.

Sebastian thanked him, and Evangeline offered her hand and said, as Wilder took it and bowed his head, "Mister Wilder. May I ask—"

"Yes?"

"We were told that injury ended your time at sea. Yet you seem . . ."

She seemed unsure of how to put her question, but he understood immediately.

"Without any obvious impediment?" he said. "I understand. The air by the river was thick with mosquitoes and biting flies. As we waited for the party to appear, all in our camp were laid low in their turn. My infection took a long time to appear and even longer to leave. Eventually I recovered my strength, only to find that my balance had been permanently affected. Now I can't take the motion of a boat. Any boat. The sea crossing home was perfect hell."

"So it left no direct mark," she said, "and yet it keeps you from the life you wanted. My sympathies."

"Thank you," Wilder said, and belatedly realized that he had not yet released her hand. He blushed.

Sebastian and Evangeline went on their way. Sebastian was thinking about those mighty steam cars, their component parts forged in Sir Owain's foundries and assembled in his shipyards, now swallowed up into the jungle and gone. Somewhere they rusted, the bones of the dead scattered all around them.

But what a sight they must have made as they set off! Like Robert's dime magazine airships and steam-driven men and ironclads of the plains, made real for this dawning age.

Once he and Evangeline were out in the open, they could see how dense the fog had become. Sebastian offered his arm, and Evangeline took it. With some hesitation, he sensed, but she took it all the same.

As they made their slow way toward the West Gate, Evangeline said, "There's a photograph of all the expedition members in Sir Owain's book. His wife and child were not among them."

"That picture was faked in a studio," Sebastian said. "Like all the others. If you look closely you can see the same man twice, in different whiskers."

"So he conjured his dead loved ones all the way out of existence? What did Sir Owain think he was doing?"

"Rejecting the reality of his situation. He finds it too terrible to contemplate, so he'd have us believe in another."

"That makes him more of a rogue than a madman."

"It's madness if he believes it as well."

As the pillars and wrought iron of the West Gate took shape in the fog before them, Sebastian said, "How goes it with your employers?"

"I've been pleading a recurrent indisposition," she said. "When concern for my health gives way to irritation at my absences, I'll stage a quiet recovery."

"I'm surprised at men of the law being so easily misled."

"The men of the law don't concern themselves with the likes of me. I only need to fool our clerk. He's a terrier with the males. But if a woman so much as touches his arm, he stammers. I've had him stammering a lot."

"Miss Bancroft!" Sebastian said, feigning shock and causing her to smile.

Although it was only a short walk to the boat pier, in the fog it was a distance to be covered slowly and with caution. The few people they saw were anonymous shapes, emerging and fading again like hulks at sea. One cart went by, its driver dismounted and leading his horse by the bridle, rapping his way along the edge of the pavement with a heavy staff like a blinded pilgrim. After its passing bulk and the noisy shaking of its iron-bound wheels over stone . . . silence.

The pier gates were closed and locked, and a notice hung upon them. Wisps of fog curled around it. It was as Sebastian had expected. No steamer captain would take passengers onto the river in such conditions. Disaster was guaranteed.

But Evangeline seemed surprised. "Oh," she said. "Are we stranded? What are we to do?"

"Don't be concerned," Sebastian said. "We can cross under the river and pick up a North Greenwich train."

"A tunnel."

"Right there." He pointed to where, visible on the embankment a few yards away, there stood a round building with a domed roof. It resembled some moon-bound projectile lifted straight from the engravings in a Jules Verne romance, a brick-and-glass bullet seated firmly on the earth.

They went across to the building, which housed lift machinery and a stairway. As they waited in the white-tiled rotunda, Sebastian could see that Evangeline was not happy at the prospect of a descent.

To distract her mind, he said, "We should look for this botanist. Summerfield or Smithfield. Whatever the man's name is."

"If he's alive. And in a fit state to speak."

The lift arrived from below. Some half-dozen people emerged, but only Sebastian and Evangeline boarded. Early in the morning, the foot tunnel would be choked with a press of workers heading from their homes in Greenwich to the docklands across the river. All would flood back again at the end of the day. The wood-paneled lift was of a size that could carry eighty or more at a time.

The old-soldier operator waited less than half a minute, and then closed the doors. During their fifty-foot descent the cage seemed to falter, like a cart rolling over a bump, and its overhead light flickered. The operator showed no reaction, but Evangeline drew in a breath.

Then the doors opened, and there it stretched before them. The quarter-mile tunnel was circular, lined with white glazed tiles, lit from above by electricity, and fog-free. Because of the way that it angled down under the river and then climbed again after the halfway point, it was not possible to see to its far end. A dozen people waited to enter the lift. More could be seen down the tunnel's length.

They started to walk. Something in Evangeline's attitude betrayed her and Sebastian said, "Do shut-in places make you nervous? You should have told me. Take my arm again, if it reassures you."

"I should not," Evangeline said.

"Why not?"

"I can't imagine your wife thinking it proper."

"My wife's American. She cares more about the way things are than the way they look."

"What have you told her about me?"

"Everything."

"Everything?"

"Nothing you need feel uncomfortable about. She works in a hospital. There's very little she hasn't heard."

He wanted Evangeline to think well of Elisabeth, and not to imagine disapproval. He said, "And but for her encouragement I might never have sought you out."

"Is that so?"

"It is."

Evangeline said, "I'd like to meet her."

"You shall," Sebastian said. "Look. You can see the tunnel's lowest point ahead of us. When we reach that, you'll be able to look up and see the far end of it."

"Let's talk about something else," she said. "Please. Where did you meet?"

"In Philadelphia. I was working for the Pinkertons then. It seems like a lifetime ago. I was alone in a new city and a long way from anywhere I could think of as home. A woman once told me that a man who can dance is always going to be in demand. So I went for dancing lessons, once a week at the Stratford Hotel. The dancing teacher's name was Alicia and Elisabeth was her best friend. She played piano for the dancing sometimes. Although her instrument was the euphonium."

"Seriously?"

"It's a sound you have to learn to love."

"And you did."

"Never quite managed that much."

At the tunnel's lowest point, just ahead of them, the slabs gleamed wetly. The tunnel floor was of great oblong slabs of cut stone, closely jointed.

Evangeline said, "What about your son?"

"Robert. How do I describe him? I won't call him troubled, because he's a happy young man. He's bright, intelligent, perceptive, and strange. In a way that endears him to all who know him, and perplexes anyone who doesn't. And the world is full of people who don't. But we finally found a place where they would understand him, feed his mind, and show him how to understand others."

"He'll have a lot to thank you for."

"Thanks aren't required. Although it hasn't been easy. When we landed in England we had just our rags and our bags, as Elisabeth put it. But we manage. Sir James got me cheap, and he knows it."

At which point, without any warning at all, the tunnel's lights failed.

THIRTY-SEVEN

THE DARKNESS WAS SUDDEN, UTTER, AND AS UNRELIEVED AS IT was unexpected. Someone farther down the tunnel screamed. Evangeline gasped, "Oh, Lord," and Sebastian said, "Don't be afraid. Take my arm."

"Where?"

"Here," he said, finding her hand and guiding it. When her fingers brushed his coat, she clutched at him. He said, "The power has failed, that's all. It might help if you close your eyes."

"It doesn't," she said after a moment. "What can we do?"

"Stay calm. We're not trapped. We're in no danger."

"There's no air."

"The air's the same as before. You're just breathing too hard. I'm going to follow the wall to the end of the tunnel."

He stretched out his hand and took one or two cautious sideways steps toward the tunnel wall, drawing her along with him at a shuffle. When his fingertips made contact with the tile, he felt a relief that he took care not to communicate. Reason was one thing. But this fear was a primitive urge and knew no logic.

With the wall to guide them, he started to move forward. Somewhere way ahead of them, someone found a match and struck a light.

"There," Sebastian said. "Look."

The match flame burned for a short while, giving them something to focus on like a distant, dying star, but the flame did not last. It burned all the way down and then, like a star, it fell.

Evangeline said, "I can't do this, Mister Becker."

"You can. You're doing well. Don't faint on me."

"I'm trying."

They kept on moving. People were shouting now, many of them calling for help. Someone else—perhaps the woman who'd screamed when the lights had first gone out—began to panic and shout. Evangeline clutched at Sebastian's arm more tightly.

"It's all right," Sebastian said. "Someone losing control of themselves, that's all. There's no good reason for it."

But Evangeline was beginning to shake, and he quickly had to put his arm around her waist to prevent her from sinking to the ground. This caused him a dilemma, because he couldn't touch the wall for guidance and hold Evangeline up as well. He shouted back over his shoulder, "Madam! You're in no danger! Just find the wall and follow it!"

But the woman only screamed back, "Please, sir, help me!"

"I am already helping someone!"

He doubted whether she heard him. Everyone seemed to be calling now, expressing their fears and not listening to each other.

Close to his ear, Evangeline said, "Sebastian. I know it makes no sense. But I feel something watching us."

"Nothing's watching us. Nothing's there."

"I know that. But it is."

"Hold on to me. Tight as you can. We're well on our way out of here."

She steadied herself and put one arm around him, which freed him to reach again for the wall. That one point of reference was enough to give him the confidence to start forward, though not without continuing hesitation. Though he knew for a fact that the way ahead was clear, he fought against a growing conviction that they were about to walk into some obstacle at any moment.

Evangeline said, "How will we get out?"

"They have stairs," Sebastian said.

And then: "Look."

He'd seen the first rays from the light of a lantern in the stairwell ahead of them, and even as he spoke the official carrying it came around and stepped into view. With that one point of reference, all of Sebastian's inclination to dread abated.

The official held the lantern high and called out, "Everybody all right down there? Come toward me."

Seconds later, the electric lighting came back on and everyone was caught in whatever attitude they'd assumed in the darkness. Most standing, some dropped to their knees, a very few people crawling on the ground. A long way off, one woman lay in a flat-out faint.

Evangeline was still holding on to him. He was still supporting her. Self-consciously, they disengaged and moved apart.

"See?" Sebastian said. "Nothing there."

Evangeline nodded. Of course not. But that was not the point.

The official said, "Can I ask you to use the stairs, please? Until the electric can be relied on."

Sebastian said, "There's a woman back there in some distress. Didn't you hear her?"

"Yes, sir," the official said, and started forward.

Instead of entering the lift, they turned to climb the stairs. The iron stairway curved up and around in a rising spiral between the central shaft and the outer wall. More lanterns had been set out to light the way, although with the power restored these were no longer needed.

They emerged on the north side of the river. After their experience underground, the fog seemed almost benign. North Greenwich Station was only yards away on Johnson Street, and a train was waiting at its single wooden platform. They climbed into a carriage and all but fell into their seats.

Evangeline threw her head back and gave a great sigh of relief.

"I've embarrassed us both," she said, although she seemed anything but unhappy.

"No," Sebastian said. "You have not."

"I know I frighten too easily. I do my best not to."

"There's no need to explain."

The train had yet to move when the ticket collector came around. Sebastian showed his travel warrant, and the guard tried to argue. "This is only for one," he said, and Sebastian said, "Are you challenging me?" and the man backed down. Evangeline's spirits were so high that she had to fumble out a handkerchief and pretend to blow her nose, lest she be seen laughing.

"You told him," she said when the man had gone.

"He's just doing his job," Sebastian said.

"Then it must be his job to annoy people."

"For a woman who's had a scare, you seem in good spirits," Sebastian suggested.

"I suppose I am," she said. "I have survived one of my nightmares."

There was a slamming of doors, and then a whistle, and then smoke and steam as their train jerked and began to roll. It left the station at a little above walking speed, and kept to it. A plate-layer sat with hut and brazier by every major set of signals, ready to place a detonator on the rail if a warning should be needed.

Sebastian said, "You were never in danger."

"I know," Evangeline said. "I even knew it then. I believe that's why it's called an irrational fear. Are you going home now?"

"If there's no message for me."

Evangeline nodded and looked out the window as the vague shapes of fogbound ships in the West India Docks went by.

"I could die for a pie," she said.

Sebastian took a moment to follow her train of thought. Messages, pie stand . . .

"No need to die," he said. "Fourpence usually does it."

"My treat. You saw to the train."

BUT THE PIE stand had closed early and was all shuttered up. The fog was not so dense in town, though it had slowed everything to a walking pace. To Sebastian Evangeline still seemed bright, almost as if excited by life itself; she'd braved fog, she'd endured a trial underground, and now she'd even crossed the river and braved Southwark.

On an impulse, he said, "Would you like to meet my family?"

"Now?"

"We're very close. It's only a few minutes' walk to where I live."

"If you think it won't be an intrusion."

"Elisabeth will be glad to see a new face. I think she's grown tired of mine."

Guests were rare in their home. Not through shame, but because their friends were so few. As they walked through the streets of the borough, and he pointed out some of the more familiar sights that he thought might interest a stranger, he had a sense of—pride?

No. Surely not. This *was* Southwark, after all.

The street door to their apartments was standing open. This was unusual, but not too remarkable. But when they ascended to the rented rooms, they found Robert alone, sitting at an empty table waiting to be fed.

"Robert?" Sebastian said. "Why was the door not closed?"

Robert looked past him, to Evangeline, noting her presence without seeming to acknowledge it.

"I don't know," he said. "Frances must have left it that way."

"Where is she?"

"I'm waiting for her to come back," Robert said. "I haven't had any dinner yet."

"Excuse me for one moment," Sebastian said to Evangeline, and went to look in Elisabeth's bedroom. She was not there. He went back to find Evangeline trying to engage Robert in conversation, and Robert increasingly unhappy at this general air of growing disruption.

Sebastian said, "Robert, tell me what happened."

"The nurse came to change Mother's dressing," Robert said. "Frances was up there with her. I heard them saying something and then Frances went out to get a cab. She ran all the way down the stairs. But it was ages before she could find one in the fog."

"Did she say where they went?"

"Nobody said anything to me."

"Was there anything else?"

Robert thought for a while.

Then he said, "Frances was crying."

THEY ALL WENT to Guy's together. They found Frances alone in the casualty waiting hall. She was alone on one of the hard benches, wiping her eyes.

Her news was not good.

THIRTY-EIGHT

WHILE LONDON SUFFERED UNDER FOG, IT WAS A CRISP October day in the West Country. Driving a pony and trap borrowed from his father's neighbor, and grateful that the pony was more experienced than he, Detective Stephen Reed made the long and lonely trek from Arnmouth to Arnside Hall at the heart of the Lancaster estate. Along the way he saw not one estate worker, nor any other living soul apart from a herd of deer that scattered away from the road as he passed by. He saw a male with broken antlers, another dragging a lame foot. Stephen Reed was no gamekeeper, but he knew neglect when he saw it.

At the Hall, he was met with silence. He tethered the pony by a water trough in the fancy courtyard and went to bang on the great iron knocker that adorned the entrance doors. It made a noise like gunfire in the yard; he imagined that it must sound like cannon fire within.

After half a minute, he banged again. Then he tried the handle out of curiosity, but the doors were locked. A minute or so after that, he heard the rattle of a key.

One door was opened and there stood Dr. Hubert Sibley, wincing at the daylight.

Stephen Reed said, "Housemaid's day off?"

"We expect a call before a visit," Dr. Sibley said.

"I'll be sure to spread the word," Stephen Reed said, and without waiting for an invitation he shouldered his way past the doctor and into the hallway.

It was gloomy within. Sir Owain was on the short balcony at the top of the Hall's paneled staircase, looking down onto the entrance-way. He seemed to hover there, like a nervous family pet; wary of visitors, but drawn by the novelty of a visit.

He called down, "Detective Reed. They told me you'd returned to other duties."

Stephen Reed drew a folded copy of yesterday's newspaper from inside his coat as the landowner descended the stairway. He said, "They've set a date to hang the tinker. Here. You can read about it." He tossed the newspaper onto the nearest table.

As he arrived at the foot of the stairs, Sir Owain said, "What can I say? I offered myself as a defense witness. I was waiting for the call."

"I know. But the man confessed and pleaded guilty. By now even *he's* convinced that he did it."

Sir Owain closed his fists and took a very deep breath, mastering a painful sense of upset.

He said, "No man was responsible. What would it take to make you believe me?"

"We know those children were not 'torn by beasts,' Sir Owain," Stephen Reed said, with his patience growing thin. "They were disfigured with a billhook. Our police surgeon found the point of it in one of the bodies. It had broken off with the ferocity of the attack."

"And this tinker—did he have such a billhook? If he did, were you able to fit the point to it? I suspect not. Beasts, I tell you."

Stephen Reed considered whether to pursue the argument, and decided against it. The fact was, no, no billhook matching the point had been found, either among the tinker's few possessions or anywhere else. But that was not the true issue, here. Arguing with a delusion simply gave it more substance in the eyes of the deluded.

Instead he said, "I take it the Lord Chancellor's Visitor judged you sane enough to remain at large?"

It was Dr. Sibley who responded. He said, "We've had no formal decision yet, but I'm optimistic."

With a glance at the doctor, Stephen Reed said, "So that'll be your job safe, then."

"Please," Sir Owain said, moving between them and placing his hand on Stephen Reed's arm. "There's no need for this. Will you come with me?"

"Where?"

"There's something I want you to see."

SIR OWAIN led the way out into the grounds. Dr. Sibley followed behind. He locked the main door after them and brought along the keys. A hundred yards from the main building, reached by a graveled path, stood the estate's private chapel. Built in stone, it was a perfect miniature of a church, complete with a porch and a bell tower. To one side of it was a small graveyard for dogs and favored servants.

The chapel was in good order. It was better than preserved; it had been fortified. There were bars on the stained-glass windows and a heavy new door with a lock that Dr. Sibley had to struggle to open.

"Please," Sir Owain said, "come," and he led the way inside.

The stone chapel was stone cold. The stained glass bathed its interior in the colors of blood, wine, and sap. Somewhere in a crypt under its floor lay generations of the family whose fading heritage had been bought out by the upstart industrialist. The upstart's fortunes had faded in their turn, and rather more quickly; but in the chapel was further proof that not everything on the estate bore the marks of ruin.

There were no pews. In their place in the middle of the floor stood a mighty cast-iron vault of a tomb, black and polished. It resembled something that Houdini might lock himself up in, more strongbox than sepulchre.

"I designed this for my own remains," Sir Owain said. "I built it to be proof against beasts. Would a man go to this trouble over a mere figment of his own imagination?"

Stephen Reed walked around it. "I've seen bank safes less substantial," he said. The tomb was wider than the chapel's doorway, and stood on feet like lions' claws. Each dark panel bore moldings of urns and draped material. Sir Owain must have had the plates cast and brought in separately, and then assembled on-site.

Sir Owain said, "I have a genuine fear of desecration. I ask you again, Detective. Would I go to such lengths as these for no reason at all?"

"I really don't know. All this can prove is the strength of your beliefs, not the truth of what you believe in. But that's a lot of iron to protect mere human remains. If a man's life is over, why fear for the flesh?"

"I can't preserve my life. But I have seen what can happen to the flesh, as you call it. I would like to preserve my dignity when my life is done."

"Anyone would think you planned on going soon."

"After all that I've lost," Sir Owain said, "I am counting my steps toward the day." He placed his hand on the metal, as if he might draw some measure of strength from the contact. He said, "I think you'll find that Doctor Sibley probably cares for my living welfare more than I care for my own."

"Well," Stephen Reed said, "the tinker's lease on life is set to end in three weeks' time. He doesn't understand much, but he understands that."

"What more can I do?" Sir Owain pleaded, in what seemed like genuine distress. "I offered my services to the law, but the law insists on taking its course."

"Sir Owain," Stephen Reed said, looking him in the eyes in a move that was often known to compel his man to sincerity. "These beasts. What are they really? Are they really out there? Or are they within?" He leaned closer. "Is this a tomb to keep monsters out, or a strongbox to contain one?"

Dryly, from over by the door, Dr. Sibley said, "I see we've moved on. After all the innuendo, that was almost an honest accusation."

Sir Owain raised a hand to silence his doctor. "Please," he said, and then he returned his attention to Stephen Reed. With one brief twitch of a rueful smile he went on, "At this point I have certain lines to speak if I wish to keep my freedom."

"I know you've been rehearsed in them," Stephen Reed said, "So let us take them as read."

"Every man is a work in progress," Dr. Sibley said quietly from by the door. "We should not look down on those who are damaged, just because they have further to go."

"And may God help the tinker," Sir Owain said, still looking at his hand, "since I cannot."

Stephen Reed said, "The girls had a camera. For taking moving pictures. They caught something strange on their film."

For a man so weary of life, Sir Owain was suddenly very interested. "Where is it?" he said.

"I gave it to the prosecutors. But it was never used in evidence."

"Why not?"

"Its images are unclear."

Sir Owain looked across the chapel to Dr. Sibley. His agitation was obvious. The doctor gave no actual sign but returned a steady gaze as if to say, *You know exactly what I expect of you at this point.*

Sir Owain suddenly said, "I think I should like to pray."

Stephen Reed could see that this took even Dr. Sibley by surprise. But what could the man do? Even the most controlling superintendent could not deny a man his prayer.

"Of course," he said, and made a gesture of invitation for Stephen Reed to join him outside.

THEY STOOD OUTSIDE, in the October air. A squirrel came bounding through the overgrown graves, froze when it saw them, and went bounding right back again.

Stephen Reed said, "Does he pray often?"

Dr. Sibley seemed bemused. "Never," he said.

"How well do you really know him?"

"He's unknowable. I've had only the most distant glimpse of what he's been through. Whatever you may think of him, respect him. A lesser man would have gone under."

"I'm sure he's a tower of strength. But would you have me believe that he never knows a moment of weakness?"

"At the beginning there were many. You know I was his doctor on the rescue ship? That was where we met. He raved. He grieved. He saw the dead, and many an apparition that was never there. By being with him from those very first hours, I secured his lasting trust."

"You were a ship's doctor?" Stephen Reed said. "I didn't know that. It explains your four years' absence from the medical register."

"I know what you think of me," Dr. Sibley went on. "You see me as some kind of leech that clings to him, exploiting his fragile state to my own advantage. Whereas the truth is that he dare not let me go."

"So are you watching over him for every minute of every day?"

Dr. Sibley gestured toward the chapel, where his employer prayed alone.

"Clearly not," he said.

"But you do seem to take your dedication to an extreme. Of the four science papers Sir Owain has published in the last ten years, your name is on all of them as co-author."

"You've been doing your spadework."

"I have. Etymology, metallurgy . . . quite a wide range for a medical man with a seafaring background."

"I had no hand in the papers. I've never claimed otherwise. The attribution was entirely at Sir Owain's insistence."

"So what do you make of his monsters?"

"All such monsters are monsters of the mind. The only person they threaten is the one who conceives them."

"Neatly said. So how do you keep them under control?"

"That's between me and my patient. I don't dominate Sir Owain. I don't control him for my own advantage. I help to keep his state of mind as close to normality as it's possible to get. That doesn't make me his master. If anything, I'm more his prisoner. I mean, I had a life before. Look around you. This is his house, his estate, his affairs. Where is my life now?"

Changing tack, Stephen Reed said, "Grace Eccles thinks you're trying to push her off her land."

"Right in one respect, wrong in another. It's not her land."

"From what I hear, her lease has been tested in court and it held up. That should be the end of the matter."

"Look," the doctor said with some exasperation. "I know Sir Owain has always let her be. But now the Lunacy commissioners are looking for any excuse to take control of his affairs, and they'll see this as proof of bad management. Her father's lease was valid, but the right to settle died with him and can't be passed on. Patents don't bring in the income they once did, and that gypsy girl's squalor diminishes the value of the property."

There was a sound from the chapel; it was of the iron latch being lifted on the inside of the door.

"Well," Stephen Reed said, "do you know something? For a moment there I almost felt some sympathy for you." And now he leaned closer to the doctor and lowered his voice because Sir Owain was coming out.

"A lease will expire and the land will always be there," he said. "Sir Owain isn't the only one who's ever suffered. Just leave Grace Eccles be."

At which point Sir Owain rejoined them, and that conversation was over.

AFTER RETURNING the pony and trap to its owners and thanking them, Stephen Reed walked to his father's cottage. It was low, small-windowed, and whitewashed, with a slate roof. With its thick walls and solid floors it had a tendency to damp, but his father kept a driftwood fire burning throughout the cold months and left every door and window wide open to air the building in the summer.

Whenever his father slipped and called him Jacky without meaning to, he wasn't sure how to feel. Jacky was the little dog his father had bought for company. The two of them were devoted to each other, that was for sure; when his father left a room, the dog sat up and watched the door until he came back. Or simply followed him. They went out together every morning, walking miles along the beach. His father had even begun to choose which invitations he'd answer depending on whether his dog was welcome.

Jacky ran out to greet him, then spun around and ran in ahead barking a welcome. He was a devoted little dog, but not a jealous one.

Stephen Reed's father, the town's onetime harbormaster, was setting a kettle on the fire to make tea. He said, "Well? Are you any further on?"

"I wasted my time," Stephen Reed admitted. "I gave him the newspaper and he showed me his tomb in his private chapel. Out of all the estate, it's the one part he seems to be keeping in repair."

"Really? I can't imagine old Owain letting his property fall into ruin."

"You might be surprised," Stephen Reed said.

Before he'd been forced to sell it, Sir Owain's steam yacht had been on a permanent mooring in the harbor. His father had known Sir Owain then, but would never claim to have known him well. He said he hadn't disliked the man. But he'd thought him a little too eager to play the stepfather to all, as if buying the land had also bought him the town and the people, like a ready-made flock.

He said, "Did he admit to anything? Or is he still insisting that dinosaurs followed him home?"

"Father."

"The man's as mad as a box of bats."

"Knowing that's one thing. Proving murder's another."

"Then what about your tinker?"

"He's never guilty."

"Everybody's guilty of *something*," his father said, and went to get the teapot.

Stephen Reed stared into the fire. The fire had been made with wood from the beach, and a little coal. After decades of public responsibility, his father's life was simple and his needs enviably few. Add to that his dog, and the rum and tobacco and his meals brought over by a woman from the Mermaid Inn, and you had it all.

Stephen Reed's own life seemed anything but simple, right now. These matters ate at him from within. He'd checked with the local grocer and learned that the coarse flour bags that had covered the two girls' faces were of the same brand as those supplied to Arnside Hall. But the same could be said of half the hotels and larger private houses in the parish. And the bags turned up everywhere, reused for everything from onions to oyster shells.

When the kettle started to boil and his father came back with the pot, Stephen Reed said, "No tea for me, Dad. I'll have to be getting back."

"Good idea."

"Why, thank you, Father. It's always nice to know I'm welcome."

"You should know what I mean. Get back to your proper police work and leave it, Stephen. Don't go sticking your neck out. If it goes wrong, you'll be made to suffer. And even if you're proved right, you'll only make enemies."

So STEPHEN REED returned to his lodgings and his county duties. He signed in the next morning and by midday was out in the marshes with two uniformed men, hunting a thief named Little Billy. Little Billy stole from boats, stripping their brass fittings when he could find nothing of portable value. The three spent a fruitless afternoon among the barges and marsh cottages, where they were met with silence and hostility. When Stephen Reed trudged home that evening, he was wet and mud-soaked and short of temper.

During the long walk back under a wide and empty sky, his thoughts inevitably strayed from Little Billy to the murdered children, and to the mystery surrounding Grace Eccles and Evangeline Bancroft.

He hadn't known Grace Eccles well. In fact, because of her father's reputation, he'd been discouraged from having much to do with her at all. But he remembered her utter and abject poverty, and wished that he'd been kinder. She'd been open and cheerful then, as if no one had yet pointed out her disadvantages to her.

And Evangeline. Sad Evangeline. The librarian's daughter. A childhood friend in more innocent times, a distant island now.

His lodging was in a house of single men, and because of the hour this was one of the few occasions when he didn't have to queue for the bathroom. Mrs. Williams had the downstairs fire lit, so there was hot water from the back boiler. He left his topcoat and other clothes out for his landlady to do with what she could, lay in the bath, and let the day's aches and chills soak away.

He grew drowsy. Later, he might read. Though his married colleagues reckoned they had it harder and their expenses were greater, the things that they always complained about were the things that many single men could envy. Home, companionship, family, and an outlet for desire. The married men, in their turn, envied the single man his freedom.

It would ever be thus, he imagined. It was one's lot to achieve one state, only to yearn for its opposite. Nothing was ever so dear as that which had been lost.

On returning to his room, he found that a note had been slipped under his door. He'd barely opened the note when Mrs. Williams came knocking to ensure that he'd seen it.

He dressed in haste and went to find a telephone. It took the operator several minutes to get the connection to Arnmouth, and a while longer for Lydia Bancroft to be fetched to the receiver.

"Stephen?" he eventually heard the librarian say. "Is that you?"

"Mrs. Bancroft," he said, "what is it? Has something happened to Evangeline?"

"It's Grace Eccles," she said.

"What about her?"

"I hardly know how to say it."

But she went on to explain. A horse had been found wandering loose on Arnmouth's main street that morning. It was a large and handsome animal, and it shied away from every approach and panicked at any attempt to get a rope onto it. No one could say where it might have come from, until someone spotted that it was missing an eye. Shy of people, and confused at its surroundings, the animal had taken some time to corner in a yard behind the Schooner Hotel; along the way it had kicked in a shop window, which had increased its agitation, and it had trampled several gardens, which had done nothing for local tempers.

Someone remembered that Grace Eccles had been treating a one-eyed animal, and she was sent for. Word came back; she could not be found, but the gates to her fields were open, her animals had scattered to the moors, and her cottage had been ransacked. The doors had been thrown wide, her few pieces of furniture upset, and there was blood on the floor. In an incongruous detail, two measured glasses of clean drinking water stood untouched amid the chaos.

Parish Constable Bill Turnbull had found her, lying in heather just a few hundred yards from her home. She was dead, and, as Lydia Bancroft put it, she had been "cruelly used."

"Stephen," Lydia Bancroft said. "Please. It's as if there's a an awful shadow that has never left this town. If Grace was not safe after all these years, then I fear for Evangeline. They keep telling us it's over. But it isn't. What can we do?"

Were it told in a romance that a female of delicate habit, accustomed to all the comforts of life, had been precipitated into a river; that, after being withdrawn when on the point of drowning, this female, the eighth of a party, had penetrated into unknown and pathless woods, and travelled in them for weeks, not knowing whither she directed her steps; that, enduring hunger, thirst, and fatigue to very exhaustion, she should have seen her two brothers, far more robust than her, a nephew yet a youth, three young women her servants, and a young man, the domestic left by the physician who had gone on before, all expire by her side, and she yet survive; that, after remaining by their corpses two whole days and nights, in a country abounding in tigers and numbers of dangerous serpents, without once seeing any of these animals or reptiles, she should afterwards have strength to rise, and continue her way, covered with tatters, through the same pathless wood for eight days together till she reached the banks of the Bobonasa, the author would be charged with inconsistency; but the historian should paint facts to his reader, and this is nothing but the truth.

ACCOUNT OF THE ADVENTURES OF MADAME GODIN DES ODONAIS, IN PASSING DOWN THE RIVER OF THE AMAZONS, IN THE YEAR 1770

LETTER FROM M. GODIN DES ODONAIS
TO M. DE LA CONDAMINE
ST. AMAND, BERRY, 28 JULY 1773

THIRTY-NINE

WHEN EVANGELINE WENT LOOKING FOR SEBASTIAN BECKER at his home, she got no farther than the funeral wreath on the door. She knocked and waited, then knocked again, but no one answered. The wreath was a striking weave of laurel, lilies, and black feathers, but in the week since the funeral the petals had fallen and the leaves were beginning to curl. This was her third attempt to reach him. Perhaps Sebastian had taken his son and sister-in-law and gone away? She made inquiries at the wardrobe maker's, but no one there could help.

Then, in a moment of inspiration, she made her way through the borough's streets to the pie stand under the railway bridge and there he was, at the stand's folding side counter. He was a figure apart from the cabbies, looking through his work messages while taking sips of hot tea from a tin mug.

He was unaware of her approach. She was almost at his shoulder when she spoke.

"Sebastian," she said, and he looked around in surprise.

Her heart lurched at the sight of him. He bore all the signs of the blow that he'd sustained. The sleep-deprived pallor of his face, the dazed look in his eyes. As if they gazed on a reality other than this one, seeing a fading version of the world that he was reluctant to leave.

He started to speak, hesitated, turned and set down his tin mug, and then said, "Miss Bancroft."

"Sebastian—" She had been pursuing him. With reluctance, but knowing that she must. But speaking to him now for the first time since the day of their return from Greenwich to find tragedy in his home, all that she could say was, "I am *so* sorry."

"Please," he said, raising a hand before she could go on. "I never had a chance to thank you."

"Thank me? What is there to thank me for?"

"The care you took of Robert that afternoon. He speaks of you often."

"How is he?"

"Confused. I know the loss has touched him. And before too long I'm sure it will show. Until then . . . he goes on exactly as before. Are you well? I'd have been in touch to ask, but I didn't know where to find you."

"I came to the funeral," she said.

"I didn't see you there."

"I stayed back. I wasn't properly dressed. But so many people!"

Elisabeth Becker's funeral service had been conducted by the hospital's chaplain in the Evelina's own small chapel. Evangeline had hurried over in the middle of the day and slipped into the nave behind some nurses standing at the back. Even greater in number than those crowded into the chapel had been the families and children that filled the passageway outside it, joining in with the hymns, bowing their heads in silence for the prayers.

Sebastian said, "Elisabeth was a good friend to many. Had it been my funeral and not hers . . . I think it would have been a much quieter affair."

"I do wish I could have spoken to you on the day. How are you, Sebastian?"

He gathered and placed the half-dozen message slips—hers among them, she noticed—inside his notebook, closed it, and put it away inside his jacket. "I get along," he said. "I follow Sir James's advice. He has the same answer to all of life's ills. 'Work, and plenty of it.' Of course, for him it's a choice. For the rest of us, a necessity."

She said, "I hesitate to raise this. But I can see no other way. Have you had any news from Arnmouth?"

"Arnmouth has not been very close to my thoughts, I'm sorry to say."

"So you don't know that Grace is dead."

"Grace Eccles?"

"You didn't know."

He shook his head. Evangeline went on, "Cruelly murdered. Close to her cottage. How much more there is to it, I don't know yet. Mother put it in a letter, but she spared me the details."

"Does it relate to the other murders?"

"I don't know. Nobody knows."

She'd hoped to ignite him with this news, and he tried to respond; but it was like an invalid's brief effort to rise, quickly abandoned.

He said, "I can't pursue this with you, Evangeline. Look at me. I don't sleep. I drag myself through the days. And if that weren't enough, I have to support three of us on half the income."

"I know," she said. "And believe me, I am ashamed to be intruding on your grief. But I've located the other survivor of the expedition. He's close to London."

"And?"

"I can get no further."

"If you can do such detective work, you clearly don't need me."

"But I do," she persisted. "He's in the Broadmoor Asylum. They've refused me a visit. That's why I've had to seek you out. I don't imagine they can turn away a Lord Chancellor's man."

"What's the patient's name?"

"Somerville. Doctor Bernard Somerville. Not Summerfield. Our master's mate had it close, but not quite right."

"I'll give you a letter."

"A letter's no use. He won't correspond and he won't agree to a visit. But he's the only man who knows what really happened in the jungle. He's our only chance of a window into Lancaster's madness. Aren't you even curious to know why the man's in a hospital for the criminally insane?"

"In all honesty? I feel very little of anything. And you're proposing that we use one madman to explain another? That'll wash, I'm sure."

But he was interested despite himself. She could see it.

"They say his behavior is unpredictable but his thinking is lucid," she said.

"Much like Sir Owain's."

"Can I walk with you? I'll tell you as we go."

Sebastian could offer no objection. They started toward the river, through the wide iron passage under the railway lines. The racket of trams and carriage wheels and overhead trains forced her to raise her voice.

She said, "After his return to England, Somerville set up house with his sister. At some point—and from what I read in the newspaper, he swears to this day that he doesn't know why—he beat her almost senseless against his bedroom wall and then chased her naked down a public street to finish her off. He claims that his violent acts and his inability to remember them are a product of his experience on the Lancaster expedition. He is judged to be dangerous to others. And that's why he's where he is now."

FORTY

S O WHEN BEDLAM WAS FULL, THEY BUILT BROADMOOR.
    Sebastian telephoned to make the appointment, and on Friday morning he and Evangeline traveled out into Berkshire on the train together. At a little station built to serve nearby Wellington College they disembarked, and from there took the carriage that was waiting to convey them to the world's first purpose-built asylum for the criminally insane.

During the ride, which took them past the village of Crowthorne and on a steady climb up the wooded hill that overlooked it, Sebastian said, "Here's an irony for you. You remember Joseph Hewlett? The man who slashed Elisabeth and then cut his own throat? He survives. The knife he used on her was filthy, and poisoned her blood. The one he turned on himself was the hospital's own, and clean. The attention he received saved his life. And on the advice I gave him, he now pleads an unsound mind. So he won't even hang."

"Surely they won't let him go free."

He looked out into the autumn woodland, where the passing trees stood like lonely soldiers. "We'll see how far he makes it if they do," he said.

She seemed startled by his tone. "Would you hunt him down?"

"I don't know. I know it would be wrong. But would it be unjust? Because hunting down men for justice used to be my living."

"You won't do it, Sebastian," she said, as their landau swung into the approach to the asylum's main gate.

"You don't know me that well."

But it was empty talk, and Sebastian knew it. His thoughts of revenge were a consolation, but nothing more than that. Most likely Joseph Hewlett would be committed to some institution very like this one, if his plea of insanity were to be accepted. Those who killed, and were judged mad, might be spared a hanging; but they were neither forgiven nor set free.

Broadmoor Asylum's main entrance had the look of some grim railway terminus, with brick towers and a big clock above the gateway arch between them. The gates opened at their approach, and the carriage passed inside and stopped. Thirty feet beyond this entrance was a second gate; the inner gate would not open until the outer had been secured. The asylum had been designed by a military architect, and built like a fortress.

For an hour the previous evening Sebastian had studied the case notes of Bernard Somerville, Ph.D. After his return from the expedition, unable to work and with his health broken, Somerville had been obliged to lodge with his sister. He slept badly, and as a consequence was hard to rouse in the mornings.

One day, following a particularly bad night, his sister had entered his bedroom with his morning tea, to find him hidden in a swirl of blankets and covers with only his big toe sticking out and visible. His sister, who sounded like a jolly sort, had taken hold of the toe and tugged on it to wake him. Whereupon he'd flown out of bed in an instant and pinned her to the wall, fixing her there with a forearm and seizing her head with the other hand to smash it into the plaster.

She managed to escape and ran from the house. Somerville pursued her, caught her in the street, and tried to finish her off with a rock. He would have killed her for certain, had he not been restrained by passersby. He'd raged in the Black Maria, and only achieved calm in his police cell some hours later.

His explanation to the custody sergeant had been that in the state between sleep and waking, he had not recognized his sister. He had mistaken her for something inhuman and malevolent. He had acted violently out of fear, and to protect himself.

"I am not," he had pleaded, "and have never been, a knowingly dangerous man."

SOMERVILLE WAS confined on the second floor, in a single room on an L-shaped corridor. Somerville had offered no threat to anyone since his arrival, saying that for the first time since the voyage home, he'd felt safe. The superintendent's deputy was to remain with them throughout the interview.

Though unmistakably a cell, with bars at the windows and an inspection slit in the door, the room was not without its comforts. It had an armchair, a writing table, and a bookcase filled with botanical and other learned texts. In the armchair sat Somerville, enormous, a walrus of a man. He did not rise as they entered, but he did close the book that he'd been reading.

In the doctored photograph at the front of Sir Owain Lancaster's book he'd been represented as a tall, spare member of the party with white hair and a long goatee. In life, his beard was a dirty gray. Combed out, it reached to his chest. He wore a smoking jacket, a waistcoat that was almost bursting its buttons across his girth, and checked trousers. One leg was extended and supported by a padded stool, recalling the infection for which he'd been treated on the voyage home. He wore a carpet slipper on the elevated foot, slashed open to relieve any pressure.

Sebastian introduced himself and Evangeline and said, "Thank you for consenting to see us."

"I don't recall consenting," Somerville said. "What I recall is the suggestion that I might be returned to the disturbed ward if I refused."

"Who suggested that?"

"Who indeed."

"If this goes well, then perhaps I can intercede for you. See if I can't persuade the superintendent to let you hold on to your privileges."

"Can we drop the charade?" Somerville said. "It's been made very plain to me. I tell you my tale or they take my books away."

"As you wish," Sebastian said, and there was a pause in proceedings as extra chairs were brought in.

When all were seated, Sebastian said, "You were in the jungle with Sir Owain Lancaster."

"I was."

"And apart from him, you were the only survivor of the party."

"Not exactly. A number of the men turned back early and missed the worst of it."

"All right, then," Sebastian said patiently. "You're the only other man who completed the journey and survived."

"I told the story for the inquest in Brazil. I was too ill to attend the court, but my account was translated and read into the record." At this point, he looked toward Evangeline. He said, "It has elements that are not pleasant for me to recall, or for anyone else to hear."

Evangeline said, "Don't be too concerned on my account."

"Very well, then," Somerville said. "Just bear in mind that these are the words of a madman. Even *I* can't trust everything that I say."

FORTY-ONE

I BELIEVE THAT SIR OWAIN HAD ALREADY SPENT TWO YEARS PREparing the expedition before I joined it [Somerville began]. The design of those great steam cars was his own. I traveled up to his estate and saw the plans there, and he took a party of us to his engineering works to see them being built. His original idea had been for the Europeans to traverse the jungle in airships while the Portuguese-speaking *camaradas* and their mules kept pace with us on the ground, but he'd been persuaded to abandon that. Not for any technical reason, I don't think, but because his wife refused to fly.

You're aware that he took his wife and child on the expedition and they didn't survive it? They appear nowhere in any of his retellings, but I don't believe there was ever any doubt that they'd accompany us. Mrs. Lancaster brought outfits for almost every occasion, but nothing for the conditions that we actually encountered. I can't imagine that he'd given her any true idea of what might lie in store.

For a man who prided himself on his thoroughness and rigor, Sir Owain came badly unstuck. He planned around his vision meticulously. But try suggesting any possibilities that were not part of his vision, and he'd give you very short shrift. I had been to the Amazon before and knew what to expect. Sir Owain had read up on the Amazon and was sure he knew better.

Take me, for example. I was engaged as the expedition's botanist. Only once we were under way did I learn that I was to perform as the expedition's doctor as well. He'd planned this to keep the numbers down. He called it good business sense.

I said to him, "But I have no more than one year of medicine. What if illness should strike?"

He said, "Then I shall expect you to go out and find suitable remedies in the local vegetation."

I argued that I had only basic first-aid skills—I could set a leg or drain a wound, but nothing much beyond that. He assured me that nothing more complicated would ever be called for. "An accident," he would quote in response to any disagreement, "is an inevitable occurrence due to the action of immutable natural laws."

Well, as you know, two of those mighty land craft broke down and never made it to our assembly point. So even before we set off inland from the coast, we were abandoning supplies. Another of them burst its boiler three days inland. That meant another two tons of goods to leave by the wayside. He wouldn't dump his family's luggage—not even that infernal rocking horse—but instead he recalculated everyone's rations with the aim of supplementing them with game from the jungle.

The plan was to travel overland to the lake headwaters of a particular uncharted river, where we'd unload our boats. The steam cars and the mules would make their way back, and the main party would navigate the river all the way down to the sea. Along the way we were to stop at predetermined points, to take measurements and make celestial observations for Sir Owain's global ordnance system.

I was traveling some way behind the engines, in the mule train. Some days I could be as much as a mile back from the leaders. As we went along I'd see sacks and boxes by the trail, opened and rifled by those ahead of me. Sir Owain continued to ride in luxury at the head of the parade, unaware of the vital supplies hemorrhaging away in his wake. When I raised it in camp the *camaradas* blamed the Indians, while the Indians either failed to understand, or pretended so.

We were a week behind schedule when we reached the lake that was the birthplace of our unpronounceable river, although Sir Owain declared his confidence that we'd make up time once we were on the water. It took us two days to prepare the boats and load our goods onto them. This involved some inevitable stock-taking, and for the first time I saw Sir Owain show concern. The boxes of staples—by which I mean salt beef, tinned hams, biscuits—were by now far outnumbered by those packed with fine wines, champagne, olives, and foie gras.

The lamp burned in his work tent for most of that night, and some harsh words were spoken. By morning he and his quartermasters had radically revised the expedition plan to suit our remaining supplies and manpower. One-third of the *camaradas* were paid off. They were sent back with the mules and oxen, which I gather they promptly stole.

Everything and everyone else was loaded onto the boats and launched across the lake. This lake stood on a level plain, with mountains behind it and the jungle sloping away below. Without wind or tide to disturb us, that first day's crossing was like a lazy afternoon on the Thames.

The river itself was another matter. It began quietly enough at the point where the lake emptied, but within the first mile it began to narrow and speed up, and then its course very soon took some rapid turns. Rocks and islands set up eddies that made the boats sometimes hard to control. Nevertheless, after two days we reached a point close to our first measuring station with some excitements but without any real mishap.

While the astronomer and the survey party hacked a trail to the spot from which they needed to make their observations, the rest of us set up camp. I took the opportunity to gather some botanical specimens, while others hunted for meat. Alas, they shot only monkeys, which most of us refused even to consider.

When our surveyors returned we celebrated with some of the champagne and tinned truffles. The next morning we broke camp and returned to the water.

On leaving the lake we'd kept the boats close together, in a kind of flotilla. But this approach had its disadvantages. In rougher waters the boats could be driven together, risking upset. Instead of using their paddles to steer, the Indians and *camaradas* had to employ them to shove the boats apart, and so for miles at a stretch all proceeded in chaos, with everyone crashing and turning and spinning midstream.

So for this next part of the journey we launched one after another, with gaps in between. Sir Owain's pilot boat would precede us all. He carried a fearsome-looking Indian whose task it was to read the river's signs and warn of any dangers ahead, while Sir Owain sat with a gun on his knees ready to shoot the Indian if he got out of hand. Where a hazard presented itself, they'd make a landing and place a signaler with a flag to warn the rest of us to paddle for the bank.

When we met a waterfall or any other obstacle, we'd have to lift our boats from the river and carry everything around to the other side of it. Around midafternoon I noticed that our boat was moving faster, the waters were boiling and heaving, and our crew was paddling harder to keep control. There was one major disadvantage in using the river's own energy to power our journey. Whatever might happen, there would be no going back.

At that point, we seemed to be moving from rough water into actual rapids. At the same time we were descending into a gorge, so there was no riverbank to head for. The gorge snaked and turned, giving us no chance to warn those who followed, any more than we could have received warning from those ahead.

The change in the water was sudden and brutal. One moment a fast, rough ride; the next, a merciless battering. Within seconds we'd lost our paddles and unsecured cargo and were clinging on for our lives, as our boat tossed and skipped down a thunderous chicane of white water and spray. Swept around the next bend, we came upon the first wreckage; one of our steel-hulled boats had lifted right up out of the water like a leaping fish, turned onto its side, and jammed itself between rocks, and now there was no sign of the men who'd been emptied from it. As we sped by I saw a wooden chest from its load caught in a whirlpool, spinning in place. I'd barely had a chance to take that in when our own boat grounded hard and bounced on a great shelf of stone, and only my grip on the side kept me from being flipped overboard.

We lost a man from our boat. I was too busy clinging on, and never saw him go. After a while, we reached quieter waters and were carried along, out of danger but with no control. We bailed out the boat with our hands and prayed that those from the wreck had survived, and that the others had fared better than we. A few hundred yards farther on, our prayers received their grim answer.

Boats, bodies, debris . . . I can hardly exaggerate the horror. We coasted through them in appalled silence. For all who'd fetched up here, more must have been swept on downstream.

Farther on, the river widened and slowed. To our left rose the sheer curving side of the gorge; it held the river in a wide loop, with a low-lying beach contained within the loop like a tranquil island. On this sandbank I saw our astronomer, waving a flag made from a shirt, and with nothing but our hands for oars we dug into the water and propelled ourselves toward him.

FIVE OUT OF our twenty boats had survived intact. Forty souls, including all in the lightly laden pilot boat, remained alive. The rest—gone. It was a true disaster. Over the next day or so we saw many of our fellows being carried by, bloated and floating high in the tepid waters and with a cloud of flies over each. Some of the cargo drifted by as well, and we rescued whatever we were able to catch. I found the medical kit, and in my capacity as "expedition doctor" did what I could to treat the minor injuries of the survivors.

Any drowned Europeans that we saw, we dragged in for burial. I regret to say that the Indians and *camaradas* were pushed out into the middle of the river and sent on their way. The surviving *camaradas* were grimly accepting of this practice, as they were the ones assigned to the digging. While searching for a suitable graveyard site within reach of the river bend, our burial party found a row of overgrown mounds with wooden grave markers. The wood was rotten, the markings illegible. Those graves could have been made ten years before, or a hundred.

I found this deeply disturbing. It meant that others had been this way before us, and had suffered a similar trial. But no record of any prior exploration of the river had been found. Which suggested to me that those who'd survived this hazard, and made these graves for their comrades, must ultimately have fallen to some other hazard yet to come.

I suggested as much to Sir Owain.

"Good God, man," was his response. "Don't breathe a word of that to the others. As if this weren't trial enough. I can't believe you're out to make it worse."

His wife and son were in a tent some way from the beach, where they would not be forced to witness the sad spectacle of the passing dead. But I saw the boy standing by the tent and staring at the waters anyway, while his mother lay prostrate inside. All the symbols of civilization—a picnic hamper, wine bottles, cruet sets, parasols, trunks with changes of clothes—passed before his gaze and were carried away, as if offered in sacrifice for the use of the drowned in the afterlife.

That evening, I overheard Sir Owain speaking to his wife and son. I did not deliberately eavesdrop. Voices carry through canvas, and it was impossible not to hear.

I heard him say, "We've suffered a setback, I won't deny it. I cannot promise you all of the comforts I'd intended to provide. But I swear to you. Our safety is not compromised and our purpose has not changed."

Mrs. Lancaster said something in return, and I could not hear what.

The next morning I looked out across the river and saw the head of that rocking horse floating by, upright and bobbing like a seahorse, badly battered and with its body mostly submerged in the water. In the same moment I saw that Lancaster's boy was in the river up to his knees, trying to reach it.

I called out, "Are you mad, boy? What do you think you're doing?" and I waded into the water and dragged him back to the shore. Though the river was slower here, it was far from safe. There were undercurrents, and there were parasites. The rocking horse was already gone.

Later that day, Sir Owain sought me out.

He said, "Simon has demanded that I dismiss you."

I thought at first that he was making some wry comment and that thanks would follow. But then I saw that he was serious.

I said, "I beg your pardon?"

"Please," he said. "If my son is ever to be disciplined, I'd prefer you don't interfere."

"I didn't discipline him," I said. "I pulled him from the water before he took the step that would see him drowned or carried away. If you want him to learn anything from this misconceived adventure, show him how to look after himself or teach him some gratitude."

I cannot tell you Sir Owain's reaction, as at that point I turned my back on him and walked away.

WITH OUR five boats, our mixed party of survivors, and our salvaged equipment, we continued down the river. In shallow water near the next night's camp, Sir Owain spied one of his instrument cases and, seeming to forget all tragedy, exulted in the possibility that he might still achieve something of the scientific purpose of the expedition.

But when the case was recovered, everything inside proved to be smashed or damaged in some way.

"Ruined," I heard him say. "All ruined."

That night some animal moved through the jungle close to our camp, smashing and breaking trees. We reached for our remaining guns and leapt to our feet. But as much as we did not want to leave the light of our campfire, the intruder did not wish to approach it and we were spared a confrontation.

The next morning we contemplated its wide trail, and two of the *camaradas* set out to follow it. Sir Owain called me over and asked for my thoughts.

I said, "There's no single animal of such a size. Not in this jungle. Unless the rumors are true and the Megatherium survives."

"Megatherium?" he said. "Never heard of it. Is it a dinosaur?"

"No," I said. "It's one of the largest mammals ever known. Believed to have been extinct for over five thousand years, but some say that the Amazon basin is vast enough and wild enough for some areas of its ancient habitat to survive unchanged."

"Herbivore or carnivore?"

"Herbivore," I said. "The Megatherium's stance was like a bear's, but it was the size and weight of a bull elephant."

He nodded, and kicked thoughtfully at the trampled ground, and then looked at all the stalks and branches that the creature had broken in passing.

"That could have done it, all right," he said.

"Could have," I said. "If one even exists."

"What do you think, Somerville? What if a man could bag such a beast and drag it home?"

He was serious. I thought for a moment that he was speaking hypothetically, but he was not.

I said, "Owain. Look at what's been lost. Forget about your standing and your reputation for once. We'll be lucky if we all survive."

He narrowed his eyes and looked at me. With the manner of a man who is judging what he's looking at, and thinking little of what he sees.

He said, "Don't make me regret bringing you along, Doctor Somerville. You can be such an old woman sometimes."

THE TWO *camaradas* did not return. I have no idea why, and nor did anyone else. I don't believe that they ran away. It made no sense for them to leave the boats. Without the river there was little chance of crossing this jungle and surviving the journey.

Sir Owain talked about going after them, not for the sake of the men but for the beast they'd followed. If he could not bag it alive, he'd have a trophy. I could see that he'd begun to look for some outcome, any outcome, that might save his face and justify his losses on our return to civilization. He was probably writing the Royal Society speech in his head. *My dear lost colleagues and loyal servants, I mourn them all; and I dedicate this triumph to their memory.*

Meanwhile, his son had begun to suffer painful eruptions on his bare legs. Though he'd dubbed me the party's physician, Sir Owain had now started to behave to me as he behaved to all critics, by sending the odd sarcastic shot in my direction ("We might have some tea, if Doctor Somerville doesn't think it too dangerous,") but otherwise choosing largely to ignore my existence. He said to his son, "It's just bug bites, boy. Get some lotion on them and stop your complaining," and so the boy came to me on his own.

He stood by me and said, "Excuse me, sir," and I hadn't the heart to let the rocking horse incident color my response.

I'd heard the conversation with his father and so I said, "Hello, Simon. Need something for those bites?"

"Father's told me to get some lotion."

I looked at his legs. I saw no bug bites. Just infected scratches. In these conditions he should have been in long trousers from the beginning, regardless of youth and social convention.

"Let's see what there is for you," I said.

There was nothing. Someone had been at my kit, and anything that might have been useful was gone. The boy was watching me now, and I didn't want to turn him away without at least making some effort to help him.

Then I had an inspiration and took out my hip flask. I soaked a pad in neat navy rum, and said, "Some of those wounds are quite raw, so I can tell you this will sting. But in a good way. Have you been scratching them?"

"A little," he admitted.

"I know," I said, "it's hard not to. We'll bind them up to stop them itching and give them a chance to heal."

I swabbed his wounds with the rum, which I know must have hurt, but he remained stoical and barely made a sound. Then I tore up some linen and bound his legs in makeshift puttees. They probably wouldn't help with the itching, but they would protect his legs and prevent him from making the scratches worse.

For the rest of the day he followed me around, offering to help with whatever job I was doing.

DISASTER STRUCK again the next morning, within an hour of continuing our journey. Our river merged with a second, faster torrent, and our pilot boat was capsized in the crosscurrent. Sir Owain, his wife, his son, the Indian, the astronomer, and two of our surveyors were dumped into the foam, along with the paddle crew. The boat was lost, but all swam to safety, or were rescued.

Which in itself would have been a comparatively happy outcome, had the boy not been dragged from the shallows unconscious. A first examination found no visible harm. But when his shirt was opened, a

spreading contusion under the skin below his ribs signaled some profound hidden injury.

We were crouched on the riverbank beside the child. Sir Owain
had his arms around his wife, who was holding the boy's hand.

Sir Owain said, "What treatment can you recommend?"

I do not think that I have ever felt so helpless as I did in that moment. I said, "None that wouldn't risk doing a lot more harm."

"Nothing is impossible for a resourceful man," Sir Owain said.

At which point I lost all restraint.

"You call on your resources and conjure me a hospital, then," I
said, "and I'll give you any treatment you're looking for. What do you
imagine you've done, here, Owain? You've cut us off from all that's
civilized."

"Please, Somerville."

"There's bleeding inside. All I can hope to do is drain it and hope
that he bleeds no more."

He said, "I've every confidence in you."

"Then it's misplaced!" I shouted. "I'll do my best, but I'm no surgeon. No more of your sunny reassurances, Owain. We're up against
it now."

We set up one of our two remaining tents and draped our last net to
keep the insects out. I went around all the *camaradas* to see who had the
sharpest knife. I sent some of the Indians out to search for leaves and
bark with reputed healing properties. Everyone was looking at me as if
I had some idea of what I was doing. I did not. I had these few materi-
als and the hope, with no belief, that I might do some small measure of
good with them.

My ignorance was medieval. All I could offer were the rituals of
medical attention, with no significant expertise at the heart of it. I
turned the unconscious child onto his side and made a cut to let out
the blood, which came out thick and dark, and very slowly. When
that stopped I placed him on his back and applied the healing poul-
tice to the wound.

I feared to see him moved. But I could foresee no good outcome if
we did not get him into the hands of someone more skilled.

I left him with his parents and went and sat by the river. I felt despair. After a while Sir Owain emerged from the tent and came over to me.

"He opened his eyes and spoke my name," he said. "I do believe he's stronger already. Well done, man." And he clapped me on the shoulder.

Through all our trials, he seemed to have learned nothing. If we can assume that Owain did not imagine them, those few words were the last his son would ever speak.

It hardly mattered whether my crude surgery had been in any way effective, because an infection quickly set in around the wound that I'd made. At the same time, Sir Owain drew my attention to the fact that the boy's mother was ailing as well.

"My dear Bernard," he said to me. "Could you take a look at Mrs. Lancaster? I'm not sure I like her color."

SOMERVILLE PAUSED. Sebastian was aware of the superintendent's deputy taking out his pocket watch and checking the time.

The botanist said, "Would it endanger my privileges if we were to continue my story tomorrow? You must agree that I have been a willing witness."

"Is there much more to tell?" Sebastian said.

"No, but what remains is the most important part," Somerville said, "and I am beginning to tire. I do not mean to be uncooperative. I only wish to do the story justice."

Sebastian looked at Evangeline. She offered no argument. All but the botanist rose to their feet. The deputy superintendent's relief was palpable. Sebastian said, "Can it be arranged?" and the deputy agreed that it could.

Evangeline said to the botanist, "Do you know why you're here?"

"I know what they've told me."

"Which is?"

"That I flew at my sister in a moment of madness. But I love my sister dearly. It's inconceivable that I would ever want to do her harm."

"And yet you did."

"I cannot explain it. Trying to makes it worse. So all in all," he said, indicating the small room into which they were all crowded, "I would rather she was safe from me, and I was here."

Sebastian said, "In that moment between sleep and waking. What did you take her for?"

Somerville shook his head.

"Who knows what I saw then?" he said. "I truly don't."

FORTY-TWO

AFTER MAKING ARRANGEMENTS FOR THE NEXT MORNING AND taking his leave of Evangeline at Waterloo Station, Sebastian made his way home. There were no messages for him at the pie stand. He hesitated at the street door to his apartments, knowing that he ought to take down or replace the wreath. Until he could afford the headstone, it was Elisabeth's only memorial. He had no mourning suit, and to be seen in a black armband was bad form on any man not in the military.

He'd deal with it another day.

He found Robert waiting at the top of the stairs, eager to give him news. Frances was in the back, preparing their evening meal.

Robert said, "Doctor Percival took me to the natural history museum."

"Just you?"

"And Frances."

"Ah," Sebastian said. "Good for him."

He did not know Dr. Percival. All of his dealings had been with the brother, Dr. Reginald. Because of all their early correspondence over Robert's education, the Langdon Down family had stayed in touch. They had even sent a representative to Elisabeth's funeral.

Robert said, "I love the museum. I could spend forever there."

Frances chipped in at that point, appearing in the doorway. "Spend forever?" she said, wiping her hands on a white towel and smiling to show that this was no complaint. "I was beginning to think he was planning to. We never got beyond the east wing."

"You should go sometime, Father," Robert said. "I'll take you.

There's a pavilion with all the creatures from Buenos Aires we've been talking about."

"I doubt that you'll find Sir Owain's creatures in any museum. Not in this world, anyway."

"But the Indians say that makes no difference. I like the idea that spirits can pass back and forth between life and dreams. Because it means that Mother's still somewhere close, even if she's nowhere we can see."

Sebastian caught Frances glancing at him. He briefly met her eyes and said, "Do you dream of her often, Robert?"

"All the time," Robert said, almost cheerily. "You should, too. Then you'd know she's always right here and you wouldn't have to be so sad."

To which Sebastian had no ready answer; and so with a change of subject that was like a crash of changing gears, he said, "And are those hands clean?"

Like a child ten years younger, Robert held his hands up for inspection.

Sebastian gave them a critical look and said, "I'd say they could use a wash before supper."

Robert looked bemused, but he didn't argue. He went off into the next room and ran the scullery tap.

Sebastian said to Frances, "Depending on what I learn tomorrow, I may have to go back to Arnmouth and finish my business there."

"All right," she said.

Belatedly, he realized what he'd be asking of her. She'd have sole charge of the household, and sole charge of Robert, for several days. Yet they'd had no discussion of such matters. Selfishly, he'd given such future arrangements no thought at all.

He said, "Are you sure?"

"Of course," she said, and added a reassuring little smile. "Leave me the rent and five pounds. Shall I pack a bag for you?"

"No," he said. "I've given you enough to do."

He went into the bedroom alone. At the foot of the bed, Elisabeth's old cabin trunk did double duty as a linen chest. He crouched before it and raised the lid. Then it hit him all at once: the scent of Elisabeth, of lavender and roses, from a sachet bag that she'd put in with the sheets and occasionally replenished with a few drops of her own perfume.

He was unprepared and, for a moment or two, incapable of anything. The sense of her returned presence was overpowering. All purpose was briefly dashed out of him.

He recovered quickly, but with his wounds refreshed. Under the lid was a secret compartment with a double-latch lock. Originally meant for the jewelry that Elisabeth had sold to buy their steamer tickets, the recess now contained a pocket-sized revolver wrapped in an old shirt, the gun's cleaning kit, and a box of ammunition.

Sebastian took out the revolver and checked it. He'd bought it from a pawnbroker to replace the Bulldog pistol that he'd carried in his Pinkerton days. In England he'd had little use for it.

The last time he'd handled a pistol had been during the siege at the children's ward. The day of Elisabeth's murder, if only he'd known it. Seated on the bed with the empty gun in his hand, he suddenly found himself all but robbed of the strength to rise. He put his hand over his eyes and waited for tears that threatened, but did not come.

He wasn't sure how, but his sister-in-law's ready kindness had disarmed him. Perhaps he could take this one moment for himself. One moment to let out a little of the pain, and with that pressure vented he'd be able to go on.

He hadn't heard Frances come in. But then he hadn't been aware of the sound he must have made, either.

She knelt down before him and took his hand in her own.

"Sebastian," Frances said. "Don't fret. She said that all would be well. I do believe she's with us, and she still intends it will."

"Frances," he said, recovering as best he could. "Aren't you the strong one?"

Releasing his hand, she stood up, crossed the room, and closed the bedroom door. Then she moved back to sit on the bed beside him.

"We must have a serious talk about Robert," she said.

"Why? Is something wrong?"

"No," she said. "Nothing's wrong. Doctor Percival thinks highly of him. He asked if we had considered what steps might be taken toward giving Robert his independence."

"Independence?" Sebastian said. "I know he has a strong and capable mind, but he thrives with the support of those who love him."

"Don't mistake me," she said, "I love Robert as much as you, but we need to face the fact that he'll outlive us both. And when we're gone, what then? An institution, Sebastian, to see out his days. He has no other family here." She glanced down at the revolver. "You spend your days in pursuit of lunatics, some of them dangerous," she said. "He's lost one parent. If he loses the other, how will I support him alone?"

Sebastian was lost for a reply. The challenges surrounding Robert had always been immediate ones. Questions of the longer term had never arisen.

He said, "What do you propose?"

Frances said, "Doctor Percival has observed Robert's phenomenal powers of analysis. He says that in the matter of employment you've set your sights far too low. With your permission he wishes to explore the possibility of finding Robert a placement in one of our scientific institutions."

Sebastian could not quite believe it. "When was this discussed?" he said.

"This afternoon. At the museum. It was one of the purposes of the visit. Imagine it, Sebastian. He might even progress to an income and rooms of his own. With a housekeeper to take care of his needs, of course."

"Does that mean you would leave me too?"

"No, Sebastian," she said. "But I've been Robert's faithful keeper for long enough. I can hope someday to be his loving aunt. I would not leave you. Unless I understood that you wanted me to."

For Sebastian it was as if doors were opening and his life, after hurtling along blindly in the wake of Elisabeth's death, were being pushed to make a necessary turn.

"Can we discuss this again?" he said.

"We will," Frances said, and rose to her feet. She steadied herself with a touch on his arm, and he responded with a supporting hand. There was a surprising solidity to her; her looks had always been so delicate that he'd imagined her to be almost without substance.

"Thank you," she said, and squeezed his hand before she stepped around him to leave.

FORTY-THREE

O N HER WAY HOME THAT EVENING, EVANGELINE STOPPED AT A post office and spent a penny-farthing on a letter card to inform her employers of a continuing indisposition. If they suspected her, let them dismiss her. She might forgo their good references, but she had wits enough to get around the problem without resorting to forgery.

The next day, she met Sebastian Becker at Waterloo Station and they made their second journey out to Broadmoor.

The same deputy superintendent met them in the carriage yard between the gates, and from there they passed on into the asylum proper. The enclosing wall was topped with spikes and broken glass. Within it stood a central hall with residential wings to either side of it, and a terrace walk for fresh air and exercise. One wing contained a women's prison, where it was said that most of the inmates had been committed for the murder of their children.

Somerville was waiting in his cell with the door open. This time he seemed pleased to see them. The tale that he had begun in reluctance had become his unburdening.

Sebastian said, "Are you ready for us, Doctor?"

"I believe I am," Somerville said.

He began—

I CAN'T SAY what it was—grief, fever, some parasitic invasion from her dousing in the river—but before long both mother and son were dying together. I was tempted to believe that the boy was dead already, rotting and breathing in some collapse of the natural order. Neither could be moved. The woman threw convulsions, and screamed if anyone touched her.

Since Sir Owain never speaks of his wife now, I shall.

I cannot say I knew her. No one on the expedition did. Most thought her aloof, and some were critical of her for bringing a child into a hostile wilderness without any grasp of what life in a wilderness entailed. But to my mind, her only crime had been to obey her husband, whose determination to treat this far-off place as but a distant corner of his own domain had led to all their sufferings.

He had to know it. When a man who demands his own way in all things is faced with the disastrous consequences of his actions, he has to know who brought them on. But can a man's mind bear up under such knowledge? I don't believe that it can. I stand before you as a living example. I may present myself in a rational manner, but I have found myself capable of acts outside my own control. Sir Owain is no different. And I believe we saw the proof of this in the days that followed.

At night, we heard those animal sounds outside the camp again. Sir Owain took his hunting rifle, and with no thought of personal danger he struck out into the darkness.

"Show yourself!" he'd call out. "You won't have them! Don't think you can hide from me!" And we heard him for some time after that, as he stumbled deeper and deeper into the jungle.

That became a routine for the next few days. I don't believe that Sir Owain slept at all. By day he sat in the tent between his dying wife and child. At night he was out there at the first sound, blaming all of his ills on that which he could not see, seeking to confront and defy it, but never being given the chance. The rifle was always in his hand, and all of us stayed out of his way; no one wanted to be mistaken and shot.

He came back to the camp on the second morning, after roaming abroad all night, and tried to tell me a tale.

"Somerville," he said. "You must listen. You must. It was a revelation. I've had a revelation."

He was wild-eyed, and close to the brink of madness. He spoke of a confrontation with the beast that had been following us and that threatened all our lives. But the details kept changing, as if he were speaking of a dream and did not realize it.

He saw it now, he said. We had ventured into the midst of a land where creatures roamed unseen, where all the things that threatened us had forms and names but stayed beyond human perception.

"So . . . ," I said. "What exactly did you see?"

"Nothing!" he said excitedly. "Because they're only there when you don't look!"

I told him that he was making no sense.

"They're waiting," he insisted. "When my guard's down, that's when they'll strike."

His wife and child slipped away that afternoon, within half an hour of each other. The first I knew of it was when Sir Owain closed up the tent and went to sit by the river. His hunting rifle was in his hand. He stood it upright with the stock against the ground and the barrel pointing up at the sky.

Everyone looked to me. I entered the tent and checked both bodies for life. When I came out, the others were watching and the news must have been written on my face. I sensed a ripple pass through the camp. Not of sorrow, but of relief. It was done. Now we could leave.

I walked over and sat by Sir Owain. I eyed the gun and tried to judge his mood. He was gazing out at the spot where the two rivers met, where turbulence had capsized his vessel. I said nothing. It was minutes before he spoke.

He said, "Were they in any pain? Do you think?"

"You saw them," I said. "They were sleeping." And then: "We need to think about moving on."

"One of the boats can serve as a funeral barge," he said. "This must be done with all possible dignity."

It took me a moment to register what he was saying.

"No, Owain," I said then. "You can't take them with you. We're not yet halfway home. There's no dignity in what a few days in this heat on the river will make of them. Do I need to explain?"

"What's my alternative?"

"You'll have to bury them here."

"No!"

"If the very idea is too painful then you can leave it to others."

"I won't leave them in the dirt of some foreign land."

"Then they'll rot in your arms. Is that what they'd want?"

It was harsh, but it did the trick. He closed his eyes, and all the fight seemed to go out of him.

"No," he said. "I can't leave it to others. This is my family. I shall be the one to deal with it."

He got to his feet. He took a deep breath and he straightened his back. Then he turned and walked back toward the camp, calling everyone together.

He stood before us all, and made a speech.

"I've decided that we shall continue downriver," he said, "as soon as my wife and child have received a fit and proper burial, as befits good Christians in a heathen land. I trust no one considers this unreasonable."

All eyed the way that he hefted his hunting rifle, and agreed that, despite dwindling supplies, creeping sickness, uncharted hazards, and invisible beasts, this was not at all unreasonable.

"Good," he said. "I shall begin my design for the tomb."

HE HAD the surveyors looking for the best site. He had it cleared of vegetation, and set our *camaradas* to dig the hole. Wherever they dug, after a foot or two the hole would fill up with water. The second choice of site was no better. The men worked, wanting to be done with this and on their way.

Meanwhile, Sir Owain had our Indians hauling flat stones out of the river, including one so heavy that it took all of them working together. Once it was on the bank, he had them hammer in wedges to split it. With a charcoal stick, he drew his funereal designs on each flat surface and set them to chipping away at the rock, flaking it down so that his designs slowly rose up in relief.

I managed to catch him alone for a moment. I said, "Owain, I'm concerned. Someone's moved our supplies."

He seemed unworried. "No one's taking more than his share," he said. "I've made sure of that."

"It was you?"

He'd a gleam in his eye when he looked at me.

"If they can't find the food," he said, "they can't desert me. I hired these men fair and square. In the time that I'm paying for, I expect them to do whatever I require of them."

I watched in dismay as, over the next few days, order steadily broke down. A few hours for a funeral was one matter; the construction of some mockery of a Highgate-style sepulchre, with control of the food supply as a means to compel obedience, was something else altogether.

The Indians responded by feeding themselves. They cut open flowering bamboo stalks and ate the grubs to be found inside. Work all but stopped on the stone carving after that, as the Indians lay around and were of little use. I guessed that there was more in the grubs than mere nourishment.

The *camaradas* roasted monkeys when they could get them and eyed Sir Owain murderously, but made no direct approach to him. He was armed at all times, and, more intimidating to our Portuguese-speaking labor force, he showed repeated signs of an increasing mental unbalance.

The bodies of his wife and son remained in the tent, sewn into canvas but getting riper and riper. At night, when he wasn't searching for beasts, Sir Owain sat with them, a handkerchief tied to cover his mouth and nose. I could hear him talking to them. Well, not so much talking. Raving.

The next morning, we found that one of the boats was missing. Five of the men had taken to the river and gone, taking their chances without any food, no doubt hoping for more plentiful and less wary monkeys downriver. There was almost a rebellion after the discovery was made, with Sir Owain firing into the air to restore order.

The European contingent held a secretive meeting and tried to persuade me to distract Sir Owain while they seized his gun and restrained him. They seemed to think I was the only person in the company that he trusted. I could not imagine how they'd reached this conclusion.

I agreed that grief and duress had affected his reason, but argued that we faced enough dangers without adding to them.

At the end of that day, we found that Sir Owain had somehow hidden the remaining boats.

SIR OWAIN asked me to perform a burial service. The tomb had been completed late that afternoon, and sunset approached. By now there was good reason not to keep the bodies from their final resting place for one hour longer than was necessary. I borrowed a Bible, chose a few readings, and concocted a service of sorts. I'd thought that it might be difficult to find bearers to fetch the bodies from the tent, but there was no shortage of volunteers. The sooner it was done, the sooner we'd be on our way.

The tomb—what can I say about the tomb? Think of those great stone monuments of our Victorian fathers. Picture the most Gothic of them, and then strain it rough-hewn through a madman's nightmare. It had four solid sides and a great slab to top it. But its angles were all wrong, its proportions strange, its decoration of urns and columns a strange mix of the primitive and the classical. A temple of skulls and bones, a pirate's tomb. And yet, entirely recognizable as what it was meant to be.

After my piece we sang "Abide with Me" and the Indians hummed and Sir Owain made a rambling, but touching speech. Mad though he was, his heart was truly breaking. He ended with a promise that our journey would resume in the morning, and revealed where he'd hidden the food. The daylight was all but gone as the *camaradas* dragged the top slab into place and we all dispersed.

Sir Owain sat alone in his empty tent, by the flickering light of a monkey-fat candle. I let him be for a while and then—cautiously, for he'd not set down his hunting rifle at any point during the service—made my way in to join him.

He acknowledged my presence. I produced my rum flask. Even a madman deserves a wake.

I said, "A sad day in a week of sad days. My condolences, Owain." I unscrewed the cap and offered the flask.

He looked at the ground, and sighed. Then he accepted the flask and took a hefty swig. He made a face as the rum went down. "You were right to be hard on me," he said, offering it back. "I should never have brought them here. What was I thinking?"

"You were thinking that all the world must be tameable," I said, waving the flask away, "because you'd already succeeded in taming so much of what you could reach."

"No," he said. "I truly believe there's a malevolence at work. They were taken. This jungle took them."

"Yes, Owain," I said, because there's no arguing with the deluded. "And nothing can bring them back. So now we have to look to the welfare of the survivors. Tell me. How did you manage to hide the boats?"

"I didn't," he said.

"Oh, come on," I said. "For boats that aren't hidden, you concealed them very well. Some of the men have been sneaking off and scouring the riverbank for as far as they could walk. Not one of them's found a sign."

Sir Owain just sat there looking at me, and offered no explanation. Suddenly I understood. Or believed I did.

"You sank them, didn't you?" I said. "They're sitting out there on the riverbed waiting to be raised and refloated. You crafty dog."

But I saw nothing in Sir Owain's eyes.

"Well?" I prompted.

He said, "I untied the lines, and shoved the boats out into the river where they were carried off."

Was he joking? Surely he was joking.

He was not.

"They're gone?" I said.

He shrugged. "I wish I'd thought of your bottom-of-the-river trick," he said, and tilted his head back with the flask tipped high, his Adam's apple bobbing as he downed the rum like so much water.

I persisted.

"So we have no boats," I said.

"No," he said.

WHEN I AWOKE the next morning, it was to find our campfire extinguished and our camp deserted. Europeans, Indians, *camaradas* . . . all were gone. They had taken what remained of the supplies, and abandoned us.

Over in his tent Sir Owain slept on, snoring in a noisy rum coma, much as I'd left him the night before. After a sleepless week, the liquor had kicked away his supports and he'd fallen hard.

Now this. Our situation was bleak. I contemplated my own with dismay. The others had seen me as Sir Owain's man, to be abandoned along with him. Such were the consequences of my caution and sympathy. I picked my way around what remained of our camp, looking for anything useful that the others might have left behind. When I came to the grave site, an appalling spectacle awaited me.

The stone tomb, so carefully and solidly built, had been pushed over by some terrible force. How had I slept through this? The slab had tipped and its walls had fallen, and the rotted bodies had been dragged out onto open ground and mauled.

At least, I believe they'd been mauled. I am no expert in the work of explosive decay.

Their canvas shrouds had been ripped head to toe. Surely the others had not done this out of spite before they left? Although as an explanation, it did occur to me before any other. But the force of it, and the fury. . . .

I felt helpless. What was I to do? Take my own chances in the jungle, and leave Sir Owain to make this discovery alone?

I *had* intended to walk away. My alternative was to stick with a madman, which would mean facing the odds with an added handicap. I'd be like a conjoined twin in a drowning pool, with the weight of a dead brother pulling him down.

Then from behind me I heard, "Holy mother of all mercy," and I knew that my opportunity to choose had already gone.

Sir Owain had risen, and came to stand beside me now. He did not blink or look away; he bore the unbearable.

We could not think of restoring the tomb. Between us we had not the necessary strength, and besides, it was irreparable. One of the side slabs was cracked, and the other completely broken. We remade the shrouds as best we could and dragged the bodies back to their hole. We placed flowers in the grave all around them and then piled on every one of the stones that we could move, plus a few more from the river. This time there was no service, no ceremony.

After that, with only the clothes we stood up in, we set off to follow the river onward as best we could and eventually, God willing, to walk out of the jungle.

WE KNEW OF only one reliable food source. Like our Indians, we were reduced to cutting into flowering bamboo and eating the grubs we found inside. Though trained in botany and able to identify some of the more extreme poisons, I had little useful knowledge that I could apply to living off the land. Disgusting though the bugs were—and we ate them alive—they sustained us and did us no harm. Whereas our one experiment with berries left us violently sick and shaking for most of a day.

Though some of the time he'd walk along for hours in an introspective silence, at his worst Sir Owain was a raving companion. At night, he would pick out sounds and identify them with total certainty as the cries of beasts that were calling to one another, plotting to capture us. By day he'd point to their traces, which I actually believe to have been made by some of our former companions moving ahead of us. It seemed only logical to assume that they would be following the river, as we were.

One time, as we rested in exhaustion after a hazardous descent beside a waterfall, Sir Owain suddenly gripped my arm and pointed across the river, saying, "See. There one goes."

All I could see was the fog of spray at the base of the falls, and the rainbow that it made.

"I see nothing," I said.

"I see the spaces where they've been," he said. "The space retains the shape. Until it fades."

Make of *that* what you can.

I began to understand why our Indians had turned so lazy. The bamboo grubs, which habit made easier to stomach as the days went by, inclined us to lethargy and fueled the most strange and vivid dreams. Taken early in the day, they induced a daze that lasted for hours. One time I stepped on a sharp rock and did not realize until much later that it had split my boot and my foot was bleeding badly.

At night, we'd pile up fronds to make a bed. Sleep came easily. Exhaustion and bamboo grubs saw to that. One morning, at daybreak, I awoke to find Sir Owain shaking me.

"Bernard," he said, using my given name for only the second time. "I've done it. I've killed one."

I blinked and yawned and raised myself. "What do you mean?"

"I followed it and killed it. Look."

He showed me his hands. There was blood on them. On his hands, on his clothes, everywhere. And on my arm, where he'd touched it.

I said, "Show me."

He led me down to the riverbank. I was limping. It was the start of an infection that would come close to losing me a leg.

Sir Owain was chattering away.

"I saw its eyes before anything else," he said. "They were yellow. And they shone, Bernard. Lit from within. I swear to you they shone like lanterns!"

Pain lanced up my leg from my wounded foot as I tripped over his hunting rifle. The weapon was lying in my way, discarded and undischarged. Had he fired a shot during the night, bug juice or no bug juice, I'm sure the sound of it would have woken me.

"Owain," I said, "look at me."

He stopped. I looked into those eyes and saw a man lost in madness.

"It was there, Bernard," he pleaded. "It was as real as you are. It's like nothing you've ever seen. Please. I can prove it to you."

We came to a clear and level spot by the river. There we found a half-built raft, and three of our former companions. The astronomer, our cartographer, and one of the Portuguese laborers. All slaughtered. They'd been hacked down and cruelly cut about. In places their wounds were to the bone. Close by lay a machete knife. They'd been using it to build the raft and I was almost certain it was the instrument that had cut them down.

Sir Owain wasn't looking at the bodies. He was scanning all around behind him, looking for something else.

I said, "Well?"

"It was here," he insisted.

"So where is it now?"

"Others of its kind must have dragged the dead beast away," he said. "It's how they keep from being discovered."

"There's no sign of any such thing," I said. "Just these men. Look at them."

"I know," Sir Owain said. "Torn by the beast."

I COULD GET no more out of him. We took their knapsacks and dined on their rations. I washed the machete in the river and we set about completing their raft. I kept the machete by me at all times. I had begun to fear that Sir Owain himself had used it on our companions, cutting down men while in his mind he fought dragons.

They'd made a rudder for steering the raft, and it had some slight effect on our course, but mostly we were at the river's mercy.

A few minutes after we'd launched, I spied a figure on the bank. It was one of our *camaradas*, standing out on a promontory. I might easily have missed seeing him, as he did not wave or call out. He stared at us and did not move.

I put my hands together before my face and called out, "Don't just stand there, man! Swim for it! We'll pull you on board!"

Perhaps he did not hear me over the torrent's roar. He certainly made no move in response.

As we drew closer I could see that he was paying me no attention at all. His gaze was fixed on Sir Owain. I leaned on the tiller in an attempt to bring our raft closer to the bank, to give him more of a chance to reach us if he swam. But the raft kept to its course, and merely began to turn around its own center. We were level with him now, and then we were passing him by.

"What are you waiting for?" I called out. "It's only a raft, it won't steer. We can't get to you!"

If he jumped now, he'd still have a chance. We'd be ahead of him, but he'd be swept along at the same speed as ourselves. He could swim to us then.

Without taking his eyes from Sir Owain, the man responded

with something in Portuguese. Then he moved back into the jungle. Presumably to make his own way; he may have reached safety, but if he did I never got to hear of it.

I wish that I could at least remember the sound of his words, so that I could repeat them to someone who speaks the language and perhaps find out what he said. All through this Sir Owain returned his gaze, but he made no move and showed no emotion.

I have thought about that moment often, and I often remember the look that passed between the two.

We did not leave the raft for three days. The cut on my foot began to fester. By then Sir Owain had grown delirious, and my own condition was not much better. I've been told that my wound turned gangrenous.

I remember him screaming that the beasts were in the water and were now conspiring to follow him home. And I remember one time opening my eyes, and in a brief moment thinking that I could see the world with equal clarity and now understood what he'd told me; that we may not see our beasts, but with practice and understanding we may perceive their shapes in the spaces where they'd been. But of our eventual rescue, I'm afraid I remember very little at all.

FORTY-FOUR

THE COASTAL MILK TRAIN GOT HIM INTO ARNMOUTH JUST after daybreak. As Sebastian was once again putting his name into the Sun Inn's guest book, Stephen Reed appeared at his side.

"Bill Turnbull told me you'd sent ahead for a room," Stephen Reed said. "Let's speak plainly."

"Let's."

They moved to the inn's part-time police office, which had been brought back into service after the murder of Grace Eccles.

"You and I know that tinker never killed those two children," Stephen Reed said. "And there can be no doubt that Sir Owain is dangerously insane. His wealth and reputation have kept him above suspicion. I believe that if Doctor Hubert Sibley doesn't actively collude, he at least looks the other way."

"Then let's catch them out on that," Sebastian said. "What exactly happened to Grace Eccles?"

"Are you saying you agree?"

"Absolutely. I know the man's history now. It's a recipe for tragedy. How did she die?"

"She appears to have let someone into her home. Someone she knew. She wasn't expecting to be attacked."

"That's a big supposition."

"The door was unlocked."

"I'd look for more than that to support it."

"She poured a glass of water for her guest. I know it doesn't sound like much, but . . . you'd have to know Grace. It was him, it has to be."

"Was there a further violation?"

"Not in the police surgeon's opinion."

"No offense," Sebastian said, "but when a missing-children case turned to murder they replaced you pretty damned quickly. How come you're back in charge?"

"That case was important to someone," Stephen Reed said. "Grace Eccles is important to no one. You've been a long time away from policing, Mister Becker. You of all people should know how it plays."

He gave Sebastian a quick account of what was known of Grace's murder. She'd invited her attacker in. Bloodstains showed that he'd turned on her once inside the house. When she fled the building, he pursued her out onto the estate. After killing her and making little attempt to conceal her body, he returned and searched the house. He might have intended to return to deal with the remains, but at that moment the search mattered more. There was no saying what he was looking for, or whether he'd managed to find it.

Sebastian said, "What's happening with the tinker? Is the execution still on, or is there a stay?"

"There's been no word of any stay. I've suggested that this new killing may call his guilt into question, but without hard evidence I can't get anyone to listen. He put his mark to a confession, for God's sake. Even his own counsel thinks he's guilty. How did the news get to London? To most people it's no more than a local affair."

"I heard it from Evangeline Bancroft," Sebastian said. "Her mother wrote to her."

"Evangeline?" Stephen Reed said. "You've seen her?"

"I tracked her down. We shared information. Her life has been marked since her childhood, but she remembers nothing of how. She sends you her best wishes. I've warned her to stay away."

EVANGELINE STOOD by her bicycle before Grace's cottage, her heart heavy, her skin cold. Her oldest friend was dead, and here was where she'd spent her final hour. Now someone was close by, moving around in the yard.

It was a man. An old man, bent and white-haired but able-bodied.

Arthur had seemed exactly the same for as far back as she could remember. At one time or another he'd carried out odd jobs for just about everyone in town. Her mother had paid him to paint their shed once. Now he was putting out feed for Grace's chickens, and hay for Grace's horses.

When he was done he came over and they stood side by side in silence for a while, watching the horses eat.

Eventually Evangeline spoke. "What's to be done with them?" she asked.

"Sergeant Reed told me to graze them until someone decides," Arthur said.

"Stephen Reed? He's here?"

"Hereabouts," Arthur said.

When the hay was gone the animals stood in their paddock looking toward the house, as if expecting Grace to appear in the doorway. After the one-eyed horse had been roped and led back from the main street, the others had returned on their own.

"Can I go inside?" Evangeline said.

"No one's stopping you," Arthur said.

She left her bicycle by the gate and pushed at the cottage door. The house had not been secured. People would probably avoid it for a while because of what had happened here, but after a few days the superstition would wear off and then anything that wasn't nailed down would be fair game. Anything that *was* nailed down would be fair game thereafter. Left unattended for long enough, such a remote building would be stripped of its lead, slates, and timbers, with the dressed stone to follow.

Unless, of course, Sir Owain took the necessary steps to safeguard his property. She knew he had designs for it; Dr. Sibley had advised him so. The house and land would need some investment to turn it into a rentable concern, but she knew that Sir Owain's advisor had some scheme in mind for that.

Perhaps if Grace had quit the property, she'd be alive now. Evangeline wondered if her defense of Grace had helped to seal her old friend's fate.

Inside the house, all was silent. The smell of damp, held at bay by for so long by a lit stove and human occupation, had quickly established itself. Someone had been in and tidied; the furniture was arranged all wrong. Broken crockery and ornaments had been swept into one corner by a wide broom that had left its marks in the dust.

Evangeline felt sick. Poor Grace. Brave Grace. As good as any of them, despised by all. Now she would never tell Evangeline—or anyone—what she'd known.

But why ransack the house after Grace's death? Why had he killed her, and what could he have been looking for? Evangeline could remember the last conversation that had passed between Grace and herself.

"That doctor friend of his . . . he wants me paying rent or he wants me out. Well, he can want. There's worse than him to watch out for."

"Like who?"

"If anything ever happens to me, I daresay you'll know where to look to find out."

At the end of the cottage, a set of wooden steps led up through a trap to the loft where, as a child, Grace used to sleep and the two of them used to play. Evangeline picked up a simple bentwood chair and climbed the steps with it.

The loft was filled with rubbish now . . . old tools, mildewed cloth, broken mirrors, broken harness. Evangeline made a space on the floor under the roof beam, set the chair down, and climbed onto it. The heavy beam, a hundred years old or more, was in two pieces with a pegged joint in the middle. Many times over the years it had been painted with bitumen to preserve it, so that it was almost black. This concealed the fact that, between the two interlocking halves of the joint, there was a gap plugged by a matching timber wedge.

Evangeline worked the wedge free, uncovering the space behind it. Their secret place. There was a box in the space that Evangeline didn't recognize.

She took it out, climbed down, turned around and sat on the chair, and inspected the box on her knees. By the faded paper label, it had once held cotton reels. When Evangeline had looked at it from every angle, she opened the lid.

The box might not be familiar to her, but some of its contents were. They were mostly childish treasures. A hat pin and a tortoiseshell comb, mementoes of Grace's mother. Some foreign coins they used to play shop with, and a pebble from the Holy Land, one of a sackful brought to their school and handed out to each child by a visiting missionary. There was a fancy livery button, and the remains of some papers; if these had been deeds or title papers of any kind, then they'd be of no value to anyone now. Mice had somehow entered the box and shredded them into a mass of pulp and little black droppings.

Evangeline closed the box and looked around. If Grace had meant for her to find something here, she couldn't imagine what it was. Perhaps it had been taken. What an irony that would be, if Grace had kept some kind of evidence to protect herself only to be killed for it.

She took the box outside and placed it in the pannier of her bicycle. Arthur had finished his work with the animals and was sitting on the stile beside the outer gate, his attitude stoical, his breath feathering in the cold air. At his feet was the rope-handled bag, made from a jute sack, in which he always carried his tools. Evangeline wheeled her bicycle through the gate and closed it behind her.

She said, "Shall we walk back together?"

"You carry on," he said.

"Are you sure? I can walk with the bicycle."

"You ride on home," he said. "Don't fret about me. I've another job to go to."

FORTY-FIVE

SEBASTIAN WAS STILL WORKING HIS WAY THROUGH STEPHEN Reed's notes when Dolly-from-the-kitchen came through with a message for him. After taking it from her and opening the envelope, he said, "Here I am trying to think of how best to confront Sir Owain, and look what shows up."

He passed the envelope and its contents across to Stephen Reed. The police detective read over the handwritten card and said, "A dinner invitation."

"It's for tonight," Sebastian said. "He must have sent his chauffeur to deliver it. The man's up to something. Do I go?"

Stephen Reed handed back the invitation with an equivocal shrug. "Lion's den," he said. "Perhaps we should both of us go."

"If he's wondering why I'm back," Sebastian said. "I'd rather keep him guessing."

"Perhaps he means to confess."

"Staking his claim to an insanity plea by confessing to the Visitor's man before the police? I suppose it's possible. But why should that require a dinner invitation?"

"His farewell to freedom."

"Unlikely. I'll keep an open mind but go armed."

Up in his room, the detective watched as Sebastian took the revolver and box of cartridges from his Gladstone. Sebastian loaded the gun with five rounds and set the hammer on the sixth chamber, empty.

"A nice short barrel," Stephen Reed observed. "That's lucky. It won't spoil the line of your dinner suit."

"Do I look like a man who owns a dinner suit?"

SEBASTIAN MIGHT not have owned a dinner suit, but William Phillips, the town's photographer, had four on the dressing-up rack behind his studio backdrop. Two were shabby, one was huge, and the other just about fit.

"You look most elegant," Phillips assured him as he stood before the studio's full-length mirror.

"I look like the headwaiter at Simpson's," Sebastian said.

Sir Owain's car drew up outside the Sun Inn at the appointed time that evening. Stephen Reed stayed out of the way. The driver held the car's door open for Sebastian, who said, "How many will there be at dinner tonight?"

"Just the three of you, sir."

"No one else?"

"No, sir."

"Do you plan to abandon me again?"

"That was a misunderstanding, sir. You can be sure my employer chastised me for it."

The drive seemed even longer at night. The landaulet's headlamps—six of them in all, including carriage lamps on the passenger cab—cast a lemon electric wash onto the bumpy road ahead. Sebastian tried to keep a mental track of their route as he remembered it—estuary, farmland, grouse moor, woodland—but after a while he gave up looking for landmarks and sank back into the leather. He did not try to speak to the driver again.

When the Hall finally came into sight, it was like a pale shining castle on the hill. Perhaps not a light from every window, but enough of them to make a startling impression from its place above the valley. A shaft lit up the waterfall that tumbled below it, and a string of bulbs illuminated the final part of the driveway that led around and up to the court.

The main doors were open and Sir Owain was waiting before them. As Sebastian stepped out of the car, Sir Owain said, "Welcome, Mister Becker."

"Thank you for the invitation," Sebastian said. "What's the occasion?"

"It's probably of no significance to anyone else. But I'm assured of my home and my liberty for another year, and it's you I must thank for it."

"Sir James made the decision."

"But you made the report."

"You don't know what my recommendations were."

"But you are a professional man. Forgive my defensive manner the last time we met. I should have trusted in your judgment."

He led Sebastian through the house. They came to a vaulted drawing room, with a wide expanse of floor on which stood a maple-inlaid piano. The back of the room was dominated by a massive marble fireplace, beside which Dr. Hubert Sibley waited to serve them with sherry.

"Look at him," Sir Owain said cheerfully. "Doctor, manager, nursemaid, and now butler. As you see, Mister Becker, there's no end to our Hubert's talents."

"Four years of shipboard living teaches a man not to stand around going thirsty for want of etiquette," said the affable Dr. Sibley as they each took a glass from his silver tray. "Your health."

"And yours," Sebastian said, struggling a little to adjust to this air of genuine good cheer. He felt like an actor who'd been invited to drop his role and meet his fellow players out of their characters for the first time. A dangerous temptation, given what he knew.

It was a good sherry, as far as he was able to tell. In Sebastian's world, sherry had always been a parlor drink for judges and old ladies. They made small talk. He asked about the Hall's extravagant lighting scheme and learned that it was the one thing on the property that came cost-free; Arnside was self-sufficient in electricity, from a hydroelectric plant of Sir Owain's own manufacture. Its turbine was driven by the very same torrent that emerged to feed the falls below the house.

A few minutes later, Sir Owain's driver appeared in the doorway. Only now he was out of his chauffeur's livery and wore a white jacket with a starched apron over.

He said, "Dinner in five minutes, please, gentlemen," and withdrew again, after which they took their unfinished drinks through into the dining room.

Another fire burned in here, keeping back the autumn night's chill. The dining room had oak paneling and green flock wallpaper. An oriental theme ran through its décor, with woven cane in the dining chairs and fringes on the light shades. The capstan table had several of its sections removed to reduce its size, and there were place settings for three.

"In case you're wondering," Sir Owain said, "our Thomas is a first-class cook."

"Though his range can be a touch limited," Dr. Sibley suggested.

"Give the man credit," Sir Owain said. "None of your fancy French sauces, but he can shoot, hang, and burn a bird with the best of them."

"And thank God for it," Sibley said, drawing Sebastian's chair out for him, "because dear old Cook wouldn't have been able to drive the car to save her own life."

"All the same," Sir Owain said, "I was sad to let her go."

Sebastian said, "What happened?"

"No fault in the woman, just sheer financial necessity. No one believes it when you sit on an estate and plead poverty, but the land and the house just suck in cash. If you don't farm and your tenants don't pay, then what do you feed it with?"

"There must be some kind of a solution. I imagine you could sell up and live well in a smaller place. Or at least rent out this house."

"See if he listens to you," Dr. Sibley said sorrowfully. "He won't to me."

"But where would I settle?" Sir Owain said. "That's the question. There's no welcome for me in London. Not since the unpleasantness at the Royal Society. And this is the only real home I know."

As well as driver and cook, Thomas Arnot was their server for the evening. The dining-room doors opened and he came in pushing a trolley, on which there was a white cloth and a plated copper tureen. He lifted the tureen onto the table and left them to it.

Dr. Sibley raised the lid on a rabbit consommé, releasing steam and an agreeable aroma, and Sir Owain said, "Mister Becker, I hope I'm not being inappropriate in mentioning it, but are you in mourning?"

"I am," Sebastian said. "How did you know?"

"We get the London papers here," Dr. Sibley said, showing some skill with the ladle.

"My dear sir," Sir Owain said. "I'm devastated to hear of your wife's passing."

"Thank you."

From then on, Sir Owain played the perfect host. Dinner consisted of a good pheasant each and a lot of easy conversation. The decanter passed around the table and Dr. Sibley was induced to tell some tales of his seafaring days as a ship's medic in the Caribbean seas, prior to his meeting with Sir Owain. One of them had a supernatural theme, but he told it with a twinkle in his eye.

Though Sebastian was itching to see their talk move on to more germane matters, a part of him was wishing for a world where all could be as it appeared, and where he could enjoy this evening as much as his companions did. He had not known such masculine company, without issues or pressure, in a long time, and had never missed it so much as he did now.

Toward the end of the ghost story, Sir Owain's man came in. He waited until the tale was over before clearing the plates and the bones.

He said to Sir Owain, "Will you need me for anything else tonight, sir?"

And Sir Owain said, "No, Thomas. Just bring us the pudding and the rest of the night's your own."

Dessert was a dish of vanilla-flavored cream. When they were done, Dr. Sibley started to collect their crockery together.

"Oh, leave it, man," Sir Owain said. "Thomas will deal with all that in the morning."

"Not on a Sunday, he won't," Dr. Sibley said.

"It can wait until Monday, then."

"So we just close the dining-room doors on all the mess? And what will your guest think of us if we do?" He said it with a wink to Sebastian, who could imagine that the mariner in him was offended by such untidiness.

With good humor, Sir Owain pushed himself back from the table and let the physician get on with his domestic business. Sibley piled up the dessert dishes with Sir Owain's barely touched portion on top.

Sebastian said, "May I have the use of your telephone? There's a call I ought to make."

"Come to my study," Sir Owain said. "You can have some privacy there."

Sebastian was led to the book-lined room where he'd conducted his first interview with the industrialist. The typewriting machine was still on the desk, but he saw no telephone until Sir Owain reached down and produced one from the drawer.

After making sure that Sebastian knew how to get a connection, Sir Owain withdrew. Within a few minutes Sebastian was speaking to Stephen Reed, who'd been awaiting this call.

Sebastian said, "All's well. But it's not the night we were hoping for."

"No confession?"

"The pair of them are being downright sociable."

"Don't lower your guard," Stephen Reed warned him.

"No, of course not. But I've watched Doctor Sibley account for most of a decent Burgundy, and if a man doesn't make a slip after that, you start to wonder if there's a slip to be made."

As if in ironic counterpoint to his remark, at that moment there was an offstage crash from somewhere in the direction of the kitchens. The sound of breaking crockery is unique and was easy to identify.

Sebastian said, "I suspect that was him."

"What should I do? Wait up for you?"

"No," Sebastian said. "They've just dismissed their driver, so I imagine I'll be offered a bed for the night."

"Be sure you lock the bedroom door."

"I'll have a chair under the handle and my revolver under the pillow," Sebastian said. "Don't lose any sleep over me."

At that point, he became aware of Sir Owain standing in the doorway. He hadn't even heard the study door open. How long had the man been there? What had he heard? Sebastian quickly finished the conversation, ending it with a few neutral pleasantries that alerted Stephen Reed to the change in his situation.

When he saw that the call had ended, Sir Owain came fully into the room and settled himself into the second chair, across from Sebastian.

"So," he said.

"So indeed," said Sebastian, uncertain of where this was going.

"There was a piece of moving-picture film? What did it show?"

"Nothing conclusive," Sebastian said. "Something or someone rushing at the camera."

"Do you know who or what?"

"I'm in no position to say."

Sir Owain said, "I know what your real suspicions are. You want to know if I could have killed those children. So do I."

Sebastian started to frame a reply, then stopped. Sir Owain seemed entirely serious. Sebastian said, "*Did* you kill them?"

"I don't know," Sir Owain said.

"But are you telling me it's possible?"

"My heart says no. But I'm a scientist. I have to start by accepting that everything is possible, and then be guided to a proper conclusion by the evidence. Evidence-based thinking, Mister Becker. The greatest single achievement of the human animal. Without it we'd be praising God while shivering in our caves and dead by the age of thirty."

"And what does the evidence tell you?"

"That I don't have enough of it to form a reliable conclusion."

Sebastian sat back in the captain's chair. "This isn't what I expected to hear," he admitted.

"Nor is it what the good doctor would want me to say. But I won't live a lie, Mister Becker. If a lie is what it is."

"What makes you suspect yourself?"

"I've examined the timings. I can't account for my whereabouts with any certainty."

"Any blood on your clothes? Your hands?"

"A man who can kill and not know it can surely bathe and not know it."

He stood up and indicated for Sebastian to follow him. Sebastian scrambled to his feet. This seemed too good to be true. He hadn't dared to hope for a confession. Much less for Sir Owain to act as his own inquisitor.

As he led the way out into the hallway, Sir Owain said, "We'll settle this tonight, you and I. Doctor Sibley is dedicated to the preservation of my health and my freedom. His livelihood depends on both. But I care nothing for either. In my time I have been an arrogant man. Experience has made me a humble one. I wish only to be judged as I deserve."

He stopped and locked the study door behind them before walking on.

Sebastian said, "And tonight's so-called celebration . . . ?"

"Was my excuse to bring you here. And a way to disguise the direction of my thinking for the good doctor."

"But the moment he sees your purpose, he'll interfere."

"I planned for that," Sir Owain said, and they entered the kitchen.

The kitchen was a tall room, two stories high, on the north-facing side of the Hall. It was tiled in yellow, with a cement floor and visible pipework. A black iron range covered the length of one wall, with ovens and griddles enough for a dozen cooks to work at once.

The range was cold, however, and there was only one figure in the room, and he was sprawled on the floor amid a mess of leftovers and broken china. Dr. Sibley lay without moving, the tray that had borne it all lying close to his outflung hand.

FORTY-SIX

DR. SIBLEY MUST HAVE BEEN AS SURPRISED AS ANYONE BY HIS collapse. It was as if he'd dropped in midstride, pitching forward and landing hard.

"Did you plan for *this*?" Sebastian said.

"Actually," Sir Owain said, looking down on his motionless companion, "I did. Although what I intended was something less spectacular. He was supposed to start yawning and take himself off to bed."

"You drugged him?"

"A few drops in his wine. They ought to have been perfectly safe. The drug came from his own kit."

Sebastian said, "I don't see him breathing."

"No," agreed Sir Owain. "Nor do I."

Sebastian dropped to one knee and checked the doctor's pulse. First at the wrist, and then again at the side of the neck.

"The man's dead," he said.

"Is he?" Sir Owain said. "Damn."

Sebastian looked up at him. "Is that all you can say?"

"It was only supposed to put him out for a few hours. I must have misjudged the dose."

"Well, you've killed him. Which makes the rest of any scheme for determining your guilt a touch redundant, wouldn't you say?"

"It *is* a setback, I have to admit."

"A *setback*?" Sebastian said, rising, and with a sudden rush of blood to the head that made him dizzy. "I'll say it is. It's all over, Sir Owain. Consider yourself arrested."

"Can you do that?" Sir Owain said. "You're not a policeman."

"Any private citizen is bound by law to . . ." He meant to go on to say, *arrest any person who commits a felony in his presence*, but his thoughts wandered right off his subject and then he struggled to remember what he'd intended to say.

Sir Owain said, "How do you feel?"

Sebastian snapped himself back into focus.

"Why?" he said. "What did you do?"

"The dose was in the decanter. That's why I only drank water."

It was a moment or so before the realization took hold. Sir Owain seemed willing to give Sebastian all the time he needed, watching him with patient sympathy. Sebastian made a start toward the door and Sir Owain stepped aside to let him by.

He felt a sudden need for the night's cold air. He seemed to float out of the kitchen and down the hall toward the main doors. He was aware of his legs working under him but not so sure they were under his control. He failed to stop himself and hit the door hard. He'd have slid to the floor, but he managed to keep hold of the handle.

He thought at first that he lacked the strength to get the doors open. But then he realized there was a much simpler explanation. They were locked.

Sir Owain had caught up with him by now.

He said, "If it's any reassurance, Doctor Sibley downed far more of it than you did. How was I to know it would be the death of him?"

Sebastian remembered the revolver. He'd been able to fit it into one of the jacket's lower pockets, in the lining on the inside. He fumbled for it. It should have come out easily. But it wouldn't. The harder he tried, the more entangled he became.

Sir Owain watched him for a while, then reached in and took the gun away, unhooking it from the lining with ease.

He said, "Mine are not the kind of beasts you can fight with one of these. Trust me. I have tried."

Sebastian pushed him away. He aimed himself toward the study, where the telephone was. He rattled and rattled at the doorknob, and then belatedly remembered how Sir Owain had turned the key in the door when they left it.

"Give in, Mister Becker," Sir Owain pleaded with him. "I can see you'll need to sleep this off before we can hope to achieve anything."

With a great effort, he knocked the older man aside. Sir Owain staggered a little. Sebastian moved without a plan, willing to settle for any route to safety, not even knowing where safety might lie.

He found himself in a corridor by the kitchen, a service way between a wall of the old house and some of the newer work; there were iron girders overhead, and glass skylight panels above the girders. Some of the glass had been smashed, and the roof was open to the night, but far too high to reach.

The fallen glass hadn't been cleared up, and crunched underfoot.

Sir Owain said, "That's what happened when the beasts tried to enter."

There was a door at the end of the passageway. It wouldn't open. Or he couldn't open it. Sebastian turned around and fell back against the door.

Sir Owain gestured toward the damage.

"They came out of the jungle and followed me all the way home," he said. "Now they wait for the dark. I do my best to fortify the building, and they do their best to find a way in. I stay up all night and I fight them off. Or do I? Do I, Mister Becker?" His face was right before Sebastian's now. "Or do I merely create powerful memories of events that never took place? The human mind is an amazing instrument of perception, Mister Becker. How far should we trust the instrument's perception of itself? That's what you can help me to find out."

Sebastian felt his legs going. Sir Owain caught him quickly and helped to lower him to the ground.

"Now," Sir Owain said, "what has all this running achieved?"

"I won't sleep," Sebastian vowed. He wasn't sure whether he was speaking aloud, or merely forming the words in his mind and getting no further with them.

It seemed he spoke, because Sir Owain responded.

"I don't think you'll have any choice," he said. "I'm not even sure what I gave you. If there's an antidote, I've no idea what it would be. We'll just need to get through this."

"Get me to a doctor."

Sebastian was terrified of sleeping at the madman's mercy. But he could feel himself sliding ever farther away.

"It would make no difference," Sir Owain said. "Sleep, Mister Becker. And when you wake up—assuming that you *do* wake up—we can begin."

FORTY-SEVEN

SEBASTIAN DREAMED OF ELISABETH. THEY WERE AT HOME. ONE of their past homes. All was well but he was possessed by a certainty that something terrible was going to happen. She was moving about the room, not looking at him, speaking; later he would struggle to remember what she'd said. He knew that this was a dream, and that unless he could work out the secret of how to remain then he'd soon be pulled out of it and back into the waking world. He tried to imagine what lay outside the door, beyond the windows. If he could only populate this place, give it geography, render it all in enough detail to snap it into the real . . . it was almost as if, by perceiving with sufficient intensity, he might dream her back into life again.

But wherever he moved his attention, the rest began to slip. It was a room on an island in a fog, where Elisabeth walked and spoke, and he would not remember her words.

He could feel the covers of a bed or a divan underneath him. His chest hurt. He knew that he was awake, but he didn't open his eyes. When he opened his eyes, that would be the end of it.

He heard Sir Owain say, "How's the head?"

Sebastian gave in.

It was daylight. He was lying flat and looking up at a paneled ceiling. From somewhere to his right, Sir Owain said, "It was touch and go there, rather. You almost stopped breathing twice."

"You could have killed me," Sebastian managed to say.

"I could. And yet I feel no conscience about it. Is that significant, do you think?"

Sebastian turned his head to look at him. He could barely keep his head lifted from the pillow. The room had painted wallpaper and heavy, masculine furniture. The bedcover on which he lay had a satin look, but was coarse and scratchy to the touch.

"Here," Sir Owain said, and put an arm under Sebastian's shoulders to lift and get him sitting upright. "Let's get you active. See if we can clear that head for you."

He turned Sebastian so that his legs swung off the bed. Then he helped him to rise to his feet and supported him walking.

"Let me sit a while," Sebastian protested.

"Trust me," Sir Owain said. "I know what you need."

They emerged from the room and into a wide gallery. This was a part of the house that Sebastian had not seen before. The gallery was formed by vaulted timbers that curved overhead, as if cut by a shipwright. It was painted in red, and its sides were lined with specimen cases and statuary.

Sebastian was helpless. He was like a drunk with a benefactor walking him home. At the end of the gallery they turned around and started back. When they staggered a little on the turn, Sir Owain said, "Forgive me. I'm not the man I used to be."

Sebastian said, "What do you think this is going to achieve?"

"I've an open mind," said Sir Owain. "But I've an idea of what I expect."

"Where's Doctor Sibley?"

"Just as dead as he was last night. That was his bed you were lying on. My dear Mister Becker, don't tell me you don't remember."

"I meant to say, what have you done with him?"

"Well, I couldn't leave an old friend just lying there on the kitchen floor," Sir Owain said. "There's no dignity in that. So I cleaned him up, and I put him somewhere fitting. It was a struggle. I had to manage on my own. I could hardly involve Thomas, could I? It wouldn't be fair. He's a faithful servant, but that's far too much to ask of a man's loyalty."

Thomas? The chauffeur. Sebastian filled his lungs and yelled the man's name at the top of his voice.

Sir Owain bore the racket patiently, so loud and so close to his ear. And then he said, "If you expect to get anyone's attention, you're wasting your time. I give Thomas his Sundays off. And it's been some time, now, since I had to let the others go."

They turned again, and started back. Sir Owain said, "That was a sad day for me. A house of this size, Sebastian—may I call you Sebastian? It takes a certain number of people just to bring it to life."

As they went along, Sebastian felt his strength returning. Movement forced the sluggish blood around his system. Soon he would be recovered enough to overpower Sir Owain. But better not to try, until he was sure.

At the end of the gallery they went through a curtained opening and across a landing. On the other side of the landing they entered a suite of rooms, where Sir Owain released Sebastian to fall onto a couch. Sir Owain's exhaustion now seemed to match his own.

"This was Hubert's study," Sir Owain said, fetching himself a chair. "Is it just me, or do you share a sense of discomfort at being in here? As if he were still alive. He so valued his privacy." He set the chair down before Sebastian, and went over to the writing desk. "Well," he said, "he's gone and there's no protecting it now."

Although not quite ransacked, it had the look of a room that had been thoroughly searched. Every drawer in the writing desk was open. On the floor was a doctor's bag, also open. Beside that was a medium-sized wooden chest with racks of glass, rubber tubing, and a Bunsen burner in a clip. Sir Owain glanced back and saw where Sebastian was looking.

"That's the kit that he kept locked away," Sir Owain said as he returned from the desk with a bound journal in his hands, "and these . . . these are the notes he was keeping on my treatment. I've been reading them. I have to say there are no big surprises."

He sat and began to leaf through the journal. He was about to speak, but one of the pages caught his attention for a few moments, as if he'd noticed something that hadn't registered with him before.

Then he remembered himself, and went on, "Did Doctor Sibley tell you how he'd been managing me? There's a list here of all the drugs he tried. Most of them will cause hallucination in one form or another. It may seem an odd form of treatment to give to a man deemed to be a fantasist, but I've been assured that the technique has a growing reputation for treating depressive illness. I used to joke with the good doctor that he was a homeopath at heart. Making me a little mad to cure the greater madness. But I don't think he saw the humor in it."

Sebastian said, "I want the telephone."

"I can imagine you do, which is why I've disconnected it. Try to concentrate on what I'm telling you. It concerns you more than you can imagine."

Sebastian said, "Sir Owain, listen to me. Yours is one of the great minds of our age, but experience has damaged it. Now it's as dangerous to others as any broken machine. You may imagine you'd be the first person to know this, but believe me. You'll be the last."

"You're wrong, Mister Becker," Sir Owain said, more seriously than before. "I do know I'm broken. I need to know *how* I'm broken. And if I cannot trust my own intellect to appraise the damage, then I must devise some other way to compare and assess. Somewhere in this fog of what is real and what is not, I have lost myself. I am desperate to find myself again. And for that I need you."

"I won't help you."

"Your consent is not required."

"You're making your situation worse."

"Not possible," Sir Owain said. "Believe me. Let me explain what I intend for you here."

Sebastian started to rise. In an instant he found himself facing his own revolver. He let himself fall back onto the couch.

Despite the gun in his hand, Sir Owain went on as if nothing had happened.

He said, "I start from a theory. When we were deprived of our supplies in the jungle, Somerville and I survived on a grub that we'd seen the Indians eat with safety. They'd lie around in a stupor and be useless for work, but show no ill effects.

"The grub caused vivid dreams. So vivid that I felt as if I were both in that terrible place and somewhere else. I felt that division of body and spirit that the Indians take for granted.

"When I remembered this and put it to Doctor Sibley that it might have been the beginning of some permanent separation, he disagreed. Not least because all the known hallucinogens are derived from plants, and not insects. But he did agree to let me conduct my own study, on the understanding that he'd share credit for any findings."

Sebastian was only half-listening. Stephen Reed knew where he was. When Sebastian failed to appear and could not be reached by telephone, he'd surely come looking.

Sir Owain said, "But I faced a problem. What *was* this grub? I knew that it developed in flowering bamboo. But to the untrained eye, one moth larva resembles another. There were no existing studies to guide me, so it was some time before I identified a likely candidate. In the end I landed on *Myelobia smerintha*, the bamboo grub that the Indians call *bicho de taquara*. I imported some eggs and bred a small colony of them in my conservatory. The larvae flourished until the glass was broken and the temperature fell. Now they're all gone."

"None of this means anything to me," Sebastian said.

"Well, it ought to," Sir Owain said. "I fed the last of them to you last night."

"You did *what?*"

"Your dessert. Take away the repugnant appearance of the insect and you're left with the texture and flavor of vanilla cream."

"As well as drugging me with wine, you fed me worms?"

"Now you're making me sound like a bad host."

Sebastian put his hand to his mouth. It was a quick gesture, and it caused Sir Owain to move back a little with the pistol, to be sure of staying out of his reach.

"I can tell you there's no point in trying to vomit up the active ingredient," Sir Owain said. "It's been several hours since the meal. Whatever reaction you're feeling now is only the beginning."

"I don't feel anything."

"I don't think that's quite true. Is it? Your skin is sallow. Your limbs are heavy. Your energy is sapped. You want to run but you can barely rise. I want you to think about it, and tell me. How does the light feel to you? What do I sound like?"

"I'm not playing your stupid game," Sebastian said. "You've poisoned me."

"Look," Sir Owain said reasonably. "I admit that I made a mistake and killed my doctor. But that doesn't mean I don't know what I'm doing now. I'm guiding you along a path that I've followed myself. Only with you I can make reliable observations, whereas before I could only interpret my own suffering.

"Shall I tell you what *I* felt at this stage? I felt as if I was on the threshold of another world of possibilities. One where there's a blurring of the line between what we know to be true and what we wish or fear to be true. I sensed the existence of a world of unseen marvels. But when that faded, it left me with the permanent feeling that I could not trust my own world anymore. I see so many things that I cannot believe are there."

Now he leaned forward.

"If you begin to see the world I see," he said, "I'll take that as a strong indication that it has some objective reality. I mourn the loss of your wife. But I can't deny that it enhances the conditions for my observations."

Sebastian said, "I'm not your experiment!"

"I'm sorry to hear you say that, Mister Becker," Sir Owain said. "Because I'm afraid that's exactly what you are."

Elsewhere in the house, not too far away, there was a sound of banging.

"There's someone at the door," Sir Owain observed. "We get very few visitors here. Can I trust you to stay quiet while I deal with them? No, it isn't fair to ask you. Of course I can't."

He got up from the chair and moved toward the medical bag. As soon as Sir Owain turned away, Sebastian launched himself from the couch, only to find that his confidence in a fast recuperation was misplaced. As the narcotic effect of the wine had worn off, the hallucinogen from the grubs had begun to increase its effect.

His legs might support him now, but his balance was unreliable. He got as far as the door and collided painfully with the jamb. He bounced out onto the landing, where he fell and hit the carpet hard.

The long gallery was to his left. The stairs were to his right. The hallway and the main door were down below. He tried to crawl toward the stairs, but the unsecured rug bunched up underneath him and he did little more than swim in place.

Sir Owain came out and knelt beside him.

"I learned another little trick from the Indians," Sir Owain said. "They put this on their arrows." Sebastian felt a sharp jab in the side of his neck, and then Sir Owain left him and went to descend the stairs. One hand held the pistol behind his back. He let something fall from the other as he walked away; it was a lancet, almost certainly the cause of that momentary pain. As he went down the stairs he dropped from Sebastian's floor-level view like a ship over the horizon.

This was a piece of luck. Sebastian hadn't expected Stephen Reed to come looking for him so soon. The gun in Sir Owain's hand could pose a problem. He had to get to the rail and shout a warning. He could do that much.

Except that he couldn't. The latest addition to his bloodstream cocktail was already having its effect. A sudden paralysis was taking possession of his body, like a fast-spreading blight.

His senses were unaffected. Enhanced, even. Sir Owain would no doubt be interested to know of it. Though he'd failed to reach the rail and could not see into the hallway below, Sebastian could hear every click and tumble of the main door being unlocked down there. The creak of the hinge as it opened. The change in the acoustics of the hallway as its enclosed space was opened to the world outside.

He'd expected to hear Stephen Reed's voice. But it wasn't the detective. It was Thomas, Sir Owain's sometime cook and regular driver.

"I'm sorry to bang on the door, sir," Sebastian heard him say, "but everywhere's locked up."

"I know it is," Sir Owain's voice came with an extra helping of irritation. "What do you want?"

"Might I have the use of the car today, sir?"

"For what?"

"Nothing you'd disapprove of, sir. And it's only for an hour or so."

"A young lady, is it?"

"Something like that, sir."

Though he and Thomas Arnot had a combustible history, Sebastian had gathered from Sir Owain's own words that the driver knew nothing of his master's current plans or past misdeeds. Though the man might not want to be disloyal, he surely wouldn't want to be branded a conspirator. Sebastian took a breath to call out to him. . . .

But he failed to draw in any air. The paralysis that had disabled his limbs was now affecting his entire body.

He could hear Sir Owain saying, "Fine, it's nothing to me. But I'm not buying your petrol."

"No, sir."

Sebastian was suffocating. He'd breathed for his entire life without ever thinking how. Now this simple gift had deserted him.

Sir Owain seemed to take his time resecuring the doors and then climbing back up the stairs. Sebastian could hear every beat of his measured tread. Sir Owain seemed to be slowing down as he ascended, and Sebastian could feel his heart slowing along with him.

"Now," said Sir Owain, lowering himself to sit on the floor beside Sebastian. "Where was I?"

Almost absently, he leaned over and pressed down on the small of Sebastian's back. Air was driven from Sebastian's lungs and, on removal of the pressure, enough fresh air rushed back in for the increasing mental fog to recede a little.

"Schafer's method of artificial respiration," Sir Owain said. "A trick from the Amazon. Saved one or two of our number after a drowning. Though little good it did them in the end."

Continuing from where he'd left off, and seeming to find nothing strange in this situation, Sir Owain said, "If those beasts are a mere projection of my madness, then it means that innocents are dying by my hand. I'm no better than Somerville, in a frenzy, chasing his sister down the street with a knife. I do harm, while convinced that I'm acting for the best.

"But I see them. I hear them. And I know them by the damage they have done to those I loved. If they have some objective reality, and there are *two* of us who know it . . . don't you see? You and I can take them on together, and make all the children safe."

He pressed down again. Without too much exertion on his own part, Sir Owain was working the bellows of his lungs as much as was needed to keep Sebastian alive, until Sebastian could once again sustain himself.

He said, "It will settle the question once and for all. If there is this invisible world of beasts and wonders, and it occupies the same space as our own, and you can see it too . . . then my sanity will cease to be the issue."

Sebastian wanted to tell Sir Owain that no experiment was required. He both was mad, and stood alone in his madness, no question about it.

But he did not yet have the breath to say so.

FORTY-EIGHT

HER MOTHER HAD ALREADY LEFT FOR CHURCH WHEN SHE WENT downstairs. Evangeline attended services in London, but never at home. Not since the vicar had spoken in his sermon of the "taint" that clung to Grace Eccles and, by implication, to Evangeline as well. By way of protest, her mother had switched her religious allegiance to a Wesleyan chapel whose congregation met in a tin shack on the beach. It was a half hour's walk to reach it, and there was no road. All who worshipped there were seen as slightly mad. When the wind blew, God showed up and rattled the roof.

Evangeline took an old newspaper and spread it out to protect the kitchen table before bringing Grace's cotton-reel box down from her room and placing it in the middle of the open pages. She lifted the lid and—well, there was nothing for it but to get her hands dirty. When she lifted out the mass of shredded pulp, dried mouse droppings pattered down onto the newspaper like tiny hail.

At least they were dry. She swept up as many as she could and put them in a twist of paper from the corner of a page. Then she began to unpick the shreds, looking for any fragment that might bear a word, a signature, or any other clue as to what the document might have been. As she sifted, from out across the rooftops came the sound of church bells ringing.

The combination of chimes and souvenirs reminded her of the time at school when, during one of the vicar's twice-weekly visits to give the children religious instruction, Grace had asked him why a God who preached humility required so much in the way of praise and worship. Was he very vain? By then Evangeline was convinced that Grace knew exactly what she was doing when she provoked authority so. She took every reprimand or beating as a kind of affirmation.

Authority might have been satisfied by Grace's punishment that day, but the damage was done. Through all the years since, Evangeline had remembered Grace's question and had yet to hear a convincing answer to it.

Her careful disentangling of the paper convinced her that this was the legal letter that, in Grace's eyes, had given her the right to remain on the land after her father's death. It had been handwritten, professionally done in copperplate. No useful part of it remained. If this was what she'd been murdered for, then she'd been murdered for nothing. Evangeline kept the few pieces with readable words on them, and swept away the rest. Then she restored everything to the box and rolled up the newspaper until it resembled a wrapped fish supper. This she jammed into the grate behind the coal for that evening's fire.

She then spent five minutes scrubbing her hands clean with hot water and carbolic soap, and a while longer sitting with the box on the table before her. She ought to pass it on to Stephen Reed. Perhaps, being a detective, he'd find some significance in this bric-a-brac that escaped her.

She wrote him a short note, to explain the circumstances. Then she got into her outdoor clothes and went out to the shed to get her bicycle. She might be accused of interfering with evidence. But her only other choice was to cycle back to Grace's cottage and return the box to its hiding place, to be either lost forever or looted by a stranger.

With the box once again in her bicycle's pannier, Evangeline freewheeled downhill toward the middle of town. She'd leave the box with Bill Turnbull at the inn.

The sudden honk of an approaching car's horn almost sent her into the bushes at the side of the road. She wobbled, she braked, and the big landaulet swerved by and stopped just past her.

She was hauling the bicycle's front wheel onto the road as the driver came back. She'd recognized Sir Owain Lancaster's car, and now she recognized his man.

She said, "You nearly scared me off the road."

"Profound apologies, Miss Bancroft," the driver said. "Sir Owain sent me out to look for you. He says, can you kindly spare him some of your time?"

"When?"

"Now, if you don't mind."

"Did he say what it's about?"

"He's put aside a burial plot for Grace Eccles. He regrets the bad feelings of these last few months. He intends her a place by his private chapel, so she won't get a pauper's grave. No more than half an hour, he says. I'm to drive you to the house."

"I've got my bicycle."

"I can put it on the back."

He directed her attention to a folding rack for luggage on the rear of the landaulet. It was big enough to take a bicycle. But knowing what she now knew, Evangeline had no intention of risking her safety out at the big house alone, and in Sir Owain's company.

She said, "I don't wish to offend your employer. But I don't think I ought to go. I mean, to the house on my own. It wouldn't be proper. My mother frowned on it the last time. She can be very old-fashioned."

"Your friend Mister Becker's there already. So is the detective. It's they who persuaded Sir Owain to send me for you."

"Really?"

That changed everything. For both Stephen and Sebastian to be at the house . . . it suggested that some swift conclusion was in the offing, and they needed or wanted her to be a part of it.

"Very well," she said, and allowed Sir Owain's man to help her up into the landaulet's cab. Then he went around the back and seemed to secure her bicycle in no time at all. She sat, feeling the vibration of the Daimler's idling engine. The driver got back behind the wheel, released the parking brake, and they were on their way.

The earliest of the morning services had ended, and Arnmouth was beginning to come back to life. They passed several family groups on the lanes, all walking home in their finest clothes. This was nothing like the resort's fashion displays of high summer, when chapel numbers were swelled by dapper city men, slim-waisted women with their straw hats decked with flowers, and children with a nanny in tow. These were just ordinary local people in their Sunday best, walking out on the one day they felt able to dress with a little pride. Soon all would go quiet again, as every household settled to Sunday lunch and the smell of boiled cabbage mingled with the sea air.

Sir Owain's man sat forward of the cab, a short windshield his only protection. Many of the cars that she saw in London now enclosed the driver and no longer owed their entire design to the horse carriages they'd replaced. Evangeline supposed that Sir Owain's crumbling fortunes forbade him any new toys. She noted that one of the car's passenger windows had been replaced with a sheet of oiled parchment. It let in the light but it was clouded, like a milky eye. It had the brightness and density of Greenwich fog.

She wondered what part she was to play here. She would be alert. Whatever hint Sebastian or Stephen Reed might give her, she would fall into the role.

She was nervous, there was no denying it. Her heart was racing now. It would not do to let it show.

Evangeline closed her eyes and mastered her breathing. She was strong. Nothing could daunt her. She told herself this, over and over.

When the jarring of the vehicle caused her to snap her eyes open, she looked out of the one good side window and saw that this was not the usual way to the Hall.

They were on the estate, but this had to be one of the less-used roads. The track became rougher as they went along it. Perhaps the chapel had its own approach? As far as she could remember, the chapel and its little graveyard weren't so far from the main house. Not that she knew the main house well. There had been a time when Sir Owain and his family had thrown open the grounds every summer to host garden parties for local people, but the house itself had stayed out of bounds.

Something was wrong here. She'd glimpsed the Hall through the trees, but they weren't making the final ascent to it. Instead they zigzagged through a screen of conifers on a track that ended at a complex of stables and estate workers' buildings, all shuttered up and deserted. She knocked on the partition window to ask the driver for an explanation, but the driver didn't respond.

She didn't know his name. Once numbering as many as three hundred souls—including stonemasons, gardeners, gamekeepers, and laborers—the estate's workers had always been a self-sufficient community apart from the town. Evangeline stared at the back of his head with a sense of growing, formless dread that threatened to coalesce into a certainty at any moment.

These buildings were not completely disused. Part of the stables was now the landaulet's garage space. But looking all around she saw broken glass and boarded windows, tall weeds, a clock tower whose face had no hands. The driver braked to a halt in the overgrown stable yard and went to open up the stable doors, ignoring all of Evangeline's attempts to get his attention. When she tried to open the door to get out, there was no handle on the inside. They'd been removed. Both of them.

Her heart pounding, Evangeline sank back into the buttoned leather. Her nails dug into the seat as she gripped it on either side of her thighs. The same disabling panic that had gripped her in the Greenwich tunnel was threatening to overwhelm her now.

As he walked back to the car, the driver glanced at her once. Though he'd been around for as long as she could remember, take him out of Arnmouth and she could never have picked him out of a London crowd. She did not know him. His was the anonymous face of the anonymous servant. And yet the past was beginning to unfurl for her now, like a dark flower in bloom.

The car rolled into the stable and stopped. The engine died, and all was silence. The driver stepped down from behind the wheel and went to close the doors behind them. Evangeline suddenly launched herself forward and tried to slide open the partition between the cab and the driver's bench, but found it locked in place.

Meanwhile, behind her, the daylight was being shut out of the stable, one half at a time.

FORTY-NINE

THE STABLE BLOCK WAS ONE LONG ROOM WITH ROOF BEAMS AND small, high windows. There were wooden stalls for long-gone horses. Evangeline could see that the walls were whitewashed and the cobblestone floor sloped toward a central drain. The unused part of the stable had become a storage area for broken-down carts and farm equipment. The two nearest stalls now served for an auto workshop.

Over by the workbench, Sir Owain's chauffeur was putting on a serviceable leather apron. He tied its strings behind him, blind, and with his attention momentarily absorbed she knew she ought to make a move; but she was hit again, this time by an overwhelming memory of sensations triggered by the sight of the apron. The male, stale smell of sweat and old leather. Like cooking bones.

She'd wasted a moment. Now he'd turned to the bench and was looking along the tools that hung there. While his back was to the car, Evangeline slid across the seat and punched the parchment out of the broken window on the opposite side. Then she reached out and groped around for the handle to let herself out.

It wasn't easy. Not hard to find the handle, but hard to turn it at that angle. By the time she'd thrown the door open and was spilling out, he'd reached her. He came around the back of the car and grabbed her, dragging her out and down onto the stones before she got a chance to gain her balance. She tangled in her skirts and went sprawling.

She was scrambling to rise, but he put his foot underneath her and hooked her over onto her back. Then he put one foot on her chest and leaned toward her, pinning her down with his full weight. She thought her ribs would break but had not the strength to throw him off or the breath to scream. She grabbed and scratched at his high leather driving boot, but it made no difference.

He said, "Where is it?"

She gasped. "What?" she tried to say, but no breath came out.

"I know you took a box from the cottage. The old man saw you. I went all over that place, and I never saw any box there. What have you done with it?"

In fear and pain, Evangeline cranked her head around and tried to look toward the car so that she could point to the pannier on her bicycle. But it wasn't there. He'd lied, and hadn't brought it.

Which meant he'd almost certainly lied about everything else; no Sebastian Becker, no Stephen Reed, no final resting place for Grace's body. He'd set out only to find Evangeline and bring her here for this. A drive through town with her bicycle displayed on the back of the car would have been a poor excuse for stealth.

With no bicycle, she couldn't appease him with the box he wanted. In which there was nothing anyway. She fought against his weight and he pressed down harder, and she felt her chest begin to crack. In her terror, she could think no more than a few seconds ahead. What could she do? What could she give him to make him stop?

Her eyes became fixed on the livery buttons on his uniform coat.

The livery button in Grace's box, the button that Evangeline had disregarded, was a match for them.

Her fear was no less. But her mind was no longer so clouded.

There was the corner where she'd once stood. He'd brought them here from the moors, later to take them out again and leave them for dead. Grace had been screaming, and young Evangeline could not bring herself to turn around and see why.

Forgive me, Grace, she thought.

He had one foot on her, the other on the floor. His stance was extended, like a fencer's in a lunge. Evangeline was pinned, but she was young and she was supple. She drew in both legs and kicked upward, feet together, hard into his jewels, which presented an open target.

The result was instantaneous and spectacular. Far more so than she could have imagined. This bit of wisdom had been shared between the sisterhood at their meetings, but few had ever seen the results.

He did not scream. It was much worse than that. He folded around the middle, turned white, and fell to the ground. There he squirmed like a cut worm, hugging himself and making tiny, high-pitched kitten sounds.

She scrambled to her feet and away, fearing his reach and recovery. As she got to the stable doors, she heard him vomit. She ran out into the yard and almost lost her footing on the cobblestones, looking all around for a way to run. She saw an archway and ran for that. Beyond the archway were derelict greenhouses. Beyond the greenhouses was woodland.

She knew what she should have done, of course. While he was helpless she should have gone to his workbench, selected a suitable hammer or a wrench, and beaten him like a jellyfish on a rock until there was no harm left in him. Now he would come after her when he was able, and he wouldn't give her the same chance twice.

He wanted the button. The button would betray him. Plucked from his uniform jacket, bearing Sir Owain's crest, kept by Grace for all these years. Grace had always known their attacker, but she'd kept it to herself—kept it from her. To what purpose, Evangeline could not imagine. She would have an angle; Grace always had. But as with her teachers, with the church, with the law, Grace had always played a defiant and potentially dangerous game.

He would follow her, Evangeline had no doubt. The beast of all their myths stood revealed, not as the monster of Sir Owain's tragic imaginings, but as a nobody with a horrific soul. Behind all the nightmares stood the reality of the cold floor, the pitiless appetite. He would deal with her and then go looking to retrieve the evidence against him.

She dared not stop. If she stopped, he would find her.

She did not even know his name.

FIFTY

W HEN SEBASTIAN COULD ONCE AGAIN BREATHE UNAIDED, SIR Owain propped him with his back against the balustrade and then lowered himself to settle on the floor beside him. Sebastian sat with his head tilted back, looking up. It was a handsome stairway, one of the finest features in the house. It was paneled up to shoulder height, with exposed light stone above. On the stone hung sets of antlers on oak plaques.

As Sir Owain settled, he said, "I'll tell you a story. This is one you won't find in the book."

Sebastian had nothing to offer in reply.

"I swear to you," Sir Owain went on, "that when I stood up in London before my colleagues to present my observations, I had no idea of the storm I'd be causing in that room, or of the grief that I'd be bringing upon myself. As if I hadn't grief enough already.

"Picture the scene. The room was crowded. I took the numbers as a sign of interest in what I had to say. But word had already spread, and they were out to deny me a hearing. They had no interest in my proposal that an expanded mind perceives a genuine extended universe. I was a fraud who was trying to sell them monsters, and that was the end of it."

He looked to Sebastian for a reaction.

"I know what Somerville says about me," he went on. "He's of the opinion that my material success made me arrogant in all things. But I swear to you, I have never taken success in business to be the measure of a man's worth. All the satisfaction that I have ever known lay in having the respect of my peers.

"That's what I lost, that night. They even booed a slide of the Amazon, as if I'd fabricated *that*. I never got to finish my lecture. I was there to be shouted down, and that's what they did. Their jeering followed me out of the building and into the street. I only have to close my eyes and I can hear it still."

At that point he noticed something, took out a handkerchief, and wiped Sebastian's chin.

Then he went on, "I rode home in a cab. At the time I had a town house just off Bedford Square. Imagine my feelings. Thanks to that one failed expedition I had lost my wife, my son, my position, and now my reputation. My fortune and my sanity would soon begin to follow.

"As we moved up St. Martins Lane, I grew convinced that my fellow scientists had pursued me on foot and that their cries were rising in the air. They became featherless leather-winged creatures that multiplied above me until they filled the sky. The cabbie heard nothing, and the horses were calm. But I saw the day grow darker and darker, as if in an eclipse.

"When we reached my door I sent the cabbie ahead to ring the bell, and then I ran inside as soon as the door was opened. I closed every shutter and drew every blind, and I forbade the staff to open them. I knew that the creatures were out there, covering my house with their wings. I understood that no one else could see them, but I never doubted their presence. If I listened, I could hear them scratching as they adjusted their grip on the walls. They did exist, I know it, and I know they still do. But *not in this world*."

Sebastian turned his head an inch or two, just enough to see Sir Owain. His captor had rested his head back against the balustrade, and his eyes were closed as he continued to speak.

"I know how I sound," he said. "Like every madman and opium-sniffer who mistakes his delusions for some important truth. But you will see for yourself, Mister Becker. I promise you will see."

Sir Owain was not a young man. By his own account he had gone without sleep the previous night, spending the long hours watching over Sebastian.

He was fading, for sure, just as Sebastian was regaining the power of movement. Soon would come the opportunity to act.

⁓

STEPHEN REED returned to the inn, crossing the street from the customs house. He'd heard nothing of Sebastian since the night before, and his attempt to place a call to the house this morning had been met with a dead line. The customs man assured him that this was nothing unusual. The telephone wire to Arnside ran across the entire estate. Sir Owain had paid for the installation himself, but of late had lacked the means to keep the line inspected and maintained.

It was almost twelve. The town's churches had now emptied, and the inns and hotel bars would soon be filling up. At the gates leading to the Sun Inn's coaching yard, Stephen Reed saw landlord Bill Turnbull with two shamefaced young boys and a bicycle. One of the boys was wheeling the bicycle, which had a wicker pannier on its handlebars. Both were in their Sunday best, a state that hadn't lasted the morning. Their neat socks had descended, their halfpenny collars gone awry.

Stephen followed them in. He was thinking that he'd ask Bill Turnbull to arrange transport out to Arnside. Though some kind of pretext would be useful, if his concerns turned out to be misplaced.

Turnbull was telling the boys to sit on the inn's rear step, to wait there while their parents were sent for. Turnbull was being stern, but Stephen Reed knew an act when he saw one.

He said, "What's going on?"

"Two young master criminals with a ladies' bicycle," Turnbull said. And then he lowered his voice and added, "I'm giving 'em a scare."

One of the boys piped across the yard, "We found it."

"Quiet, you." Turnbull leaned the bicycle against an empty ale cask and looked in the basket for some clue to the owner.

Stephen Reed said, "I need an excuse to go out to Arnside."

"You don't need an excuse."

"All right, then, I need a way to get there."

"Fancy a bike ride? This one's going spare."

Stephen Reed was about to speak, but then he looked again at the bicycle.

"Haven't I seen it before?" he said.

Turnbull had found a folded note in the pannier along with an old cotton-reel box. After a glance at it he looked up in surprise and held the note out.

"It's addressed to you," he said.

Stephen Reed took the note and read it, saw the signature, and went over to the boys.

"Stand up," he said, "and tell me about this bicycle."

The boys stood nervously. The ire of Big Bill Turnbull was bad enough. But this cold-eyed, well-dressed stranger was trouble of an unknown magnitude.

One of the boys said, "We thought it was thrown away."

The other added, "It was buried right down in the hedge, honestly. We was taking it to the meadows to try riding it."

"How did it get there?"

"Don't know, sir."

Stephen Reed pushed it, just to see. "I think you do," he said.

The second boy admitted, "We thought he was throwing it away."

"No such luck, my friend," Stephen Reed said, and he leaned forward to put himself more on their level. "Now," he said. "Do you want to be two boys who stole a bicycle, or the two young heroes who made sure it got back to Miss Bancroft?"

The two boys exchanged a glance. He'd offered them a way out of their trouble, and after only a moment's hesitation they took it. Now he had to slow them down, to keep them from talking over each other and making no sense at all.

They'd seen a woman with a bicycle talking to a man with a big car. They didn't know the woman. They knew the car, it was Sir Owain's Daimler, and the man was Sir Owain's driver. Sometimes, when he was out and about in the vehicle without his employer, he let the local children look at the engine, or stand on the running board to look through the glass at the luxury inside.

After a short conversation, the woman had climbed into the car. The driver had wheeled her bicycle around to the back of the vehicle and then, to the boys' surprise and delight, had lifted it by the frame and pitched it wheels-first over the hedge. After the car had driven away they'd waited a decent interval—a whole ten minutes—and then retrieved the machine. They'd been caught wheeling it through town.

"Right," Stephen Reed said. "Sit back down."

He went back to Bill Turnbull. Turnbull had opened up the box and was looking through its contents. He said, "She says in the note, this box was hidden away in Grace's cottage."

"I know," Stephen Reed said. "How did we miss it?"

"By the looks of it, we didn't miss much," Bill Turnbull said, poking critically through the litter in the box.

Stephen Reed said, "Do you know Sir Owain's driver?"

"I do," Bill Turnbull said. "His name's Thomas Arnot. His father was the old coachman up at Arnside Hall. When the professor bought his first car he sent the son off to train as a mechanic. Why?"

"The boys reckon they saw him dump Evangeline's bicycle. What else do we know about him?"

"Can't really say. He's one of those people who's always around, but you never really notice." He tilted the box toward Stephen Reed to show him the contents. "Can you see anything of use to us here?" he said. "I can't."

Stephen Reed looked.

"No," he said, and then returned to the subject of his interest. "Where will I find him?"

"He lives on the estate," Bill Turnbull said. "Over the garage where the stables used to be."

FIFTY-ONE

Sir Owain didn't stir when Sebastian rose. Nor when he took the revolver from his hand, or patted down the material of Sir Owain's dinner jacket in the hope of finding keys. Perhaps they were in the door; on legs that were still unsteady, Sebastian went downstairs to see. There were no keys to be seen.

He returned to the landing and stood before the older man on the floor. He held his revolver at the ready, just in case. Whenever Sir Owain had spoken, he'd been earnest and benign. His actions, however, had been another matter. Drugged wine, a dish of mind-changing grubs, and a poisoned lancet signified a less affable host, and one not to be readily trusted.

"Sir Owain," he said, and saw no response. Sebastian nudged him with his foot and spoke his name again.

The man was showing all signs of life, other than consciousness. His color was good, his breathing steady. But nothing Sebastian did seemed to rouse him.

He went back downstairs and found his way to the study, thinking that he might reconnect the telephone. But the study was locked, too, and there was no point in trying to break in. Two inches of oak and a brass lock. He'd seen less substantial doors on bank vaults.

So then Sebastian went back and searched the entire entrance hall, as best he could. Sir Owain had come straight upstairs after speaking to his driver on the doorstep, so the key had to be somewhere within reach. But Sebastian couldn't find it.

He looked into the kitchen. Dr. Sibley's body was gone, and the mess had been cleaned up. The cement floor was dry. The woodwork shone, the copper gleamed. It had occurred to Sebastian that something was different about the house, and there it was: its general air of shabbiness had somehow receded during the night, like the lines of age falling away. When he turned to look back along the corridor behind him, he saw more of the same. The rug was fresh, its colors bright. The paneling was newly polished. He could smell the beeswax.

He could almost imagine the place inhabited again, with the staff and family somewhere just out of sight. Was someone playing the piano?

He raced through to the drawing room, but no one was there. He must have imagined it. Correction: he surely had imagined it, because the great house was locked up tight and only he and Sir Owain were inside. He wasn't sure of what he'd heard, or whether he'd actually heard anything at all. It was as if the thought of music had crossed his mind, and his senses had immediately conjured some momentary evidence in support of the notion.

There was the danger. He took a deep breath and steadied himself. This was some progressive effect from whatever intoxicant he'd been fed the night before. It had to be. He realized now that he dare not fully trust his senses.

There was no way out of the kitchen. An unlocked door led to some stairs and a basement scullery, but there was no way out of that, either.

Behind a concealed entrance in the library he found a billiard room with a full-sized table set ready for play. He even thought that he could smell the cigar smoke in the air. On the walls were caricature sketches of famous past visitors to the house, with one wall dominated by a painting of a sea engagement involving one of Sir Owain's battleships. As he looked at it, the seas around the ships began to roll and the sky to darken. He quickly turned away.

As he made his way along a lower gallery, a great shadow slid along the wall before him, though there was nothing to cast it. Butterflies in cases began fluttering excitedly on their pins as he passed by.

He grew more desperate. From a fireplace in an alcove he took a cast-iron poker and walked holding it before him, like a sword. Poker in one hand, gun in the other. If any danger should arise to threaten him in this new, malleable, and shifting world that he'd been thrust into, he would be ready to take it on.

Sir Owain had made the Hall into a lunatic's prison for him. But he'd be no man's specimen.

EVANGELINE HAD run through the woods, along pathways and carriage drives that had been laid out for beauty and long overgrown, until she reached the twelve-foot wall that bounded the formal gardens. Her boots were wet and her skirts were torn. She started to follow the wall along, but it had been solidly built and had no breach. No matter, she thought, she could follow it to its end; but then the inadvisability of this occurred to her. All that Sir Owain's man would need to do, if he were sufficiently recovered, would be to go to the place where the wall ended and wait for her there.

Hiding was not an option, so far from the world. She needed to get off the estate. But when she moved, sudden eruptions of game birds betrayed her position to anyone with the wit to observe them. The advantage that she'd gained was slowly being lost. She could not leave the immediate grounds unseen. Even if she were to manage it, there would be miles of open land still to cross. She needed some closer refuge. She made the decision to approach the house.

Sir Owain might be mad, but she knew now that he was not her tormentor, nor had he ever been. His concern was authentic, his sadness real. And though Dr. Sibley might be mean and his manner unpleasant, he surely would not turn her away without a hearing. There was a chance that they might not believe her. But if she could beg the use of the telephone, she was in no doubt that Stephen Reed would.

The formal gardens had been laid out at a time when there had been a fashion for all things Japanese. But this was Japan as the English saw it. Her climb to the house was through an unkempt fantasy garden of streams, grottoes, and thick stone pavilions all but buried in wild undergrowth. When she reached the back terrace behind the Hall, she hesitated. It was but a step out of hiding and a walk across the courtyard to the door. She saw no sign of life anywhere about the property, and heard no sound other than the steady filling and draining of the drinking trough provided for visiting horses and fed from some distant spring.

Evangeline waited as long as she dared. What finally induced her to break cover was the far-off sound of a car's engine, down in the valley below the house. If Sir Owain's man was searching for her in the car, then he couldn't be watching for her here.

With relief, she emerged from hiding and started toward the doors. She was almost halfway across the courtyard when she heard him sprinting behind her.

She didn't look back, but instantly broke into a run with the aim of reaching the door ahead of him. Alas, she did not. He caught her arm and spun her around, almost popping the joint in her shoulder. He had a disheveled, furious look to him. He tried to drag her across the courtyard and away from the house. She dug in her heels, and after a yard or so her feet shot from under her and she sat down hard.

It didn't make him release her. But he couldn't do anything with her, either. So he let go of her arm and hit her, aiming the flat of his hand at the side of her head, with Evangeline managing to deflect some of the blow as she threw her own hands up to cover her face.

"Where is it?" he said.

"What?"

"You know what I mean," he said, and raised his hand to hit her again.

"I know!" she said quickly. "I know what you want." She fumbled in her coat.

He held off from hitting her and leaned in close, breathing hard and making a low, tutting, hissing sound through his teeth that was like the impatient tic of an eager snake. When she had to switch sides, he followed her hand.

When he had the button, what then? He'd have one piece of necessary business left, the disposal of the witness.

"Here," she said. Looking up at him, showing a face that was eager to please, Evangeline brought her hand out of her coat. He leaned forward as he saw the glint of metal in her hand. She looked away and rammed her suffragette pin all the way into his left eye.

It was nine-karat gold. With imitation amethyst, peridot, and seed pearls. Though for Sir Owain's man, the important element was the two-inch steel pin that came at him ahead of the rest.

He screamed. Like a hare being torn by dogs. But he didn't let go of her, and he didn't fall. He clapped his hand over the damaged eye and went at her with redoubled fury. She'd expected to disable him but had only increased his rage to a degree that overcame all pain. He was cursing, calling her names, laying into her with one fist and then with both; she rolled over and made herself as small as she could and drew her arms up to protect her face, taking most of the punches on her back and feeling that her heart would burst in her chest at each jarring blow.

Then he stopped. She wanted to scramble away but she couldn't move. He was rising to start kicking her now, she knew it. She wanted to call for help from the house, but he'd beaten the breath out of her.

Instead of receiving a kicking, she felt herself seized by the collar and hoisted into the air. He was dragging her across the courtyard like an ungainly sackful of limbs, aiming with purpose for the horse trough. She realized his intention and tried to fight back. But he managed her easily, never letting her find her balance or gain a purchase on the ground.

She did not get a chance to take a breath. When they reached the trough he plunged her in headfirst and held her under. The shock was enormous. She tried to grip the rough edges of the trough and force herself back, but she hadn't the strength. He was going to hold her down until she was fully subdued, or worse.

Evangeline let her hands fall from the edge. She stopped fighting and tried to relax. If she could deceive him into thinking that she'd lost consciousness while she still had a spark of it left, she might yet prevail.

Was that her plan? Or was she in fact merely clinging to hope while experiencing her life fading in reality? Some people said that drowning sailors experienced bliss, though how those people came by the knowledge, never having drowned nor spoken to anyone who had, she could not imagine. She felt no bliss, only panic and fear.

Her ruse was not working. She could not manage the necessary stillness. Once more she started to resist, but he'd taken the opportunity to force her farther under. She opened her eyes. The water was cold and foul and silty, swirling about her like Greenwich fog. She was there once more, on the terrace of the Trafalgar Inn, watching for Sebastian Becker's boat as the ghost ships passed by. The heavens split, and it started to rain.

The rain was red. It fell slowly through the fog all around her, like hot cinders through half-frozen slush.

THE SMELL should have warned him. There they stood, their heads fused, their arms around each other. Freaks out of their bottle. Their skin was soft and pliable and completely without color, much as he imagined those bamboo grubs to have been. Rank spirits of alcohol were pooling around their feet. Sebastian couldn't work out what they wanted.

When he'd asked for their forgiveness, they hadn't responded. So it wasn't that.

The face they shared had no expression. All bent out of shape, it was like a reflection in an oily puddle. No clues there. But then one arm came up and beckoned, and the pair attempted an awkward turn. They didn't lead him onward, for which he was grateful. The smell of their preservative almost overpowered him as he eased by them. Once past, he did not look back.

This corridor led to the conservatory. Along the walls hung more of Sir Owain's sentimental art collection; pet dogs, girls in gardens, boats at sea. On a plinth stood a strange piece of marble. It was of a child wrapped in a thin shroud, a stone carver's technical exercise with the child's features showing through the folds in the cloth. From the corner of his eye he saw the stone child turning its head to watch him as he passed.

The conservatory opened out before him. A soaring structure in cast iron and glass, a temple of light and dense, humid air. Within it was contained an entire world in miniature, a jungle facsimile of palms, orchids, lianas, and ferns. A pathway wound through to its center. Sebastian's heart was beating, faster and faster.

My dust would hear her and beat, had I lain for a century dead.

Elisabeth was waiting.

There she stood, her back toward him. She wore a plain high-collared blouse and a long, light dress the color of smoke. Not as he'd seen her last, in the somber luxury of a chapel of rest, but as in life, unharmed. She seemed not to be aware of his approach. Her head was tilted, as if listening to music.

As soon as he saw that, he heard the music too. He remembered another Sunday in Willow Grove Park, a trolley ride out of Philadelphia, with Sousa on the bandstand. He'd worn a suit and a straw boater. They'd been younger then and, had they only known it, very happy. It seemed to him that Elisabeth looked exactly as she had on that day.

It took him a surprising amount of courage to speak.

He said, "A woman once told me that a man who can dance is always going to be in demand."

She didn't look at him. But she showed no surprise. She'd known all along that he was there.

Reaching out to touch the dull, spiky flowers on the towering grasses that grew beneath the palms, she said, "A wise woman. What happened to her?"

"She left when I wasn't looking."

"That's not your fault."

"It feels that way."

She let the drab petals trail through her fingers. "Did you know," she said, "that when bamboo goes into flower, it flowers at the same time all over the world? No one can explain it. But somehow it knows." And she started to move away.

"Wait," he said. "Please."

Elisabeth stopped. She looked at him then, with those large gray eyes he remembered so well.

"What?"

"I know it's too much to ask," he said. "And I know it can't happen. But I so want you back."

"Good-bye, Sebastian," she said. "This hour must pass. It's time to let me go."

"Not yet," he said. "Please. I don't want to."

"I know," she said. "But you must do it anyway. For both of us."

FIFTY·TWO

Sir Owain was awake and alert when Sebastian finally returned to the stairs landing and dropped back into his place on the floor beside him. The man didn't seem to have much strength for rising, and didn't try. But his manner was eager enough.

"Well," he said, "did you see them? The monsters?"

Sebastian took a deep and heavy breath; when he let it go, it was as if a small measure of his pain was washed out of him with it.

"No," he said. "Not monsters."

"What, then?"

Sebastian looked down and made no reply. Sir Owain went on, "You've seen her. Haven't you? You can see her too? I've always known she was out there. But she always runs from me. What did she say? Did she mention me at all?"

Sebastian looked at him then. He knew that Sir Owain was speaking of his own wife, not of Elisabeth. But he was willing to let Sir Owain believe that his were the only ghosts that haunted the premises.

He said, "What would you want her to say?"

"Don't just tell me what you think I want to hear," Sir Owain said. "Tell me honestly. Did she say if I can ever be forgiven?"

Sebastian hesitated, and considered his own experience. Then told him, "She said to let her go."

"Let her go? She said that? What does it mean?"

"What do you want from her?" Sebastian said. "She can't come back to you. Stop wondering when the pain will go. It won't. It's part of what she left you. You'll have to learn to love it."

"What about my son?"

"From what I know, your son is happy," Sebastian said.

"Did *he* have a message for me?"

"I'm sure he wants you not to worry. You've suffered enough. Believe that he forgives you."

Sir Owain lowered his head, and his shoulders began to shake with silent weeping. Sebastian had mixed feelings about the lie, but no conscience. What mattered, here? He had his own consolation, rooted in a new and very shaky faith; let Sir Owain now have his.

He put his hand on Sir Owain's shoulder.

"It's over," he said. "Now, please. Where did you hide those keys? I need your telephone."

THE KEYS WERE in the hallway cabinet, the one that contained the warship model. The glass lid lifted, and the keys were inside one of the steamer's funnels. Sir Owain unlocked the study door and reconnected the telephone, which took him no more than a minute.

Sebastian placed his call, and as he waited for a messenger to return with someone from the Sun Inn to speak to him, he became aware that Sir Owain was no longer standing in the doorway. He felt a twinge of alarm. Sir Owain was subdued now, but far from harmless. Dr. Hubert Sibley lay dead, somewhere hereabouts. That might not be enough to save the tinker, but it would remove Sir Owain from human society.

Dolly came to the telephone. Not Stephen Reed, not Parish Constable Bill Turnbull, but the Sun Inn's cook. She began to tell him that the two men were already on their way to Arnside Hall; they'd made a troubling discovery, but she did not know what it was. While she was still explaining, Sebastian heard a shout. It came from outside. Sir Owain must have taken the keys and opened the main door.

Sebastian heard, "Monster! Monster!" and then the sound of a gunshot, ferociously loud in the courtyard. "Oh, Lord," he said. He abandoned the telephone and ran into the hallway, skidding when he hit the rug, but not stopping as he dived onward toward daylight and the open air.

Sebastian had once seen half of a man's head blown clean off, gone from the eye sockets up.

Much the same thing had happened to Thomas Arnot, Sir Owain's chauffeur, as he'd stood trying to drown a young woman at the horse trough. Only he didn't seem to know it yet. His body was still standing, half turned toward Sir Owain. Sir Owain stood in the middle of the courtyard with his hunting rifle half lowered. Arnot, his brains gone, seemed perfectly capable of carrying on without them. He seemed about to release his victim and start a jerky walk toward his would-be executioner.

But then the pretense crumbled, and the chauffeur's body fell. His legs gave way, and he slid to the ground like a rotten building falling into its own foundations. Sir Owain still held the rifle, but Sebastian had a more pressing concern. Arnot's victim remained half submerged and had ceased to struggle.

The water in the trough was all befouled with blood and fragments of bone. Even after Sebastian had pulled her out of it and lowered her to the courtyard floor, her long hair streaming like a mermaid's, it was several seconds before he recognized Evangeline. He froze in horror. She did not move, or breathe.

"Here," Sir Owain said, thrusting the hunting rifle into Sebastian's hands and shoving him aside. "Delay can be fatal."

He moved with purpose. He rolled Evangeline to lie facedown and drew up one of her arms so that her forehead could rest upon it, keeping her head clear of the ground. He placed his hands against the small of her back and pressed on it, in a more thorough version of the technique he'd used to keep Sebastian alive. Water streamed from Evangeline's nose and mouth, as if squeezed from a goatskin. She showed no discomfort, or even awareness. Though she drew in breath when Sir Owain removed his weight from her, she gave no voluntary sign of life at all. Sir Owain repeated the action, again and again, the abdominal pressure forcing her diaphragm upward to act upon her lungs.

Sebastian looked down at the rifle in his hands. It was a large-bore, single-shot buffalo gun. Little wonder that it had caused such damage at this range.

"You see?" Sir Owain said, with a sideways glance toward Arnot's body. "They do. They walk among us. Invisible to all."

Evangeline suddenly spasmed and began a coughing fit just as the vehicle bringing Stephen Reed made its noisy entrance into the Hall courtyard.

Stephen Reed jumped down from the wagon and was arrested by the sight before him. Sebastian with the hunting rifle. The bedraggled sea creature that was Evangeline. Sir Owain crouching over her.

And the body of Thomas Arnot, his head topped like an egg, his body's blood now snaking across the courtyard stones in search of a drain.

Sebastian laid down the rifle and helped Sir Owain to lift Evangeline to a sitting position. She was dazed and seemed not to know where she was.

"Who did this?" Stephen Reed said, torn between the fascinating sight of the mutilated chauffeur and concern for Evangeline.

Sebastian was about to speak, but Sir Owain spoke first.

"I did," he said, and a peculiar little smile played about his lips.

He said, "I slew the beast."

FIFTY-THREE

IT WAS A BRIGHT SPRING DAY IN LONDON AND STEPHEN REED was walking up Bell Yard from Fleet Street, behind the Royal Courts of Justice on his way to the chambers where Evangeline Bancroft worked. They'd arranged, by letter, to meet that day during the half hour she had for lunch. But Stephen had taken a room in a boardinghouse off the Strand and was intending to spend several of his leave days in town. He was hoping that she might consent to allowing him to spend some of that time in her company.

He had much to tell her. The tinker had been freed, without apology. A billhook in Thomas Arnot's workshop had been matched to the broken piece held in evidence. With Arnot gone, piecing his story and his motives together proved difficult. He had become public property, with one person's theory as good as any other's. A number of learned men, some of them from distant parts of Europe and all eager to dissect the psychology of this very twentieth-century phenomenon, had descended upon the resort and been thoroughly fleeced of their cash in return for interviews and information. Some of the information fed to them was even based in fact. One of the few conclusions that could be agreed upon was that it must have been as a child that Arnot had first noticed Grace; barely out of childhood himself, he'd watched her when her father and his own had done some dealing in horses.

A search of his living quarters above the former stables had revealed accommodations that were both squalid and austere, as if a monk had elected to live in a pigsty. A small collection of well-thumbed French postcards had been found hidden above a beam and, behind the laths of the wall, items of children's clothing. They suggested other assaults and disappearances of which the police had known nothing.

Despite knowing of Arnot's guilt from the day of her own assault, Grace had not given him up. Such was her nature. She never gave anything to the authorities, her lifelong enemies. Whatever knowledge Grace had, she hoarded for her own advantage. When the time was right, it appeared that she had blackmailed Arnot. Unable to make a living in a dying trade, she'd set out to supplement her income from his.

In her own mind, there was probably a certain aptness to this. He'd done her harm, and now it was his time to pay, with money he earned by the machines that were wiping out her livelihood. Little matter that the evidence she could threaten him with—nothing more than her own word and a livery button from his uniform—was so insubstantial. It had been enough to compel him.

The rest was guesswork. The most credible theory was that when Sir Owain's fortunes declined to the point where he could no longer pay wages, Arnot was trapped. Grace cared nothing for his difficulty—it was his problem, not hers. Let him steal if he had to. Evangeline spoke of "poor Grace," but inside poor Grace was a heart of flint. Only such a heart could let more children suffer, knowing what she knew. She had survived; so must they. And if they did not . . . such were the laws of the human jungle.

Unable to pay, unable to preserve himself by any other means, Arnot had silenced Grace and searched for the evidence she'd claimed to hold.

Stephen Reed now reached the Inns of Court. He asked for directions of one of the servants of the Inn, and quickly found Evangeline's building.

He was early. As he waited in the square, watching the benchers pass and the workers in the boiler rooms of justice going about their secret business, he rehearsed the speech that he intended to follow.

He meant to offer himself to Evangeline, if she would have him.

And if she would not, he could wait.

At around the same time, in a belowground passage built some thirty years before to serve temporary exhibition grounds in South Kensington, Sebastian was heading for an appointment of his own. He, too, was thinking of Evangeline May Bancroft, and the lightless shaft under the Thames where he had once done his best to sustain the young woman's spirits. This tunnel was wide and spacious, with a faint breeze drawing through.

Sir Owain Lancaster had been tried for the manslaughter of Hubert Sibley. He had insisted on representing himself in court, which had all but guaranteed the trial's outcome. After Sir James Crichton-Browne spoke on his mental condition, the jury returned a verdict of not guilty by reason of insanity, and Sir Owain was detained indefinitely by order of the Crown. The Arnside estate and his remaining assets were placed under the control of a Master of Lunacy appointed by the Lord Chancellor's office. His late wife's family petitioned for control over what remained of his dwindling wealth, but their petition was denied.

Sir Owain had applied to his administrators to be allowed to make a cash gift to Sebastian, as a sign of gratitude. He hoped that it might enable Sebastian to move his family into more suitable housing. The Master of Lunacy had forbidden the gift, deeming it improper, but Sir James had felt moved to raise Sebastian's pay in consequence. For the moment, Sebastian remained in Southwark.

As far as Sebastian was aware, Sir Owain had adjusted to his lot, rediscovered his faith, and spent his days in the serene anticipation of an eventual reunion with his loved ones. For his own part, Sebastian suffered occasionally from vivid and emotional memories in which he relived the involuntary delirium that Sir Owain had inflicted upon him. But these episodes were always brief and had begun to diminish.

He ascended the stairs to leave the passageway at its newly opened entrance before the natural history museum, the so-called Cathedral of Nature dedicated mostly to the display and worship of bones and taxidermy. Its iron galleries and terra-cotta detailing made for a unique blend of industry and Byzantium. He'd been here several times, mostly at weekends, since Robert had made his first visit with Dr. Percival.

Today was different, and somewhat special. Percival Langdon

Down had arranged an interview for Robert with the Keeper of Paleontology. Despite the boy's lack of formal training, Langdon Down had persuaded the Keeper that his depth of interest and effortless power of analysis might fit him for employment here. As a boy attendant to begin with, perhaps moving on to become a junior assistant in the Department of Geology. He surely had the necessary ability. Robert even had the Latin, entirely self-taught.

Sebastian was to meet the three of them in the Great Hall, but only Frances was waiting there. She had her best coat and bonnet on.

He said, "Am I late? I didn't think I was."

"You're not late," Frances said. "The Keeper sent a message down and Robert went up early."

"Shouldn't we be there?"

"No, Sebastian," Frances said. "He isn't a child. He went off perfectly happy with Doctor Percival. He doesn't need us."

She noted his discomfort, and it made her smile.

"It'll soon be over," she said. "And I'm sure he'll do well. Let's walk for a while. Take your mind away from it."

They walked out of the Great Hall past Huxley's statue, down the gallery of the East Wing. Pier cases of specimens made a series of alcoves to either side, from early man to the mastodon. For once, they didn't have to stop every few paces while Robert picked out some fossil and launched into an eager lecture. They passed the exhibits by, their thoughts elsewhere.

"I wish Elisabeth could be here to see this day," he said.

"I know you do. This will be everything you both wanted for him."

"Everything *she* wanted," he said. "I'm not sure I had her faith."

"She had her doubts too, you know. She believed in him. But I think she would have found it hard to let him go."

He looked at her. "Really?"

Frances nodded. "You knew her best. But I knew her longest. She was the same when we were children. She could deal with disappointment if it was her own. But she always suffered at the thought of it being borne by anyone else."

The gallery ended in a square pavilion with no exit. On pedestal number ten, near the center of the room, stood the plaster skeleton of *a Megatherium from Buenos Ayres,* an enormous extinct animal with a frame resembling that of a giant sloth.

This was the exhibit that Robert had first led him to see. The Megatherium was the unseen beast that Sir Owain had imagined he might bag and bring home. Its skeleton was thick-boned and barrel-chested, and it had been set in a rearing position with a plaster tree to balance against. As a result of its raised stance, its skull was up almost as high as the ceiling.

They turned to walk back. There was no way of knowing how long the Keeper's interview would take.

"You know," Sebastian said, "if Robert gets this job, he'll be the one member of the family with a reliable weekly income."

"One step at a time, Sebastian."

"But you're right. He deserves whatever the world can offer him. And you, Frances. I owe you so much. But do you never wonder how your life might have been without us?"

"I'd miss Southwark."

"Really?"

It took him a moment to realize that Frances was teasing him. He hadn't been expecting it. His credulity amused her no end.

They began their return to the Great Hall.

"Life will be better than this, Frances," he said. "I promise you it will."

She took his arm.

"I don't mind," she said.

POSTSCRIPT

THERE IS, IN ONE FINAL PIECE OF BUSINESS, THE MATTER OF A short length of moving-picture film.

The camera negative was returned, in due course, to Florence Bell's family, who could bear neither to view it nor to throw it away. It was kept in an attic where the nitrate stock began to deteriorate, as nitrate stock will. When the film can was rediscovered and finally opened, some decades later, the core was a solid lump and the outer layers were crumbling. All else within the can was dust, rust, and vinegar.

The print that Sebastian Becker turned over to the Crown Prosecutor's office went into a government archive. The archive was thinned and most of its silver was reclaimed for the war effort in 1915.

No clear understanding of the brief sequence's content was ever agreed upon.

ABOUT THE AUTHOR

STEPHEN GALLAGHER is a novelist, screenwriter, and director. He is the author of fourteen novels, including *Nightmare, with Angel; Red, Red Robin;* and *The Spirit Box*. He lives in England.